UNDER THE ITALIAN SUN

Sue Moorcroft writes award-winning contemporary fiction of life and love. *The Little Village Christmas* and *A Christmas Gift* were *Sunday Times* bestsellers and *The Christmas Promise* went to #1 in the Kindle chart. She also writes short stories, serials, articles, columns, courses and writing 'how to'.

An army child, Sue was born in Germany then lived in Cyprus, Malta and the UK and still loves to travel. Her other loves include writing (the best job in the world), reading, watching Formula 1 on TV and hanging out with friends, dancing, yoga, wine and chocolate.

If you're interested in being part of #TeamSueMoorcroft you can find more information at www.suemoorcroft.com/street-team. If you prefer to sign up to receive news of Sue and her books, go to www.suemoorcroft.com and click on 'Newsletter'. You can follow @SueMoorcroft on Twitter, @SueMoorcroftAuthor on Instagram, or Facebook.com/sue.moorcroft.3 and Facebook.com/SueMoorcroftAuthor.

By the same author:

The Christmas Promise
Just For the Holidays
The Little Village Christmas
One Summer in Italy
A Christmas Gift
A Summer to Remember
Let it Snow
Summer on a Sunny Island
Christmas Wishes

Under the Italian Sun

Sue Moorcroft

avon.

HarperCollins*Publishers*
1 London Bridge Street
London SE1 9GF

www.harpercollins.co.uk

HarperCollins*Publishers*
1st Floor, Watermarque Building, Ringsend Road
Dublin 4, Ireland

A Paperback Original 2021
1
Copyright © Sue Moorcroft 2021

Sue Moorcroft asserts the moral right to
be identified as the author of this work.

A catalogue copy of this book is available from the British Library.

ISBN: 978-0-00-839302-1

Typeset in Sabon LT Std by Palimpsest Book Production Limited,
Falkirk, Stirlingshire

Printed and bound in UK by CPI Group (UK) Ltd, Croydon CR0 4YY

MIX
Paper from
responsible sources
FSC™ C007454

This book is produced from independently certified FSC™ paper
to ensure responsible forest management.

For more information visit: www.harpercollins.co.uk/green

Acknowledgements

It was an out-of-the-blue idea to write about a character whose search for her past included finding someone whose name she shared. This idea carried me off on an engrossing and emotional journey to Italy at a time when flights of the imagination were particularly valuable. As always, I shamelessly tapped others for help and I'd like to extend my thanks to each of the following wonderful people:

Maureen Duckworth and I were at school together in Northamptonshire, England. It was fascinating to hear of her search for birth parents, half-siblings and aunts, and the disappointments and unlooked-for consequences. I'm indebted to her for her openness and setting me on the correct track for so many aspects of Zia's story.

During my research, I watched the touching, evocative *Irene's Ghost* made by Iain Cunningham of forwardslash-films.com, documenting his search for the truth around the early loss of his mum. I found him on Twitter to say how much I enjoyed the film and that I was writing about the same subject. He generously offered to chat and brought out many things I hadn't thought of to enrich

Zia and make her a more nuanced character. Iain also signposted me to Action on Postpartum Psychosis, an invaluable source of information and personal experiences.

Isabella Tartaruga was so generous and kind with her time when I was unable to get to my writing retreat at Arte Umbria in the Apennine Mountains or revisit the vineyards. She answered many, many emails about Italy and read my first draft to pick up errors. Her knowledge immeasurably increased the book's authenticity.

My brother Trevor Moorcroft helps me with much of my research – fact-finding, fact-checking and collecting the right information for me to read. I turned to him for particulars on Brighton, residency and citizenship in Italy for British subjects, vineyards, winemaking and a myriad of other details. Thanks also to Lisa Verroken for getting us information on tattoo artists; and the social media friends who answered questions that began, 'How would you feel if . . .?' or 'Does anyone know . . .?'

I also did a lot of reading around the subject of single mothers and how the UK treated them during the twentieth century. Some of this information was absorbed into the background of Vicky and Tori's stories and left me with an admiration for women who had to find ways of coping in less tolerant times.

Mark West has been a first reader for almost all my books and *Under the Italian Sun* was no exception. I always enjoy reading his perspicacious and pithy comments and he usually spots something no one else does.

The members of Team Sue Moorcroft are a constant source of pleasure and support, and frequently contribute names for minor characters and places. I consider myself so fortunate to have a street team.

Book bloggers: I love you! Please don't change a thing.

I was amazed to realise that this is my tenth book with Avon HarperCollins. I couldn't get them to you without the wonderful Avon team, my awesome agent Juliet Pickering, who meets every challenge calmly, and all at Blake Friedmann Literary Agency. Big thanks to every one of my publishers around the world.

And thank you for reading *Under the Italian Sun* and my other books. My job is a delight because of you.

To the readers joining me on this escape to a rocky plateau above a sun-drenched valley in Italy. Our journey begins on page one.

Chapter One

Zia Chalmers backed out from the storage space on all fours, dragging a cracked brown suitcase. 'Ouch!' She rubbed her burning scalp where she'd caught her ponytail on the frame of the tiny access door. 'One of the benefits of an attic flat is the eaves storage. You just have to be size zero to access it.'

Ursula, lounging on the carpet of Zia's spare room – currently Ursula's room – peered at the suitcase. 'How long's it been there?'

'Six years, since Gran died. I should have sorted through it then but I was twenty-four and felt too young to be left alone in the world, let alone clear Gran and Pap's bungalow ready for sale.' A perfunctory swipe at the dust then Zia sprang the suitcase's old-fashioned clasps with a *phut!* The hinges groaned as she threw back the lid and paused to absorb buff folders jammed beside faded red document wallets. A blue and white quilted beach bag took up one corner. She patted it. 'I found this on top of a wardrobe. It's full of Mum's letters but reading them felt intrusive so I stuck it in here.'

Ursula frowned down at the jumble. 'Will looking through this stuff upset you?'

Zia shrugged. 'Maybe, but if I want clues about my father it's the only place I can think of to look.' She toyed absently with the beach bag's zipper. 'Gran and Pap always denied knowing his name. It wasn't a popular subject because they didn't like Mum being a single mother and a "free spirit", as Gran called her. We visited them in Spain when I was a kid but I think they were duty visits for Mum. Shame, because Gran and Pap were wonderful after she died.' She blinked away the memory of her shocked ten-year-old self clinging to Gran.

Ursula laughed. 'They might have had old-fashioned values but your Gran was mischievous and kind and Pap was really smiley. I loved going home from uni with you on the holidays. It made my homesickness a bit better.' Ursula's own family was back in Ireland. She'd come to England for her degree and stayed. Zia's closest friend, Ursula was as blonde as Zia was dark, a beanpole where Zia was curvy, an arty and unconventional tattoo artist whereas Zia had a corporate client relationships role in asset finance. Nevertheless, they found the same things funny, loved the same books and movies and completely got each other. When Ursula and her husband Stephan hit a rocky patch, Zia had instantly offered Ursula somewhere to stay.

Zia thought wistfully of tall, bony Gran with salt and pepper hair drawn neatly back and Pap's blue eyes and shock of silver hair. 'When I first went to live with them Pap showed me how to make a sort of whistle from cow parsley stems. It made a rude noise and he said it was called a keck-fart but not to say so in front of Gran. Then she saw it and said, "Has Pap made you a keck-fart?" It was the only thing that made me laugh that summer.' She touched the folders, dry and smooth, filling the room with a comforting smell of old paper. 'I probably kept way too much of their stuff.'

Ursula slid her tattooed arm – she had one inked and one clean – around Zia's shoulders. 'But you loved them.'

Zia nodded jerkily. 'Gran and Pap gave up their life in Spain when Mum fell off that ladder and got her head injury.' Zia remembered the clatter and the shriek of pain. Mum staggering to her feet inexplicably angry and disorientated, then violently sick. In quick succession had come the neighbours, the ambulance, and the end of Vicky Chalmer's life and Zia's childhood as she knew it.

Ursula planted a consoling, lipstick-scented kiss on her cheek. 'If you find your daddy you might find a whole other family just waiting to welcome you.'

'Living relatives might be nice but you know that's not why I'm interested in finding out who he is.' Zia stared at the mountain of old paperwork as if it might magically form itself into the key to her life.

Ursula sighed. 'I know. You're after an Italian passport, Zia-Lucia Costa Chalmers. Jeez, we might even find out why you have that mouthful of a name.'

Zia managed a smile. 'You know the story Gran told me – my dad was from Italy and a lady called Lucia Costa had once been kind to my mother. When I began to learn Italian and pointed out that Zia means "aunt" she just shrugged.' She sighed. 'When I asked other questions, she said she only wanted to concentrate on the happy memories. I didn't persist in case it made her sad. Mum was thirty-five when I was born and by the time they took me on Gran was seventy-five and Pap seventy-seven.' Zia climbed to her feet, rubbing stiff knees. 'Ouch. Let's take this lot through to the dining table.'

She heaved the cracked brown suitcase along the hallway of her airy Brighton flat. At the top of what once had been a Georgian town house the apartment gazed over the gardens of New Steine and the flowing silver figures of the AIDS monument. All the buildings had been converted into apartments or boutique hotels and most wore gracious pastel colours, though one was a jolly turquoise. Her tall sash windows opened onto a balcony with curlicued black railings. If she glanced right, she could watch the sea switch from blue to grey and to the left ran busy, bustling St James's Street. She adored her home, a gem in trendy, quirky Brighton on England's south coast, and thought Gran and Pap would approve of her selling their bungalow to buy it.

Ursula settled her long limbs at the table near the white marble fire surround. OK. What are we looking for?'

Zia pulled out the first few document wallets. 'Anything that might lead to filling in the blank on my birth certificate where my father's name ought to be. If he really was Italian it would be the easiest route to Italian citizenship.'

'But you said anyone can apply for Italian residency,' Ursula objected, pushing back the lock of blonde hair that dangled perpetually over one eye.

'That's right. Residency first, then maybe citizenship after a few years. It's just that those applications will stand miles more chance of success if I can prove I have an Italian parent or grandparent.' She pulled a face. 'If dear McPherson & Partners had been obliging enough to make me redundant before Brexit I could have easily tried living in Italy – *and* I'd have avoided the relationship with Brendon.'

Sadly, her three months with Brendon, though they'd begun promisingly with flying sparks of attraction in the euphoria of a New Year's celebration, had ended with his infidelity, particularly insulting as it had always been him trying to rush her into commitment. She'd been stupid to get involved with him; not only had he been a work colleague at the time but he was also the best friend of Stephan, Ursula's husband. The latter fact had created an expectation that the two couples were a foursome and in the same place on the commitment scale. The former . . . Zia had always assumed that colleagues who dated kept their relationship out of the workplace but Brendon had been open about them sleeping together. She hadn't enjoyed being exposed to nudge-nudge-wink-wink office gossip.

Then McPherson & Partners made staff cuts of which Zia was a casualty, while Brendon hung on to his job. When, hot on the heels of that disappointment, Brendon had cheated, Zia ended things – and there had been a ripple of relief beneath her shocked humiliation. Next, a drunken exploit of Ursula's had prompted Stephan to demand their marriage was put 'on a break'.

Horrible as both Ursula's problems and Zia's redundancy had been, at least Zia was no longer tripping over Brendon.

'But Brendon's still calling you,' Ursula observed now. 'Any chance of a reconciliation?'

Zia wrinkled her nose. 'No, I was having doubts about us before he got caught in the act. He says he's sorry but I suspect he's only after forgiveness so he can feel better about himself. Unfortunately, I don't find cheating easy to forgive. I only stay polite to him because if you and Stephan get back together, we'll end up back in the same friendship group.'

Ursula sighed mournfully. 'Don't know if that will happen either.' Her second sigh was longer and more mournful than the first. 'I would have chucked myself into Devil's Dyke without your shoulder to cry on these past couple of months. I'll so miss you if you go away. You're my rock.'

Perturbed by Ursula's frequent descents into woefulness since her marriage hit trouble, Zia hesitated, chest tightening at Ursula's anxious expression. Her friend's emotional state was a worry. Ursula had scarcely come out of her room when she'd first moved in, until an understanding doctor and a little medication – plus a heap of TLC from Zia – had persuaded her that life was worth living. Privately, Zia cursed Stephan for refusing to attend couples' counselling. Instead he occupied the marital home like the moral high ground, dishing out judgement on his sorrowful wife. 'It's not even definite that I'm going,' she hastened to reassure her. 'Maybe I've romanticised my whole history into something it's not. Perhaps Lucia Costa was Mum's midwife so she named me after her. My dad might have just worked at the local Italian restaurant and Gran assumed his nationality from that.'

Ursula's forehead remained crumpled. 'But you look Italian with your golden skin and shiny dark hair. I bet we discover your dad's an Italian millionaire. He'll spirit you off to his empire in Rome and it'll be Ferraris and Armani all the way.'

Zia rolled her eyes. 'Ha. More likely I'll spend a bit of my redundancy payout on a holiday in Sorrento. You can come too.'

'It's a deal,' replied Ursula, but without the grin Zia had hoped for.

They flicked through files in silence for several minutes.

Then Ursula managed a half-laugh. 'This seems to be correspondence relating to your grandparents selling their Spanish house. There's a letter about the buyer asking for a price reduction and someone's written, "Fat chance!" at the bottom.'

'Gran, I expect.' Zia giggled, taking the paperwork to see for herself.

Ursula jumped to her feet. 'I wish I could be as don't-mess-with-me as she was. Want coffee?' She headed for the kitchen while Zia steeled herself not to put the correspondence in the 'keep' pile just because Gran had written a pithy comment on it. Outside the windows, gulls swooped like kites, crying out as if to tempt her into the bright May afternoon.

Ursula returned with two steaming coffee mugs then, turning back to the paperwork, happened on a folder of school reports, which actually made her laugh aloud. 'Listen to this teacher's comment: "Once we established who was in charge of Class 10, Victoria and I got on well." And, "Victoria Chalmers is more interested in decorating the cover of her maths book than adding work to its pages." She did tap dancing. Look at all these certificates.'

Zia craned to study the faded colours on thick card. 'Were teachers too stuffy in those days to call her Vicky? No one ever called her Victoria.' She picked up another folder and opened it. 'Here's a second batch of reports. She must have got loads. "Victoria Chalmers has settled well in Year Seven and is working hard." Maybe she liked senior school better than primary. And water had become her thing because this folder's full of swimming certificates.' A large buff envelope caught her eye. It was marked in her gran's careful cursive handwriting: *Vicky.* Her laughter faded and her heart misstepped as she picked it up. 'I know what's in this – Mum's birth and death certificates.'

'Aw, Zia.' Ursula's eyes filled with sympathy as Zia withdrew a long piece of stiff, crested paper from the envelope and unfolded it. Navy blue handwriting over red watermarking declared Victoria Chalmers to have been born in The Royal Exeter and Devon Hospital in April 1956 to Joyce Mary Chalmers and Alfred John Chalmers. The writing blurred before Zia's eyes. 'I was cheated of a lovely mum; always smiling, always busy with whatever house she was doing up. Telling me we were moving – again.'

'But doing up properties was the way she made her living,' Ursula excused the absent Vicky, though her voice oozed sympathy.

'Yeah. But I attended five different primary schools before I moved in with Gran and Pap.' Zia blew her nose and read from the death certificate, dated July 2001. 'Victoria Chalmers died of traumatic subarachnoid haemorrhage, or, in normal language, a bleed on the brain.' Carefully, she refolded the certificates, slid them into the envelope and placed it on the 'keep' pile.

The afternoon drew on, the sun moving behind the building so that the vivid colours of the garden outside dulled, though it didn't stop people from parking themselves on benches to eat a snack or consult a phone. Finally, Ursula stretched and yawned. 'That's every folder checked and there's not a hint of anything to do with your dad. I think you need to look through those letters of your mammy's. Maybe she talked about him with her friends.' Ursula only used words like 'mammy' for effect or when she went home to her big cheerful family near Dublin.

'I suppose so.' Slowly, Zia pulled the beach bag from

the otherwise empty suitcase. The white areas were slightly grey, the blue faded. She remembered discovering it, right at the back of the wardrobe top, as if retrieved from Zia's mum's things when she died and then forgotten.

Slowly, she slid open the zip and took out a sheaf of letters, spilling them across the oak table. Her fingertips wandered over envelopes: blue, pink, white and buff. Inside each was either lined writing pad paper or occasionally decorated sheets; paper that had lain undisturbed for more than twenty years. Zia felt tingly and comforted, all at once. 'Some people might say I'm intruding. But suddenly I feel almost as if I'm going to meet her again. I deserve a chance to know her better, don't I?'

'Of course you do,' Ursula approved.

'I'll sort them into some kind of order first.' Zia spent the next fifteen minutes flipping through envelopes while Ursula switched on a couple of lamps against the encroaching evening then vanished into the kitchen, returning after some clattering about. 'I've stuck chicken and jacket spuds in the oven.'

'Mm,' Zia answered absently, her attention still on the old letters spread out like tarot cards in front of her. 'There are lots of letters from Gran and Pap and some from friends. The earliest's dated December 1991. I'd been born the previous October and we'd just moved from Devon to Northamptonshire. The letters continue as we move to Bedfordshire and Huntingdonshire.' She neatened the rows.

Ursula resumed her seat, picked up the bag and peered inside. 'Is this empty?'

Absently, Zia nodded, pausing to prepare to poke her nose into her mum's life. 'It's quite nice that everyone wrote to each other in those days.'

Ursula pulled a brown envelope from a pocket in the

beach bag. 'Here's another envelope but there's nothing written on it.'

Zia continued her own line of thought. 'No one will ever find a bag of our letters, will they? We're all emails and WhatsApp. It'll just vanish. It's a pity. Maybe that's why people keep journals.' When Ursula didn't answer, she glanced up.

Mouth half open, Ursula was clutching a piece of paper in each hand, eyes enormous. 'Oh!' Her voice was breathy with alarm as she stared at them. 'Oh, Zia!'

Zia craned, but couldn't see what was making Ursula look as if she'd just discovered her bank account had been emptied. 'What on earth's up?'

Slowly, hazel eyes glittering oddly, Ursula turned the two pieces of paper and laid them before Zia. 'These are birth and death certificates for Victoria Chalmers, too. But the dates are different.'

'Different to . . . the other lot? How can they be?' Zia stared at the two documents. Heart thumping, she tried to take in the words unknown registrars had written in flowing fountain pen, forcing her reluctant brain to accept the evidence in front of her eyes.

Ursula was right.

Here were a separate set of birth and death certificates for Victoria Chalmers. With trembling fingers, she dug out the certificates she'd examined earlier and laid them alongside. Ursula shifted her chair closer so she could compare them, too. From the kitchen the oven timer pinged, insistent in the silence, but neither woman answered its summons.

Zia moistened dry lips. 'I can't believe what I'm seeing. There were two Victoria Chalmers, both born in Devon. Mum died in 2001, in Cambridgeshire, aged forty-five. The other died in Exmouth in 1991, when she was eighteen.' She scrabbled for the folders of school reports and certificates and examined them with fresh eyes. 'I didn't notice before but these are from different periods! What the hell?'

Ursula's voice was thin and uncertain. 'So, your mum was seventeen when the other Victoria was born.' She propped her chin on her hand.

The oven timer continued to ping in counterpoint to the gull's plaintive calls but Zia heard the *shush-shush* of her heartbeat louder than both. As spooked as a child at a horror film, she had to force her breathing to be even. 'Could the second Victoria have been my sister, or half-sister? One Mum gave up for adoption, maybe, because she was too young to cope? That might explain why the baby was registered with the same name as Mum – the adoptive family chooses the baby a new name anyway, don't they, and the adopted baby gets a new birth certificate?'

'I don't know. But . . .' Ursula arched her brows at Zia. 'The second Victoria might not be your sister. Could she be . . . your mum?'

'No,' Zia whispered. 'That can't be. Why would Mum hide the fact my real mother had died? Why would Gran and Pap?' Ignored, the timer stopped pinging of its own accord.

'Same goes if she was your sister,' Ursula pointed out. 'The letters might give us clues.'

Silently, they gazed at the stack of envelopes. Tentatively, Zia reached for the topmost and unfolded it, recognising the bold, black, sprawling handwriting. 'From Gran.' She swallowed a lump at the sight of the flimsy air mail writing paper that had winged its way from near Valencia in Spain.

11

14th December 1991
Dear Vicky,
    How are you? How is Zia-Lucia? Are you coping with her?

Zia paused. 'It's a bit weird to see baby me being discussed.' She returned to the letter.

Your father and I think we'd better come back to live in England and give you and Zia-Lucia some support. We can't imagine how you feel with poor darling Tori gone. How terrible it all is. Oh, darlingest darling, we grieve for you and with you! You've always gone your way but won't you let us help you this time? Can't we weather this together? We all loved Tori.

Zia swallowed. 'Gran used to call me "darlingest darling", too.' Had she loved the unknown Tori enough to call her the same? It gave her a twirly feeling to think it.

Ursula interrupted with the eagerness she usually reserved for solving sudoku. 'But 1991's the year the second Victoria died. Tori must be her – it's another short name for Victoria. I'll bet your mum was known as Vicky and this younger Victoria as Tori.'

Zia considered, stretching cramped legs beneath the table. 'Makes sense. Obviously, she was in touch with Mum at the time of her death and Gran and Pap too. That doesn't work with the adopted-baby idea – unless she'd traced Mum, of course, and either the adoptive parents hadn't given her a new name or she wasn't using it.'

Ursula looked intrigued. 'I wonder who her birth father was.'

Zia tried to laugh but it caught in her throat. 'My past seems littered with mystery fathers.' She started on the next letter. The handwriting was different. 'Pap's written this one.' They read it together.

3rd January 1992
Dear Vicky,
From your last letter it seems you don't want Mum and me to come back but we are worried about you. I'm going to be honest – we think what you're doing is crazy and sooner or later you'll have a lot of explaining to do. It's not too late to reconsider.

Zia skimmed the rest of the letter, 'Then there's a load of stuff about Pap's garden and Gran teaching Spanish to new ex-pats. But what do you think Mum would've had to explain about? It's like one of those games where you get clues in fragments.'

The next letter was dated a couple of weeks later and Gran had taken up her pen again, beginning with anxious enquiries.

Are you sure you're managing? Do you need money? Are you getting enough sleep? It's all very well burying your grief in the baby, darling, but tinies are exhausting.

Then Zia gurgled a laugh. 'Here comes Gran's usual bluntness. "*Exactly how long do you think you can keep this up? We thought you were flouting convention when you lived with that Harry Anstey but that was nothing compared to this current caper.*"'

'What caper?' demanded Ursula.

Zia was already rifling the stack of envelopes. 'Harry Anstey! There are letters here from him too, amongst some from Mum's friends. I didn't know they'd ever lived together. He visited us about once a year and it was like a mini-holiday. Mum would cook big dinners and we'd go on days out to parks or beaches but I don't remember them acting relationshippy.' She found the letters she wanted and pulled out the one with the earliest date. 'This is January '92, around the same time as Pap's letter.'

The letter read:

> *Vicky, babe, I can't bear it. I'd gladly take time off work to stay with you and help with Zia but I'm sure you hate me. Do you? Can you ever, ever forgive me?*

Zia met Ursula's fascinated gaze. 'Why would Mum hate Harry? They were mates.'

'Old flame?' Ursula suggested. 'All that "babe" and "forgive me" stuff? And living together? Perhaps he did a Brendon and got caught with his pants down.'

'Maybe.' Zia read on, quickly. 'But, no, this doesn't sound as if Harry's begging forgiveness for straying. Listen. *"If only I could relive that time when Tori disappeared! I'd sit up with her all night."*'

'Tori disappeared?' Ursula breathed, eyes saucers of astonishment.

Then Zia read the next few lines and almost stopped breathing. '*"Lucia Costa has been here again. I wish Tori never gave her this address. I was in the front garden and suddenly she was there, asking about Tori, ranting that you should never have taken Zia-Lucia from her in Montelibertà. Nightmare! I was as gentle as I could be,*

14

repeating what I told her last time, that we'd lost Tori and you no longer lived locally. I do feel sorry for her because she was obviously fond of Tori but if it wasn't for her sniffing around maybe I could bring you both home."'

'Jeez!' yelped Ursula.

Zia's breath escaped as a gasp. 'Lucia Costa! Who on earth *was* she? Why was she looking for me? And what the hell does he mean about taking me from somewhere called Montelibertà?' She grabbed a discarded A4 envelope and turned it over, scrabbling for a pen. 'Let's list significant points and try and piece the story together.'

They spent the rest of the evening at the task, picking at their overcooked meal absent-mindedly as they puzzled over the letters. By midnight their bullet points filled the back of an A4 envelope.

Weary eyes burning, Zia ran her gaze down the list. 'So, this is what we have.' She used her fingers to mark the points. 'Gran and Pap thought Mum was doing something wrong but shared her grief over Tori's death.' Another finger. 'Harry suffered guilt over her death. Probably Tori is the second Victoria Chalmers. Mum had been to a place called Montelibertà in Umbria, Italy and fetched me from this woman, Lucia Costa.' She reached the last finger on that hand as she came to the final point. 'Just after Mum and I moved to the Midlands, Lucia went to Exmouth looking for me but no one told her where I was.' She paused to rub tired eyes. 'This is like a TV drama.'

Ursula grabbed another letter and read aloud from it. 'Then in 1999 Harry says, "*Oh, Vicky, that bloody Lucia Costa turned up again after all these years! I told her I knew no more than I had when you first moved away. BLOODY woman!*"'

15

'And the last few letters from him are asking why Mum's not answering his letters any more,' Zia rounded out. 'He sounds so sad. The very last says: "*I didn't tell Lucia where you live, Vicky! Why would I betray you now? I've kept your secrets all these years.*"'

She laid down the letter, blood rushing in her ears. 'Holy shit. What did Mum do?'

Chapter Two

Piero Domenicali swung his silver Alfa Romeo into the rocky gap that formed the entrance to his property, Il Rifugio, passing the turning to Lucia and Durante's place, Bella Vista. Parking in the shade of the cypress trees as June in Italy prepared to burst the thermometer, he yanked off his tie and flung it on the seat. When he'd knotted the blue silk this morning, he'd indulged in a sneaking hope it would win parental approval and help him strike some miraculous bargain: 'Look, Papà, I'll wear a tie and you accept I don't want to sell my home . . . but I'm willing to sell the vineyard.'

The miracle hadn't happened. Salvatore had talked persuasively, lifted supplicating hands, hugged Piero and acknowledged the sacrifice he was asking his youngest son to make. Big brother Emiliano had followed suit. Of course, his father and brother wanted to accept the deal and sell everything; Emiliano's home was safely down the hill in the town of Montelibertà and Salvatore planned to buy a smaller place and spend much of his time travelling. It was only Piero's home and that of Lucia and Durante that the Binotto group were insisting on buying before they'd commit to buying the family vineyard.

And Il Rifugio wasn't *just* Piero's home. His workshop stood on the other side of the house, representing his first passion but his second business. He'd make it his only business if he could ever find a way to sell the vineyard and winery without losing this place. It was what he should have done all along – watched functional but beautiful wooden structures take shape in his hands.

He'd nearly burst an artery today when Graziella, his father's girlfriend, had sneered, 'Oh, your precious workshop,' and dismissed it with a wave of her hand. Almost without taking breath, she'd moved on to emotional blackmail. 'Family is family, Piero. Lucia and Durante are only neighbours.'

'They're friends, not just neighbours,' he'd snapped, thinking of Lucia and Durante's warm, undemanding company at the end of a long day. Rather than add, 'And you're not family, Graziella,' he'd turned to Alberto Gubbiotti, the dark-suited representative of the Binotto Group, a quiet, shadowy man who Piero disliked for his unsmiling air. 'We were promised time to consider your organisation's offer. No one's supposed to be exerting pressure, remember?'

Alberto Gubbiotti had inclined his head but Piero knew impassioned speeches bounced off him. He just listened as the family argued, probably calculating how long it would be before the Binotto group, impatient to diversify all over other people's land, got its hands on what it wanted.

Moodily, Piero slammed the car door. The current turmoil was enough to make him wish his family had stayed in America. Salvatore had moved them there when

Piero was two then, ten years later, had inherited the vineyard and winery of Tenuta Domenicali from a cousin. Piero and Emiliano's mother Elvira had been alive then and had allowed herself to be persuaded by a Salvatore fired up by the prospect of a new adventure. Twelve-year-old Piero and Emiliano, fourteen, who were settled in school and speaking English as easily as Italian, hadn't been consulted. Salvatore had just dragged the family back to Umbria, the green yet rugged heart of Italy.

He strode past his house to the edge of the rocky shelf on which it stood and gazed down into the sweep of the fertile valley, the view of Tenuta Domenicali that usually soothed his soul. Endless rows of vines sloped away dizzyingly. The breathtaking carpet of green and brown surrounded the golden stone home of his teenage self, where his father still lived, the winery buildings huddled around it like a mother dog with puppies. The Umbrian Apennine Mountains in their dusky purple and green summer clothes passed the other end of the valley like a herd of great migrating beasts. At one side of Il Rifugio the drop from the plateau was gentler and a track had once run down into the vineyard from his home, long overgrown.

He was looking at the three things Binotto's wanted; what the whole horrible battle was about. Tenuta Domenicali. The view. And access. How he wished they didn't want the latter two.

He dropped his head and turned away.

A couple of hundred years ago some ancestor had seen this plateau as a perfect site for a beautiful stone house – Piero's home, Il Rifugio. At a respectful distance had been the vineyard manager's accommodation and workers' cottages, now known as Bella Vista and owned by Lucia

19

and Durante. The boundary between Il Rifugio and Bella Vista was marked by a row of cypresses like artists' brushes upended in the landscape. A path had been trodden through the trees and scrub that provided dappled shade and he turned and made his way along it now, past the gazebo he'd built so lovingly.

On the other side of the cypresses Lucia and Durante had coaxed the land into terraces of lavender and rosemary. A mighty wisteria swirled along one side of the house and a small olive grove baked in the afternoon sun. The old workers' accommodation had been transformed by Durante into holiday cottages. Villino Il Pino and Villino La Quercia had two bedrooms and Villino Il Tasso one. With no pool and being a couple of miles out of town, their guests were mainly adults seeking a quiet haven.

As said guests were generally directed to park their vehicles the other side of the Bella Vista gazebo – Piero had made that, too – it gave him pause to see a dusty red car parked directly outside the house. Lucia's sister-in-law Fiorella who helped with the cleaning drove a red car, but Fiorella would never have left it with its nose inserted into Lucia's lovely lavender hedge.

A woman stood beside the car. Her dark hair was captured in an elegant updo and a smart red and black dress swirled down to her knees. His mind instantly leaped to the possibility she was from the Binotto empire. Had it been a two-pronged attack? While Gubbiotti had been pressuring the Domenicalis this woman had come to pester Lucia and Durante? She turned and regarded him from behind black sunglasses.

That he felt an immediate tug of attraction as he noted the curves above and below a neat waist only abraded his ruffled temper. He called out in Italian, 'If you're from the

Binotto Group I'm going to be upset. And can't you park without crushing Signora Costa's garden?' He gestured at the lavender which was responding to its maltreatment by issuing its delicious spicy scent.

A blonde woman jumped from the other side of the car, more casually dressed in shorts cut high enough to grab second looks from any heterosexual man. She glanced at the dark woman and demanded, 'What's up?'

The sound of English and her touristy clothes brought him up short. Too late, he realised the car's steering wheel was on the right; the dark woman he'd barked at had been standing at the passenger door. There would probably be a British number plate buried in the lavender.

The dark woman glanced at the blonde. 'He doesn't like your parking.' Though she looked like an Italian businesswoman, she too sounded like a British tourist. Turning back to Piero she lifted one eyebrow in a way that made him wonder whether his collar was askew and his hair tangled by the wind. '*Lei non parla italiano.*'

He switched to English. 'Sorry. I mistook you for someone else.'

The blonde's long legs carried her to the front of the car and she blushed as she inspected the lavender bed. 'Sorry. It's her car and I keep forgetting how big it is. We're renting a cottage here and we're supposed to be asking for Signora Costa or Signor Roscini. We have a mobile number but no one's answering.'

He exerted himself to create a better impression. 'The signal's spotty.' It wasn't true but seemed better than saying, 'The phone's probably off for siesta.' He moved towards the terrace steps. 'Why don't I show you to a seat? I'll see if I can locate your hosts.'

He led them up the terrace steps, enjoying the way they

halted open mouthed as the swooping rows of vines and purple mountains came into view. Bougainvillea on the rustic rails blazed cerise beneath a perfect blue sky and nowhere was the vista more stunning. He left them lost in admiration.

A drinks fridge stood in the open hallway just inside the terrace doors, access to bottled water being a courtesy extended to guests. He passed out a couple of bottles to the women and left them admiring the landscape while he ventured further within the stone walls, over the tiled floor to the foot of the stairs. He called up, 'Lucia? Durante? *I vostri ospiti sono arrivati.*'

An exclamation greeted his words and in a few moments, Lucia peeped over the bannisters, her dark, silver-streaked waves hanging either side of her face. 'The guests have arrived? They're early!' she hissed.

He grinned. 'I put them on the terrace.'

She blew him a kiss. '*Grazie mille. Due minuti.*'

'*Prego.*' Swooping up a bottle of water for himself, he returned to inform the women that Lucia would arrive in two minutes.

The dark woman just nodded but the blonde smiled and said, 'Thanks.'

Belatedly, he said, '*Benvenute in Italia*. I'm Piero Domenicali and I live just through the trees. You're English?'

'I'm Irish,' corrected the blonde.

The year he'd spent in the UK learning about the wine trade there had taught him the difference. 'The Republic?'

Her smile broadened. 'Yes. I'm Ursula and my friend is Zia.'

The dark woman smiled too. 'I'm English.' She hadn't removed her sunglasses.

Then Lucia's voice rang out from behind them. '*Buongiorno*! I'm sorry not to have heard you arrive. Welcome. I'm Lucia Costa.'

Ursula and Zia turned to greet Lucia. Even in beige shorts and a prettily flowered top, small, round Lucia was always uncreased, as if she were still a businessperson. Ursula made introductions and answered Lucia's friendly questions about their journey – they'd driven from the south of England and been three days on the road, which made it odder still that Zia was dressed in what Piero saw as office clothes. He noted how Ursula spoke for them both and that some of Zia's composure seemed to have slipped since Lucia's arrival. Lips slightly parted, she took quick, shallow breaths as Lucia explained Durante would soon arrive to show them to Villino Il Pino. Did she always look as if she were quivering with tension at meeting someone new? She must find life exhausting.

Lucia, in contrast, always had an easy manner. 'You are Zia?' she asked her. 'Is it a common name in England?'

The tension in the dark woman's expression seemed to intensify. 'It's not common but there are a few of us.' She smiled then. 'I expect it seems odd as I know it means "aunt" in Italian.'

Whatever Lucia might have replied was lost as Durante strolled from the house – he rarely hurried since retiring. His shorts were crumpled and hugged his paunch. '*Buongiorno*! I am Durante.' After introductions he added, 'I show you your accommodation.'

The guests rose as Lucia added, 'You'll find a map of the area in your cottage but ask questions any time.'

Piero stood beside Lucia, who only reached his shoulder, and they watched Durante herd them away. The moment they'd disappeared down the steps she turned to him. 'What happened at the meeting?'

Wearily, he dropped into a terrace chair beside a pot of nodding pink geraniums. 'More pressure. Alberto Gubbiotti upped the offer, so he'll no doubt be contacting you with a similar increase. I was asked to vote for it. At least, Papà asked. Emiliano hoped and Graziella demanded.'

Lucia dropped into another chair, resting her head on her hand so the softening flesh pulled to one side. 'Oh, Piero. How I wish they'd just leave us alone. Or that Salvatore and Emiliano weren't your family.'

He nodded but added fairly, 'Or that I didn't want the vineyard to be sold too.'

Though her mouth quivered as if she might cry, she reached out and took his hand. 'You, my friend, are in an impossible position.'

Chapter Three

Stunned by meeting the Lucia Costa she might owe part of her cumbersome name to, Zia sat silently as Ursula drove down the slight slope past Bella Vista's olive grove, bearing right and then halting at Durante's direction. He beamed, looking like an ageing cherub with his big tummy, wide smile, turned-out sandals and a ruff of pale grey hair above his ears. When they'd climbed back out of the car, he opened the close-boarded door of the nearest of three cottages. 'Here is your little house for two weeks.' Quickly, he showed them the cooking and showering facilities. 'In the past, workers from the vineyard live here and bring their water from the well.' He had little trouble communicating in English but he stuck with the present tense and uncomplicated sentences whereas Lucia spoke more fluently, with only the occasional awkward phrase.

'I'm glad we don't have to do that,' Ursula joked. The booking had been made in her name and they'd agreed in advance that she'd do most of the early talking. Sooner or later, Zia knew, the hosts would need to take a copy of their passports but the longer she could put that off, the longer she could lurk in the background and assess Lucia Costa. Was she the Italian lady Gran had said had been kind to Zia's mother? Would she know something about Zia and the conundrum of the two Victoria Chalmers?

Durante chuckled. 'The well is closed.' He placed one hand on top of the other to demonstrate then picked up a fold of paper from a low table. 'Here is your map and you see Lucia marks to you the supermarket. Other things also. Church. Shops. Piazzas.' He tapped a fresh point on the map. 'Here is Bella Vista. You see a line of cypress trees on the boundary? Please, you do not go through because it is Piero's land.' He folded the map again. 'The patios in front and behind the cottage are for you. There are sun loungers. Lucia gives you a small welcome—' Durante indicated a bottle of red wine and an uncut loaf of bread in the kitchen then opened the fridge to display oil, cheese and a pack of parma ham. He treated them to another beaming smile. 'You like me to carry in your luggage? No? Please, we ask all guests, when the car is empty, park behind the gazebo.' Via the open door he pointed out a wooden structure of such elegance and size that Zia might have called it a pavilion. Villino Il Pino was too small and set-back for them to see much but the mountain tops but the gazebo, set on the lip of the plateau, must offer awe-inspiring views of the valley. Durante said goodbye and pulled the door behind him as he left.

Zia plummeted onto a small grey sofa, thankful she no longer had to hold herself together. 'Holy hell. I feel like someone put me through the spin dryer.'

Ursula curled up beside her. 'Do you think she's the same Lucia Costa your mum knew? Did you feel any connection?'

26

'A tall order to know from one meeting.' Zia fought to even out her breathing. 'What bond could I sense with someone I met when I was a baby, thirty years ago? We've probably driven for three days for nothing and I've interviewed for a front-desk position in a property management company in Montelibertà – which looks ghastly, by the way – and fibbed about already having applied for residency.' She kicked off her interview shoes and pulled up her interview dress to allow the air to cool her. 'Maybe we should have tried harder to track down Harry and ask him.'

'Yeah, rude of him not to still be living at the Exmouth address he wrote to your mum from over twenty years ago. Anyway,' Ursula mused, 'his old letters gave us Montelibertà as a starting point. Google can find only one Lucia Costa currently in the area – isn't it useful that Italian women don't take their husband's surnames? She speaks English. She looks the right age to have been an adult when you were a baby. She and her husband run holiday cottages in an Italian paradise and we've enjoyed a fab road trip across France and Switzerland to get here. And the interview for the ghastly job was only a fact-finding mission for if you do decide to try and move out here so why worry?'

Spirits lifting at this pragmatic view, Zia nodded. 'True. We've seen everything from cities to farms to mountains and stayed in cute hotels in Nancy and Lucerne. The worst that can happen is that we'll drive home again at the end of two weeks, no wiser.'

'Hey, now!' Ursula wagged a manicured finger. 'Don't you be telling me you're not going to try and talk to Lucia.'

'I didn't say that.' But Zia's belly did a wild dive off

27

the high board at the thought. If Lucia was the wrong Lucia Costa then Zia's enquiries could be easily brushed aside. But what if she was the right one? She'd know why Vicky Chalmers had once fetched Zia from Montclibertà. Part of Zia yearned to know but what if it proved hard to hear? Her memories of Vicky, the mum who'd died far too young, were golden. How would she feel if fresh knowledge tarnished them beyond redemption?

A knock fell on the front door. With a creak, it swung ajar and Piero Domenicali was revealed, his stunned gaze zeroing in on her bare legs where she'd hitched up the hem of her dress. Mortified, she scrambled to cover herself.

He cleared his throat. 'The door opened as I knocked. I didn't mean to . . . intrude.'

Zia was busy blushing like a furnace so Ursula was the one to uncoil from her place on the sofa and answer. 'That's OK. I expect Signor Roscini didn't quite shut the door when he left. Come on in.'

He seemed to remember the wine bottle he was clutching and held it out. 'I brought an apology for being grouchy earlier. It's from my family vineyard, Tenuta Domenicali. Orvieto Classico is one of the white wines of our region.'

Collecting herself, Zia rose too. 'That's kind but we didn't expect anything. Is your family vineyard the one we can see below? The vines look beautiful, swooping down the hillside.'

He nodded. 'My father owns half and my brother and I inherited the other half from our mother. Papà and Emiliano manage the vineyard and the winery and I sell the wine.'

Ursula scrutinised him. 'You sound as much American as Italian.'

His sudden grin chased away the lines from his forehead

and brought light into dark eyes. Somehow it looked more at home on his face than his earlier frowns. 'We lived in California when I was a kid. I got a year in England in my twenties, too, working with a wine importer.' His gaze moved to Zia. '*Tu parli italiano.*'

'*Sì, ne ho imparato un po'. Vorrei migliorare,*' she answered. *Yes, I've learned some. I'd like to be better.* 'I'm not fluent. I'm afraid that on our side of the channel we're lazy. Lucia and Durante speak English well, too,' she added, thinking she might as well gain a little background if she could. Piero seemed on easy terms with them.

He nodded. 'Lucia particularly. She owned a ceramics factory that exported all over Europe and speaking English is an advantage in business. Durante managed a car hire place and Montelibertà is a tourist town.'

'Are there other homes up here?' Zia already knew there weren't from the satellite view on her map app.

He shook his head. 'Just us. The properties used to belong to the vineyard and Lucia, Durante and I bought them to modernise. I think there are guests at the other cottages but otherwise we're pretty quiet up here.' He stepped back towards the door. 'I hope you enjoy your stay. *Arrivederci per ora.*' Then, to Ursula, 'Goodbye for now.'

Moving to the open doorway they watched him stride away across the paving and up the slope, arms swinging easily beneath his white shirt. 'He's hot,' Ursula murmured.

'Hey, you're a married woman!' Zia teased, giving Ursula a small shove and choosing not to admit that she'd noted his back view in well-cut trousers, too.

Still, the interlude had dispelled Zia's negativity about their mission and she found herself once again delighted with Italy and curious to discover what history she might have with Montelibertà. They unpacked the car and Zia swapped her 'interview dress' for shorts and a bandeau top. Driving over, apart from meaning they'd have a car while they were here, had allowed her to pack generously in case she chose to prolong her stay. Ursula had taken all three weeks of her remaining annual leave and they'd planned that she'd fly home if Zia wasn't ready to go at the end of it.

Villino Il Pino's rooms were painted white and the small windows were edged with stone. Its floors were terracotta, beautifully cool to bare feet, and crisp white sheets covered the beds. Ursula appeared in the doorway of Zia's room, brandishing her phone. 'Just got a text from Durante reminding us copies of our passports have to be taken for the authorities.'

Knees turning to jelly, Zia dropped onto a corner of the bed. 'Potentially a turning point if Lucia notices my full name.'

Ursula came to perch beside her, legs long and smooth. 'I could take the passports and try and shrug off questions . . . but you *want* information, don't you?' Her eyes were sympathetic but also puzzled.

'I do but it's scary. You're being fantastic with my dramas.' Zia hugged her friend's willowy frame, breathing in the smell of the high-factor sun lotion she used on her pale skin.

Ursula hugged her back. 'Sure, you know I love a good puzzle.'

'How about I take the passports and play it by ear?' Zia suggested.

Though looking faintly disappointed that Zia wanted this tricky moment under her control, Ursula agreed, 'Sure,' and passed hers over.

The late afternoon sun blazed as Zia followed the dusty pathway past the olive trees, climbing the steps to the terrace and knocking on the door to the main house. Durante answered, his fringe of hair wafting like grey candy floss. 'Ah, you have the passports. *Grazie*. Lucia buys printer ink now so I scan now and print later. OK?' He led Zia into the cool interior of the house to a small office where a well-used desk looked spacious enough for two. It was old-fashioned but the black printer-scanner and streamlined aluminium computer were bang up to date.

Durante opened the first passport – Ursula's – and slid it under the scanner lid. The machine hummed and sighed into action. 'You like Villino Il Pino?' He flashed one of his ready smiles. 'You like Italy?'

'I love both,' Zia answered promptly. 'I've been to Italy often but never to Umbria. It's beautiful.'

Durante looked pleased as he removed Ursula's passport and reached for hers. Zia held her breath so hard her heart knocked on her breastbone but Durante turned to the correct page and placed the passport face down on the glass plate with barely a glance. 'Umbria is called "the green heart of Italy", yes? We are born in Montelibertà, down in the town, and go to school there. In the past, I work in town and Lucia close to Deruta, where the transport links are good. But this is our home and the cottages our retirement business. Just a little work to keep us from trouble.' He twinkled at her.

It was impossible not to smile back as she took back her passport, not sure whether to be glad or sorry at Durante's lack of reaction. 'Have you visited England? Ursula and I live on the south coast.'

'Yes, I visit a few times. Lucia, many times, on business, selling to the UK.'

They ambled together to the terrace door, passing the opening to a salon, its furniture old and eclectic, dark varnished wood or painted green and cream and decorated with pink roses. Polish scented the air. 'You have a lovely home. Traditional and elegant.'

'We love it. It's a big house for just two but we like the space.' And Durante heaved a sigh.

Zia wondered at that but his smile returned as she said goodbye. She retraced her steps, drinking in the hum of bees and the dance of butterflies around the lavender. Ursula was waiting on a lounger in the uber-posh gazebo, gazing out over the valley. Zia settled next to her murmuring, as if they were secret agents, 'Lucia's out so I saw Durante. He scanned my passport without really looking at it.'

'No further forward then,' Ursula murmured back absently without removing her gaze from the panorama. The vines were taking on a sepia cast as the sunset painted the landscape from its own palette, the nearest mountain dark green, the next purple and the most distant lavender-blue. Cicadas whirred and a bird of prey rode the wind on outstretched wings.

Zia inhaled the woodsy smell of the sun-warmed gazebo and, transferring her gaze right, tried to see where Piero Domenicali might live. The last cottage, Villino La Quercia, blocked her view even before the trees and bushes. She winced at the memory of the door to Villino Il Pino swinging open to leave him staring at her legs before she'd yanked down her hem . . . but she also remembered his eyes were like chocolate flecked with demerara sugar.

'I really want some of that wine.' Ursula sighed.

Zia glanced at her. 'We can fetch it.'

'No, you know I've put myself on a self-imposed alcohol

ban since falling prey to hen-party cocktails and that white knight delivering me home, paralytic.'

'As it's the reason you moved into my spare room, I know only too well,' Zia murmured. Stephan had been incandescent, suspecting Ursula of sleeping with the unknown stranger or 'white knight', as Ursula called him. Hungover the next day, she'd made the mistake of trying to laugh it off. 'Does a guy carrying me home because I'd passed out count as "sleeping with"?' Then, when Stephan raged into fresh accusations, 'Look, women generally know if they've had sex – full docking manoeuvres, anyway – and I don't think I have.'

Far from finding the statement mollifying, Stephan had been so distraught that Ursula, in the untenable position of not knowing whether she'd sinned, had yielded to Stephen's demand that she get out. In the space of one fraught week in March the two couples – Zia and Brendon, Ursula and Stephan – had fragmented. Out of the four, only Zia was ready to move on.

As if following a similar train of thought Ursula murmured, 'I don't know if Stephan reacted so badly because it was only a few days after you'd caught Brendon having drunken stranger sex at a party but what he did is *not* the same.'

Zia patted her arm. 'No. I *know* Brendon's guilty. As far as we know, all you did was get drunk.' Still, she didn't fetch the wine. If being dry would help Ursula cope with the as-yet unresolved situation with Stephan, Zia was happy to go along with it. Ursula, though sometimes red-eyed and subdued, seemed to harbour hope. Even three months after she moved out, she was still having long, intense telephone conversations with Stephan from which she often emerged more red-eyed than ever.

Ursula changed the subject. 'Let's have breakfast here tomorrow, drinking in this view.'

Though spellbound by the sunset, Zia pointed out, 'If we don't get to the supermarket before it closes at eight, we won't have any coffee with breakfast.'

'Suppose,' agreed Ursula reluctantly. But still they remained where they were for another half hour, perched on the edge of the world looking out at an apricot sky.

Chapter Four

The atmosphere in Tenuta Domenicali's office crackled like the air before an electric storm.

Salvatore's grey eyebrows quivered in rhythm with his brush-like moustache as he frowned. Age was grinding lines into his face like the creases on a walnut shell. 'Has Graziella done something wrong?' he demanded when Piero joined him and Emiliano in the white, high-ceilinged office they all knew so well, traditionally Salvatore's domain though he'd relinquished much of the vineyard's day-to-day business to his sons now.

'We three are the shareholders. Emiliano doesn't bring Jemma,' Piero pointed out. He'd rather have Emiliano's pretty wife at business meetings than his father's girlfriend, Graziella. Jemma wasn't overbearing.

'But Jemma has her own job,' Salvatore returned. 'Graziella helps me with the computer.' Salvatore didn't like computers whereas Graziella was tech-savvy.

As today's battle was all about saving his home, Piero moved on. 'We had agreed selling to Binotto's was too big a decision to be hurried but now we're being pressured.'

'Graziella—' Salvatore began.

Piero lifted a hand. 'I know Graziella is in a hurry. But why are you?'

Salvatore bristled. 'I'm seventy. I want to retire, to travel and enjoy life.'

Piero got up and crossed to the drinks station. Espresso greased the wheels of any meeting. He sent his father a level look. 'You could take eight round-the-world cruises without selling a stick or stone. You could leave the running of Tenuta Domenicali and have plentiful income from your share.'

Emiliano jumped in. 'But you don't want to work here, Piero. Two years ago, the only way you'd stay was if you could work four days a week instead of five.'

Piero conceded the point. 'It's no secret that I want to sell Tenuta Domenicali. But not at the expense of my home and that of Lucia and Durante.' He passed the first espresso to Salvatore but looked at his brother as he continued. 'I can see why the deal's attractive to you. You want to stay. They've offered you the role of winemaker. You'll get a huge lump sum, a salary and a reduction in responsibility.' Piero paused. 'And keep your home.'

Emiliano scratched his close-trimmed beard. Although he was mature in most ways, happily married to Jemma and a father to Cristian and Camilla, he had a boyish tendency to follow the glossy magazines when it came to trends.

Salvatore beetled his brows. 'We understand you're being asked to make the greatest sacrifice Piero but the vineyard has been on the market for over a year and the Binotto deal is the only one on the table.'

'I'm being asked to make the *only* sacrifice,' Piero corrected softly. He passed an espresso to his brother and stared out of the window at the stone buildings of the winery or *casa vinicola,* its great stainless-steel tanks visible through the open door. Although his role wasn't wine-making he knew every corridor, every step and stone, where every barrel and closure waited. The voices of winery workers filtering into the office accompanied his every working day.

Salvatore said heavily, 'The vineyard is steep and small. The grapes have to be harvested by hand and we can't compete with the prices of wine from the big vineyards.'

Piero collected his own coal-black espresso. 'We produce a quality, boutique product, which hand harvesting is part of. We don't compete for the supermarket shelves. We have prestigious clients like Harvey Nichols and Harrods in London and restaurants all across Europe.'

'But there's no other deal,' Emiliano circled back obstinately. 'What if there never is? Papà retires, you and I carry on, bearing all the risk as the market dwindles until we can't afford to grow grapes. Nature takes back Tenuta Domenicali and we're left with nothing.'

Piero paused. It had happened to other small vineyards.

Salvatore made good on the hesitation. 'Binotto's wants this as a working vineyard for wine tourism so whether the wine is produced at a profit becomes secondary.'

Piero took his seat again. 'I know all that.' He couldn't blame his brother or father for wanting easier lives and Salvatore wanting to enjoy time with Graziella. When she and Salvatore had met Piero had welcomed it. Elvira, his mother, had died with a kidney problem when Piero was twenty and he didn't begrudge his father a life. In fact, he'd been wryly amused. That the then sixty-eight-year-old Salvatore had attracted a fifty-three-year-old woman, and a willowy and attractive woman at that, was impressive.

Graziella and her ex-husband had owned three small hotels and sold out to a chain when they divorced. Graziella still liked to dabble in business. But it was a damned shame she saw fit to 'dabble' in Tenuta Domenicali and an even worse shame that his father and brother were letting her.

'I won't be rushed.' Piero looked at his father, meaning, 'Call Graziella off.' Salvatore's eyes narrowed but he nodded.

Less than an hour later, Piero was in his own office on a video call when, to his fury, Graziella bounced in wearing a yellow dress and gold sandals, both designer, her carefully cultivated corkscrew curls flying. Ignoring the virtual meeting he was in the middle of she cried, 'Piero, I won't have you upsetting your father. You're making him ill—'

It was all Piero could do not to leap to his feet and bellow, 'Get OUT!' Luckily, Salvatore appeared on Graziella's heels, hooked his arm around hers and bustled her back up the corridor.

Breathing hard, Piero returned to his computer screen where the woman who'd been pitching the environmental and economic benefits of moving cargo by barge in Germany was looking surprised but fascinated. '*Scusi*,' he muttered. Inwardly, he seethed.

Then he checked his thoughts. Why had Graziella picked on his father's health as a lever? Did she know something?

It became impossible to concentrate. He wound up the call then strode up the narrow corridor to the big office. As so often these days, he found Graziella and Salvatore sharing his father's ancient desk, Graziella's finely manicured fingers on the keyboard and Salvatore peering through his glasses at the screen.

'Are you ill, Papà?' he asked tautly.

Salvatore looked uncomfortable. 'I'm tired, that's all.'

'You're sure?' Piero regarded his father narrowly, checking for telltale signs that all wasn't well.

'I didn't say he *was* ill. I said you'd *make* him ill.' Graziella tilted her nose in the air.

She'd said he 'was making' his father ill but he left the room and returned to his own desk without pointing that out, knowing he'd been sent on a guilt trip. Salvatore and Emiliano could reconcile themselves to him giving up the home he loved on the shelf above the valley, a prospect that gave him a bellyful of lead.

And if he accepted the deal it would sell Lucia and Durante down the river as the lawyers said that if he sold, they'd be forced to sell too. They couldn't reach their property without crossing his.

The rest of his day passed in resolving supply chain issues. Salvatore and Graziella had driven off somewhere, to Piero's relief. The more contact he had with Graziella, the less he wanted. Emiliano was out on the vineyard.

Unable to concentrate, Piero quit his office, striding out into the sunlight. High up in the vineyard he could see Emiliano doing what he'd do frequently until the October harvest: inspecting grapes with Dino, a member of vineyard staff. He set off up the slope. When Emiliano caught sight of him, he said something to Dino and headed down. The brothers met in the middle of a row where their only companions were hovering insects and the breeze that rustled the vines.

'*Ciao*,' Emiliano greeted him guardedly.

Piero jumped in. 'What are your views on the way Graziella's acting? She told me off today.' He recounted the incident of Graziella storming into his office.

Emiliano laughed in disbelief. 'That's unacceptable.'

'Agree.' Piero felt a flutter of relief. They'd grown up as allies and his big brother setting himself against Piero was almost as disquieting as Salvatore listening to Graziella ahead of his own son.

Cautiously, Emiliano said, 'Papà's in love. We'd be unwise not to accept it.'

Piero shrugged. 'I accept his right to love a woman who's not Mamma. It's . . . *this* woman. Or, at least, the way she's trying to force an issue that isn't hers to force. She's changing him. He's not the impetuous, quirky man he used to be, going his own sweet way. He's letting himself be influenced.'

'She's forthright,' Emiliano conceded, turning over a vine leaf to inspect its underside.

'Bossy. Pushy.' Piero amended. 'Selfish.'

Emiliano waggled his eyebrows. '"Forthright" would be more diplomatic.' Then he pulled Piero in for an understanding hug. 'We've put you in a crap position. It's unfortunate the offer suits Papà and me but not you.'

'No kidding.' Cheered by brotherly love that could survive being on opposite sides of a fence, Piero made his way downhill again while Emiliano rejoined Dino up the slope.

After returning to his desk to pick up his laptop, Piero drove home.

There, he threw off his office clothes and pulled on a pair of shorts and work boots. Taking a bottle of cold water, he quit the house in favour of the workshop at the side of it, glancing over at the hazy mountains as he rolled open the green doors as if sliding the uncomfortable day from his shoulders. The smell of cedar wood welcomed him in from the drifts of sawdust that gathered despite the extractor system and his sweeping the floor often. Well, sometimes. He opened the doors at the other end of the workshop too so the breeze could wander through. Trees and a slice of spiky mountain were visible through one door and the drive through the other. Inside, his wood-working machinery stood foursquare and businesslike and his hand tools were racked on the walls.

On his bench stood a square lantern roof destined to provide the crowning glory to an orangery, half-glazed with greenish antique glass. He was good at these small, specialised, creative commissions. The contractor was a joiner called Antonio who'd send someone to pick the lantern up once glazed. The hill that began as Via Virgilio in Montelibertà climbed right past Il Rifugio and the rocky opening to his drive was large enough for trucks.

Contentedly, he set to work, fitting the remaining glass with generous squeezes of mastic and delicately pinned wooden beading. Once finished, he sent a photo of the gracefully peaked structure to Antonio, who confirmed collection for Wednesday.

Phone still in hand, he noticed Lucia had texted: they were hosting drinks on the terrace for their guests. Would he like to join them? After a rubbish day he didn't feel like chatting with tourists but his fingers paused before he could tap out a suitably polite refusal. Maybe Zia would be there? He'd found it hard to scrub from his mind the image of her on that sofa. Her ludicrous expression of dismay as the door swung open to reveal her in a hiked-up business dress had been far sexier than Ursula's mini-shorts and tight top. He'd gaped like a teenage boy, lust exploding through him. Add in Zia's full mouth and swept-up hair . . .

He checked his workshop clock. Still time. *Great,*

thanks, he texted back. A quick shower and change later he set off through the trees, crossing the Bella Vista drive to the terrace to locate the gathering.

'Piero! *Vino o birra?*' Durante called as he saw him, rising from the table.

'*Birra, per favore,*' Piero answered and, '*Buona sera,*' to the guests. He smiled at Zia and Ursula and took the vacant seat beside Zia, who'd abandoned business wear in favour of white shorts and a lacy top, her hair swinging in a ponytail. Lucia introduced him to the guests he hadn't met: two women and two men in their sixties wearing cloth sun hats, Dutch but speaking good English.

The party sipped drinks and helped themselves from a dish of olives as they made small talk. Zia, Piero noticed, seemed adept at kicking off the conversation and then listening. She said to Lucia, 'Durante told me you travelled.' She wore sapphires on her ring finger, right hand. If she'd been an Italian woman it would have meant she was engaged but he knew British women usually wore engagement and wedding rings both on the left, as Ursula did. Zia's third finger on her left hand was bare.

'Yes, yes, when I owned a ceramics factory. Like Piero. He travels around Europe selling wine.' Lucia lifted her glass of white to illustrate.

Piero grinned. 'I travel less, now. Video conferencing's taking over.' He didn't mind that Lucia had made him sound like a rep rather than the director of sales and transportation. Essentially, he sold wine.

After a rambling digression about personal meetings versus video calls, Zia gave the conversation another nudge. 'Which parts of Britain have you visited, Lucia?'

'London, often.' Lucia answered. 'Also, Edinburgh in

Scotland and other places. Sometimes for trade shows, sometimes to meet buyers.'

'Ursula and I live in Brighton, in East Sussex,' Zia popped in. 'But I was born in Devon.'

Lucia sipped her wine before replying. 'I visited Devon a few times.'

Did Piero dream it or did Zia exchange a quick glance with Ursula? She moved on so smoothly to a polite enquiry about whether Lucia had family in Montelibertà that Piero wasn't sure. Then Durante pulled him into a conversation with the Dutch tourists who wanted to cycle around Lake Trasimeno. He joked, 'All of it?' But was happy to talk about the beauties of the lake.

After an hour, Ursula's phone rang and, saying breathlessly to Zia, 'It's Stephan. See you later,' she excused herself.

Zia smiled and nodded then continued to chat to Lucia while the Dutch couples asked Piero and Durante about trains to Orvieto. Living in a tourist town they were used to these conversations and were happy to explain the new public transport fare system. Durante pushed another beer into Piero's hand. The sky turned from lavender to navy and the terrace lights came up.

The Dutch guests eventually left to seek dinner in Montelibertà and the instant they'd exited down the steps Lucia gave Durante's arm an urgent shake. 'Listen!' she demanded dramatically. 'Zia, she knows property law. She thinks they're lying.'

Piero's gaze flew to Zia, whose brows shot up. 'I didn't exactly say that,' she countered quickly. 'I just said I wasn't sure what you told me sounded correct. I'm not an expert.'

'But tell them what you think,' Lucia demanded. A sheen had broken out over her face, clinging to the furrows in her skin.

Caution entered Zia's brown eyes. She said to Piero, 'Lucia said you've been told that because she and Durante need to use Il Rifugio's drive to reach their place, whoever owns the land can stop them gaining access.'

Piero nodded. He wasn't sure how deeply Lucia had gone into things with Zia but he wasn't sure he liked it. Salvatore and Emiliano could appear in a bad light. From the outside, it might be hard to see how family members could desire completely different things yet still love each other.

Zia frowned. Rather than making her look older, as it had Lucia, it emphasised her thoughtful intelligence. 'I think the reverse is true. I worked for a company dealing with leaseback and often the real estate concerned was in Italy or Spain.'

Durante's brows lowered. 'What's "leaseback"?' He stumbled over the word.

Zia shifted her gaze to him. 'My company would buy, say, an Italian supermarket – but just the property, the real estate. The supermarket would then have the proceeds of the sale to inject into their business while continuing to trade from the premises, for which they paid us rent.'

'Providing the return on your company's investment,' Piero clarified.

She nodded. 'I worked on a purchase that was complicated by an easement of passage issue – *diritto di passaggio* – and, putting it simply: Italian law allows people to get on and off their property.' As Durante was still frowning, she repeated it in Italian, making a pretty good job of it too. When she'd termed herself 'not fluent' it had been verging on false modesty.

Durante drained his beer and slapped the glass on the

table. 'Then why did the lawyers tell us whoever owns Piero's land can make ours worthless?'

'Because it's what they want us to believe!' Lucia cried, her lips trembling. She gripped the edge of the table as if ready to hurl it at someone. 'We will take them to court and fight.'

Noticing increasing unease shadowing Zia's face, Piero assumed the voice of reason. 'Let's not get carried away. Zia makes sense but we've been given the complete opposite information – though we don't have much experience with the law firm in question.' For Zia's benefit he added, 'It was thought our local firm wouldn't have the expertise to handle such a complex situation so someone recommended these guys to my father.' Someone called Graziella, who said the same lawyers had acted for her and her ex-husband when they sold their hotels to a bigger chain. A spectre of uneasiness loomed in his mind.

Zia's eyebrows still held a thoughtful quirk. 'How long ago did you buy your land?'

He calculated. 'I was twenty-two, so sixteen years. Lucia and Durante a little earlier.'

'So, what do the ownership papers say about the access?' Her gaze was still on Piero.

The spectre of uneasiness looked at him as if he were a mug. 'The buying act? I haven't seen for myself. I was young and Papà and the notary guided me. The papers were put in the company safe. Now they're with the lawyers.'

Another small movement of her finely marked eyebrows. 'The originals? I would have thought copies . . .' She smiled. 'But, as I said, I'm no expert.'

Durante put in, 'And our papers are lost in earthquake

45

damage a few years ago. A water pipe bursts and the basement of our lawyer is flooded. We request copies from the *Ufficio del Registro* but we wait.' He looked as Piero felt: abashed.

Lucia groaned. 'We've taken the word of lawyers who do not even work for you and me, Durante. We must be mad.'

In growing disquiet, Piero gazed at Zia. 'You disclaim expertise but you seem to know more than us. Would you come look at Il Rifugio? I have questions.' He'd have invited Lucia and Durante but Zia had looked unnerved when Lucia started throwing about words like 'lying' and 'court'. He didn't want her too spooked to share whatever information she possessed.

Zia regarded him for a moment, then nodded. 'I'll text Ursula to explain in case she finishes her call and comes looking for me.'

'Of course.' He waited while she swiftly sent her text then they fell into step as he led her up the drive, her head level with his shoulder and her ponytail swinging. As they passed between banks of yellow-blooming broom that perfumed the early evening air, the noise of traffic grew louder. 'The drive we're walking on belongs to Bella Vista. It's maybe eighty metres,' he explained. They stepped onto the section that connected with the road. 'This part's the issue. I own it and they pass over it.' They continued for another twenty strides until they reached the public road and he had to lift his voice over rumbling engines and tooting horns as he gestured to each side. 'This opening's natural and, as you can see, the rock's several metres high.'

Her eyes caught the flicker of headlights as she gazed at the towering rocks, studying the way the public road had been sliced from the mountain, leaving a sheer face in either direction. 'I guess Lucia and Durante wouldn't be allowed to blast away at the mountain to make direct access further along, even if it made financial sense.'

'Exactly. Let me show you the rest,' he suggested. This time he took her down his own drive, passing his Alfa Romeo and then the house, to the open area that provided the same glorious vista as Lucia's and Durante's terrace. 'It's getting dark but I think you can make out the vineyard and winery owned by myself, Papà and my brother Emiliano.' The buildings were a cluster of lights and the mountains mere shadows in the twilight. He embraced the valley he loved with widespread arms. 'The estate, the company and the wine label, they're all called Tenuta Domenicali. Now Papà's older, Emiliano takes the lead in the production cycle, planting vines, nurturing them, harvesting the grapes, seeing the wine through fermentation and bottling. Orvieto Classico's our main focus but we produce some Sangiovese.' He grinned. 'When Papà was the winemaker he flew by the seat of his pants. All his life's been like that – trying things and somehow making them work. Emiliano, though, he's a winemaker of repute, very measured and insightful. My role's about developing the brand and getting the wine to buyers.'

She listened, nodding, following his gestures with her gaze.

He let his eyes rove over the vineyard and the buildings, one of which had once been the home where his mother Elvira had helped her sons with their homework one moment and hosted a big party the next. Generous, open-hearted, Elvira had been a stark contrast to the woman who lived there now. 'Lucia's obviously explained a big organisation wants to buy Tenuta Domenicali, Il Rifugio and Bella Vista to create a centre for wine tourism. The houses and the cottages would be for high-end guests who'd enjoy the exclusivity and the view.'

'Agriturismo for rich folk?' She smiled faintly.

'Exactly. And, most of all, Binotto's want my access. You can't see well in this light but down the side of the vineyard—' he pointed '—there's a connecting track. They could upgrade it to make a road to bring in coaches of the tourists who "follow the wine" through Umbria, Assisi, Montefalco and Orvieto. Visitors could tour the winery and buy the bottled product. Tourists have money to spend. Binotto's would advertise in the right places to the right clientele.'

She tilted her head. 'Why's this access important? People must drive into the vineyard now.'

He pointed again, though she had no chance of seeing the lane into the vineyard. 'There's a rural road further down the valley. As a small producer, being serviced by small and medium-sized trucks is no problem. But . . .' he drew out the word, 'the road past the end of my drive is major and links to Orvieto and Rome to the south and Arezzo to the north. Coaches could come across Il Rifugio to the vineyard.'

She gazed down at the buildings and their shining lights. 'If Tenuta Domenicali isn't making enough money from wine production, your family could do many of the tourism things you've mentioned, bringing in the tourists in minibuses on the existing road.'

'If only it was that simple.' He looked down into her face. She was beautiful. He could smell her perfume on the evening air and around them fireflies were beginning to glow like hovering fairy lights as if vying with the stars popping out above them. It was a wildly romantic setting and since he and his ex, Nicoletta, had split up and she'd gone to Milan, he'd brought a few women here with seduction in mind. Now, though, he needed to focus on the turmoil that filled his every day and threatened his future. 'We all want to sell; Papà to travel, Emiliano would stay and continue to turn grape juice into wine and I have another passion. There's been no interest in the vineyard except for this one deal. None!' He paused to collect his thoughts. 'I've always been on great terms with my family but it's becoming tricky. Everyone's sorry I'll lose my home but . . . If I sell, do you think the Binotto organisation has deep enough pockets to ensure they get everything they want regardless of the law?'

'Bribery happens,' Zia said pragmatically. 'And regardless of my experience, you should bear in mind that lawyers don't usually lie, as such.'

It wasn't what he wanted to hear but he accepted it with a sigh. 'And I've never had to question anything Papà told me.'

Zia stroked back wisps of her hair that danced in the evening breeze. Her hand was elegant, the nails painted lilac. She frowned, answering obliquely, 'Dealing with family is delicate. They tell you things – or avoid telling you – and you don't quiz them. You trust them. There's plenty in my life I wish now that I'd questioned.' She smiled and he watched the way her lips drew into a bow, then she checked the time. 'I'd better find Ursula. We plan to eat our evening meal in Bella Vista's gorgeous gazebo.'

'You like the gazebo? I made it.' He couldn't resist telling her, enjoying her eyes widening in surprise.

'The one by the cottages?'

'I have one here, too, though you can't see it in the dark. Spare me another minute?' He took her across the front of the house and around to where his workshop still stood open to the evening breeze. Switching on the lights, he watched her blink then focus her gaze on the lantern roof that was awaiting Antonio.

'That's gorgeous!' She stepped closer to stroke her finger-tips along the grain of the wood and reach up to touch the onion-like finial.

He couldn't suppress a note of pride. 'I like to make beautiful things. This will be the topmost point of an orangery roof. The joiner has the tooling and manpower to build the main structure, which I don't, and I have the patience and time to design this artisan touch, which he doesn't.' He took out his phone and flicked through his photos until he found what he was looking for. 'I made this for Emiliano's kids, Camilla and Cristian.'

Zia stepped closer to inspect the image of two children beaming beside a child-sized wooden house with a green door and jaunty little windows. 'A play house? How awesome! Not many children have anything so wonderful. It's like a fairytale cottage. Look at the curly bits around the roof.'

'That's what Americans call "gingerbread trim".'

She passed the phone back. 'You must be Uncle Popular with your niece and nephew.' Even in the harsh overhead lights her skin was as smooth and brown as a hen's egg. Then her phone rang. 'Do you mind if I take this?' she asked.

As her conversation was obviously with Ursula about dinner he began to switch off lights. When she'd finished he said, 'I'll show you the shorter route back, through the cypress trees.' And, contrary to his usual policy for Bella Vista guests: 'Come to Il Rifugio at any time.'

Chapter Five

On Friday morning Ursula was ready for the holiday to begin. 'How about a walk to the market in the centre of Montelibertà?' she suggested.

Zia laughed. 'Three miles each way? Coming back uphill? You? In flip flops? You'll have sprouted blisters before you've covered the first mile.'

Ursula trailed a finger wistfully over the Google Earth-generated landscape on her phone screen. 'You're too practical. I was enjoying a romantic notion of drifting through vineyards and olive groves.'

Zia examined the image, too. 'I'm not sure the owners of said vineyards and olive groves would welcome us as I don't see footpaths. And it's already thirty degrees Celsius at ten a.m.' She jingled her car keys temptingly.

Ursula put away her phone, eyes dancing. 'A gentle stroll around the piazzas might be nice too . . . with pauses for vino and gelato of course.'

With an answering grin, Zia grabbed her bag. 'Durante recommends parking on Via Virgilio just before we get into town. It's free and will give us just a little walk.' Soon they were joining the public road where she'd stood with Piero the evening before, traffic buzzing in both directions to reinforce his comments about it being a major route. Rock ran alongside the road for nearly two miles then gave way to a country park crowded with pine trees shedding needles into dusty beige drifts. Cars were parked in the shade and she caught sight of picnic tables in glades.

'Lunch there one day for sure,' Ursula declared, peering back over her shoulder as they passed.

Then the road curved and Zia gasped, 'Oh!' She slowed and pulled to the side of the road to let the traffic whizz on without them. Below nestled sun-drenched Montelibertà, the land rising like an amphitheatre around three quarters of the town and falling away in the last part. Church steeples poked up between terracotta-tiled roofs, buildings were painted cream, ochre or apricot, the major structures gracing the town centre while houses huddled on the slopes like children hatching mischief. These last were what caught Zia's eye – normal homes for average families. She wondered whether any of those families was hers.

'Pretty,' she breathed. 'I can see why the tourists love it.'

'It seemed more ordinary when we came from below and passed through,' Ursula observed, gazing at the sunlit jumble of buildings.

Then a scooter beeped angrily as it buzzed close by the car windows and Zia stirred. 'I'd better park properly.' In a few minutes she was able to slot into a space near a hotel called Casa Felice.

'Happy House. Even I can translate that,' Ursula said as they locked the car, scooter engines whining by and trucks changing gear. They wandered downhill along busy pavements, passing restaurants, bars and shops interspersed with houses graced by balconies and shutters. Occasionally there was a small garden behind a wall. The scent of lavender accompanied the musical sound of Italian, tourists adding a percussion in English and German. Crates of plump, shining pears and apples stood outside a shop on the corner of a side street so narrow Zia felt she could touch both sides at once like the vine that formed a living arch above. She peeped up at two elderly ladies enjoying lunch on a shady wrought iron balcony barely big enough for them and their table, apparently unconcerned by people milling beneath or a van nosing along within inches of the walls. She murmured, 'They look so civilised drinking red wine up there.'

Ursula was more interested in a shop that devoted its entire frontage to ceramic goods. 'Are these what Lucia used to make?' She traced the brightly coloured geometric designs on a plate with her artist's soul shining from her eyes.

'Maybe. Ask her later.' Zia admired an oil pourer decorated with deep purple grapes and though she said, 'This would be good in my kitchen,' she didn't buy it. The Georgian and Regency buildings of Brighton felt a long way from a noisy Italian street where the sun kissed her shoulders.

They drifted on past shops selling leather goods and fountain pens. Eventually they reached the cobbles of Piazza Roma where cream-canopied market stalls were surrounded by buildings with arches beneath. Through the biggest lay another square, Piazza Santa Lucia, according to the map. 'It's nice to be away from the traffic,' Zia observed as they started up the first row of stalls.

Ursula made a beeline for a stall selling more ceramics.

There were jugs shaped like startled chickens' heads with open-beak spouts standing beside butter dishes shaped like lemons. For seven euros she bought a candleholder with an open sunflower to catch the wax, then they wandered on past glowing olive wood jewellery, inexpensive clothes, bread, cakes and colourful pyramids of fruit.

Eventually they turned to the cafés and selected one with a table half in shade and half in sun. Zia loved to be baked in golden light but Ursula preferred the protection of a nice parasol.

Once they'd ordered sparkling water and let the first half of it cut through the dust in their throats they settled back to study the menu. 'The platters look good,' Zia said.

Ursula grimaced. 'The pizzas look *good*. The platters look healthy.'

Zia solved this conundrum. 'How about we order a pizza and a salad and go halves on each?' She smiled at their waiter, neat in a green waistcoat and white summer shirt, and exercised her Italian-speaking muscles. The money she'd spent getting a native Italian speaker to chat to her for an hour a week paid off whenever she travelled to Italy. When you were used to the real rhythms of a language rather than the English version, it helped a lot.

Ursula, typical tourist, was content to let the whole dialogue flow over her head while she watched the market stall holders begin to pack up. But after the waiter had whisked off she proved she hadn't lost sight of their reason for being in Montelibertà and switched her gaze to Zia. 'So, what next with Lucia? She seems nice. Are you going to ask her if she's a piece in your family jigsaw?'

Although Ursula smiled, Zia could read uncertainty in her eyes. Last night's conversation with Stephan hadn't gone well, apparently, and Ursula's hopes that he'd calm down and accept there was no evidence she'd betrayed him were fading. It was a shame that their relationshp was in jeopardy at the same time as Zia was digging for her Italian roots. Ursula might feel there was a danger of losing both her husband *and* her best friend. She presented a brash front to the world with her body art and make-up but was actually petal-soft and insecure.

'I'll definitely talk to her. Or probably, anyway,' she added, trying to be honest without appearing too unflatteringly eager to do something that could distance her from Ursula. From the direction of Piazza Santa Lucia the rich tolling of church bells began rolling around Piazza Roma and Zia took the opportunity to change the subject. 'That must be Santa Lucia church. I expect Lucia was named for that saint.'

Ursula refused to be deflected. 'Definitely probably? Are you sure you don't want to throw a "maybe" in there?'

Zia laughed, pausing to smile her thanks at the waiter who delivered a basket of deliciously fresh-smelling bread. She selected a piece to dip in oil and balsamic vinegar. 'But it sums up how I feel. One moment I think I'll say to Lucia, "My mother died when I was young but I believe I have a connection with someone called Lucia Costa from Montelibertà. I wonder whether it could be you." But the next I worry I'll find out something awful, like Mum stole me away. Then suddenly I'm itching to know, regardless.'

'Tricky.' Ursula gave Zia's arm a consoling rub.

The pizza and salad arrived and Zia selected some of each for her plate, watching the delicious molten cheese drip from the side of the thin crispy dough, as she arranged leaves and slices of tomato and onion alongside. 'It is,' she agreed. 'And my mind keeps circling around the question of the two Victorias. I might look up private investigators who could find out what happened to Harry Anstey so I can see what he knows. According to his letters, my mum Vicky Chalmers collected me from Lucia, here in Montelibertà. Why? Why did Lucia then travel to Devon asking about Tori, who Harry describes as "lost" and "disappeared" and Gran as "gone" and grieved for? It does sound like Tori is the younger Victoria Chalmers who we know died at about that time.' She paused to consider, fork poised. 'Her birth and death certificates were in Mum's bag so she must be linked to Mum. Could she be a cousin with the same name? One I don't know of?'

'Or could a male in the Chalmers family have married a seventeen-year-old who happened to also be called Victoria?' Ursula supplied.

Zia felt a worm of turmoil wriggle in her belly. 'Or Tori Chalmers *was* my birth mother,' she admitted. 'Making Vicky Chalmers my grandmother and Gran and Pap my great-grandparents.' She glanced at Ursula, comforted by her sympathetic expression. 'Sitting here in a gorgeous old Italian town in the sunlight, part of me wants to just enjoy the holiday then go home to find a new job. Maybe meet a new man, one who won't cheat on me.'

'Giving up the idea of living here?' Ursula probed, picking up a slice of pizza.

'Not really ready to.' Zia exhaled hard. 'As usual, that brings me back full circle – everything's easier if I can prove my father was Italian. And if Vicky Chalmers took baby-me from Lucia Costa who lived in Montelibertà, then chances are she can throw light on my father's identity. What the hell was I doing here so young when I was born in England?'

She fell into pensive silence. Ursula began to check out

her phone. After a few minutes, again feeling that a change of subject would be welcome, she ventured, 'Fancy a look at a nineteenth century theatre with a neoclassical interior? All that pretty gold stuff? According to this tourist site they have a gelateria and Il Caffè Teatro.'

Before Zia could reply her phone began to ring. She dug it from her bag and pulled a face when she saw who was calling. 'Brendon.'

'Shall I make myself scarce?' Ursula suggested.

Zia shook her head as she answered. 'Hi Brendon.' She aimed for coolly polite rather than welcoming.

His voice came down the line rising and falling on the rhythms of North East England where he'd spent his childhood. When they were first together at the beginning of the year, his voice had ignited flames inside her but at that time she hadn't caught him having sex with someone else. He said, 'I thought I'd call and say hello. Are you out of the country? I got the single ring tone.'

As Stephan knew where Ursula was and with whom, Zia was pretty sure Brendon would be clued in. 'That's right. Italy.'

'I know the attraction there.' He sounded indulgent, friendly, eager to curry favour.

She chose not to discuss her daddy issues. He knew her background . . . at least what she'd thought was her background until a couple of weeks ago. 'It's a fantastic country. Are you calling for anything in particular?' A flock of pigeons were helping clear up the square in the wake of the market and she watched them pecking amongst the cobbles, sticking out their self-important chests and remarking 'Brrrroop,' to each other. A laughing blond boy charged at them and they clattered into the air, only to settle again in a different place. Ursula had gone back to her own phone, tapping and scrolling while Zia took the call.

'I was hoping to talk,' said Brendon. He gave a nervous, unconvincing chuckle. 'Obviously, I didn't realise I'd be interrupting your holiday.'

Although she wanted to say, 'Yeah, right, like Stephan didn't tell you,' she maintained a civil veneer. 'Talk about what?'

Another chuckle. 'To make sure you know how sorry I am for what happened. Again.'

Yet again, he meant. It felt uncomfortable, as if he thought there was a route back to her if he just rattled the door often enough. 'I know you are. But it doesn't change what happened.'

Brendon cleared his throat, loud down the phone. 'I wondered . . . well, I mean, why . . .' It took another breath and then the sentence came out in a rush. 'I've been talking to Stephan and I'm trying to work out why you're supporting Ursula when she made a mistake but won't forgive me.' His voice became husky. 'I love you. I can't believe you won't give me another chance.'

Zia rolled her eyes but tried to stay patient. 'What you did and what Ursula did isn't the same.' Ursula looked up so sharply her blonde forelock danced. Zia continued. 'Yes, you both got drunk . . . but only you were unfaithful.'

Like a politician, Brendon chose to address only part of her reply. 'Of course she was unfaithful! A guy doesn't bring a woman home paralytic when there's nothing to it.'

Ursula tapped out a message on her Notes screen and turned the phone so Zia could read it. *Fishing for info on behalf of Steph?*

In case he was, Zia let him have information with

both barrels. 'So, the guy had sex with Ursula then calmly delivered her back to her husband? He'd have to have immense front. I think he saw a woman who'd become incapacitated and helped her out. Nice people do sometimes do that kind of thing. I can understand Stephan being upset and angry at the state she was in—' Ursula made a faux-hurt face '—but why does he refuse to believe she didn't cheat? I've never known her to be seeing two guys at the same time, even when we were students, and I definitely don't believe she's capable of two-timing her husband. Steph's her everything and he should know it.'

Ursula abandoned her pout and blew a kiss instead.

Tightly, Brendon said, 'But that's the point. People act out of character when they're drunk. I'd never have done . . . *that* if I wasn't.'

The memory of *that* didn't soothe her. She'd walked into that bedroom with a group of friends worried he'd passed out and found him very much on his feet and enjoying sex against the wall – and that wasn't the name of a cocktail. He'd been pinning the woman's arms above her head. Zia had never gone in for that 'hold me down and make me powerless' stuff and her first reaction hadn't been, 'Why is he having sex with another woman?' so much as 'Why is he having sex with another woman *like that*?' It felt like an added betrayal. Brendon and his hook-up had frozen, a tableau of undone clothes and tumbled hair as if the sex had been stormy and frantic.

Tightly, she said, 'Even alcohol doesn't excuse you having so little respect you'd "do that" while I was at the same party. You stomped into a minefield and our relationship blew up.' She added, 'We were going through a tricky time anyway.'

59

'Erm . . .' he interrupted, as if ready to argue.

She ploughed on before he could. 'We wanted different things. We'd only been exclusive a couple of months and you all but suggested I use my redundancy as a career break to have your kids.'

A long silence. Then he said stiffly, 'Somewhat of an exaggeration but if I was insensitive, I apologise. But I'm not giving up on us. You keep going to Italy searching for whatever connection you think you feel with the frigging place but you're a wonderful, intelligent woman who has a man pining for you in England. Why can't you forgive me? I promise I won't push you to come and live with me.'

She recoiled. 'Good, because I love my flat. It's something I can rely on.' Aware her voice had sharpened she smoothed it out. 'Brendon . . . I can't forgive you. Forgiving someone isn't a choice. It's a reaction, something that comes from within.' She said a brusque farewell and ended the call with a stab at the screen.

Ursula whistled. 'That sounded as if it went almost as well as my last chat with Stephan.'

Zia's hands were sticky with sweat. "Fraid so. He thinks if he's persistent enough it will revive the relationship, I'll take him back and that will be tantamount to me admitting I overreacted to his teeny tiny mistake.'

'I suppose he could also genuinely miss you and care for you,' Ursula mused fairly. Then she heaved a sigh. 'But as I exploded my own relationship by getting wrecked, I suppose I would go easy on him. Thanks for sticking up for me. He might pass it on to Stephan.'

'Hopefully,' Zia agreed. She drew on a determined smile. 'Now, let's pay our bill and get off to that neo-thingy theatre and eat ice cream. Chocolate, with nuts.' She wanted to banish the memory of Brendon's dogged attempts to rekindle past flames.

All the warmth she'd once felt for him had been left on the other side of his infidelity.

Friday was a workshop day for Piero. Today, rather than being enveloped in the roar of the machines, he was working on a drawing. From outside the open doors came the whistle and chirp of birds and a wild boar snoring beneath a bush. Last year he'd caught glimpses of piglets too, striped like the bark of the trees they were learning to forage around. Better they were up here than learning to eat grapes down in the vineyard.

He was drawing out a hexagonal garden structure for an elderly English woman who'd made her home in Fabro, twenty minutes down the mountain. At the end of her half-wild garden of lemon trees and stone paths would stand this elegant structure in which to sit – shady in summer but with glazed panels for fitting in the cooler season. She called this a 'summer house' and said they'd always had one in the English garden of her childhood, practical in view of changeable British weather.

He deliberated as he drew lines and calculated measurements. Could he market British summer houses to other customers? Montelibertà was at an altitude of almost six hundred metres, just about high enough for snow. He was not a fan of cold and imagined making similar panels for his own gazebo, giving him somewhere to listen to music while gazing out over the valley, winter sun amplified by the glass.

If he was still at Il Rifugio come winter.

A shadow slipped over his mood and though part of his brain continued to be occupied with angles, sizes and supports, the remainder wrestled with the clash of his love for his family and the legal issues.

When lunchtime arrived, he ate in a patch of dappled shade, browsing the internet for *diritto di passaggio*. It was depressing to read about people who'd thought the law was on their side but found themselves to be small fry when up against sharks. Lucia and Durante might have the right to continue to access their property but could the Binotto Group still find a way of making it better for them to sell?

After some research he selected a lawyer in Orvieto and used the online facility to make an appointment. Then, having spent ten minutes gazing down at his family vineyard, family winery and family home nestled in the lush green valley, cancelled it.

He should talk to Papà and Emiliano again first.

At about three p.m., having called through an order for the materials he'd need for the summer house, he headed off in search of Lucia and Durante. The drone of bees kept him company as he brushed past bushes and trees. About to cross the Bella Vista drive, a flash of white caught his eye and looking past the olive grove he could just make out someone in the gazebo. He watched a hand put down a sheet of paper and pick up another, long hair tumbling over a shoulder. Zia.

Executing a swift change of direction, he turned down the footpath edged with grass already turning to summer gold, obeying a compulsion he hadn't felt since first drawn to Nicoletta. The way that had ended, Nicoletta disappointed and frustrated while he was exasperated and puzzled, had put him off dating local women who might – quite reasonably – come to expect commitment. Tourists were accommodating: here, then gone. Zia was a tourist.

How much impact could a tourist have on his life in a couple of weeks?

She noticed him when he was a few strides from the gazebo and glanced up with a flash of her arresting smile. A blue and white bag rested against her smooth brown leg and she held what looked like a handwritten letter. A bundle of envelopes lay in the mouth of the bag.

'Busy?' he asked.

'Just reading. Ursula's fallen asleep in the shade behind Villino Il Pino.' Then, as if realising that what she held in her hands was perhaps not usual holiday reading, added, 'These are letters to my mother, Vicky. They mention Montelibertà. She obviously came here once. I'm trying to discover more about her because she died when I was ten.'

'I'm sorry.'

'At least I had lovely grandparents to bring me up.' She tilted her head enquiringly. 'Do I look as if I might be of Italian descent?'

He took the question as an invitation to linger, stepped into the gazebo and sat on a lounger. 'I thought you were Italian when I first saw you. In fact, I thought you were probably from the Binotto Group, come to bother Lucia and Durante. You looked like a business person.'

Her eyes sparkled. 'I'd had an interview for a job in Montelibertà.'

Surprise shivered through him. 'You're staying to work here?' So, she wasn't a tourist?

The smile faded. 'It's not that easy any more. I haven't even applied for residency. I just wanted to see what might be involved, what an employer would ask for.' She added, 'I was always told my father was Italian but not who he was. If I could prove I have an Italian parent, I might get Italian citizenship by descent – *jus sanguinis* or "right of

63

blood". I thought if I found him . . . well, it's why I'm here, really.'

'Here at this address?' His gut tightened, roughening his tone. 'Please don't say it's Durante! The last thing Lucia needs just now is to discover her husband fathered some illegitimate kid. She's upset and frightened enough.'

Zia snatched off her sunglasses. 'Of course it's not Durante—!' Then she checked, retreated slowly behind the sunshades and muttered stiffly, 'I don't have any reason to suspect it's Durante and I'm not here to embarrass anyone.'

Acutely aware that through protectiveness towards his friends he'd made an illegitimate child sound shameful when the illegitimate child in question was sitting right in front of him, he looked for a way to shuffle back from the precipice of bad manners. 'Sorry. I just meant – they must have been married when you were born. It would mean Durante . . .'

'Cheated,' she finished for him. 'I share your disgust at that.' Without another word she pushed the letter into the bag, gathered up her things, rose and headed off for her holiday accommodation. He called a polite goodbye but didn't catch her response.

Like a dog in disgrace, he slunk off towards the terrace which, in summer, got more use than the house. The door stood open, flanked by a blooming passionflower. Piero pushed aside the fly curtain and called out, '*Ciao.*'

'*Siamo in ufficio,*' Lucia called cheerily. *We're in the office.*

He went through the cool hall to find her and Durante sharing the desk.

'Paperwork,' Durante grumbled. 'The government wants too many forms.' He clicked his computer mouse and behind him the printer hummed into life.

Lucia had printouts and envelopes spread over the desk and patted her husband's arm as if she'd heard it all before. 'Any news?' she asked Piero.

'I've done a bit of reading. Unfortunately, where it concerns big corporations, much of it seems to be about people who lost cases they thought they should have won.'

'Money talks.' Lucia propped her fist against her double chin, the soft flesh spreading across her fingers, looking towards the door as a figure ambled past. She called, 'Fiorella, *caffè per tre, per favore.*'

Piero turned in his chair to smile at the older woman in the doorway. '*Ciao*, Fiorella.' Having lived next door to Lucia for so long, he knew many of her large family and her sister-in-law was a familiar figure in her wrap-around apron, her grey hair drawn back. Most had given up even part-time work by their late seventies, the age he judged her to be, but Fiorella supplemented her pension by helping in the house or cottages. It was likely the euros Lucia put in Fiorella's pocket were more than was adequate recompense for the light work, and food and drink usually came as part of the deal. Lucia was big on family and Fiorella and Lucia's eldest brother Roberto had never been well off. Roberto also picked up casual work where he could.

Fiorella returned Piero's greeting, repeating, '*Caffè per tre,*' and shuffled off in dusty flip-flops.

Durante scrubbed his hand over his face and returned to their interrupted conversation. 'So still everything we worked for can be taken from us.'

Piero nodded, the knowledge like a rock in his stomach. 'I suppose,' he said cautiously, 'that you could negotiate the highest price you can and give in, rather than spend years fighting lawsuits.'

'Unless you refuse to sell your land.' Durante stuck out his chin.

Lucia gave her husband a look. 'He's in a horrible position,' she chided.

Piero groaned. 'There's certainly no good choice. Talking to Zia last night I began to hope we might have enough leverage to stop the sale. But today I imagined telling Papà that. It would be hard.' He raised his hands and let them drop.

Durante looked as if he might cry. 'We should be making plans for the cottages next year but how we can we? Lucia wants to try running courses – maybe a week in June and one in September. Some tourists like writing holidays or painting holidays so why not ceramics? But we'd need to start advertising in September. Get it on our website.'

The printer stopped and Durante reached for the sheaf of papers it had churned out then passed them to Lucia.

'If only there was another buyer for the vineyard on its own,' she said drearily, picking up the top sheet of paper. Then she froze, her mouth dropping open. The sheet began to shake in her hand. '*Zia*,' she breathed.

'What? What, Lucia?' demanded Durante.

Piero regarded Lucia with concern, not liking her pallor and the blank shock in her eyes. 'I saw Zia in your gazebo on my way here. What's the matter?'

But Lucia was already scrambling out from behind the desk. Almost sending Fiorella and her tray of coffee flying in the doorway, she ran from the room.

Piero and Durante exchanged glances then set off after her.

Chapter Six

Zia had finished her bottle of water and needed a new coat of insect repellant against the late afternoon bug patrol. That's why she'd returned to the cottage, she told herself, not because Piero had made her feel as welcome as a turd at a pool party.

But when she stalked into Villino Il Pino she found Ursula on the sofa with red-rimmed eyes, clutching her phone. Ursula gave a huge sniff. 'Steph's just phoned in a filthy temper. That bloke – you know, the white knight who brought me home from the hen party? – turned up at our house.'

Ire forgotten, Zia let the bag of letters slip from her shoulder and thud to the ground. 'What the hell for?'

Ursula wiped her eyes. 'To ask if I was OK. He'd got to hear that another girl in the club that night had something put in her drink and woke up naked under the trees in Preston Park.'

'No,' Zia breathed, feeling sick as she plumped down beside Ursula. 'Was she . . .?'

'I don't know. Steph didn't ask. He raged at the white

67

knight so much the white knight took off. Stephan rang me to rage some more and I said he had no business chasing the white knight away. If someone was roofied that night the police might want to talk to me in case I was roofied too. It would explain why I didn't think I'd drunk enough to pass out. I might know something to help prosecute the scum who did whatever they did to that poor woman and left her to come round alone and naked in a public place.' She shuddered. 'Can you imagine?'

'Barely.' Zia shuddered too. The idea was terrifying.

Ursula hiccupped. 'Steph sneered that I was grasping at straws to excuse my own behaviour. I told him to fuck off, he told me to fuck off, and that's the state of our marriage. And as being teetotal since Stephan threw me out has got me precisely nowhere, I'm about to have a nice big glass of wine. Join me?'

'Definitely.' Zia hugged Ursula hard and went to fetch the white wine from the fridge. 'I can see why you cut alcohol for a while but, let's face it, a glass of lemonade can be spiked as easily as a cocktail.' She took down two glasses and took them to the low table.

She'd just poured when an urgent *blam-blam* fell on the front door. 'What on earth?' she gasped. Bouncing to her feet she raced to answer the summons, half-expecting there to be a fire. She flung open the door to find Lucia Costa on the dusty paving, sweat beading her forehead, thick silver-streaked waves flying in the breeze, a sheet of paper clutched in one hand.

'Zia-Lucia,' she whispered.

Zia's heart somersaulted as she realised the paper Lucia was gripping was the printout of her passport's photo page. She stared into Lucia's dark, emotion-filled eyes and, wordlessly, their gazes locked. Piero jogged up, eyes wary, with portly Durante puffing behind.

'*Cosa c'é*? What is the matter?' Durante gasped and twitched the paper from Lucia's hand. He skimmed it. Then, slowly, he turned to gaze at Zia with wide, astounded eyes. He grasped Lucia's arm. 'I didn't read it! I just scanned the page for the authorities.'

Lucia swayed.

Piero got his arm beneath hers. 'Zia, perhaps if you were to let Lucia sit down . . .?'

Blood hammering in her ears, Zia shook herself from her stupor. 'Of course. Yes. Come in.' A voice inside her said, *It's the right Lucia!* She felt as if her head and her heart were trying to meet in her throat. Desperate yearning to know whatever Lucia knew warred with an equally desperate fear that Zia would be worse off for knowing.

Ursula, her own woes set aside, cleared things from the seating area and, like obedient children, Zia and Lucia plummeted onto opposite sofas. Durante took the space beside his wife, linking his fingers with hers and staring at Zia with stunned brown eyes. Dimly, Zia was aware of Ursula whispering, 'Do you want me to go? I could sit on the patio and you call me if you need me.'

Piero, his gaze flicking from Zia to Lucia to Durante, evidently had no intention of leaving Zia alone with his friends. That, together with his insensitivity in the gazebo, made her mutter through numb lips, 'Stay, please.' Ursula sank down at her side.

Piero perched on the arm of the other sofa. They were like two teams, staring at one another, the low table between them.

Lucia spoke first. 'Are you Tori's daughter?'

69

The words ripped through Zia, the possibility she hadn't wanted to face suddenly feeling like the truth. 'I don't know,' she whispered. 'Am I?'

Lucia's lip wobbled. 'Your name . . .' She gazed down at the now crumpled sheet in her hand.

Zia cleared her throat. 'All I've been told about my name is that a woman called Lucia Costa was once kind to my mother. From letters, I think she lived in Montelibertà. I've been told my father's Italian but I don't know who he is.'

Slowly, Lucia's round, homely face collapsed and she burst into tears. Durante slid his arms around her, cradling her as she sobbed, but he didn't take his gaze from Zia. His voice was husky. 'In the past, Lucia loves Tori. Tori lives in Monteibertà for a few months. When Tori's daughter Zia-Lucia is only a few weeks old Tori brings her to us.' He shook his head sorrowfully. 'Tori is changed. Very strange. Upset, frightened.' He creased his forehead and muttered something in Italian that Zia didn't catch.

Piero translated, 'Hysterical.' Now dawning under-standing had replaced wariness in his eyes.

Durante nodded. 'Yes. She is . . . she is crazy. She ask Lucia to look after the baby – you – for a short time but she disappear. We do not know what to do so we look after you and wait, two days, three, four, five. Then, Tori's mother Vicky comes.'

Zia nodded and sipped shakily from her glass, steadied by the alcohol.

Like a hostess remembering her duties, Ursula fetched more glasses and the rest of the wine. Soon, all five of them sat around the low table clutching drinks like the first guests at a party.

Lucia pulled a tissue from her shorts pocket and blew

her nose. 'Tori was not at all the same.' She shook her head mournfully. 'What happened to her? We never knew. She left here a lovely girl, though a sad one, and returned scarcely able to talk sense.' She closed her eyes for a moment. 'An angel must have watched over her when she drove all the way from England in that state.'

Alcohol or not, Zia found herself trembling. 'You think I'm Tori's daughter. But I always thought I was Vicky's.'

Lucia and Durante exchanged shocked looks. Lucia lifted bewildered hands. 'Tori had a daughter called Zia-Lucia who would be your age. Tori's mother was called Vicky.'

Slowly, Zia put down her glass and rose, persuading her trembling legs to take her to fetch the blue and white bag she'd discarded by the door earlier. Then she dropped back down onto the sofa, unzipped the bag and fumbled her way into the inner pocket. Drawing out four stiff, formal pieces of paper she positioned them on the table so Lucia, Durante and Piero could read them. She touched the first pair. 'These are the birth and death certificates of Victoria Chalmers, who I knew as my mother, Vicky. She died when I was ten.' She moved on to the second set, the parchment-like paper cool beneath her fingers. 'This person was also called Victoria Chalmers. She died a few weeks after I was born and I've only just discovered she existed. Vicky and Tori are both short names for Victoria.'

Lucia's chin wobbled. 'I went to Tori's home in England. A man, Harry, he told me Tori had died but I didn't want to believe him. It was a very, very difficult time. There were secrets . . .' She hesitated.

Zia replied bitterly. 'I seem to be at the centre of all these secrets but I don't know any of them.'

71

Lucia closed her eyes once more. Tears eased from beneath the lids and tracked down her cheeks like streaks of silver in the late, slanting light.

Durante took her hand. '*Penso che dovresti spiegare.*' *I think you should explain.*

At length, Lucia opened her eyes and began to speak. '"Zia Lucia" is what my nieces and nephews call me. Aunt Lucia. When Tori first knew Gerardo she spoke so little Italian she didn't realise "zia" means "aunt" so she thought my name was Zia-Lucia with a hyphen. When I explained, she laughed a lot.' Lucia smiled reminiscently, the apples of her cheeks lifting. 'She always called me Zia Lucia, like Gerardo and the others. And she named the baby Zia-Lucia after me but also because she liked the sound.'

Zia held her breath. Finally hearing the truth was like standing on the high diving board and wondering whether you really wanted to launch yourself into thin air. The slap of the water when you landed could really hurt. She licked her lips. 'Who was Gerardo?'

Lucia gave a watery smile. 'Gerardo is my nephew. We have always had a special bond. Tori came to Montelibertà when she was eighteen. School was finished for her for a while and she wanted to travel. She worked in a bar where many tourists go and she met Gerardo. He was also eighteen.'

Vaguely, Zia registered Piero's still presence. Like Ursula, he'd assumed the role of spectator.

'Tori fell in love. Gerardo . . . for him it was different.' Lucia gave a pained smile. 'It is uncomfortable to tell you this but she knew he did not love her. She told me. Also, his parents would not accept a future for him with a British girl with no shared religion or background. Gerardo learned English at school but my brother Roberto and his wife, Fiorella, knew little. His parents felt she would take his mind from his work as a printer's apprentice. He had to be up early, not staying out late to meet Tori when the bar closed. The family needed him to earn his wages because they were not rich. He was also attached to the university in Perugia, studying at home and attending exams.'

'That's a heavy workload,' Ursula observed.

Lucia agreed. 'He did not finish at university. Gerardo was the second of eight children. They wanted him to help his younger siblings, not romance a girl who would return home at the end of the summer.'

'So, your nephew Gerardo's my father?' Zia whispered, closing her eyes against a dizziness that threatened to overwhelm her. 'I can hardly believe I finally have the information after thirty years of wondering. That makes you my great-aunt. And there are grandparents and uncles and aunts and perhaps cousins?'

Durante stirred. 'If you are Zia-Lucia, the daughter of Tori, then yes, Gerardo Costa is your father.'

Was it fanciful or did she catch a whiff of doubt in Durante's voice? 'Either Gerardo Costa is my father or he isn't. Either Tori was my mother and the second Victoria Chalmers or she wasn't. I need to be sure.'

'Durante.' Piero finally spoke. 'Do you know the birth date of the baby Zia-Lucia? From memory, not from Zia's passport.'

Durante screwed up his face in thought. 'She is born in autumn, the year of the first regional football championship, *Campionati di Eccellenza*. I remember. I like football a lot then and support team Deruta.' He glanced at Lucia for confirmation. Though her mind was spinning, Zia noticed their closeness, the way they automatically turned to each other.

Durante took out his phone and perused it for several seconds. 'So. The internet says first championship 1991.' He returned the phone to his pocket. 'When Tori returns with Zia-Lucia we are maintaining the hire cars and that programme always begin in the middle of November when most tourists are gone. Zia-Lucia was maybe one month old, so I believe her birth date to be the middle of October.'

'I was born on the 17th of October 1991,' Zia choked out.

Lucia turned the copy of Zia's passport towards Durante so he could confirm it for himself. She turned back to Zia, 'Tori lived in Exmouth in Devon, England.'

'That's where I was born.' Zia's throat had tightened so impossibly that she could hardly squeeze out the words.

Ursula slid an arm around Zia's shoulders. 'Sounds like you found your family, honey.'

Zia nodded. Then a sob burst out of her, an eruption of grief over the lies she'd been told, for 'Mum' being her grandmother and Gran and Pap being great-grandparents. For her mother being a teenager who behaved 'crazy' and died far too young – a mother whom Zia would never know. After a lifetime of having hardly anyone, she had a family . . . but most of them didn't know she existed and might not want to.

And Gran and Pap must have known the truth and never told her.

She cried so hard her sinuses burned. Lucia murmured to Durante that perhaps they should leave for now. The kind words finally made her get a grip.

'*Per favore, resta,*' she said. 'I'm sorry. I just—'

'I can tell you more another time.' Lucia sounded

worried but also . . . what? Pleased? Excited? A smile even pulled at the corners of her mouth.

Zia gazed at the older woman through tear-swollen eyes. 'I want to know everything. Anything. I've yearned to know all my life. It was just the shock.' She drained her wine glass as if to demonstrate her willingness to fortify herself.

Lucia looked torn for several seconds. But then she nodded and carried on. 'Gerardo found it easier to let his parents think he was no longer seeing Tori. It was not true.' She sighed. 'Durante and me, we decided not to have children. We had many nieces and nephews to love and I was a businesswoman with no yearning to be a mother. But we had sympathy for Gerardo and Tori. It was wrong to go against my brother but . . .' She shrugged again. 'We let them meet in our garden, even when we were not at home, after his work ended and before hers began. We lived in town then.' She gestured vaguely in the appropriate direction and wiped a tear that teetered at the corner of her eye. 'After some months, they came to me. Tori was pregnant. Gerardo was scared. Tori wanted that they should go to England together. In England they would be OK but in Italy Roberto and Fiorella would be very angry. Gerardo had lied to them about Tori and gone against the teachings of the church. They were strong in their beliefs in those days.'

Zia nodded. 'My grandparents – or great-grandparents – weren't religious but they had traditional views. Unfortunate,' she reflected with a small smile, 'as first their daughter Vicky and then their granddaughter Tori had babies when they were single.'

Durante put in. 'Gerardo, he does not want to live in England. Tori in love, yes. Gerardo . . .' He paused.

'Wasn't,' Zia finished for him.

Nodding, Lucia pushed back her loose curls. She fidgeted, apparently finding it hard to meet Zia's eyes. 'He knew abortions were OK in England and saw it as the answer to the problem. He didn't want to give up his life in Italy or break with his parents. Tori was desolate.'

Zia's heart gave a great thud as if Tori's pain toppled Zia into a horrible, sickening realisation. 'So, my father didn't want me to live at all, not even in another country?'

Lucia stumbled over explanations, evidently unwilling to be too hard on the nephew she loved. 'He was young. Young not just in years but in behaviour.'

Zia wasn't so willing to let him off the hook. 'Immature and scared of his parents.'

Durante gave a 'maybe' waggle of his head. 'Scared of the upset, the argument, the change to his life, maybe. Not a bad boy. Just young.'

So, both Lucia and Durante were prepared to be understanding of Gerardo. Zia couldn't really blame them for their love for a favoured nephew, no matter how hard it was for her to hear the bald truth about him being more 'scared of the upset' than caring for his daughter. She herself hadn't wanted to upset Gran and Pap with questions after Vicky's death . . . but being sensitive to someone's sorrow and aborting a baby weren't on the same page.

The sun was level with the windows now, encompassing them all in an apricot glow. Piero got up and brought water to everyone. He'd been so still that Zia had half-forgotten he was there.

Lucia took up her tale again. 'She left Montelibertà, Tori. We exchanged letters. She sent me a photo of herself once.'

'Do you still have it?' Zia interrupted. The young woman

who'd given her life seemed to bound from a name on pieces of paper to physical form.

'In our album,' Durante said softly. 'We make a copy for you.'

Zia found her eyes boiling once more. 'Thank you! Please go on,' she begged.

Lucia looked on the brink of tears herself so it was Durante who took up the story. 'She ask about Gerardo often but he will not look at the photograph. It is better to forget, he says, Tori's mother accept the baby and Tori is OK in England. She soon forgets too.'

'He didn't ask about me? Or was he just disappointed she hadn't had the abortion?' It was shocking to think of herself as so disposable.

Durante shrugged. 'It is difficult to know. He begins to see us less. Maybe he is embarrassed or guilty.'

'When the baby was born, Tori sent us a card with a picture of you,' said Lucia. 'That was when we knew your name – Zia-Lucia Costa Chalmers. We thought it was so funny and sweet to call a baby "aunt" but she said she thought Zia made a pretty name.'

Durante twinkled suddenly. 'Imagine. If you are a boy, she might call you Zio-Durante Costa Chalmers. Zio . . . uncle.' He laughed.

Little humour lurked in Lucia's eyes, though. 'A few days later another letter came from Tori but she did not sound like herself. She was confused. Repeating things. Scribbling phrases over and over. "Please make Gerardo come. Please make Gerardo come. Zia-Lucia my baby. Zia-Lucia my baby."'

Durante sobered. 'Then she arrive in a car. We are so shock. She drives all those kilometres with you and is exhausted.'

'But, also, moving, walking, hurrying all the time,' Lucia added, waving her arms wildly to illustrate energy. 'She wanted Gerardo to see his baby and fall in love. Then he would love Tori too and all would be well.' Her expression crumbled. 'But, instead, Gerardo was horrified. He was seeing an Italian girl. Tori got more and more wild. Her eyes were like this!' Lucia sat up very straight and opened her eyes like golf balls.

'She talk, talk, talk, cry, cry, cry.' Gravely Durante shook his head. 'We want her to see a doctor but she says no.'

'I asked Gerardo to talk to Tori, face the situation,' Lucia continued. 'He agreed so she left you with me while she and Gerardo talked alone. Durante was working. They went into the countryside but she returned alone after maybe one hour and drove off without the baby.' She spread her arms, her quivering lips transmitting the long-ago shock. 'What to do? I waited. No Tori. Durante came home. We waited for several days. We tried to get the phone number of the address we'd been writing to in England but we could not. If there was one, it was not in Tori's name.'

Durante said sombrely, 'Lucky, we help look after babies in our family so we can take care of you.' He gazed at Zia as if gazing down the years. 'Gerardo asks we do not tell his parents. We do not want to tell the police because it will expose Gerardo and make trouble for our family. Thirty years ago, we do not have these.' He brandished his phone. 'We send a telegram to Tori's address.'

Lucia grabbed the narrative once more. 'Then on day number five, Tori's mother Vicky came to tell us Tori had arrived home again. "I'm Zia-Lucia's grandmother," she said. "Tori is mentally ill and I have to take her baby home." Tori had given your passport to her but I did not

78

know what to do.' Lucia assumed a bewildered expression. 'What if the things Vicky told me were not true? You had been left with me. I asked her to phone Tori so I could get permission. Vicky said Tori wasn't capable of understanding and she took you – right from my arms! Just, grab, like that!' She thrust out her arms and then hugged them to her. 'She took the buggy from the hall and left in her hire car.'

'Wow,' Zia breathed, trying to picture her smiling, gentle mother – no, *grandmother* – snatching her like that. 'Did you call the police?'

Lucia sank back in her seat. 'Gerardo did not want it. He said it was good. The baby should be with its family.' Lucia shook her head. 'Maybe I should have told Roberto and Fiorella but we had kept Gerardo's secrets for so long.' Her gaze dropped to the row of birth and death certificates still lying on the table.

'And what good?' Durante contorted his shoulders in an enormous shrug, spreading his arms. 'Roberto and Fiorella are not sympathetic. Maybe they say the baby is not Gerardo's.'

Zia flinched. Every time Lucia or Durante indicated how unwanted she'd been she felt pierced by a new pain. It was weird to know that though she'd grown up loved, first she'd been abandoned.

'I flew to England,' Lucia went on sadly. 'I visited Tori's address in Devon. No one answered at the door. A neighbour said there was a family death.' Her eyes darkened with pain. 'I could not lose you from my heart, Zia-Lucia. Were you well? Was Tori still unhappy in her mind? Had Vicky really had permission to take you? I returned a few weeks later and that time a man opened the door.' She put a hand across her mouth, quivering on the edge of fresh tears. 'He said his name was Harry, a friend of Vicky, and Tori had died. Vicky was looking after you very well but lived somewhere else now.'

Ursula murmured to Zia, 'That ties in with Harry's first letter.'

Zia nodded. 'Was he kind to you? Harry?' she asked Lucia huskily.

Lucia shrugged. 'Yes, yes, I suppose,' she admitted grudgingly. 'But he would not tell me where you were and when he shut the door, I cried. A neighbour invited me into her home to drink a cup of tea.'

Zia managed a watery smile at this Englishness.

Lucia heaved a huge sigh. 'The neighbour agreed Tori had died. She had an illness. I cannot remember the name but it comes to a few women after a baby.'

'Post-natal depression?' Ursula hazarded.

Lucia frowned. 'Perhaps. It was long ago,' she added apologetically. 'But it made her ill in her mind. She did not see reality. She had wandered during the night and fallen a long way. That was how she died.'

Wandered during the night and fallen a long way . . . For a moment, Zia felt as though she might throw up. Her face and hands went cold and clammy. She had to force herself to listen.

Lucia continued. 'The neighbour said Vicky would care for you well. They knew each other for many years. I went home but I was troubled. Ill in her mind, maybe, but Tori had given you to *me* to care for and I let you be taken away.' She had to stop and blow her nose again. 'Several years later I was at a trade show in Devon. Not Exmouth but Ex . . .' She wrinkled her brow.

'Exeter?' Zia suggested.

Lucia nodded. 'I think so. I called again. Harry was not

patient, this time. He said Zia was fine, living in another part of the country. I should not to be upset and I should not visit again.' Slowly, she pushed herself to her feet and opened her arms. 'Zia-Lucia, I never found you but now you have found me.'

And then somehow Zia found herself on her feet and in a warm, soft, loving embrace.

Despite every crappy thing she'd heard today, it made her glad she'd come back to Montelibertà.

Chapter Seven

Saturday mornings had once been spent wandering through Montelibertà hand-in-hand with Nicoletta and maybe meeting friends for coffee. Now Saturday morning was workshop time for Piero.

It was peaceful. At first, he'd missed Nicoletta but he'd never missed the pressure she brought with her. Reflecting on this, he was careless as he swung a piece of oak. The end collided with the lantern roof waiting for collection by Antonio's men . . . and a crack appeared across the glass as if dashed there by an unseen hand. 'Balls!' he exploded into the empty air.

'Oops!' said a female voice. He spun around to see Zia standing in the doorway wearing red shorts and a black top that showed red bra straps, her hair piled up on top of her head. The corners of her mouth twitched. 'You swear in English?'

He leant the length of oak against a bench and smiled at her. 'I left America at an age when saying "H-E-double-hockey-sticks" was daring but in England I had a colleague who swore like a trooper. English has great swearwords.' Courteously he added, 'Sorry. Didn't know I had a guest.'

'As I'm an uninvited one I can hardly complain.' She smiled and drifted a few steps further into his space. '*Il tuo inglese è migliore del mio italiano.*' *Your English is better than my Italian.*

It seemed an odd thing for her to visit him to talk about but he answered her in Italian. 'In America we spoke English everywhere except home, where we spoke Italian. When we came back here to live, our parents wanted us to keep our English up so we switched round – English at home and Italian outside it. We visited either the UK or the US every year and there are always tourists to talk to in Montelibertà. But your Italian's very good.'

She gave a modest shrug. 'Conversation helps a lot. I used to chat to an Italian woman in Brighton.' She switched back to English. 'Bad luck about the glass.'

Ruefully, he examined the cracked pane. 'It's being picked up on Wednesday so there isn't time for new glass to be delivered. I'll have to take a long lunch hour on Monday to sprint to the industrial zone in Perugia and pick some up.'

She'd leaned her behind against a workbench and crossed her bare legs at the ankles. She'd been wearing black and red the first time he saw her and the combination looked good. Her sunglasses were hooked in the front of her top, drawing his eye to an inch of cleavage. 'Perugia's on our list of places to visit,' she said. 'The old city on the hilltop's picturesque and Ursula's never been so we're going to park at the bottom and take the Minimetrò. Where's the industrial zone in relation to that?'

He noted she was sufficiently familiar with Perugia to know the Minimetrò, the unmanned passenger cars that coasted up the steep rails to the city of Perugia. 'Not far. Just off the RA6.'

'I have my car. We can pick it up for you.' She was subdued this morning. The puffiness around her eyes spoke of a sleepless night or a lot of tears. Or both. After the emotional reunion in the cottage, she'd gone off with Lucia and Durante for a date with their photograph albums. Neither he nor Ursula had tagged along. Zia had looked to be in a trance. Emotional overload would do that.

'Really? That would be brilliant,' he said frankly. 'Monday's probably going to be difficult enough without losing two or three hours.' His stomach sank at the reminder that he had to tackle his father and brother yet again. 'I'd be happy to meet the cost of your fuel, obviously.'

She waved that away. 'The offer doesn't come without strings.' She paused and examined her fingernails, which were navy blue today. He imagined her sitting in the sunlight outside Villino Il Pino while she painted them. 'Thing is . . .' She lifted a clouded gaze to his. 'It's a bit of an imposition.'

As she seemed to be struggling to find a way to go on, he suggested gently, 'How about you come in for coffee?' He usually discouraged people from intruding into his workshop hours but he couldn't find it in himself to ask if it could wait until evening. Aside from her volunteering to save him at least an hour each way on Strada Pievaiola on Monday, her mouth was too vulnerable, her eyes too troubled.

She didn't even try to demur for the sake of politeness but followed him out of the workshop and into the glaring sunlight and the thrum of the ever-present cicadas. He made casual conversation as they strolled. 'The house has

84

doors front and back with an upper terrace above. One has a view and the other has a drive. I don't have much of a lower terrace apart from this bit of paving.' He indicated the mossy stones they were crossing, then pointed at where the vine that clung to the house was threatening to cover windows and block the gutter. 'Living here isn't like living in a town house with a square garden and a straight path to a rectangular drive. Here, man has built a house but nature keeps the rest.' He opened the door for her and let her step first into the cool kitchen.

'You live here alone?' She gazed approvingly at the terracotta floor tiles and traditional unfinished stone walls.

'I had a girlfriend but it didn't work out.'

Politely, she didn't ask for details but looked through the open door into hallway. 'What beautiful stairs.'

He followed her gaze towards the lower flight, which led up to the door that opened from the other side of the house. Like so many houses built into the mountain it was split-level. The stair treads were of plain terracotta but the risers boasted pretty hand-painted tiles of dark blue and white. The bannister wood was nearly black with age and a blue glass ball on the newel post caught the light. 'The house is about three hundred years old. I've been told that Papà's cousin who ran the vineyard before us had a particular female friend who lived here once. Maybe that's why the property was named Il Rifugio, The Escape.'

'"A particular female friend",' she repeated thoughtfully, cocking one eyebrow.

He smiled, not about to apologise for the alleged misbehaviour of an ancestor. 'Nobody had lived here for a while when I bought it from the company. I upgraded the water and electricity systems and modernised the kitchen, knocking two rooms into one. It's one of my favourite rooms.' He gestured to encompass the three windows that looked out to the valley and the simple wooden cabinets he'd fitted beneath plain work surfaces. Nicoletta had wanted flamboyant additions but he'd resisted. It summed up their relationship: Nicoletta wanting and Piero resisting.

While he started to make the coffee, Zia settled herself on a stool, hooking a foot over a rung. 'Durante said they were refused permission to knock down walls in the cottages.'

'That only happens if you ask,' he answered gravely.

Laughter gleamed in her eyes. 'They seem lovely people, Lucia and Durante.'

'The best,' he agreed. His coffee machine was the kind with pods and it didn't take him long to make two cups. He popped a plastic caddy of sugar on the table and a milk carton in front of Zia then straddled a facing stool. 'So, Lucia's your great-aunt.'

'Apparently.' She opened the sugar and added half a spoonful to her coffee, then a dash of milk. 'It feels unreal. Lucia's one of six and just one of those siblings, her brother Roberto, has eight children. The Costa family's massive.' She gazed at the table top, rubbing the grain of the wood with a fingertip.

He refrained from remarking that she could have called Roberto her grandfather. When she remained silent, he said, 'So, about the imposition you mentioned . . .?'

Immediately, her shoulders seemed to scrunch up. 'You'll probably think it's weird that I've approached you. We only met recently.' She sent him an uncertain look. 'But the whole thing with Lucia and Durante yesterday rocked me. I talked to Ursula but she could only listen, if you see what I mean. She couldn't add.'

He tried to find a foothold in the conversation. 'Add . . . what sort of thing?'

She didn't immediately answer but stirred her coffee long enough to dissolve the entire container of sugar. 'Context,' she said at last. 'And objectivity, maybe. Lucia and Durante are so closely involved . . . I can't expect them to . . .' She was obviously struggling to express herself and he remained silent while she searched for words. Then she burst out, 'All my life I've felt different. Separate from people. I thought it was because I didn't look much like Mum – Vicky, I mean – and we moved around a lot, which really affects lasting friendships, and I didn't have a dad. When Vicky died, Gran and Pap took me on. I'll be forever grateful for their sacrifice but I still thought: *I'm not getting the life I should have had*. Now I learn I didn't get the life I should have had *twice* and it's not just that I didn't know my dad – I didn't know my mum either. I've been up half the night trying to make sense of it. I actually put the light on to look in the mirror and ask myself "Who the hell are you?" I read internet articles and one said the human brain develops most in the first few weeks of life, which makes me one big fuck-up. Unplanned, unwanted, dragged across Europe, abandoned, wanted, snatched then left motherless. All before I was six weeks old.'

He liked the sudden F-bomb. It felt like a sign she was comfortable with him because he'd seen enough of her to know profanity didn't litter her conversation. He couldn't resist her vulnerability. 'How can I help?'

She held his gaze for several moments. 'Do you know him?'

'Gerardo? Your father?' he stalled, wishing she could have asked him something easier.

Her mouth twisted wryly. 'The "father" who wanted me aborted.'

'He was frightened and immature,' he observed fairly. 'His parents have mellowed a lot now but teenagers having illegitimate children . . . It doesn't surprise me they would have been scandalised thirty years ago. I imagine my grandparents would have been the same and you acknowledged yours were.'

She didn't argue but fidgeted with her cup. 'You're not related to him or one of his friends?'

He shook his head. Gerardo wasn't someone he'd choose to hang out with.

Again, that steady gaze. She had pretty eyes, like a tiger's eye ring Nicoletta had liked to wear. Not as dark as his, Zia's irises were gold as well as brown. Bare of make-up, her lashes were thick silk fringes. Nicoletta wouldn't have gone out in public without several thick coats of mascara, even when on holiday, but Zia suited the natural look. Even unadorned, her eyes were dramatic and her skin was smooth. She dropped her voice to a whisper as if inviting him to share a secret. 'What's he like?'

'Well,' he began, blowing out his lips. 'He's about fifty.'

'Forty-eight,' she amended. 'Lucia's already told me he lives in an apartment on the edge of Montelibertà with his wife Ilaria. They have three children – Riccardo, Laura and Caterina. But what's he *like*?' Her gaze focused in on Piero as if wanting to extract every drop of meaning from whatever he had to say.

Piero drank a mouthful of coffee, rich and black, while he thought. Carefully, he said, 'I don't think he's a particularly strong person.'

'He's ill?' Her fine eyebrows met quizzically.

'No. He's just . . .' He touched her hand to soften what

88

he was about to say. Her fingers were slender, her skin soft. 'He's not good at keeping a job or looking after money and doesn't spend much on new clothes or haircuts. He has a favourite bar.'

Her eyes darkened. 'He's a waster?' she demanded baldly.

'I didn't say that.' But it was pretty much what he thought. He chose to hint. 'In every country there are people who work only sometimes. And then for cash.' That was why he avoided Gerardo, who'd accost any likely employer with requests for cash-in-hand work, then prove unreliable. Piero had only known Zia a few days but what he'd seen made him suspect that this would disappoint her.

The way she wrinkled her nose only confirmed it. 'Is Ilaria like that, too?'

Piero shook his head. 'She has a regular job. I should think she keeps the family afloat.'

Her lips had parted distractingly as she listened. She licked them before speaking again. 'And what about . . . his children?' She didn't call them her siblings. It was as if she somehow had no right to claim the relationship.

'I know he has children but I don't remember meeting them.'

'Oh.' She picked up her coffee and sipped, staring thoughtfully out through a window. At this time of day, the mountains were more green than purple, like immense slumbering lizards. The vines were greener still, though only a segment of the vineyard could be seen from here. When the harvest began, people would look like ants working along the lines of vines seven days a week and Emiliano would be concentrating fiercely on sugar levels and picking at the perfect time.

'I see why Lucia was reticent,' she said quietly. 'She loves him and doesn't want to acknowledge his weaknesses.' She gave a humourless laugh. 'I suppose I'd harboured a secret hope that if I ever discovered my father, he'd be a wonderful man who'd welcome me, introduce me proudly to the family, give me grandparents, aunts, uncles and cousins. He'd help me adjust to who I really am and bring context to how I was created. For some reason it never occurred to me he'd have wanted me aborted.' A tear glistened but she didn't let it fall. 'Seems unlikely I'll be able to claim Italian citizenship via my father if I'm his shameful little secret.'

'I'm sorry,' he murmured, wishing he knew her well enough to comfort her with a hug.

She drew in a long even breath and asked with forced brightness, 'What are my grandparents like these days? Do you know them?'

He rasped his stubble. He didn't bother shaving ahead of a day in his workshop. 'Ah, yes. Didn't Lucia tell you? Fiorella helps in their house.'

Horror swept across the features she turned on him. 'My grandmother comes to their house? Holy shit. I feel faint.' But she didn't look faint. She looked upset and edgy as if she needed to race around and crash things together.

Here at least he could offer some positivity. 'She and Roberto have moved with the times, I'd say. I like them.'

It didn't seem to comfort her. 'Thanks for being candid,' she said dismally. 'I hope I haven't made you too uncomfortable.' Then her brow furrowed as if struck by a thought. 'You wouldn't have met Tori?'

He smiled. 'If you're thirty then I would have been eight and living in California the summer she was here.'

'Right. Of course.' She paused. Slowly, she extracted a photo from her pocket. 'Durante made me this print.' She laid it on the table and turned it to face him.

Curious, Piero examined the photo. It was typical of a new print of an old picture: faded colours overlaid with a fresh gloss. The girl – young woman – who gazed back at him was very English-looking with pale skin and freckles. Her fair hair curved back from her face like flower petals and her blue-striped blazer fell open either side of a large baby bump hugged by pale pink dungarees. Wow. She barely looked sixteen, let alone eighteen. She would have made the ideal cover model for the tear-jerking novels he remembered his mother reading: a woeful girl beseeching life to improve, abandoned by someone who should have been on her side.

'Seeing this must be emotional,' he said, actually feeling a lump in his throat.

Sadness weighed down every word of her response. 'Beyond anything I've ever experienced. I feel giddy with it. It's done something to my sense of identity, given me something I never knew was missing . . . but that something's already out of my reach. It's hard to accept.' Her head came closer to his and he was aware of the smell of honey, maybe from her hair. 'I'm bursting with so many questions my head hurts. Do I look like her? Ursula thinks I do.' She looked at him so he could study her.

He looked into her face, trying to concentrate on answering rather than on how strikingly her features fitted together. 'I can see a likeness in the shape of your mouth. And the eyes,' he agreed.

'But she's kind of pink and freckly.' She pulled out another print. Much more recent, it depicted a man in his late forties in a suit, maybe at a family wedding, his dark hair brushed into a man-bun. It was the Gerardo of today, though an exceptionally tidy version. 'I get my colouring from him.'

Piero agreed. 'The Mediterranean skin and hair has won out.' He smiled. 'English rose meets Latin looks. It's a winning combination.'

She slid both prints back into her pocket, appearing deaf to the compliment. A catch in her voice, she said, 'To suddenly have this knowledge is overwhelming. Obviously, I'd considered the possibility that Tori would turn out to be Vicky's child and my mother but then all but dismissed it. Why on earth would Vicky pretend I was her daughter instead of simply telling me my real mum had died? Why would Gran and Pap perpetuate the lie? Surely I was entitled to know about the fabric of me? I *am* overwhelmed.' She shook her head. 'Yet, at the same time, hungry for answers.' She got to her feet.

'There's no one you can ask?' He rose too, accompanying her to the door and feeling the familiar oven-like blast as he opened it, the sun heading towards its noon-day height.

She paused on the threshold, the sun lighting the coppery strands in her dark hair. 'Do you remember seeing me reading a load of letters? Most were from Gran and Pap but some were from Mum's friends. One in particular, Harry, the one Lucia had mentioned meeting, obviously knew a lot of the story. I've already been back to the address on the letter but it was from twenty-two years ago and he wasn't there. None of the neighbours I tried even remembered him, nor Vicky, though I think she may have lived there too at one time. One of the things I did during the night was to research private investigators who might be able to find Harry. It's a giant pain to do it yourself and every register you look at costs a bomb.' She paused and gave a pensive smile. 'Sorry. I've been all me-me-me. How's everything with you?'

He followed her through the door. 'I'm preparing to speak to Papà and Emiliano on Monday. Hoping for a miracle.'

'Good luck.' She produced her phone and held it out. 'Put your number in. I'll send you mine then you can text the details I need to pick up the glass. I'll have it here sometime in the evening.'

He took the handset, warm from her pocket, and quickly added himself to her contacts before handing it back. 'You're doing me a big favour.'

'You've done me a much bigger one. Thank you. I hope the conversation wasn't too tricky for you but I'm one jangling ball of emotions at the moment.' Her fingers got busy on her screen, his phone buzzed and he saw her details had arrived. As he saved the number, he heard her say, '*Ciao*,' and when he looked up again she was already walking away towards the cypress trees.

'*Ciao*,' he called after her as she approached the rocks and scrub, her shorts a splash of red in the landscape. He watched until she was out of sight.

A couple of hours later, Piero realised that a SatNav wouldn't tell Zia which door to use once at the glazier's unit in the Perugia industrial zone so he sketched a diagram and took it over to the cottages. He could probably shove it under the door if Zia and Ursula were out.

But as he rounded the corner of Villino Il Pino he spotted Zia lying motionless on a lounger by the front door, the wind stirring her long dark hair and pressing her top against her body like a caressing hand.

93

On the next lounger sat Ursula, watching something on her phone. She was blonde and pretty but, like her tattoos, it was on the surface. Zia's beauty took more absorbing, from her slow sensual smile to the way the light played in her eyes. Ursula must have caught his movement because she glanced up, held a finger to her lips, slipped her feet into flip-flops and stole towards him.

He halted out of earshot of the sleeping Zia and waited for her to reach him. She murmured, 'I think she's exhausted with all the bullshit.'

He nodded. 'Not surprised.' He held out the sheet of paper and explained his sketch. Before she could just take it and turn away, he asked, 'Do you think Zia will be OK?'

Ursula grimaced. 'She's strong and self-contained but finding out the truth has been a big deal. She's grown up without much family. It's a bitter blow to know she missed out on her birth mother and that her birth father viewed her as a disaster.' She shaded her eyes, her expression regretful. 'I'm afraid she's had few constants in her life. When I got pneumonia she completely overreacted and bellowed, "Don't you dare die!" at me in hospital. I was down afterwards because it took ages to return to normal and my husband didn't seem to get that. But Zia was there for me.' She gave a wistful smile.

'You seem to be there for her, too.' But he thought of Zia telling him about looking in the mirror in the middle of the night and asking herself who she was. Alone. 'I'm afraid I wasn't able to give her a reassuring picture of her father.'

'She told me, before she nodded off.' She sighed. 'I have a big family and great parents and I tend not to appreciate them. When I lived in Ireland they were in my face, all over my life, up in my business. I craved privacy. But when I look at Zia, I realise I was lucky.'

'Much the same for me. Is there no man in Zia's life?' The casualness of his enquiry belied the level of interest he felt in the answer. He wasn't stupid enough to have put too much reliance on Zia not wearing a wedding ring. She might easily have a significant other. Not everyone was Nicoletta, yearning for a band of gold.

Arching a brow, Ursula said, 'Not just now. There was until March but then he – well, there was a situation. He'd like to patch things up but . . .' She shrugged, her blonde hair falling into her eyes. Cut the way it was, so long in front, it did that a lot.

'Then maybe things will be patched up,' he said experimentally. As he said it, he realised that he wouldn't even resent such a reconciliation because if ever a woman was short of people to care about her, it was Zia.

She grimaced. 'I don't think Zia's in the mood to dish out second chances. She's never wishy-washy or codependent about relationships.'

It seemed as if there was a lot more to the story but he didn't press it. He said his goodbyes and left, feeling comfortable that he could invite Zia to dinner one evening without treading on anyone's toes.

Chapter Eight

Piero set off for the vineyard on Monday morning wishing he could spend all week in his workshop. He drove downhill to Montelibertà town, cut across its suburbs and took the lane to the vineyard. A mile as the crow flew became four miles by road, but in all the time he'd owned Il Rifugio he'd never felt tempted to make the old track into Tenuta Domenicali functional, though it was used by vineyard machinery further down its length. He loved his isolation and Binotto's plan to upgrade the track to a road felt an affront.

He parked his car between the office and the winery, inhaling the familiar earthy, herby vineyard smells, stronger when, as today, storm clouds sat on the mountaintops like vast grey-purple cushions. A warm wind tugged his shirt as he crossed to the offices and took the three steps up as one.

His father's desk in the big office was vacant as he passed through. Emiliano's voice floated from his own space, already involved in a phone conversation about *vendemmia,* the harvesting of the grapes, which would take place around early October when the sugar levels would be highest. Piero's first job when he reached his desk was to phone the order through to the glazier and text Zia the information she needed to pick it up.

She returned: *Will bring it over later.*

Usually, his glass order was delivered by two sweaty blokes in a Fiat truck. A beautiful woman with expressive eyes beat the hell out of that.

Emails took up the next hour. Monday's inbox was always gruesome because Friday's messages had gone unattended. As he worked, he kept an ear open for Salvatore's rich, rolling voice but instead he got a WhatsApp message from Graziella. *See your father and me this morning.* He swiped it from his screen as if swatting a wasp, infuriated, especially when seeing his father was exactly what he wanted. Ignoring the message, he sent his own to Salvatore and Emiliano. *Possible to meet about ten this morning, please?*

Emilio: *Sí.*

Salvatore: *Graziella and I are available.*

OK, typed Piero, thinking it was not OK, wondering whether Salvatore had actually written Salvatore's message or if it was Graziella 'helping'.

The four of them met in Salvatore's office at ten, politely offering each other coffee and ensuring everyone had a seat, though the tension was palpable. Someone apart from Piero had an agenda and he suspected it was Graziella.

He jumped in before she could. 'The lawyers' advice regarding the access situation may be in doubt.' He watched Graziella's face drop as he gave them a summary. As he'd spent most of Sunday on the internet researching, he was confident he sounded informed. He concluded, 'I know the lawyers were recommended to you, Papà, but I believe we should ask more questions.'

Salvatore and Emiliano, clearly bemused, gazed at Piero. Outside, the sky darkened until the light inside the office was grey. Thunder rumbled like a growl from a big dog. Nobody moved to put on a light.

Emiliano turned an enquiring glance on Salvatore. 'Were the lawyers clear?' He sounded unsure, as if, like Piero, he'd simply accepted what he'd been told.

Salvatore looked at Graziella and Piero's heart sank as he realised he was expecting her to supply the information.

Graziella's lips turned down. Stiffly, she said, 'My interpretation of the lawyer's advice is that the owner of Il Rifugio controls access to Bella Vista.'

Emiliano sat up. '*Interpretation?*' he repeated, clearly horrified. 'I thought it was solid legal opinion.'

Salvatore's eyebrows twitched as if in response to the flicker of surprise in his eyes. Noting his father's reaction, Piero pressed, 'Papà? What's your own interpretation?' At the same time, he was absorbing the fact that the assistance Graziella rendered Salvatore because she could type at hurricane speed and flip from app to app like a gymnast had morphed into her providing 'interpretations'.

Salvatore cleared his throat. 'I would have to read the email again to remind myself.'

'Emiliano and I should read it too.' Piero fought to keep his voice level. Lightning flashed and thunder rumbled closer. A gust of wind threw rain at the window and the lowering sky beyond the glass promised the kind of deluge that meant Umbria wasn't ready to turn from green to summer gold. July and August could be completely dry in the Apennine Mountains so a few good thunderstorms in June were welcome and this one entirely suited his mood.

Salvatore shifted, his gaze sidling to Graziella once again. In a rush of fury, Piero realised his father didn't know where to find the correspondence from the lawyers. His father wasn't paying proper attention.

Salvatore was known to grab the right opportunities; he was the father Piero had trusted all his life. But he apparently had an Achilles heel . . . and she was called Graziella. Whether he'd been swayed by his feelings for her or just welcomed someone taking care of the onerous stuff, he'd shown blind trust.

Piero, too, was guilty of not asking enough questions but he was going to remedy that. He indicated the computer. 'Could you call the email up?'

Reluctantly, Salvatore entered his password. Again, he glanced at Graziella.

Graziella let her head fall back, rolling her eyes towards the uneven ceiling in a gesture of frustration.

'Is there a problem?' Emiliano demanded. His gaze flicked to Piero with a fierce 'what do you know that I don't?' expression.

Salvatore, eyes on the computer screen, clicked the computer mouse. Outside, vineyard workers called to one another and the familiar hiss of a downpour could be heard through the windows.

Graziella vented a sudden, frustrated wail. 'I was just trying to protect you, Salvatore!'

'By doing *what*?' Emiliano demanded, sounding more frustrated by the minute.

Salvatore swung around to regard his girlfriend, features rigid.

Tears began to trickle down Graziella's lean cheeks but Piero wondered if they were of disappointment and rage rather than sorrow or remorse. She continued to aim her explanation at Salvatore, the person likely to give her the most sympathetic hearing. 'I just wanted you free of the endless, endless pressure of this place. You don't have many years left, Salvatore, I want you to enjoy them. Travel, relax. *La dolce vita*. I'm sorry. Very sorry. But I was worried about you.'

Not too worried to make the seventy-year-old sound as if he were on his last legs, Piero thought savagely as he bit back the scornful observation that travel and *la dolce vita* just happened to be exactly what Graziella wanted herself. She'd obviously been trying to 'free' Salvatore to go with her – and no doubt foot the bill. It would be far better for Salvatore and Emiliano to see this for themselves, though, so he sat on in granite silence as Graziella wept.

'I just presented the circumstances a certain way,' she wailed. She swept Piero with a vicious glare. 'Your family is selfish.'

With a gasp, Emiliano saved Piero the bother of pouncing on that remark. 'Selfish? *The vineyard belongs to us three.*'

As Emiliano and Graziella launched into a spat loud enough to rival the thunder, Piero's attention remained on Salvatore. His father's entire face drooped with disappointment. But disappointed by what? Or in who? Piero sighed. This wasn't over.

'Papà.' He spoke over the rising, passionate exchange between Emiliano and Graziella. 'I would like Emiliano and I to read all correspondence between Tenuta Domenicali, the lawyers and the Binotto Group for ourselves.'

Graziella stopped in the middle of a shrill accusation that Emiliano had no consideration for an old man.

Salvatore nodded. 'We'll send the files—'

But Emiliano's attention had shifted from Graziella. 'Piero and I will do it. It's important that all the members of the family—' he lingered over the word as if to highlight that Graziella didn't come into that category '—should be confident we have equal opportunity for seeing and understanding everything.'

Piero remained silent but inside his chest his heart was drumming with triumph. It felt like a turning point, no longer him against the others, anxious that questioning Graziella was, by extension, questioning his father. Everyone had woken up to the fact there was a problem. He couldn't quite hide his smile.

With a show of offended pride, Graziella rose to her feet, tossing corkscrew curls. 'Excuse me.' Tucking her designer bag beneath her arm, she stalked through the door. Judging by how soon they heard the engine start up followed by the swish of tyres, she must have broken into a sprint across the yard to escape the hammering rain.

Slowly, Salvatore turned back to his sons. He looked older than Piero had ever seen him as he gestured for them to take his place at his computer. Piero hoped that at least his father's stone-faced embarrassment presaged change so far as Graziella's role was concerned.

The day proved arduous.

The first thing Piero did was to disable remote access on his father's machine. He wasn't saying that anyone would log in remotely and change or remove files . . . but saw no downside in making sure they couldn't.

A major discrepancy came swiftly to light. In line with Zia's thoughts on the matter, the lawyers had *not* given the opinion that the owner of Il Rifugio could control access to Bella Vista. In fact, they'd advised the opposite

– access was properly agreed, documented and difficult to overset.

'But the Binotto Group has money. They could probably force the issue,' Emiliano observed in a tone that suggested he were making a wish.

Stung by the hint of hope Piero retorted, 'Or they could creep up on Lucia and Durante and slit their throats because their heirs might be happy to sell. Unethical, unlawful but cheaper.'

Emiliano looked abashed.

Salvatore was almost silent, perhaps shocked by his girlfriend's deceit and mortified that he hadn't seen it coming. He contributed to discussions only when necessary, his words slow and heavy. By the end of the day the lines on his face all seemed to be pointing south. With a jab of alarm, Piero patted his arm. 'Tired, Papà? I'm sorry if I forget you're seventy.'

Salvatore managed a wintry smile. '*Only* seventy.' The smile faded. 'I need to sleep on all this.' He offered no opinion on what might happen after that.

'Good idea. My brain's fried,' Piero said in English. A popular phrase when they'd lived in California, it had never fallen from the family lexicon and anyway the three of them moved between Italian and English almost without thinking. It was part of their shared family landscape, like the photo above Salvatore's desk of their old red Ford Mustang outside the modern winery Salvatore had presided over in California and the framed photo next to the computer of Piero and Emiliano brandishing baseball mitts.

'I think we've gone over everything anyway,' Emiliano contributed. Then he broached what was at the forefront of Piero's mind. 'Papà . . . would you consider changing your password? I'm not comfortable with Graziella having unrestricted access to company files.'

Silence. Sometime in the afternoon the rain had stopped and a watery sun was burning through the cloud. Salvatore's gaze flicked between his sons.

Piero held his breath.

Then Salvatore gave a single nod.

Zia and Ursula picked up the small glass unit for Piero then parked near the Minimetrò and enjoyed a glide through the tunnels to Perugia's historic centre. It was a relaxing way to spend a Monday, eating gelato as they strolled past the medieval Palazzo dei Priori and the Gothic cathedral. They leaned on the city walls and took photos of the lowlands laid out like a toy-strewn carpet. Then they explored narrow winding roads between tall buildings and lunched at a restaurant within sight of a carved marble fountain, Fontana Maggiore.

When an approaching thunderstorm darkened the afternoon, Zia suggested they make a dash for the Minimetrò but the storm beat them there. They dived instead into a bar enoteca on the city wall.

'Wow, awesome view,' said Ursula, getting her breath after their sprint out of the rain and admiring the panorama through floor-to-ceiling windows. They enjoyed lattes while the lightning tried to crack open the sky and gusts of rain marched across the landscape like distant armies. It was so awe-inspiring they stayed for an early dinner.

When they finally turned off the hill up from Monteliberta, Zia said, 'I'll take the drive to Piero's house and drop the glass straight off.'

Ursula stretched and smothered a yawn. 'Great. I haven't seen his place yet.'

It was almost dark but there were no lights showing in Piero's house and his silver sports car was absent. Zia pulled up, conscious of a dart of disappointment. She realised she'd been looking forward to seeing the calm, confident man who'd not only given up time to sharing insight into Gerardo and family but done it so kindly that his thoughtful sentences had felt like hugs. It wasn't often she trusted anyone so quickly. 'Doesn't look as if he's here. I'll find somewhere safe to leave the glass.'

Ursula hopped out of the car and regarded the shadowy bulk of the square stone house. 'He's got quite the place here. It's bigger than Bella Vista.'

Zia opened the boot and carefully lifted the glass in its white protective wrap. 'Let's try his workshop.'

They wended their way past scrubby shrubs and a gnarled and stunted olive tree. Ursula, grumbling that the mosquitos were like fighter jets, lit the way with her phone and tried the door. It swung open and she reached for the light switch. 'Wow,' she breathed, as light flooded the room, bouncing from hulking green machinery with grinning blades. Fresh wood chippings scented the air.

'Hot Piero certainly gets his manly-man on, doesn't he?' observed Ursula, gazing at the racks of well-used power tools. 'When we first met he looked like a business type but I can imagine him in here, being good with his hands.' She giggled. 'Do you think he is? Are you planning to find out?'

The lantern roof still stood on the bench. Zia lowered the glass carefully beside it then texted Piero to tell him where it was. She tucked her phone away with an air of unconcern. 'I've only had a couple of conversations with him.'

'So?' Ursula nudged her. 'He checks you out when he

thinks no one's watching . . . *all* the time. And I told you he asked if there's a man in your life.'

As Zia was still processing her feelings towards Piero she didn't answer as she switched off the lights and waited for Ursula to step out before rolling the door back into place.

Ursula heaved a great sigh and turned to head back towards the car. 'Just as well you didn't wet your knickers over him. I told him about Brendon and he lost interest.'

'*What*?' Zia swung about.

Her friend executed a little jig on the gravel. 'Har, har. Gotcha,' she crowed. 'Actually, he just smiled . . . but in an interested way.'

Despite interrupted sleep, on Tuesday morning Zia woke early so she could steal out to sit outside Villino Il Pino and watch the coming of a peacock dawn.

Fruitlessly, she wished back loved ones she could no longer consult, though she could imagine her grandparents' reaction to her search for her father. *Why stir things up? He walked away from his handiwork before you were born and again when you were tiny. Doesn't that tell you enough?* She imagined Gran's lips pursing and Pap's white brows meeting in a scowl.

And what about Vicky? How would she have explained the little matter of having pretended to be Zia's mother? There must be a reason smiling, honest Vicky acted out of character. She'd been the person Zia had thought she could rely upon most; and now it turned out she couldn't.

Then there was Tori . . .

Zia ached with a retrospective feeling of loss. What force had impelled that young mother to stick a newborn in a car and make a mad dash across several countries, only to abandon her? That rosy, freckly face half-smiling for the camera provided no clues, no matter how long Zia gazed at it.

Thank goodness for Lucia and Durante. What would have happened to baby Zia-Lucia thirty years ago, if not for them? It sounded unlikely that Gerardo would have ensured her care. She had an icy vision of being handed over to authorities and her mum – well, 'Vicky Mum', as Ursula had taken to calling her – searching for her, having to prove the right to return her to her birth country. And if she'd failed to find her . . .? She was deeply grateful to Lucia and Durante for ensuring that had never come to pass. She was sorry too that their kindness had gone unacknowledged, any further contact with Zia denied. She was beginning to feel a real connection to the kindly couple – though she hadn't quite managed to entirely regard them as relatives. Or maybe she didn't dare, in case of disappointment.

When she was tired of trying to make sense of the nonsensical, she went indoors to get ready to meet the day. After breakfast, Durante called round, his soft grey hair fluffing around his ears and his bare feet and sandals already dusty, and invited them to lunch.

They accepted and arriving at the main house at noon they found Lucia in a summer dress printed with tiny blue birds and Durante sporting clean shorts and sandals. 'We've located the rest of our photo albums,' Lucia greeted them. With a smile, she indicated a stack of albums of various sizes and colours on their heavy, dark wood dining table. 'Shall we look before lunch?'

When they'd all chosen seats, Lucia produced a large drawing pad and turned the pages to show Zia an extensive family tree. 'I've been busy constructing this. Maybe it is helpful?'

Slowly, Zia took the pad into her hands. These names written in stylish handwriting related to people whose DNA she shared. A few names she already recognised – Gerardo and his parents Roberto and Fiorella; his wife Ilaria and their kids Riccardo, Caterina and Laura. Then a host of other names. Giancarlo. Maria. Alessandra. Bianca. Carmen. Isabella. Another Laura. Gianni. Antonio.

The others fell so silent that Zia was conscious of the birdsong from the colourful flower garden visible through the dining room window at the front of the house, a contrast to the wildness around Il Rifugio. Overwhelmed by the volume of names on the family tree, she picked up Lucia's pen from the table, turned the page and created a list.

1 parent
2 grandparents
3 half-siblings
7 uncles and aunts plus spouses
18 first cousins, some plus spouses/kids
5 great-aunts and uncles plus spouses/kids

She halted, unnerved by applying familial relationships to strangers. 'All my life I've had one mum and two grandparents and an unknown father. Now . . . this! And none of them, except you and Gerardo if he hasn't expunged me from his memory, even know I exist. I doubt Gerardo ever told any of them.'

Lucia shook her head, looking uncomfortable. She laid her hand on the top photo album, ivory with age. 'There are two more pictures of Tori.' She hesitated, her dark eyes searching Zia's for a reaction. 'With Gerardo.'

Zia's palms began to sweat. 'May I see?' Lucia opened

the album at the right page. Ursula, too, craned to see as Zia gazed on the same freckled English rose beaming up at her. Beside her was a gangly, youthful Gerardo with dark eyes, golden skin and dark hair. His grin was out-of-proportion wide, as if he'd yet to grow into it, hair short, centrally parted and flopping to each side. In one picture the pair cuddled up on a garden bench; in the other they were standing with their arms around each other, faces crinkled with laughter.

Her parents.

Who?

Zia stared at the image of the people who'd given her life but never been in it. She glanced at Ursula through misty eyes. 'I need to get on with finding a private investigator.'

'What is that?' Durante asked.

'A person you pay to find someone.'

He cocked his head like a friendly gnome. 'We know where to find most of these people.'

But Lucia had understood Zia's meaning. 'You want to know what happened when Tori returned to England?'

Zia tried to explain, tripping over her words. 'What you've told me, these photos you've shown me, they've switched something on inside my head. I need to know *everything*. Vicky's friend Harry evidently knows the reasons she avoided you. She was usually so sweet and giving, she must have felt justified at the time.'

'Humph,' Lucia said.

Zia flicked through other albums but few photos meant anything, except Lucia pointing out Roberto and Fiorella. Strangers. More strangers she could have called aunt, uncle or cousin smiled for the camera at weddings and parties, lunches and picnics. Gerardo and his brothers and sisters had obviously given official school photographs to Lucia and Durante. She wondered suddenly about Tori's school photos. Did Vicky destroy them? Had Zia inadvertently thrown them out when she sorted through Gran and Pap's things? Yet she'd easily identified and kept an album from Vicky's childhood and one from Zia's own.

'Always, I loved my nieces and nephews,' Lucia commented, breaking into her thoughts. 'Every summer they would come to our garden all together to eat and play.'

Durante's smile was nostalgic. 'My brothers move away so I do not know my own so much but when the children of Lucia's sisters and brothers arrive, it is a party. And their parents say thank you.' He laughed. 'A day off for the parents and tired children ready for sleep.'

Zia's heart gave a curious little prickle. They were such generous, dear people. 'But you never wanted children of your own?'

Durante made a face, puffing his cheeks, lifting his hands in a very Italian gesture. 'We like children to go back to their Mammas and Papàs. We like our work and we like our play.' His eyes twinkled.

Lucia put her hand over Zia's. 'If we could have, though, we would have kept you.'

The prickling transferred itself to Zia's eyes at the thought they would have relinquished the lifestyle they'd loved for her. 'Thank you,' she croaked, her heart full. 'You wanted me. Vicky wanted me. Gerardo didn't want me and Tori gave me away. Bit of a contrast.'

Durante shook his head sadly. 'Tori, she has great, great trouble in her head. She love you very much but she is not . . .' He cycled his hand, looking at Lucia for help.

Lucia considered. 'The world she was seeing, it was not the true world. Her mind had been altered. Perhaps,' she added thoughtfully, 'in some way she realised she could not do well for you.'

'But she could trust you?' Regret clutched Zia's heart as she gazed at the young, fresh-faced English girl who had lived and loved in Montelibertà. And gone home to die. 'I haven't decided whether to contact Gerardo. I don't want to disrupt his life and hurt his family just for my own ends.'

Lucia didn't try to pretend. She sighed. 'It is difficult.'

Durante's mobile features arranged themselves in an expression of doubt too, mouth twitching from side to side.

Oh, well. At least they weren't guilty of bullshitting her.

Ursula, though, was frowning. 'I don't see why Gerardo shouldn't do this one thing for you. He's done nothing else.'

Zia managed to raise a smile at her friend's mutinous scowl. 'Maybe not but his wife would probably not open any champagne. His children might think less of their father for a teenage pregnancy and his parents are bound to be hurt by thirty years of deceit. They'd be made unhappy when they've done nothing wrong.'

'You've done nothing wrong,' Ursula pointed out.

Zia shrugged. 'I exist.' She stared at the photo again, trying to read the young Gerardo. If he hadn't returned the love of the laughing girl in his arms it was a shame, but there were no rules. 'What was Gerardo like in those days?'

Lucia's smile broke across her face like sunshine, betraying the soft spot she had for her nephew. 'Lots of girls liked him. Charming.'

'He love fun times,' Durante contributed.

'Did he give Tori the idea they'd have a future together?' Outside, a car crunched over the gravel and halted but nobody looked out of the window to check it out.

'Possibly,' Lucia admitted, fidgeting with the golden rings that had worn grooves into the soft flesh of her fingers. 'It would explain why Tori was so shocked when he didn't face his responsibility.'

Responsibility – Zia, in other words. Although she recognised Lucia's loyalty to Gerardo, Zia felt unfairly frustrated that they wouldn't condemn the boy who'd been old enough to have sex but not to face the consequences. He'd let – no *encouraged* – a teenage girl to return alone to her home country and decide whether to abort, keep or give away her baby. She shut the album with a snap.

Then she heard the front door open and, at the same time, the car outside drive away.

'*Ciao*!' came a creaking, high pitched voice. An elderly lady in a flowered wraparound overall came into the room and halted when she saw Lucia and Durante weren't alone. Her apologetic smile showed a missing tooth. '*Buongiorno. Scusate.*'

In Italian she told Lucia and Durante that her car had broken and she'd had to rely upon her husband to bring her to clean the floors. He couldn't do it the next day, Wednesday, the arranged day, so she'd come today instead. Zia understood, though the accent was broad and the delivery rapid, but most of her brain was coping with the shock of recognition. The woman was in the pages of the photo album in her hands.

Fiorella.

She took in the seamed, lively features, the dark grey hair in a ponytail at the nape of her neck, the flip flops worn thin. Faintly, she answered, '*Buongiorno,*' and heard herself and Ursula introduced as guests at Villino Il Pino. She listened to Lucia explain that lunch was planned on the terrace and Fiorella suggest she begin upstairs to leave them in peace, followed by an apology for being in the way.

'*Non ci dai fastidio,*' Zia heard herself reassuring her. *You're not in our way.*

Fiorella beamed before hurrying off. Lucia turned apprehensive eyes on Zia. 'That was not planned.' Then, quickly, 'If she would take the money without doing the work, we would give it.'

Zia nodded absently. 'Perhaps she'd rather earn it than take it. I would. She seems a nice woman.' Her head throbbed. How bizarre to speak to her grandmother without identifying herself. But how could she?

Suddenly she appreciated the ways in which Lucia was being torn. Betray Gerardo? Or keep secrets from her brother and sister-in-law? Encourage Zia to have a chance to know Gerardo? Or hope Gerardo be permitted to leave his mistake in the past?

'Lunch, I think.' As if aware of the same enormous emotional can of worms Lucia turned to practical matters and bustled off to clatter in the kitchen. Zia and Ursula, their offers of help refused, decamped to the terrace table in the shade, while Durante ambled in and out with oil and balsamic vinegar, paper napkins in a metal box, glasses, wine, water and cutlery.

'How're you doing?' whispered Ursula when he was on one of his trips indoors.

'Head spinning,' Zia murmured back.

Ursula edged closer. She smelled of coconut suntan cream. 'That was your *grandmother,*' she breathed.

112

'Apparently.' Zia realised her fists were clenched and forced herself to let them relax.

Then Durante reappeared with a platter of antipasti and Lucia a salad bowl and warm crusty bread that smelled mouth-watering. The conversation turned to easier topics than family conundrums.

Lucia launched into an explanation of the courses on painting ceramics she planned for next year. 'Here, where it's shady.' She waved at the tiled overhang they sat beneath. 'And there is also a storeroom to be turned into a studio. Participants will stay in the cottages and at the end of the house we have a tiny apartment, also. It's not ready for guests yet but by next year, yes. In the past it was maybe for a relative.'

'A granny annexe,' Ursula put in, helping herself to large slices of glowing red tomato glistening with olive oil and herbs.

'A what?' Durante demanded and laughed when Ursula repeated it.

'We will employ someone here to cook and I will teach.' Lucia looked pleased at the idea. 'Painting ceramics was my training when I was young, before I owned the factory and was a businesswoman.'

Durante helped himself to slices of salami and an enormous hunk of warm bread. 'Her designs are beautiful,' he confirmed. 'She won prizes.'

'That sounds fascinating.' Ursula's artist's soul was obviously intrigued and she questioned Lucia as they enjoyed the rich meats and crumbly cheeses before them.

Lucia sighed. 'Let us hope we are here next year.' Then she slapped the table. 'No, we will not be driven out!' Her scowl switched to a smile. 'Especially now Zia has told us things may not be as black as we feared.'

With a wriggle of alarm, Zia replied, 'As I told Piero, I'm no expert. You need to see a lawyer.'

Lucia nodded. 'On Monday.' Then she pointed her fork at Zia as if the sound of her neighbour's name had reminded her of something. 'It's Piero's birthday on Friday and we're giving him a lunch. Would you like to join us?'

A picture of Piero flashed into Zia's mind, the smile that told her he was aware of her, his easy walk, his obvious discomfort over his own family situation.

'Others come, too.' Durante wiped up herb-speckled oil with a corner of bread and popped it into his mouth. 'Two ladies Piero likes.'

Ah. Zia said nothing.

Ursula flicked a glance in her direction before asking casually, 'Oh? Is one Piero's girlfriend?'

Eyes crinkling, Durante shook his head. 'I think no.'

Lucia washed down her mouthful with a sip of rich red wine. 'I think he has no girlfriend since a year. He was going to be married—'

'Ha,' interrupted Durante.

Lucia frowned him down. '*Perhaps* he was to be married. But, then . . .' She walked her fingers in the air, miming someone going away. Zia would have liked to know more but Lucia began to question Ursula about her interest in art, so Zia just enjoyed the delicious food and glorious view as she listened to Ursula talk about life as a tattoo artist. Little clouds hung like puffs of smoke in front of big clouds, chasing their shadows over the mountains. It was like a moving watercolour painting. How would the mountains look in winter with snowy peaks? Zia couldn't imagine them being any more beautiful.

As the afternoon wore on, noises from the kitchen indicated that Fiorella was now working in there and it distracted Zia from the conversation. She was wondering whether she should screw up her courage to wander in and strike up a conversation when she heard tyres on gravel once again. Fiorella shouted something cheerily and Zia caught the word, 'Roberto!'

She sat up. It hadn't occurred to her that if Roberto had dropped Fiorella off the likelihood was that he'd pick her up again.

The engine cut. A car door slammed. A shuffle of feet heralded the appearance of a tall, rangy man climbing the terrace steps, bald on top but the rest of his hair and moustache pearly white. He greeted Zia and Ursula, gruff but polite, nodding and smiling. Then Fiorella hurried out of the house, complaining he was early. Roberto smiled again and shrugged.

Zia caught Lucia's glance flicking anxiously to her. Fiorella and now Roberto had met their granddaughter without knowing it. Lucia did know it. Had always known it. Had never told them. Though he was as tall and lean as Lucia was short and round, he was her brother and the easy connection between them as they chatted was obvious.

Zia grappled with the unhappy sensation of being excluded. It made her want to leave them to their conversation and jokes but she didn't want to be rude and make an abrupt exit. Then she realised Lucia was nudging her brother and his wife back towards their vehicle. It made her uncomfortable, especially when Roberto cast a look at the table as if he might have expected to be invited to sit down and enjoy a cup of coffee.

'Let's leave as soon as we can say goodbye,' Zia murmured to Ursula, suddenly aware of how much she was disrupting Lucia and Durante's lives. She was a mistake. A jinx. A black cat who might bring ill fortune by crossing their paths.

She should enjoy the last week of her holiday and go home. It was only fair. She'd tell them now of her decision, expressing deep gratitude to them for sheltering baby Zia-Lucia. When Lucia and Durante trod back up the terrace steps, she grasped the chair arms, ready to rise, steeling herself to say the words.

Then Lucia flopped into her seat. 'So,' she pronounced with the air of one who'd thought long and hard but was now happy with a decision. 'If you wish, I will tell Gerardo privately that you are here. If he wants to come and meet you, he is welcome.'

Durante added, 'Of course, he is not force to accept.'

'That is a risk,' agreed Lucia, patting Zia's hand. 'You tell me "yes," I will speak to him. Say "no," and I will not. You take your time and think about it.'

'Oh.' Zia sank slowly back into her chair, her resolution to say thank you and goodbye flying from her mind. This was a whole new decision to wrestle with.

Chapter Nine

Two days later, Zia was still undecided. Toasted by the afternoon sun, she'd positioned a chair and table to the side of the cottage to avoid eavesdropping because Ursula was indoors on the phone to Stephan. Her friend's cross voice still reached her occasionally. Reconciliation was evidently a way off.

Though her laptop was open, Zia's gaze drifted down to a small tractor crawling between Tenuta Domenicali's green vines while the possible consequences of meeting Gerardo swooped around her like the swallows above the cottage. How would Zia feel if Gerardo passed on the opportunity to meet her? Was it worth risking rejection for the chance that she might one day get an Italian passport? Maybe she should just go home and request a Resident Permit or *Permesso di Soggiorno* and, if she was successful, live in Italy for the required period. Then she could apply for citizenship. It wasn't impossible for her to achieve it without the golden key of 'by descent' . . . just less likely.

Maybe living in Italy was a pipe dream anyway. She

could go home to dear old Brighton and get a job utilising her Italian language skills before she ran out of money. Such a role might mean business trips to Italy and that would be something.

The rumble of the tractor drifted to her on the breeze. A figure on foot before it moved steadily from vine to vine. Curious suddenly, she turned back to her computer, adjusted the folder she was using as a light shield and tapped *Tenuta Domenicali* into a search window. A website flashed up and she chose the English language option.

Tenuta Domenicali is the vineyard and winery that has been at the heart of generations of the Domenicali family. On the south and west-facing slopes and terraces of the Orvieto wine region, above the town of Montelibertà in Umbria, the grapes are grown that produce the off-dry Tenuta Domenicali Orvieto Classico and the medium white Tenuta Domenicali Sangiovese.

In the past decade Emiliano Domenicali has taken over from father Salvatore as the winemaker. He says, 'In our small vineyard we use the best of old and new methods to ensure a characterful product. Our grapes are harvested and sorted by hand but fermented in temperature-controlled stainless-steel tanks to preserve the hallmark freshness.' Next to his quote was a picture of a slightly older, less sculpted version of Piero.

Salvatore, still very much involved in Tenuta Domenicali, is proud his sons are continuing to produce wine in the traditional way. A picture of an older man with beetling brows and a lurking smile in his eyes.

The commercial side of Tenuta Domenicali is in the hands of younger son Piero who developed the story around the wine. It's he who finds the restaurants and other clients to appreciate it. Piero appeared more relaxed than his brother and father, his hair falling over his forehead and lips quirked on a half-smile.

The information about the *Denominazione di origine controllata* or DOC classification, roughly equivalent to the French *Appellation d'origine contrôlée* that defined quality standards, proved less interesting.

Zia returned to her task of choosing a private investigator to find Harry; he who might know why Tori had left Montelibertà a bright, lively, loving girl and reappeared as a wildly unbalanced young mother. Some organisations called themselves 'tracing agents' rather than private investigators but they all offered results via *information from national and local registers, credit applications, company appointments, utility and phone billing, marketing surveys and Post Office redirects*. It dispelled her visions of someone pounding the pavements in a trilby and trench coat.

Finally, she selected a site and entered her details, ticking *Trying to trace family member/friend* then entering Harry's name in the space reserved for *target*. The term gave her an uncomfortable feeling, as if she wished Harry harm instead of just wanting to talk to him about Vicky and Tori. Consulting one of his old letters, she typed in his last known address.

She'd just realised her credit card was still in Villino Il Pino so she couldn't pay and submit without intruding on Ursula's privacy, when she caught sight of a familiar figure crossing the drive. The figure waved and changed course towards her. Suppressing an urge to smooth down her clothes, she smiled as Piero drew near.

'*Ciao*,' he called and took the other seat at the table, brushing back his hair as the wind's fingers combed it mischievously into his eyes. 'Thanks for leaving the glass

119

in the workshop. You saved me a long trip on a tricky day.'

As he'd brought the subject up, she felt able to ask, 'How did the family conference go?'

He snorted. 'Apparently, Graziella's been interpreting lawyers' emails in the way she thought most likely to result in the Binotto deal going through. The law firm agreed with your view of the access question all along.'

She watched him. The set of his lips didn't speak of satisfaction and a V between his eyes suggested tension. 'So . . . that's good?' she asked experimentally.

He shifted restlessly. 'It seemed as if it would be, because Papà and Emiliano were initially shaken by discovering the truth. But they still want to sell and Binotto's is still the only offer, so Papà's talking to them again but from a different angle now he knows the facts.' Then, as if sick of the subject, 'What have you and Ursula been up to?'

'Wandering around Lake Trasimeno today. Yesterday we did the tourist thing in Orvieto then later hit a night-club in Montelibertà. It made me wonder where Tori used to work, so I asked Lucia this morning. It's a bar/restaurant, now called Altarocca, and we're going into town to try it for dinner. It's just off Piazza Santa Lucia.'

'I know it.' His gaze dipped to her lips and she thought he was about to suggest he accompany them but, instead, he said, 'I understand I'll see you at lunch tomorrow. You'll meet Paola and Priscilla.'

Constantly mulling over the Gerardo situation, maintaining a smile for Ursula's sake as they played tourist, she'd forgotten there would be other guests. 'So I understand. Are they particular female friends?' she asked, remembering the phrase he'd used once before and lingering over the word 'particular'.

He laughed. A pause, then he laughed again. 'Not *particular* female friends but they're wonderful women. I'm sure you'll like them.' Then he jumped up, tossed, '*Ciao!*' over his shoulder and loped off in the direction of the main house, still grinning. Zia didn't see what was so funny.

'Do you realise I have to be back at work on the 1st of July, one week from today?' Ursula pulled a tragic face as they locked Villino Il Pino that evening and crossed the paved area, rounding the gazebo to the car.

Zia tried to sound as if it wasn't a million-dollar question. 'We'll have to decide whether we're driving back together. If we are, that gives us three more days here and three for the journey.'

As it was her turn to drive, Ursula perched a pair of oversized Ted Baker sunglasses on her nose and started the car, the tyres crunching on the stony drive. 'You stay on,' she suggested quietly. 'Give yourself time to decide what to do about your father. It's too big a decision to rush.'

Zia waited while Ursula negotiated the junction of the drives before accelerating onto the main road to join traffic swarming down the hill like insects with headlights. She said slowly, 'If I were to do that then we would need to arrange your flight and find me somewhere to stay. We've only got Villino Il Pino until the 30th of June. Then it's booked to someone else.' Under the purpling evening sky, they passed the country park they still hadn't managed to visit and parked at the top of Via Virgilio ready to stroll into town.

Ursula swatted bugs trying to make her their evening meal the moment they left the safety of the car and gestured towards the pretty Casa Felice hotel. 'You could book in there, maybe?'

'I could check availability,' Zia agreed. She imagined herself eating breakfast in Il Giardino, the café outside. It held appeal.

It was a lovely evening for a stroll into town. The breeze felt like velvet and the heat of the day had sunk into the pavements. They weaved between other pedestrians, watching the ceramics shops bringing in their wares ready to close up. A ten-minute meander saw them at Piazza Santa Lucia and they passed the church Lucia had attended as a child, beautifully rendered in creamy yellow with enormous wooden doors.

'Lucia's saint's church.' Ursula smirked. 'If she's named for the saint of virgins it's no wonder she had no kids.'

'A bad joke for a good Catholic girl,' reproved Zia. Then she turned the corner and stopped as her gaze fell on Altarocca, the bar where Tori had worked. It was built of stone with amber-coloured rendering and a big window beside the door, a popular place judging by the number of people inside.

'I'm a bad girl, according to Steph,' Ursula grumbled as they stepped through the open door to an interior of red-tiled floor and white-painted walls. 'Wow. This place is bigger than it looked from the outside.'

Zia agreed as she gazed at the many rows of wooden tables going back from where they stood. 'Lucia said thirty years ago it was a bar all the young people came to. It looks like a *tavola calda* now, where you choose your meal from the counter and pay for it then wait for it to be ready.'

The lady behind the till nodded and murmured, '*Buona sera.*'

'*Buona sera*,' they chorused, then chose pasta from the heated cabinet and salad and bread from the chilled one. Food plated and drinks poured, they bore their trays to a table near the door to a garden where cane parasols were threaded with fairy lights. The garden was pretty but Zia wanted to sit in what used to be the bar where Tori worked.

'Looks popular with students and tourists,' Ursula observed, looking around at the teeming, noisy tables as she put down her tray.

'It's good value. The whole bill was less than twenty-five euros.' Zia tasted her pasta, enjoying the crusty baked topping speckled with herbs. 'I wonder what the place was like thirty years ago.' As they ate, she gazed at the long stone bar with glasses racked above and tried to mentally animate the two young people frozen in time in Lucia's photograph album – the English rose being chatted up by a local Romeo. Going on dates. English rose hurrying to finish work. Local Romeo waiting outside for her when the bar closed late in the evenings. Afternoons in Lucia and Durante's garden. Two young bodies meeting in the sun, screened from the neighbours by cypresses and roses.

Contraception failure.

Panic.

Abandoned baby.

A lump grew in her throat and she had to put down her fork.

Ursula's voice came, warm with compassion. 'You need to work stuff out,' she said, without having to be told why Zia had stopped eating. 'Drop me at Perugia Airport on Wednesday morning for the flight to Stansted. I'll travel by train to Brighton ready for my first client at the tattoo parlour at nine on Thursday. Easy.' She gave Zia's forearm a stroke. 'We've prepared for this. You packed to stay a month or two if you decided to. Do it. You have unfinished business here.'

Zia gave a strangled laugh. 'You're right, mind-reader. I'll look for a hotel—' A thought struck her. 'I wonder if Lucia and Durante would rent me that apartment at the side of their house? I know they said it's not ready for guests yet but it might be OK as temporary accommodation.' Zia felt both lighthearted and lightheaded at the prospect of staying on in Italy, possibly for weeks. Without so much of a time pressure, she could think more about what she could or should do.

Her appetite returned and after another glass of wine and a pistachio semifreddo, she linked arms with Ursula and rambled back to the car feeling a hundred per cent better now the decision was made.

Chapter Ten

Never had Ursula sounded more Irish than on Friday lunchtime when she halted at the head of the terrace steps and exclaimed, 'Nuns!'

Zia had been prickling with irritation that her phone had just beeped with an email from the private investigator to say her enquiry was still pending; she'd forgotten to complete the transaction after she'd been reunited with her credit card. Ursula's dramatic exclamation distracted her and she looked up from her phone to regard the lunchtime revellers already seated at the table. Whatever birthday guests she'd expected to see, it certainly wasn't two women wearing black habits and beaming smiles. No wonder Piero had laughed when she'd asked whether his other guests would be 'particular female friends'. She blushed.

'Zia! Ursula!' Piero called now. 'Come meet Sister Paola and Sister Priscilla.'

'How do you greet a nun?' Zia hissed. She hadn't been brought up in a particular religion.

Ursula started forward. 'Sure, you shake hands. Do you know nothing?'

'Not about nuns,' Zia murmured, following. '*Buongiorno*,' she called, wondering whether the black habit and coif with the close-fitting white cotton cap was comfortable in the summer heat. Though the table was situated in the shade, temperatures were well over thirty degrees Celsius.

Piero rose and kissed both Zia's and Ursula's cheeks – a new development. '*Buon compleanno*, Piero,' Zia said, examining the sensation of his lips brushing her skin.

'Yes, happy birthday!' Ursula beamed.

'Thank you,' he said. 'Sister Paola and Sister Priscilla were just telling me how life's going on at the Benedictine monastery.'

Sister Paola, who had very fair eyebrows and grey eyes responded in heavily accented English as she shook hands with the newcomers. 'All is well. We have many guests this summer, enjoying our simple life.'

Zia liked her smiling eyes. 'You have guests at a monastery?' she asked Sister Paola as she took the seat beside her.

'Yes, they come to volunteer. In exchange for four or five hours' work a day we provide a bedroom and meals. They join us in prayer if they wish. People come when they're tired of modern life, I think.'

Sister Priscilla joined in. 'But we have internet. Without internet I think no volunteers.' She laughed. Her brows were thin and grey over dark eyes and she looked at least twice the age of Paola.

Zia laughed too. 'Tell me more. I know people take working holidays but I've never heard of them being at a monastery.'

Lucia and Durante arrived bearing jugs of iced water and bowls of olives. Sister Paola waited for them to greet

126

the newcomers before continuing. 'Anyone is welcome. From any country, any religion.' She leaned forward as if imparting a secret. 'Both genders! We're not so unworldly that we can't speak to men.' She seemed to have picked up on Zia's uncertainty and wanted to put her at ease.

Zia giggled at the gentle teasing. 'Have you known Piero, Lucia and Durante long?'

The closely covered head nodded. 'More than ten years. We experienced—' She hesitated and turned to Piero, 'What is it called, the shaking of the ground?'

Piero was pouring out water, each glass sparkling in the light. 'It was a tremor. The earthquake was further north.'

Sister Paola nodded. '*Sì*. The monastery was a little damaged and members of Lucia's factory helped us with repairs. She also asked Piero to repair a wooden building in our grounds.' Her eyes twinkled in her round face.

Zia found herself thinking how incredibly normal the nuns were. If she'd ever thought of those in religious orders, she'd vaguely imagined them gliding around in silent seclusion with their eyes cast to heaven. In contrast, these bright, engaging women chatted enthusiastically of volunteers, cultural experience, open minds and convivial mealtimes. 'We're grateful to the volunteers,' said Sister Priscilla, taking up a bread stick. 'They improve the condition of our house. They paint window frames or work in the garden or the kitchen.'

Ursula said, 'I think a cousin of mine has done something of the kind in Spain.'

Lucia looked interested. 'You are Catholic, Ursula? Today I will return with Sister Paola and Sister Priscilla to look at some nineteenth century painted tiles in their guest house. Several have cracked and I offered to provide replicas. My old factory will fire them for me. Would you like to come?'

Beaming, Ursula pounced on the opportunity. 'I'd love to! Zia?'

Zia was glad something might distract Ursula from her unhappiness over Stephan but that message from the private investigator was on her mind. 'I'm sure the monastery's beautiful but I won't get in your way. I have an email I need to answer.'

She helped Durante bring out the lunch of salad, chicken, pasta and crusty bread. It was followed by dessert of *torta gelato*, chocolate sponge with stracciatella and chocolate ice cream. 'Mm,' she groaned approvingly as she devoured her portion.

When the plates were cleared, against the constant background of rustling breeze and droning insects, her dining companions chattered about Italian ceramics, British seaside cities and Umbrian vineyards. She listened as she enjoyed the magnificent view of the valley, hugging her pleasure that she was to remain in this wonderful place for a while.

This morning she'd approached Lucia about renting their annexe, phrasing her request so as to make a gracious refusal easy. 'I'd like to stay in Montelibertà a little longer and before I look elsewhere I thought I'd ask about your apartment—' Then she'd found herself enveloped in a huge hug while Lucia crowed, '*Sí, sí*, of course! Durante, listen! Zia-Lucia is to stay longer with us!'

Durante had barrelled into the office from the kitchen, exceeding his customary speed in his eagerness to give her smacking kisses on each cheek. Then they'd all tumbled into the apartment to inspect its dusty interior. 'The walls need paint, the bed a new mattress and bedclothes,' Lucia had proclaimed.

'I don't need all that,' Zia had protested. 'I'll just buy bedclothes and a shower curtain—'

'You will not.' Lucia had hugged her again. 'The apartment is not occupied except for when Durante's brother comes and we will make it nice for you. Durante was to do this soon, anyway.'

Ever since that conversation, Zia had been experiencing bubbles of joy whenever she remembered the warmth of their welcome. Much as she loved Ursula, she'd shared her living space with her for three months now and liked the thought of having her own patch for a while.

Whether she would ever meet her birth father or trace Harry were questions for the future. It was enough to know that instead of packing up the car and embarking on the long drive home across Europe on Monday, she'd drop Ursula at Perugia airport on Wednesday and return to this ravishing spot. She'd eke out her redundancy money and savings while she explored the full potential of this wonderful summer in Montelibertà.

Ursula had moved on to talking about her tattoos and her job as a tattoo artist which, Zia was the first to admit, called for great artistic skills, but was quite different to replicating nineteenth century wall tiles. Then Zia realised: Piero had his gaze on her. She flushed, wondering whether she'd looked particularly vacant, lost in her thoughts.

His eyes were hard to read, so dark and deep.

As if divining Zia's thoughts, Lucia said, 'Piero, do you know that Zia—' But then the telephone rang inside the house and she excused herself to answer it.

Zia, guessing Lucia had been about to impart the news

about her extended stay, opened her mouth to tell him herself but then Sister Paola asked him how the grapes were doing this year and he turned to answer her.

When Lucia returned, she brought with her a prettily wrapped birthday gift for Piero, an olive wood sommelier set, which made Zia feel better about the pewter drip collar for a wine bottle that she and Ursula had bought him in Orvieto. Not knowing him for long, they'd gravitated towards something to do with wine and, though it was engraved with an attractively bold, masculine design, they had then wondered if they'd been unimaginative. It was comforting to know Lucia's mind had run along the same lines. Ursula had been shocked when they didn't buy Piero a birthday card but Zia knew cards weren't so commonly given in Italy. He thanked everyone and kissed their cheeks but Zia noticed his eyes gleamed most over Sister Paola and Sister Priscilla's gift of *pinoccate*, diamond-shaped sweets made of sugar, pine nuts and dark chocolate, which looked delicious.

Soon, the table was cleared and the party broke up so Lucia, Ursula, Sister Paola and Sister Priscilla could leave for the monastery. Durante headed indoors for a nap and Piero and Zia left the terrace. On the steps they paused to wave as the Dutch guests from Villino Il Tasso and Villino La Quercia drove up the drive. They'd gone out so much that Zia had barely been aware of them. Now she was to remain at Bella Vista she'd see lots of guests come and go. She turned to Piero to tell him the news but he was already speaking.

'You know, of course, that's it's an Italian tradition that when it's a man's birthday he can ask a beautiful woman out to dinner and she has to say "yes"?' His expression was solemn except for his eyes, which danced with laughter.

'You just made that up,' she retorted, but her pulse gave an extra throb.

He assumed an injured air. 'Italian men never lie. Will you have dinner with me this evening?' He smiled a slow, wide, sultry smile that crinkled his eyes. Something odd happened to Zia's legs. Wow, was it genuinely a thing that a handsome man could make a woman weak at the knees?

'You're not spending time with your family?' she asked, to give herself time to get used to the knee situation.

He turned his palms up. 'How could the beautiful-woman tradition be observed if I did?'

A spurt of laughter escaped her. She knew Ursula wouldn't mind being left to her own devices so she said, 'Dinner would be lovely.'

'I'll pick you up. Seven thirty?' When she agreed, he once again kissed her cheeks. His lips brushed her skin like a breath, his hand grazing the bare flesh at the sensitive base of her neck for just an instant. He murmured, 'I look forward to this evening,' and made off towards his own property with long strides, leaving Zia to head back to Villino Il Pino with butterflies somersaulting in her tummy.

It's just a date, she told herself. *It's not like it's my first one. It's just the first one since Brendon.* A break from men had been a natural reaction to catching her boyfriend cheating but an evening with Piero Domenicali's flashing smile and dark eyes was definitely a good way to end it.

She let herself into Villino Il Pino's shady interior. Her laptop waited on the table and she'd just taken out her credit card when her ringtone danced onto the air. She faltered when she saw her phone screen. Stephan? He and Zia weren't in the habit of chatting since she'd broken up with his best friend and he'd hit the pause button with hers. He knew where her sympathies lay. She completely understood him being rocked by some stranger bringing his unconscious wife home but to dump her *just in case* she'd cheated? That didn't sit well. In fact, Zia had a whole issue around him throwing Ursula out as if she didn't own their house every bit as much as he did. Stephan keeping Ursula in limbo, not exactly ending his marriage but not exactly not ending it either, put Zia's back up too.

'Hi, Stephan.' As she waited for him to speak she opened her laptop with her free hand.

'I just tried to ring Ursula,' he said, without saying 'hi' back.

'Oh?' Zia opened the email from the private investigator to locate the link to the payment screen.

'Her phone seems to be off,' he said tentatively. 'I thought you might know where she is.'

Zia clicked the link while she considered his motives. The temptation to be unhelpful was enormous because, in her humble opinion, Stephan deserved a little shirtiness. Or even shittiness. It wouldn't make things easier for Ursula, though. 'She's gone to visit some nuns,' she said.

'Nuns?' Stephan sounded astounded.

'I don't think she's entering holy orders. She's become interested in painted ceramics.' She explained the trip to the monastery.

'Oh . . . I see.' Stephan sounded relieved.

Zia put down her credit card without tapping the numbers into the relevant boxes. 'Is it the first time you've called her when she hasn't answered? I suppose that could give you a nasty moment.' She checked the antipathy that had crept into her voice. Until he turned on Ursula, causing her grey, woebegone moods, Zia had counted him as a friend. She thought of evenings in pubs or days sampling Brighton's delights as part of the same group and continued more softly. 'Stephan, you know she won't moon around waiting for you to calm down forever, don't you? She got in a bad situation, probably through nothing she did herself, and you've meted out a harsh, overlong punishment. She's a wonderful woman and men find her attractive. Clearly, she's going to come around to realising those things if you keep this up.'

More silence.

The credit card form on her screen timed out and she sighed. 'Just saying.' She refreshed the page. 'I expect she'll put her phone back on soon. I don't know if I'll see her myself this evening because I'm going out but I'll text her and tell her you called. Bye, then—'

'With a man?' Stephan put in swiftly. 'Are you going out with a man?'

The suspicion in his voice took her aback. 'I'm not answerable to you,' she said brusquely, annoyed she'd hesitated as if feeling guilty. She'd been single for four months.

'No. Sorry,' he replied. But he sounded winded. Maybe he thought that if she was dating then she might drag Ursula into a foursome. Or maybe he felt possessive on behalf of his big-buddy Brendon?

She had her answer when, not a minute after exchanging brief goodbyes, her phone rang again and this time it said *Brendon* on the screen.

She was completing the credit card transaction and waited for it to be accepted before she picked up with a tart, 'If you're ringing to get goss on Ursula for Stephan, she's behaving impeccably.'

'It's not about Ursula,' he said soberly. 'Stephan says you have a date tonight.'

'Yep.' Between the two of them they'd made her too irritated to be gentle about it.

'What kind of date?' he asked. He sounded wounded.

Zia laid her credit card on the table, her back prickling. 'That doesn't concern you now.' She tried to sound neutral but knew she hadn't managed it.

He sighed. 'After our last conversation I had a word with myself. I decided not to call you again till you got home but I have to say it, Zia. I truly, truly feel we can get over things if we give ourselves a chance to talk now the anger's gone.'

Zia tipped her head back, staring at the smooth white ceiling. 'What makes you think the anger's gone?'

It took him several seconds to answer. 'I get you,' he said in a small voice. 'You're the one with the anger so I can't say whether it's gone or not, right?'

'Right,' she agreed. She glanced at her email inbox. No receipt yet. 'I'm not sure why you're calling.'

'Please don't sleep with him,' he blurted. Then, in a voice of dawning horror, 'Have you slept with anyone since we split?'

'Stop,' she said flatly, not even attempting patience now. 'Please, stop. You're alternating between playing the victim and trying to control the uncontrollable. Neither is appropriate.'

She heard him suck in a long, deep breath. When he spoke again, his voice held a calm-down-woman note that made Zia grit her teeth. 'Let's not confuse the issue. I rang about the date. As you've been there only a short time it must be with a man you don't know well so he'll just be using you for sex.' He gave a self-deprecating laugh. 'Call it male protectiveness but I'm looking out for you.'

'OK, *let's* not confuse the issue,' she parroted. 'If I have sex with my date I'll be using him as much as he'll be using me. And what you call protective, I call meddling. Even when we were together, we butted heads about whether you had the right to tell me what was safe for me – the answer is "no". And . . . well, just, how dare you?'

'How dare I?' he echoed. Astonishment vibrated across the airwaves.

'Yes! How dare you express an opinion on my life? Call another man out on their sexual behaviour? Have you any idea how it felt to see you having sex with another woman and panting that she was "the best fuck of your life"? With our friends there to hear?' She'd buried this particular insult in the chaos of the moment but now felt a good moment to dig it out and brandish it in his face.

He made a sound as if he'd just swallowed his tongue. 'Zia, I didn't mean it literally! Men will say and do anything when they're drunk.'

Zia fell silent, mentally replaying his words. Outside, the crunch of tyres on the drive heralded the approach of a vehicle. Doors slammed and she heard the Dutch guests calling to each other in their musical language. She selected her iciest tone. 'So, you're saying that when alcohol's involved I could never trust you, even if I did give you the second chance you keep asking for?'

He made the tongue-gulping noise again. 'I didn't mean that precisely . . .'

'I don't suppose you did. Not precisely. It's interesting that you think you should be forgiven but Stephan thinks Ursula shouldn't, isn't it? Or are you going to claim you were roofied, too?' Shaking with a mix of anger and outrage, she added with studied politeness, 'I'll say bye Brendon. I don't expect to hear from you again.'

'*Don't sleep with other men*,' Brendon half-shouted, as if that would stop her ending the call.

It didn't. And it didn't do much to calm her outrage either.

Chapter Eleven

Piero had sacrificed the rest of the afternoon of workshop time in favour of preparing dinner, one eye on Ferrari's progress in the Formula 1 practice sessions. Now it was time to fetch Zia, however, he was second-guessing himself. Was bringing her into his home instead of taking her out too much of a seduction scene? The table was neatly laid on the upper terrace . . . conveniently close to his bedroom. He wouldn't be a straight man if he wasn't up for more than dinner with such a beautiful woman, but did this look as if he felt entitled? He didn't want to be that guy. He sighed. A tourist, she couldn't have an expectation of a date or two leading to an actual relationship but he shouldn't have amended the original arrangement without checking. He took out his phone and called her.

'*Pronto*.' She sounded lightly amused at giving him the Italian greeting.

He smiled at her funny, pretty English accent. 'Do you mind a change of plan?'

Her voice dropped a tone, carefully neutral. 'You can't make dinner?'

He corrected her swiftly. 'I absolutely can. But do you mind if it's at Il Rifugio? I thought you might like to try the family wines and if we eat here then I don't have to drive. But we can go into town if you'd prefer.'

'Oh.' He could almost hear her examining the idea and looking for flaws.

'If I turn into a creep you can set Lucia on me,' he offered gravely.

Her laughter trickled over his senses. 'On that basis I suppose I'm safe. I'll bet she can be scary.'

He turned and began to head towards the cypresses. 'I'm on my way to walk you over.'

'I'm sure I can find my way.'

'I don't want to give you time to change your mind.'

They remained on their phones, exchanging teasing remarks until their paths converged near the cypress trees. She sauntered out of the lavender dusk in a strappy black maxi dress, picking her way between rocks and wild rosemary. The dress, though plain and understated, hinted at her curves, more alluring than many a figure-hugging dress. Red toenails and red sandals completed her outfit and her glossy hair was piled on top of her head. Her beauty hit him so hard he felt as if every nerve ending was reaching out to her. It shook him. Managing to disguise his reaction, he took her hand and shortened his stride to match hers. 'Are you happy to eat on the terrace?'

One eyebrow quirked as she glanced at him. 'That little patch of paving by the creeper?'

'No, the one on the first floor. Well, kind of first floor because the house is built into the slope. It's one flight up from the front, two from the back.'

She nodded. 'I should think it has a fantastic view over the valley.'

'The best.' He'd left the door from the drive standing open and guided her up the steps to the French doors, which he'd also left ajar. They stepped out onto the broad terrace that ran most of the width of the house.

'How beautiful,' she breathed, dropping his hand to approach the terrace wall and gaze out. The valley was fading into the twilight, the winery and Salvatore's house shadows behind clusters of yellow pinprick lights, the vines thick, black ropes sweeping down the slope. Only the very peaks of the mountains were still bathed in apricot and pink as the sun sank.

He, too, caught his breath at the view – her rear view in the terrace lights. Her dress wasn't as plain as it first appeared because it was backless except for laces criss-crossing her bare brown skin. He had to drag his eyes away and step forward to join her, catching the scent of honey again and wondering if it was body lotion.

If ever a body was worth taking care of, it was hers.

When she turned back from gazing out at the view, he guided her towards the end of the terrace where a cane sofa stood beside a small table. 'I thought I'd give you a private tasting of the wines of Tenuta Domenicali.'

'Sounds fantastic,' she murmured, seating herself on one half of the sofa.

He stooped to open an aluminium-fronted cupboard. 'The disadvantage of the terrace is it's a long way from the kitchen so I had insulated cupboards installed. Once the heat of the day's over they keep things at roughly the temperature they go in, if you don't mix hot and cold.' He drew bread, cheese and two bottles of wine from one and two more from the other.

'Four bottles?' she exclaimed, eyes widening.

He grinned as he carried them over to the table. 'We

should drink it at room temperature but I chilled some in case you prefer that.'

'White wine? Room temperature?' She lifted a dubious brow.

He dropped his voice as he set the chilled bottles in a cooler. 'Truthfully, I prefer it chilled but if you tell Emiliano I'll deny it.' He took up the Sangiovese and opened it. He took four glasses from the cupboard and poured small measures into two. 'We should taste the Orvieto first as it's the lighter wine but it will go better with dinner so let's begin with the Sangiovese.'

'But Sangiovese's red,' she commented, accepting a glass.

'Frequently, yes, but it's possible to produce a white wine from red grapes. It's the skins that colour wine so we remove them at the beginning of the winemaking.' Gently he stayed her hand as she went to raise the glass. He often put on tastings to impart product knowledge when visiting call centres that handled Tenuta Domenicali wines. 'We take a little bread first to cleanse the palate. And then a sip of water. Now, we take a moment to appreciate the wine's colour . . . though the terrace lights aren't good for that,' he conceded ruefully.

'But naturally the colour would prove exactly right if we could see it,' she answered with exaggerated enthusiasm.

'Naturally.' He enjoyed her entering into the spirit. 'Swirl the wine to release the vapours . . . now we put our noses over the rim and breathe. Enjoy the bouquet.' He suited his actions to his words. 'Is it pleasant?'

'Mmmm,' she said, closing her eyes. For a moment he lost his train of thought as the sensual sound hit him low in his belly.

He realised she'd opened her eyes again and collected

his thoughts back up. 'And now we take half a mouthful. We let it slide from the front of the tongue to the back. Then side to side.'

'Aren't we supposed to try and suck in air at the same time?' She tilted her head enquiringly.

He agreed. 'You'll see the experts do it. But I don't want you to choke.'

She wrinkled her nose. 'A likely outcome.'

After nibbling more bread, this time with cheese, and sipping water, they repeated the ritual with the Orvieto Classico. 'Mmm-*mmm*,' was Zia's verdict this time. 'Now that's a wonderful wine.' The terrace lights were glowing more brightly as the sky turned black and moths had begun to dance as if celebrating her presence.

Her enjoyment pleased him. 'I agree. I shouldn't admit this either but I'll drink Orvieto Classico with anything. It consists of a minimum of forty per cent Grechetto grapes and twenty to forty Procanico – that's what we call the Trebbiano grape in Umbria. The remainder's Malvasia Bianca. The Sangiovese's a single varietal wine so contains only Sangiovese grapes.' He laughed. 'Now I sound like what I am – a wine salesman.'

'Sold,' she declared. 'I'm already wondering how much I can fit in my car to take home.'

'I'll bring you some from the vineyard.' He glanced at his watch. 'Time for the food. You sit there and—'

But she was already jumping up. 'I'll come with you. I'm not great at doing nothing.'

So, they ended up side by side in the kitchen, taking herbed chicken wings, beef cannelloni, cheese tartlets, and stuffed mushrooms from the oven and salad from the fridge.

When they began ferrying food upstairs he switched on

the lights for the other end of the terrace and was satisfied when she admired the olive wood table set with shining glasses and gleaming cutlery. 'Beautiful.' She ran her hand over the wood. 'Olive wood has such a gorgeous, satin feel.'

'It has.' He had to swallow. Her nails were freshly painted the same red as her toenails, not talons but pretty ovals tipping each elegant finger. He imagined them gliding over his skin.

She studied the table's ornately turned legs. 'Did you make this?'

He felt suddenly bashful. 'I'm not a furniture maker but yes, I did.' He left her to carry the remainder of the wine to the table while he brought the last of the food upstairs. Taking his seat opposite her he could no longer brush shoulders as they had on the sofa but he had a better view of her. He said, 'Using the terrace lights at least keeps the moths above our heads. Otherwise, I would have gone for romantic candlelight so we'd have a better view of the stars.'

'Romantic?' She paused in helping herself to small amounts of everything on the table, clearly not a woman to nibble on a lettuce leaf.

He met her gaze. 'Of course, romantic. I invited you because I'm attracted to you.' He'd always been transparent with women. Sneaking up for a sudden pounce wasn't his style.

She popped a piece of cheese tartlet into her mouth, chewed and swallowed, then sent him a faux-frown. 'You said you invited me because it's your birthday.'

He grinned at the teasing light in her eyes. 'I'm attracted to you *and* it's my birthday. Eating together is a good thing to do with someone you like. Do you know the

Italian saying "I have not eaten beans with you"? It indicates that if you haven't eaten together you can't know each other. I want to know you.' He topped up their wine glasses.

Rather than reply to that she returned to his earlier comment and looked out into the night. 'We can see a few stars.'

'But without the lights we'd see a million. Some evenings I sit up here and watch them come out. There's little light pollution and Italian stars are quite a sight.'

She helped herself to another cannelloni, offering him one too before putting down the plate. 'They're not Italian stars. We see exactly the same stars wherever we are in the world.'

'You're spoiling my lyrical comments,' he complained, liking her quick intelligence and sly smile. 'And people only see exactly the same stars if on the same latitude. Otherwise, the celestial horizon changes.'

They continued teasing and joking as they gradually cleared their plates. Piero wondered how long it was since he'd enjoyed the company of a woman so much.

Dinner was over and Piero had disappeared downstairs to make coffee. That was clearly a job for one so Zia had returned to the sofa to listen to the pulse of cicadas in the night, her mind full of Piero and the way his dark eyes had glowed as he'd listened to her. She'd caught him watching her mouth as if wondering what it would be like to kiss it and had watched his in return. He was such a presence, with his lithe body and quick, sure movements. She felt like one of the terrace moths being drawn inexorably to his flame.

Her thoughts were interrupted by the ping of an

incoming text. In case it was Ursula checking she was OK, she slipped the phone from her bag. But it was Brendon. *Accuse me of double standards if you must but if you sleep with other men you're making it impossible for us to get back together. xx*

She glared at the message. What didn't Brendon get about 'we're over'? Her shoulders rose and fell on a sigh.

'Problem?' asked Piero as he reappeared with a gleaming white porcelain coffee pot and gold-rimmed cups. Placing the tray on the table brought him close enough for her to catch his woodsy scent. She wondered whether it was from the shower or his workshop.

'Not really.' She thrust the phone away, watching him pour her coffee before helping herself to sugar and milk.

He poured his own coffee then paused with his hand beside a switch beneath a plastic cover. 'Shall I put out the lights to show you the Italian stars?'

She smiled. 'Sounds lovely. Living in a city, even a small one like Brighton, makes you forget the stars are there.'

A click from the switch and they were plunged into darkness. Piero must have already turned off the house lights and they were too far from the public road for its illumination to reach them. She heard him feel his way around the table then his weight settled beside her on the sofa. His voice came from a few inches away. 'It'll take several minutes for us to get our night vision. We can talk while we wait.' He hesitated before adding, 'Durante mentioned they've offered to tell Gerardo you're here and see if he wants to meet.'

'That's right.' The silvery sliver of moon was looking brighter already, as if realising it could properly show off its light without competition from man-made illumination. 'I haven't decided.' Briefly, she ran through all the unwanted consequences she'd thought of – Gerardo's relationship with his wife and kids and Lucia's with Roberto and Fiorella. 'It was freaky to meet Fiorella and Roberto. My other grandparents saw to half my upbringing but these don't even know who I am.' She paused to register an ever-growing number of stars twinkling into her vision. 'Gran and Pap gave up their retirement in Spain because they thought I'd deal with Mum's death better in England. They'd come to school concerts when they'd rather be watching TV or get up in the middle of the night to do jigsaws with me if I was crying too much to sleep.'

His fingers found hers and curled around them. 'You're in a tricky situation.' After several moments, he added, 'Of course, Fiorella and Roberto would have gone to your concerts and stuff, given the opportunity. They've been cheated out of a granddaughter.'

She gave a mirthless laugh. 'Have you seen the Costa family tree? They have enough grandkids.'

'And they love them all, from what I've observed.' He lifted her hand and cradled it in both of his now, warm and slightly rough. 'Have you thought about why Tori included "Costa" in your name? It might have been to honour Lucia but maybe she wanted you to feel entitled to it.'

The idea tingled over her like a static shock. 'No, I hadn't thought of that.' But then she sighed, the instant's pleasure draining away as reality hit. 'I guess I'll never know. I wish I did. I wish I felt part of Tori, felt a connection with what I lost. I've started to dream I can't find her, which is stupid because she's gone, so obviously I can't.' She tipped her face up to gaze at the black satin sky spangled with a million diamonds. 'I don't think I've ever been able to see so many stars. And the longer I look, the closer they seem. Some are big and bright; some so tiny I have to concentrate to see them at all.'

'Their brilliance has travelled for light years to twinkle down on this mountainside, on us, on this night.' He stroked her fingers.

Conscious of the whisper of skin on skin she continued to gaze up, lulled by the night's sounds. A buzz. A whirr. A flutter. A man breathing beside her. Her thoughts turned in his direction. He was like the black coffee he drank: strong, bold, straightforward; but cream and sugar graced the coffee tray presumably because he'd remembered she liked both. It was a tiny thing but she knew that if Brendon had taken coffee black, he wouldn't have brought the cream and sugar. She would have had to ask and he would've been surprised her need was different to his. And it wasn't just the tiny things he felt entitled to control either. That bloody text telling her that if she didn't come to heel he'd end things had been an attempt to seize power by making it his decision. It rankled. *She'd* made that decision months ago. Attempts to control her had always been a bone of contention, so why the hell did he think the correct response to losing her was to escalate that crap?

Her ideal man valued a woman as an individual . . . without making the mistake of treating her as if she were another a man. Her ideal man definitely knew how to make her feel all woman. Could Piero?

She felt her blood quicken as she realised what she was actually thinking about.

She was attracted to Piero. Her senses heightened when he was near. Her hand reacted to the touch of his. How exciting would it be to experience his hands on other parts of her body? And his mouth. His lips looked soft and sensitive. She risked a sideways glance. Her night vision had come in now and she could make him out, head back, gazing at the sparkling sky.

As if catching her movement, he turned to her, making her breath skip. He murmured, 'I suppose if you're going to meet Gerardo you're running out of time . . . this trip, anyway.'

She realised she hadn't told him that she was staying on after Ursula went back. 'Oh, but—' she began. Then she felt her phone buzz again from within her bag, nestled in her lap. She picked it up. 'Rude of me to check this out but it's probably Ursula because I keep forgetting to text her.' She'd been too irked with Brendon's message last time she'd had her phone in her hand.

This time it was Ursula. *OK? x*

She hurriedly typed back: *Fine, thanks. Oops, forgot to text. x* 'Sorry,' she said to Piero.

He waved her apology aside. 'I understand.' He didn't add, as Brendon would have, 'Women need to keep in touch with each other to be safe,' which, obviously, women knew without him pointing it out. Instead, he quirked an eyebrow. 'I'm just glad it's not a boyfriend.'

The half-question, half-statement hit the right note with her too. He wasn't accusing her of anything but it was a gentle hint that his personal code was to stay away from someone committed elsewhere. 'My *ex*-boyfriend texted earlier,' she admitted honestly. 'We split in March. He got drunk at a party and I walked in on him with another woman.'

'That must have been horrible.' His voice was deep and sympathetic.

'It hurt,' she admitted. 'He didn't even know the

147

woman's name. He's apologised a hundred times and I know he considers himself a good man who made a bad mistake, but I can't forgive him and he doesn't like that.' She didn't share with him that Brendon had the audacity to instruct her not to have sex with whomever she was seeing tonight. Piero had stopped stargazing in favour of gazing at her and her skin was tingling.

He angled his body towards her and the weight of his gaze felt still heavier. One of his hands drifted from hers to stroke her forearm on its soft underside. Huskily he said, 'I'm sorry you were hurt but I'm not sorry you're not seeing anyone. I've never wanted to kiss a woman more than I want to kiss you at this moment.' He waited, not crowding her, giving her the option to shut him down.

Instead, she made an instant decision to go with her own desires. 'Then . . . let's.' She leaned closer to his warmth to let their mouths touch, lifting her hands to his shoulders, closing her eyes to enjoy that first tingling brush of his lips and the heat that shot down her spine as they deepened the kiss. His breathing stepped up and his mouth opened in invitation beneath hers. She didn't need his arms tightening around her to know he was in the moment as deeply as she was. She pressed against him and suddenly she was fighting for breath, not because he was one of those vacuum-her-up kissers but because her heart was doing the most extraordinary things in her chest. It seemed to beat the air from her lungs.

'Wow,' he breathed against her mouth. Then he lifted her onto his lap and homed in on her mouth again, lips softly seeking, tongue caressing, his stroking hands making her feel as if he were trickling handfuls of warm sand over her skin. She broke off with a gasp, overcome by sensation.

His mouth travelled to her throat, the hollow of her shoulder, seeking out the sensitive spot beneath her ear, licking, nipping, kissing, nibbling. She nuzzled and kissed his collarbone and he groaned aloud. 'Oh, yeah.' His fingers were stroking her through the laces that criss-crossed her spine. 'I hadn't realised a back could be so sexy till I saw you in this dress.'

Her breath fluttered on a laugh. 'You like it?'

His fingertips explored her spine. 'I love it.'

They kissed on and on. She ran her fingers through his hair and liked the feel of it, liked the beat of his pulse against her lips, the way his tongue lazily explored inside her mouth as if nothing could be more pleasurable.

She turned around in his lap to straddle him, enjoying the deep rumble of appreciation in his throat as he took the opportunity to nibble and lick at the swell of her breasts above her neckline, drawing from her a tiny yip of pleasure.

'Are we . . .?' He stopped to groan as she shifted against him. 'I mean, do you want . . .?' His breath seemed about to choke him and she laughed in satisfaction that she could prevent him from forming entire sentences. He cupped her face, halting her from another nuzzle into the delicious area where his neck disappeared beneath his shirt's open collar. He sucked in an audible breath. 'I don't want to take anything for granted but you've got me not knowing which way's up.'

'Well,' she drawled enjoying a liberating feeling of wildness. It wasn't *because* Brendon had forbidden it but there was definitely satisfaction in refusing to toe the line he somehow felt entitled to draw. 'I'd like to if you would.'

He groaned. 'I would. I really, really, would.' And he reached behind her and gave the bow in the lacing of her dress a tug, grunting in satisfaction when it tumbled undone. 'I studied whether you'd knotted it as well,' he confessed, stroking smoothly up her body to hook her straps slowly over her shoulders. 'You can tell that a woman really turns you on when you mentally undressed her fifty times while making the coffee.'

She shrugged and the straps began a slow descent down her arms, causing the fabric of the dress to sag. The warm night breeze rushed in to caress her naked breasts, turning her skin to goosebumps and drawing her nipples to tight points. Piero dipped his head and sucked one slowly into the scalding heat of his mouth. She whimpered her pleasure. He moved to the other breast, caressing, sucking, licking until Zia could hardly breathe. Frustrated by how many clothes they still had on she managed to undo the first couple of buttons on his shirt to stroke the tight skin over his collar bones.

He showed no signs of suffering the same impatience, apparently happy to take his time easing the skirt of her dress up her thighs so he could investigate her underwear, groaning when he discovered a brief pair of Brazilians, following them round till he could palm her near-naked buttocks.

'I'm usually a big fan of visual stimulus but feeling our way around is sexy,' he murmured. Then, lifting her, he stood them both up so he could ease her dress further down and send it whispering to the floor. 'But there's a perfectly good bedroom a few yards away if you'd rather?'

She shook her head, sucking in her breath as she laid her hand on the front of his trousers and found a whole lot of hardness. 'How about out here, under these Italian stars of yours?' With a quick movement she dealt with the button at his waistband then, slowly, slooooowly, pulled down the zip and slid her fingers inside, finding him straining hot and hard against his underwear.

Galvanised, he shoved down his trousers, kicked them off and yanked his half-unbuttoned shirt over his head. 'Don't move.' Almost tripping in his haste, he pulled away and fumbled his way through a nearby door.

Zia waited, heated, aroused, left hanging as she listened to him swearing as he crashed around somewhere nearby.

Then he was back. 'Didn't want to destroy my night vision by putting on the lights and it took ages to find a quilt.' He flung it onto the terrace floor along with two pillows.

She let out a breathless laugh. 'I don't need to ask if you had the same issue locating the condom because I can hear the wrapper crinkling in your hand.' She let him guide her down to join him on top of the quilt. His hands stroked up her legs and suddenly her panties were sliding down. She dragged down his boxers and took him in both hands to explore his velvet hardness. When he gasped, his heated breath brushed her breasts, where his mouth soon followed.

Their movements became urgent. Hands, hearts, half-spoken words, questing mouths, skin, joy, pleasure, heat. He fumbled for the clips in her hair, sliding them free with gentle, sensuous movements that tingled through her scalp. Her long locks slid down around her shoulders and breasts and he buried his face in the mass, breathing her in. 'Jeez, you're beautiful,' he groaned, then set about exploring her with his mouth. She'd never known a man who used his tongue and lips so much or with such devastating effect, drawing burning trails on her body with lips, tongue and teeth.

Soon she saw a few more stars to add to the million in the summer sky above.

Chapter Twelve

Sunlight outlined the internal window shutters. Slowly rousing, Zia took stock of her surroundings: stone walls and a tiled floor. She was in Piero's bedroom, she realised, and she wore nothing save the heaviness of his arm across her hip. The day already promised to be hot.

Everything about last night had been hot, too.

Piero had refused to be hurried. Slow or fast; hard and deep or teasing and gentle, he'd spent so much time inside her she'd become exhausted but so aroused she couldn't stop. Even caressing her instep he'd made her feel as if sparks must be coming off her skin. He'd been intent on searching out every erogenous zone, some she hadn't known existed and some she'd never before admitted to. Encouraged by his uninhibited pursuit of what she liked she'd explored him in return, cupped him, held him, stroked and sucked him, tried him and taken him.

After he'd exploded inside her the first time, they'd laid in each other's arms beneath the glittering sky. 'Do you know the names of the stars?' she'd asked, her head pillowed by his shoulder, her legs entangled with his. 'I only know Orion's Belt.' She pointed to three stars neatly lined up like buttons on a shirt.

He'd pulled her more securely against him, his skin damp and hot, lifting an arm to point up. 'That third star from the moon, that's called Zia's Perfect Body. Next to it is Zia's Hot Mouth. And over there is Zia's Fantastic—'

Convulsed with laughter she'd dealt a playful shove to his chest. 'You can't give lewd names to stars! They're too beautiful.'

His hand had slipped over her skin. 'Your body's beautiful.'

When both bodies had begun to protest at the hardness of the terrace despite the quilt and pillows, they'd moved indoors to his bedroom. She'd offered to return through the trees to Villino Il Pino but he'd said, 'Only if you *want* to,' in such discouraging tones she'd texted Ursula that she wouldn't be home and sunk down onto his cool sheets instead.

They'd woken when dawn turned the stone bedroom walls to gold and he'd growled, 'Now I can see as much of you as I want.' They'd made love again until, finally sated, he closed the shutters and they plummeted back into sleep.

Now, feeling his comatose, sinewy body against her, Zia was satisfied – in all ways – with her choice of first-man-since-relationship. She'd got to know him a little before sharing her body and who knew what might happen now she was staying for a while?

Piero stirred and opened his eyes, blinked and smiled. 'Mmm, great start to the day.' He nuzzled her neck and kissed her good morning. His dark hair was rumpled, his eyes heavy with sleep but when he smiled he was one of the best-looking men she'd ever seen. He smothered a yawn. 'What time is it? I'm meeting Emiliano to taste the wine that's due to go out. I usually work here on Saturdays but this is a nice little ritual for a quiet moment.' He found his phone and checked the screen. 'Already turned ten. Want to come with me? See Tenuta Domenicali?'

She kissed his chest, his skin pleasantly salty. Though the idea of more time with Piero gave her a tight, tingling feeling in her abdomen, she said, 'I would, but I can't just keep dumping Ursula.'

He kissed her temple. 'Invite her.'

'OK.' She rediscovered her bag beside the bed and made the call while Piero opened the shutters on his way to the bathroom and she watched his naked back view disappear.

Ursula answered on the first ring. 'I've been watching for you to do the walk of shame past the olive grove,' she hissed, as if Piero might be able to overhear.

Zia smothered a laugh. 'Soon. I was calling to invite you to Tenuta Domenicali for a look around the winery.'

'Aw.' Ursula sounded torn. 'Lucia's offered to show me how she plans to do tile-painting for next year's courses. It's just with enamel paint because it doesn't need firing but that's what'll work for a craft holiday. She's invited us both to have a go.'

'As I don't have an artistic bone in my body, I'll stick to the wine.' Zia glanced in the mirror, feeling a ripple of shock that not only was her long hair tumbled and tangled but her neck and breasts were red with stubble burn. Definitely time to say a quick bye-for-now to Piero and slip off to Villino Il Pino to shower and change.

Less than an hour later, wearing a fresh summer dress of hazy greens that brought out the bronzes in her now-tamed hair, she was ready when Piero's Alfa Romeo purred over the gravel to pick her up. After a pause for several breathless, drugging kisses they drove slowly back past the terrace where Lucia and Ursula sat at the table in the shade, their heads close together. They all waved and Zia wondered self-consciously if Lucia could tell she and Piero had slept together.

Deciding there wasn't much to be done if she could, she settled back to enjoy being driven briskly down Via Virgilio, turning off before the centre of Montelibertà. After a couple of miles, the road led to a lane of gravel and dust and they passed a sign made from black iron letters on white-painted wood. *Tenuta Domenicali*. The lane rose steeply, vines stretching away on either side. 'Why is there a rose bush on the end of each row?' she asked, struck by how pretty they looked, like a corsage alleviating the formality of a suit.

'They're sensitive to disease and pests so the roses give us an early warning that something might be attacking the vines.' Piero slowed as the lane widened into a yard surrounded by several buildings of golden stone. A man called, '*Ciao!*' to Piero and, with an interested lift to his eyebrow, '*Buongiorno*,' to Zia.

She returned, '*Buongiorno.*'

Piero introduced them in Italian. '*Lui è Gioele, che gestisce la vigna. Gioele, lei è Zia.*' This is Gioele, who manages the vineyard. Gioele, this is Zia. Then Piero asked after his brother. '*Dov'è mio fratello?*'

Gioele grinned. '*E' dal vino.*' With the wine.

They left the sunny yard for a cool, barn-like building where cylindrical steel tanks stood twice Zia's height. They almost bumped into a man who Zia recognised from their website as Piero's brother Emiliano, though he wore a short beard now and his body was more thickset. Emiliano began, 'I thought you'd forgotten—' He broke off when he saw Zia.

Piero looked amused at his brother's evident surprise. 'Zia, this my brother, Emiliano, the winemaker with the magic touch.'

Emiliano shook Zia's hand. 'Welcome to Tenuta Domenicali.' Like Piero, when he spoke English, he sounded American. 'Piero doesn't bring people to the vineyard every day.' He shot his brother a questioning look.

'Zia's one of Lucia's guests. Her friend's painting with Lucia so I've brought her to see Tenuta Domenicali,' Piero explained smoothly, as if no steamy night connected them.

'Of course.' Emiliano smiled at Zia. 'Do you know that in Italian Zia means "aunt"?'

She grinned. 'I do. At least it wasn't anything more embarrassing. Imagine if it meant "elephant" or "slime".'

For the next hour she followed the brothers around the winery from the enormous fermenting tanks, double-skinned for temperature control, to the traditional French oak casks for the maturation of the Sangiovese. Emiliano's obvious passion flowed as they passed square cages full of wine bottles without labels in the cellars. 'In Umbria, Montefalco is also popular but Tenuta Domenicali sticks to Orvieto Classico and Sangiovese. The Orvieto is *abboccato* or off-dry, white with crisp acidity and peach notes. You might also pick up white flowers and green apples. In the past, Orvieto Classico was popular with popes. We're a little more than an hour north of Rome. Now, our white Sangiovese is growing in popularity. You know how we make white wine from red grapes?'

'You separate the juice from the skins at the start,' Zia replied.

'Ah, Piero's been educating you.' Emiliano sent his brother another searching look but Piero merely listened like a polite tourist on a vineyard visit, hands in pockets. Emiliano led the way out of the winery and across the yard into the vineyard, walking through the vines as if they were friends to watch over. 'Our terroir is calcareous clay and sandy soil, rich in minerals. A wine's taste comes from soil, geographical origin, climate and grape type. We've plenty of sunlight thanks to our elevation.'

Zia gazed at the vines that stretched their arms along wires, proffering unripe bunches for the insects to buzz busily between. If she let the rows lead her eyes up the slope she could make out the rocky shelf on which she was presently staying, glimpses of the buildings' terracotta and stone amongst the tangle of trees.

Emiliano went on. '"Our story", as Piero would say, is estate-bottled wine from those who grow the grapes.' He flashed Zia a smile much like his brother's. 'Shall we open a bottle of the Orvieto Classico that's about to go out? It's from the harvest two years ago.'

'Finally, you get to the point,' Piero joked.

While Emiliano vanished in the direction of the winery cellar to fetch a bottle, Piero grabbed his laptop from his car then the brothers showed Zia across to a building with steps up, holding the door for her. They passed through a large office with an empty desk and several chairs and took a short corridor into a smaller room. 'Emiliano's office,' Piero said, pulling up a well-worn green chair for her. He opened his laptop on the desk. 'I need to write new vintage notes for the call centre scripts and website text.'

Emiliano produced three glasses and opened the wine with an economic one-handed movement. Zia had noticed Piero using the same technique the night before.

In silence, Emiliano poured and the brothers lifted their glasses to the light. Self-consciously, Zia followed their example. It was exactly the colour of white wine. Good start.

After the wine swirling and inhaling of the vapours, she took her first sip. 'Mm,' she said approvingly. She felt vaguely foolish when Emiliano sent her an absent smile. They were still inhaling vapours and discussing top notes while Piero tapped at his laptop.

They went through the entire Orvieto tasting three times, each time with fresh glasses, until Piero felt happy that he had the right words and phrases and the scent of the wine filled the air. He and Emiliano hadn't been swallowing much but Zia had and she felt relaxed. As they chatted, she looked at a picture on the wall entitled *La Vendemmia. The Harvest*. She let the idea of helping with the harvest filter into her mind, of joining those workers who dotted the rows in the yellow autumn sunlight to tenderly divest the vines of their fruits.

But no, Emiliano had mentioned the grape harvest taking place in late September or early October. Her permitted stay of ninety days would be up before then as it was still only late June.

A fly buzzed dolefully at the window and she was about to ask if it was OK for her to let it out when she realised that the voices of the Domenicali brothers were no longer low and conversational but raised and rapid, gazes locked across the desk.

'When did the email arrive from Alberto Gubbiotti?' demanded Piero. He'd switched to Italian and it took Zia a moment to follow the switch and compute what he'd said.

Emiliano answered tightly. 'Yesterday. We didn't think

you'd want to talk it over on your birthday but I'll forward it on Monday.

'Forward it now,' snapped Piero and, with a sigh, Emiliano opened his own laptop.

Zia rose. 'I could wait outside.'

Emiliano hesitated, obviously awaiting a lead as Zia was Piero's guest, but Piero rubbed his freshly shaven jaw and returned to English. 'Actually, Emiliano, I've talked to Zia about this because she has experience with commercial property in Italy.'

Uncomfortable at Emiliano's surprised expression Zia hurried to add context. 'The company I worked for dealt in leasebacks. I led deal execution from the client relationship side. Others put the deals together and worked on legal matters. I know just enough to have questioned the advice you were given, that's all.' Her cheeks heated because Emiliano didn't look thrilled.

However, when his gaze rested on his younger brother compassion entered his eyes. He admitted, 'Piero and I have different goals because with the deal on the table I could stay as winemaker.'

Piero nodded. 'Emiliano's the one who doesn't let the wine turn to vinegar.'

'Right.' Zia smiled to see the brothers support one another even though they'd found themselves on opposite sides of a fence. She asked Emiliano, 'So you've already seen your post-takeover contract?'

Emiliano frowned, returning sharply, 'Not yet. You're saying I should be asking to see it?'

She flushed. 'It's not my place to say.' On the other hand, she had a little knowledge and it might be wrong not to share it. 'When large organisations acquire small ones it's common for key personnel to be kept on to smooth the transition. It's just—' she hesitated but then decided to plunge on '—there might be a minimum term. Your contract should stipulate that.'

Emiliano looked thrown. 'How long they have to keep me, you mean?' He paused, probably absorbing, as Zia had hoped he would, that being kept on didn't mean indefinitely. 'I suppose the detail comes later.' Then, as if defending his position, he added, 'It's the only deal on offer, you see.'

Zia furrowed her brow. 'Piero mentioned that. It seems odd, doesn't it? Was your agent's plan to market directly to other larger growers and producers?' It felt good to stretch her business muscles. She'd packed them away upon redundancy.

Piero rubbed his jaw, a mannerism Zia already recognised as meaning he was thinking. 'I've been too busy to ask these questions. You're making us look naive about business.'

'I don't mean to,' she said swiftly. 'But big companies aren't like family businesses.'

Emiliano began to gather up the empty glasses.

'Thanks for the gorgeous wine,' Zia said to him, wanting to lighten the mood. 'And for the personal tour. It was fascinating.'

But even as Emiliano made to reply Piero exclaimed, 'Shit!' He glared at his laptop screen and then switched that glare to his brother, whose eyes widened apprehensively. 'I can see why you didn't want me to see this email from Alberto Gubbiotti until Monday.' He turned to Zia, expression tight. 'Now we've questioned the right of way, Binotto's has abandoned that leverage and want to go ahead with the vineyard and my land without Bella Vista.'

160

'Oh . . .' she said, seeing instantly that this wasn't good news for Piero.

Emiliano confirmed her thoughts. 'Graziella's delighted. She says you've been hiding behind the pretext of protecting your friends and you can't do that any longer.' He lifted his hands, still full of glasses, in a resigned gesture.

'I can fucking imagine,' said Piero savagely, snapping his laptop shut. 'And what does Papà say?'

With a dark flush, Emiliano mumbled, 'He says perhaps we should seize the day.'

Piero swore again. 'I'll just bet. This move has called to his impetuous and opportunistic instincts.'

In a very few minutes after that Piero and Zia said their farewells to Emiliano and were soon back in Piero's car, the air conditioning blasting as if he felt the need to cool his temper. As soon as they were out of sight of the winery, he slapped both hands on the black steering wheel. 'Fuck!' He drove too quickly, as if his mood had affected his road sense, bumping the car along the winding lane between the vigorous green of growing vines and sunny yellow roses. 'Now Binotto's have said they'll go ahead without Bella Vista my position's weak. If I refuse to sell Il Rifugio the deal falls through and that's not fair on Emiliano and Papà.'

For Zia, all pleasure had gone from the day. She clung on to the door handle, her words jumping about in accordance with the uneven terrain. 'I'm sorry. I should have kept my mouth shut. Questioning the advice about the right of way just made Binotto's rethink their attack.' She suspected they were seeking a division in the family in order to conquer and Piero was hurt that they might have hit on the very spot – Salvatore Domenicali's spontaneity.

'It is . . . unfortunate,' Piero admitted tautly. 'But please

don't apologise. It's an unintended consequence, that's all.'
Then he stamped on the accelerator and the engine note
sounded as angry as she knew he was, despite his effort
to keep his tone even.

'But I am sorry,' she muttered. She'd actually been
planning to share another option with him once they were
alone. To her, there was a glaringly obvious avenue none
of his family seemed to have peeped down. But now,
smarting under the realisation that she'd broken the golden
rule that the unqualified shouldn't dish out advice, she bit
her tongue. *A little knowledge is a dangerous thing*, she
could remember Gran scolding, if ever Zia had over-
reached herself as she apparently had now.

Disappointment sloshed like cold custard in her stomach.
Last night had been magical, when Piero had shared the
stars with her and they'd made love half the night. It could
have led to a summer romance . . . if his following of her
well-meant advice hadn't backfired.

In silence they drove onto Via Virgilio, up the hill and
in through the gap in the rocks. Feeling he might prefer
his own company, she said, 'Ursula will be thinking I've
deserted her. Park at your place and I'll walk through.'

He sighed. 'I need to visit Bella Vista anyway to tell
Lucia and Durante about the email.'

'Right. Yes.' She supposed the lovely couple at Bella
Vista *might* just appreciate knowing their home and business were safe from immediate threat.

He parked so that the terrace shielded them from anyone
looking out from the house but before she could take a
breath to say she understood his anger Durante popped
out of the olive grove. Cheerfully, he rapped on the window.
'Piero, save me. The women are painting flower on
everything.' He roared with laughter and Zia and Piero

had little choice but to quit the car and follow him up the terrace steps where Lucia and Ursula sat surrounded by ceramic tiles painted with a proliferation of rosebuds, grapes, sunflowers and strawberries.

Ursula's blonde forelock was pinned out of her eyes, the way she wore it when tattooing, and her eyes were alight. 'Zia, isn't this grand? Lucia's been showing me traditional designs. The techniques are simple but the product looks amazing. Look, if you take a square brush and dip one corner in the sienna and one in yellow, then press . . . twist . . . and flick, you get these awesome streaky sunflower petals. So textured! You know, we could sell tiles like these in The Lanes back in Brighton.' And she burbled on about angled brushes, square brushes, round brushes and liner brushes and cheapo tiles that cost around four pence.

From the corner of her eye, Zia watched Piero murmur to Lucia and Durante and the three slipped off indoors.

Smothering a sigh, she made admiring noises while Ursula demonstrated how to create a bunch of grapes with a wine cork dipped in purple paint but most of her attention was on the low hum of voices drifting out through the salon doors. After ten minutes, she touched Ursula's arm. 'Piero brought Lucia and Durante news about the people trying to buy this place. Maybe we ought to clear up and clear out?'

Ursula glanced around, apparently surprised to find that they were alone. 'Oh, right. I'll wash the brushes but leave the tiles because they'll take days to dry. Will you bring mine to the UK with you when you drive home?' She began swishing brushes and wiping them on rags. 'You don't fancy going down to Montelibertà for a late lunch, do you? I want to look at the ceramics shops again and get ideas.'

163

'Sure,' Zia agreed. 'A lot of the shops close at one so we can fit in lunch before they reopen at three-thirty.' Piero showed no sign of reappearing. A dragging weight of unhappiness settled on her to think of him giving up the kitchen he'd made, the tiled stairs, his peaceful workshop amongst the trees . . . the bedroom with the broad terrace beneath the stars. It was all so Piero.

'Shall we get off now, then? I've left Lucia a thank you note.' Ursula proudly displayed a tile ornamented with *Grazie mille, Lucia* in swirling writing and a rosebud in the corner.

Jolted back to earth, Zia managed a smile. 'OK, Arty Pants. Let's go.'

It wasn't really the way she wanted to leave things with Piero but it looked as if he had plenty to do with the rest of his Saturday anyway. In case her leaving smacked of sneaking off in disgrace, she texted him. *Going for lunch with Ursula. Thanks for the private tour and the starry night. x*

They were eating salad in Piazza Lucia an hour later when she received the reply. *Your pleasure was my pleasure. x* It gave her a skippy feeling inside but she couldn't help but notice the word 'was'.

Chapter Thirteen

On Sunday morning Zia awoke before seven, tossing and turning like a guilty child who'd broken someone else's toy. To take her mind off whether she and her clever ideas had unwittingly hindered Piero in his mission to keep Il Rifugio, she got up and found Ursula's bedroom door ajar, her bedclothes tossed back. She wasn't anywhere to be seen in the cottage or outside. Surprised that her friend had beaten her in the early rising stakes, Zia showered, dressed and took her toast outside.

She was checking her phone for messages as she ate her breakfast when she heard Ursula yell, 'Zia!' and, looking round, saw her bounding across the paving in yellow camisole pyjamas, hair on end, eyes blazing with excitement.

'I've been in the gazebo, talking to Stephan,' Ursula gabbled. 'He texted to say he missed me and I saw it when I got up for a pee so I rang him to say I missed him, too. We've talked and talked.' She did a little shimmy, her face radiant. 'Things are looking better. He admits he overreacted but he was wild with jealousy when that feller dragged me in rat-arsed. But he says his life's empty without me. Oh, Zia!' She dragged Zia up and gave her a huge hug, disregarding the toast crumbs. 'Isn't it grand?'

Laughing, glad that there had been a breakthrough in negotiations, Zia hugged her back. 'Super-grand! I hope he's been thoroughly miserable.' This glowing, sparkling Ursula was a vast improvement on the dull, unhappy one Zia had grown used to in the last months.

'I'm starving.' Ursula vanished indoors in search of coffee and a pastry and almost immediately Zia's phone buzzed with a text from Piero. She opened it, tummy flipping with apprehension.

Do you have plans? Fancy morning coffee at Piazza Lucia? Ursula invited too. x

It was as if a tiny grey cloud had lifted. After yesterday lunchtime's brief text exchange and then not hearing from him she'd resigned herself to the fact that there would be no more dates for them. Although her heart's *dudda-dud-da-dudda* belied it, when Ursula returned with her breakfast, she adopted a casual air as she exhibited the message.

Ursula giggled and shoved the phone back at her. 'Go 'way! Like I'd be a hairy gooseberry while you and Signor Bedtastic make eyes at each other. Told you he wasn't miffed with you. He didn't have to take your advice, did he? Anyway,' Ursula continued. 'Stephan's only gone off because he's promised to take his nephew swimming. Soon as he's available we're going to FaceTime so I want to shower and sort my hair.'

She finished her pastry and bounced off to the bathroom while Zia replied to Piero. *Ursula's otherwise engaged but I'd love to. x* They arranged that he'd pick her up in forty minutes and she rushed off to change out of her shorts and into a cotton dress with turquoise flowers splashed on her favourite colour of red. Then she wove her hair into a fat, fishtail plait to swing glossily down her back.

When she slid into his car's passenger seat, she found her smile had suddenly turned shy. A lot had passed between them in the previous forty-eight hours.

He leaned over and brushed a kiss on her mouth. 'You look gorgeous in red. You were in a red and black dress the first time I saw you and you took my breath away. Have you visited a café called Don Peppi in Piazza Lucia, by the church? They bake their own pastries in the morning.'

His manner was so normal that Zia gladly followed his lead, though she had made a promise to herself not to poke her nose into vineyard business in the future. 'I don't think so, though Altarocca where Tori used to work, where she met Gerardo, is just off that piazza.' She was hyper aware of the proximity of the golden skin of his bare arm as he turned the car and began back up the drive.

He glanced over as the car brushed the last of the yellow broom. 'I never asked what happened there. How did it feel?'

'Odd,' she admitted. 'We had a reasonable meal but I kept trying to bring them to life in my mind then feeling sad because I couldn't. I wish Lucia had a video of Tori as well as those few photos.'

He covered her hand with his for a moment then drove down into Montelibertà, demonstrating acute spatial awareness by parallel parking in a small space in Corso Sant' Angelo. They strolled hand-in-hand down Corso Musica, past the theatre and into Piazza Lucia to find an empty table with a view of the comings and goings of the square.

Piero glanced at his watch, plain but for the Dolce & Gabbana symbol. 'The church bell tolls at the end of the service. I love the sound. Simple, but rich.' They chatted as they waited for coffee and pastries. Piero told her he'd just been given the green light on a new project, a wooden playhouse. Zia told him about things looking better for Ursula and her husband Stephan, sitting back to let the waiter unload his tray of cornetti, biscotti, espresso for Piero and cappuccino for Zia. Piero offered her the plate. 'I'm pleased for Ursula to have something so good to go home to.'

Zia took a deliciously moist and citrusy cornetto while Piero took a biscotto and dipped it into his coffee. She began, 'Ursula will be going home before—' She was about to tell him that she was planning to stay on in Lucia and Durante's apartment, but before she could get the words out a furious woman stormed up to their table.

'Piero, *ti voglio sposare*!'

Piero's jaw dropped. 'Nicoletta!'

Zia gaped at the woman, at her short dress and long, groomed hair. And the tears standing in her eyes. Had she just said *Piero, I will marry you*?

Then the woman gazed from Piero to Zia and the tears welled out onto her cheeks. '*Bastardo, non hai aspettato che tornassi da Milano.*' There was no mistake this time. *You bastard. You didn't wait for me to get back from Milan.*

As if announcing a funeral, the church bell began a single, sombre toll. The noise in the square increased as the church doors opened and a chattering throng streamed out. Zia thought she glimpsed Fiorella and Roberto with another couple of their age but she was too stupefied by what was happening in front of her to check.

Nicoletta fixed her huge, luminous eyes on Piero. 'You had to amuse yourself with a *tourist*?' She covered the word with scorn.

Piero kept his voice low. 'Nicoletta, what do you think you're doing?'

'*Un'altra donna*,' Nicoletta interrupted in tragic tones.

Another woman. Her? The words galvanised Zia. She shoved back her chair and leaped to her feet. 'I'm no one's other woman. Excuse me.' She spun on her heel.

'Zia!' Piero called, sounding shocked.

She glanced back but didn't halt. 'This sounds like something you should stay and sort out. I'll call Ursula to fetch me.'

Piero hesitated. A waiter rushed over, perhaps worried they'd all storm off and no one would pay the bill. Nicoletta began to hurl insults after Zia, much to the interest of the audience of café patrons and churchgoers. As Zia hurried, she heard Piero snap, 'Stop it! Leave her alone. She's going home soon anyway.'

It sounded as if his fiancée had come home unexpectedly and caught Piero cheating.

With her.

She sped over the cobbles, dialling Ursula as she went. Ursula, though sounding surprised, said, 'I've finished FaceTiming Steph so I'll come straight down. Can you walk to Via Virgilio so I can find you?' She'd been Zia's bestie for too long to ask a load of questions. She just did as she was asked.

Questions would no doubt come later.

Piero could have tossed some euros on the table and raced after Zia but decided it might be better to put a stop to Nicoletta's game, especially as she'd dropped down into

Zia's vacated chair and was looking around as if for a waiter.

Not enjoying the frankly curious gazes from fellow patrons of the café, Piero sat down too. 'What the hell are you playing at?' he hissed.

Nicoletta turned beseeching eyes on him. 'We were going to be married, Piero.'

'No, we weren't,' he reminded her brutally.

Her eyes dropped. 'But you know how I hoped . . .' She gazed down into her lap. A tear dropped onto her light blue dress and made a darker spot. It was followed by another.

She could have mopped the tears at source and Piero knew she could be a drama queen but his heart softened. He and Nicoletta had been together for two years. He'd considered himself in love with her at one time, gauging 'in love' by experiencing the strongest feelings he'd so far felt for a woman. The passion had faded and marriage had been far from his mind but Nicoletta had been hurt.

'You're visiting Montelibertà?' he probed gently.

She shrugged. 'Living here again. My job in Milan's gone. The economy's bad in the north and I couldn't afford to keep my apartment while I looked for another job. I hope to get work in Montelibertà because my sister says there are still tourists.' She flicked a glance under her lashes at the word 'tourists' as if she expected him to look embarrassed. She must have heard Zia speaking English because she didn't stand out as non-Italian on looks alone.

'You're living here?' he repeated, not sure how he felt about the news.

A fresh tear rolled down her cheek and hit her dress. 'With my sister.'

That explained a lot. There was a healthy sibling rivalry

between them and it would rankle with Nicoletta to have to be beholden to her.

A waiter took her order for espresso, eyeing her tears with interest. Piero didn't ask for a fresh cup for himself but found it hard to be so rude and unfeeling as to leave Nicoletta to cry into her coffee alone. He felt guilty about Zia but was sure that when he explained, she'd understand.

It was half an hour before he could find the right moment to express his sympathy at Nicoletta's plight but gently remind her that their relationship was over. He drove back to Il Rifugio and jogged through the cypresses, only to find Zia's car absent and Villino Il Pino locked up. He was frustrated but not shocked. It couldn't have been nice when Nicoletta descended, making wild claims. Zia and Ursula were almost at the end of their holiday and had probably gone out for the day.

He tried to phone Zia but his call went straight to voicemail. Standing outside the locked cottage door, he left a voice message. 'Zia. I'm sorry that happened. There's nothing between Nicoletta and me now . . .' He hesitated, then added, 'But I'd rather explain in person if you'd let me know when you come back.' He repeated the same information in a text then changed and went to his workshop to occupy himself while he waited.

The call never came.

Euphoric didn't begin to describe Ursula's emotional state on Monday morning.

'Now, you're sure that you don't mind?' she kept saying as she pranced around, flinging things into her suitcase.

'Well, seeing as you've already changed your flight to just a few hours from now, don't you think it's a bit late to ask?' she teased. 'Honestly, I'm really happy for you,

Urs.' Zia treated her friend to a big hug to prove it. 'You would've been going home on Wednesday anyway.'

'But now Stephan has held out the olive branch I can't wait.' She treated Zia to a leer. 'Just think of the make-up sex.'

'Mind if I don't?' Zia joked. Inside, she was disappointed to lose Ursula two days early but wouldn't for the world dampen her joy by saying so.

For about the eighteenth time, Ursula checked she had her passport. 'What about you and Signor Bedtastic?'

Her mask carefully in place, Zia shrugged. 'Over, I expect.' Despite Piero leaving her messages, Zia hadn't replied. After her ignominious flight from the café yesterday she'd suggested to Ursula that they drive off to Città Della Pieve and they'd returned home well after dark. It had been a temptation to do as Piero asked and listen to his explanation but while she was wavering, she'd received a text from Brendon.

> *After uncomfortable soul searching I realise nothing I've said in the past few days has helped our situation. I SHOULD NOT be judgy as I have no moral high ground (but please spare me details if you slept with him). I SHOULD keep telling you that I love you and can't imagine my life without you. If you ever think you can come back to me, I'll be the happiest man in the world. Xxxxx*

Despite noting spooky similarities to the phrases Ursula attributed to Steph, Zia found this dramatic message harder to read than all Brendon's attempts to rekindle their relationship. His tacit acceptance that she had the right to sleep with Piero had the bizarre effect of making her half-wish she hadn't. She'd thought she could handle a casual hook-up – OK, an incredible night of sex – but the miserable nausea she'd felt when confronted by a sobbing Nicoletta had shocked her. She wasn't in danger of feeling too much for Piero, was she? That would cast her in the Brendon role. Uncomfortable.

The unpleasant things Nicoletta had said, the contempt with which she'd obviously viewed Zia and the fact that Piero had remained behind with his ex, had all kept her awake last night. But now she shook herself. No. She refused to be this disappointed in a man she'd only just met.

She conjured up a smile and made a show of checking the time. 'Ursula, if we're going to make it to the airport in time for you to catch your flight, you'd better get your arse in gear.'

'Okay, huneeee,' Ursula half-sang, giddily fastening her luggage.

They were just hoisting Ursula's suitcase into the car when Piero hurried out of the trees, his frown a slash across his forehead.

'You're going?' he called as soon as he was near enough.

Ursula lifted her sunglasses to give Zia a questioning look. 'Shall I go back indoors?'

Zia watched Piero's long strides eat the distance between them. 'I suppose it might be best.' Then, raising her voice and ostentatiously checking the time, 'We only have five minutes so I won't be long.'

Piero paused to nod his thanks in Ursula's direction but then his eyes fastened on Zia as he came close enough for her to smell his shaving foam.

He didn't try to touch her but plunged into an explanation the instant the cottage door closed behind Ursula.

'I'm sorry about Nicoletta. As you haven't replied to my messages, I guess you're pretty pissed with me but I have to explain before you leave. You must be thinking I'm a rat.' His speech was low and rapid, his eyes intense. 'We were together for two years but Nicoletta wanted . . . things. Her sister found a rich man who loved her, married her and gave her kids.' He rubbed his jaw. 'I think she saw me as a way to get the same. I was already having misgivings about her moving in with me. When she gave me the ultimatum to marry her or it would be over, I chose for us to be over.' He shifted awkwardly. 'The relationship was one-sided. I didn't want to hurt her but . . .'

As Zia had found herself in a similar situation before Brendon's unwitting sex show, she nodded her understanding as his words tailed off.

He moved a step closer and took her hands. 'She took a job in Milan. Moved away. The company folded and now she's back, witnessing her sister enjoying all the things she wants for herself. She lost her temper when she saw us together and said irrational crap like that dramatic "I will marry you," even though I never proposed. We split up a year ago. I was completely free to be with you. I'm sorry I didn't come after you but I wanted to leave her in no doubt there's no way forward for us.'

She nodded again because she was the first to admit that exes sometimes acted irrationally. 'Why was she so sneery about me being a tourist?'

He grimaced. 'Some locals view tourists as unfair competition. Tourists, in the holiday mood, behave however they want, then leave and go home. Locals who behave in a similar fashion might be judged.'

'I imagine tourists are handy when locals want a fling, though,' she observed coolly, recalling how Piero had

174

emphasised how temporary Zia was in his life, the creeping-skin mortification of Nicoletta hurling insults like *puttana* after her. 'That's what you meant when you told her I'd be going home.'

He gestured at the luggage piled into the open car boot. 'You are going home. I hate for us to have such a sour ending, though.'

He looked sincere, she thought. Creases of concern had consumed the laughter lines that usually lurked at the corners of his eyes; the pucker at the bridge of his nose spoke of disquiet. But, gently, she withdrew her hands. 'If I was here to stay, would you still have slept with me?'

His frown deepened. 'But we both knew you weren't here for long. We each made the same decision. Didn't we?' He sounded genuinely thrown.

She considered his emphatic use of 'both' and 'each', aware she'd never actually told him she was staying for a while, not sure she wanted to face the bald fact that he might not have slept with her if he'd known.

But then Ursula peeked out of the cottage and mimed glancing at a watch on her empty wrist. Zia beckoned her, saying flatly to Piero, 'I accidentally misled you. Lucia and Durante have said I can stick around to decide what to do about Gerardo. I tried to tell you a couple of times but we got interrupted. Ursula's moving back in with her husband and I'm taking her to the airport then coming back.' She jingled her car keys as Ursula, who, obviously judging a hug goodbye with Piero inappropriate, gave him a quick smile instead and jumped into the passenger seat.

Piero stood in silence, looking wrong-footed.

Zia stepped towards the driver's seat. 'We weren't both making the same decision but that's not your fault and I don't suppose it matters.' She opened the car door and got in, throwing behind her, 'Sorry again that you listened to my advice and it went wrong.'

As she turned the car and drove over the gravel, she was conscious of Piero, still unmoving, still watching.

'So how did that go?' Ursula asked tentatively.

Zia swallowed hard. 'He just came to say goodbye.'

Ursula said, 'Yeah, really?' but didn't argue. Best friends knew when you didn't want to talk.

Chapter Fourteen

You let Piero distract you from the reasons you're in Italy but now the dalliance is over, Zia lectured herself sternly as, two days later, she surveyed the interior of the cute apartment on the side of Lucia and Durante's house.

Her things stood in the middle of a floor that needed sweeping. Lucia had planned to ask Fiorella to clean the apartment but Zia had protested it as inappropriate. As neither Lucia nor Durante would hear of charging rent, she'd insisted on refreshing the apartment in lieu and had also declared her intention of making herself useful at Bella Vista. With that in mind, she left the apartment as it was for now and returned to Villino Il Pino to help Lucia and Fiorella change the bedding and clean.

Lucia looked shocked to see Zia and her gaze flickered in the direction of Fiorella, who'd said only, '*Buongiorno,*' and carried on wiping kitchen surfaces.

Zia murmured in English, 'I'd like to help but is my being here . . . is it a problem?' She was asking whether her proximity to Fiorella would make Lucia edgy.

Lucia considered for several moments. Then she shook

her head. 'It's OK.' This time the glance that flickered towards Fiorella was more calculating, as if it was dawning on Lucia that Zia couldn't let slip the opportunity to make some kind of connection with her grandmother.

Once she realised Zia spoke passable Italian, Fiorella chatted as they shared the chores.

Zia ventured to smile and say, 'You speak quickly. I have trouble with the translation sometimes,' and Fiorella obligingly slowed her delivery. It enabled Zia to tune into the strength of Fiorella's accent and keep up her end in a conversation about Zia liking Montelibertà and not having a job at the moment. In return, she heard about the Montelibertà Festival, which would begin in less than two weeks on the tenth of July.

'First we have music in Piazza Roma,' said Fiorella, shaking pillows into their cases. She paused impressively, before adding, 'Free! We take our own chairs and food.'

Lucia kept her attention on the table she was dusting but Zia felt she was acutely aware of the conversation, and bore any discomfort Zia and Fiorella being together might cause her stoically. By the time the cottage was ready for its next guests, Zia had decided Fiorella was a likeable old lady, free with her opinions and open in her curiosity about others.

For most of the week that followed, Zia worked on the apartment. She painted the walls and visited a homeware store on the edges of Montelibertà for yellow curtains, white bed clothes, a shower curtain, crockery and cutlery. She oiled the hinges on the terrace door so it no longer squawked in protest when opened. Durante produced an old table with two chairs from an outbuilding. Zia painted them green and arranged them at 'her' end of the terrace. It made her happy to think the setting up of her temporary

178

home would help Lucia and Durante when the time came for them to let the apartment out next summer.

The property management company where she'd interviewed on that first day emailed to ask whether she'd yet established her right to work in Italy. Feeling guilty she'd misled them into thinking she'd even begun an application to live, and therefore work, in Italy, she replied that she'd made no progress so couldn't take the job if offered. Then she turned her hand to fitting a blind of green leafy fabric at the kitchen window.

Zia knew through an ecstatic call and a series of texts that Ursula had removed her things from Zia's flat in the New Steine and was cosily re-established in her own terraced house up near Brighton race course with Stephan. She rang again on Wednesday evening and Zia took the call on the terrace, her feet up on the railings, watching the sun set fire to the mountaintops as they talked. 'I'm surprised you have time to ring me,' Zia teased.

Ursula giggled. 'I haven't forgotten you but I am kinda taken up with my own stuff. My man here's even buying me gifts.'

Zia heard the rumble of a male voice and Ursula giggled louder. 'Well,' she clarified, 'it's all sexy lingerie so they're joint presents, really. Anyways, are you missing me?'

'I am,' Zia agreed, wistful despite the joy in Ursula's voice. 'Having lived together since March I got used to your ugly mug.'

Ursula dropped her voice, making it hollow and mysterious. 'And have you heard from the private investigator? Or met Gerardo?'

'The investigation's underway. I expect to hear something soon.' Zia freed her feet from her flip-flops and wiggled her toes in the warm evening air. 'And I'm still to decide about Gerardo, though I think about it a lot. I've seen Fiorella several times. I'm trying to get a sense of why Gerardo found her so scary. She does hold strong opinions, I guess, and she's not afraid to share them.'

'Plus, everyone changes in thirty years. She could once have been much scarier.' Ursula's voice dropped again. 'And Piero?'

Bearing in mind that Stephan was probably still within earshot and not wanting him to carry tales to Brendon, Zia answered lightly. 'Lucia and Durante are his friends so he often arrives at the end of the day for a beer or a glass of wine. We're polite to each another but then I find a reason to drift back to the apartment.' Seeing him was unsettling. She found herself watching his hands and remembering what they could do or noticing afresh his ebony lashes. 'I love living in the apartment, Ursula! It's so cute and my bedroom opens onto the terrace. There are new tourists in the cottages; all Brits. One couple are on a retirement trip around Europe and have a little brown dog. Lucia doesn't allow pets but they just turned up with her.'

Ursula utterly disregarded the side-chat. 'And Piero's happy to pretend nothing happened?'

Zia undid her hair from its clasp and let it fall down her back for the breeze to play with. 'He called once and asked to talk but I said now I'm staying I have to focus on other things.'

Stephan must have been close because he chimed in, breathy and close to the mic with a snarky, 'Sounds like a good idea.'

Ursula hissed, 'Private conversation, Stephan!' She sounded mortified when she returned to Zia. 'Sorry, honey. Honestly.'

'No prob, I understand Stephan is Bren's mate.' Zia tried to sound breezy for the sake of harmony in Ursula's newly resumed marriage. Naturally, Stephan's unasked for opinion nettled her but she understood why he stuck his oar in on behalf of his friend.

When they'd all said goodbye, she stayed out to watch the twilight fall. She missed Ursula's laughing, chatty understanding, her willowy presence, bright clothes and pretty body art.

She missed Piero as well, though she'd tried hard not to. She hardly knew him – if you could 'hardly know' someone you'd been upside down on top of. They'd met only three weeks ago and that was very little time in which to develop feelings . . . wasn't it?

Determined to look forward rather than back, she spent the rest of the week varnishing the terrace doors, visiting the country park she and Ursula had never got around to exploring and provisioning the tiny kitchen in the apartment. Pleased with her efforts, she arranged to prepare a meal for Lucia and Durante on Friday.

Unfortunately, when Friday evening came and they were laying down their cutlery after emptying the dish that had held pasta, Piero turned up.

Durante waved him to a chair. 'Zia is our hostess this evening! A delicious meal. I have a second helping and leave you none, my friend. I do not know you are coming. Sit down and take a glass of wine.'

After a hesitation, Piero sat, pouring himself half a glass of the Cerasuolo d'Abruzzo Zia had chosen for its gorgeous clear pink. She was shocked to discover that despite a polite smile, his eyes were . . . hurt? Usually, if his visits happened to coincide with a mealtime Lucia and Durante would simply continue to eat. Did it feel different to him because Zia had cooked tonight? She tried and failed to conjure up a way of saying, 'I should have invited you. It didn't occur to me. I wasn't deliberately excluding you to make the point that things have cooled between us.' She was left listening to the others talk and nursing a chilly twinge of conscience.

Presently, two of the cottage guests came to hover at the top of the terrace steps – Zia thought they were the couple from Villino Il Tasso with the little dog – and Lucia went to the edge of the terrace to talk to them. Then she called to Durante, who, grumbling beneath his breath, joined her.

Zia's heart lurched. She didn't want to be left alone with Piero and began gathering plates until he laid a hand on her wrist, gentle, light, yet hard to ignore.

He said, 'I'm sorry I was clumsy over Nicoletta and if I acted as if you leaving would be a good thing. I think you feel it devalued what we shared.' Lucia said something to the guests and Durante laughed. Piero went on in a rush. 'The way things went with Nicoletta, the pressure, the way she bad-mouthed me because I wouldn't give her what she wanted, the issues at Tenuta Domenicali, they all felt like good reasons to avoid—'

'Entanglements, yes, I agree,' she said. 'I'm on a boyfriend break myself. I came to Italy for a reason and I shouldn't have become distracted.' She knew she was withdrawing to protect herself but she couldn't fall for someone who didn't want to be fallen for. She didn't enjoy Brendon trying to make her have feelings she didn't have and she wasn't going to put someone else in the same disagreeable position. She steeled herself to speak airily, like an adult who knew that casual encounters happened all the time. 'We had a lovely night together. Let's keep it as a memory.'

His dark eyes widened and he released her wrist.

She rushed on. 'Also, I was wrong to give you half-informed advice. It went badly.'

His brows drew together. 'You keep apologising for that. Please stop. I was angry at the situation and the way things are stacking up against me, not at you.' Then Lucia and Durante said goodbye to the guests and headed back to the table, still discussing something to do with the guest's dog, who was a yappy Jack Russell who saw it as his task to warn his humans that people were occupying other cottages. Piero rose to his feet and began to move off, raising his voice in a genial, '*Ciao!*' as if leaving for no better reason than his after-work wine having been drunk.

'*Ciao*, Piero!' they called as they returned to the table.

Zia's eyes followed the smoothly striding figure until he disappeared through the tall cypress trees that stood like inky brushes against the purpling sky.

A few hours later, playing Tiwa Savage on her laptop to fill the silence, Zia got into bed, trying to make the most of what breeze there might be by leaving her windows open and the fly screens shut. Checking her emails, she found a message from the private investigator. With a hand that suddenly felt as if it belonged to someone else, she clicked to open it.

It was a short missive, topped and tailed by legalese and disclaimers, but there it was.

Enquiry target: Harry Robert Anstey DOB 14.05.1949
Currently residing at: 4a Herbert Road, Chichester PO19 5PZ UK
Time at this address: 5 years+
No other registered occupant of this address.

She stared at it, heart hurrying . . . before dropping to a walking pace.

Oh. No phone number. No email address.

She checked the private investigator's website and saw that at no time had those contact details been promised as part of the package. A google of Harry's name along with the address failed to render much more, not even a social media profile. But, Chichester? That was only an hour away from Brighton.

She read and reread, considering her options. She could write – but Harry could ignore a letter. Or Ursula might use part of a day off to drive over if asked. But, no, Zia should handle this in person, she quickly realised. This was her backstory she was trying to unravel. How could she know how Harry would react to her when she didn't know what happened to sever his friendship with Vicky in 1999? She had faded childhood memories of a kind man but that wasn't much of a guide for more than two decades later.

By the next morning, she was tired from lying awake thinking about the blank patches in the painting of her life. It was the Saturday of the opening of the Montelibertà Festival and when Lucia invited her to go, she jumped at the chance.

'Durante is helping some of the musicians,' Lucia explained. 'Two of his friends are in a jazz band and play at the jazz festival in Orvieto every year. Durante enjoys being involved.' She pulled a face. 'As long as it's not me hauling around big speakers in this heat, I don't care.'

Durante had been gone for some time when Zia and Lucia drove into town. Lucia knew the owners of Caffè Roma and had cheekily reserved a table looking out onto the piazza. Zia grinned as she sat down and inspected the crowd gathering on the cobbled square. 'Best seats in the house.' It was so hot that even she was pleased the entire table was shaded by an ivory-coloured parasol.

Lucia produced a lacy fan and began to waft it before her face, her expressive features creased in delight as she gazed at the raised stage where the market usually stood. 'From here we can see everything.'

The stage was shaded with an enormous green canopy and bulky black speakers lined the sides like a row of bodyguards. All sizes and shapes of garden chairs were being arranged to face the stage and marshals were fighting a losing battle trying to encourage their owners to set them out in rows. Zia heard waves of loud, laughing Italian, as people shared beer and lemonade from cool boxes, waving and calling to friends. The pigeons that usually crowded the cobbles lined nearby rooftops, maybe rubbing their wings together at the thought of all the crumbs being dropped for them to peck up later. She caught sight of Durante bumping a sack barrow of unwieldy boxes, roaring with laughter when the top box flipped off, spilling cables like fighting snakes on the cobbles.

Every table in Caffé Roma was taken so they had a wait for their food while a hubbub of tuning and testing noises came from the stage. The jazz band was to be on first, according to the flyer they'd found on their table.

'The mayor is to open the Festival,' Lucia read, pulling a mock impressed face. 'And we'll have fireworks after the last band.'

'How late?' Zia asked.

'Ten o'clock,' Lucia replied, her eyes still on the colourful flyer.

'*Ciao, ciao*,' called a high voice and Zia turned to see Fiorella and Roberto beaming at them over pots of geraniums, green folding chairs hanging from Roberto's shoulders.

'*Ciao, ciao,*' she replied, smiling.

Then Zia became aware of Lucia giving a little jump and a man stepped from behind the older couple, beaming. Zia knew him instantly. The man from the photo album. Her father. Well, the man who made Tori pregnant, anyway.

'*Ciao*, Zia Lucia!' He twinkled like a child who knew his smile would open doors. His grey-streaked hair was tied back in a ponytail and dilated pupils as much as the aroma of beer suggested he was enjoying the festival.

It took Zia a frozen instant to realise he wasn't addressing her, 'Zia-Lucia' with a hyphen, but Zia Lucia as in Aunt Lucia.

There was only the most infinitesimal hesitation from Lucia before she cried, 'Gerardo!' and rose to embrace him across the geraniums.

Zia watched Gerardo chattering with his parents and aunt, laughing just a little too loudly, his movements just a tiny bit loose. With his untidy ponytail and creased clothes, he looked like actor Steve Buscemi in one of his more dissolute roles. She was introduced to him as Zia, one of Lucia's guests from England.

His loud laugh rang out again. 'Zia means "aunt" in Italian!' His English was heavily accented but passable. He didn't betray with even a flicker whether he remembered a baby that a young English girl had named Zia.

His baby.

Instead, he returned to his aunt and switched back to Italian. 'Where have you been? None of your beloved nieces and nephews have seen you. Not once have I been invited for a delicious lunch.'

Lucia's colour rose. 'We're busy with guests this summer.'

Fiorella looked perplexed. As she helped service the cottages, she'd know whether this summer was busier than any other. Zia felt a jolt of guilt. Lucia must have withheld invitations to family so Zia wouldn't be blindsided – as she had just been – by her blood relatives wandering about the place in blissful ignorance of her identity. Breath quickening, she watched Gerardo, assessing what she felt, searching inside herself for a speck or spark of feeling. What flipped into her mind wasn't *this is my father* but *this man tried to erase me before I was born.*

Her gaze shifted to Fiorella and Roberto, beaming at their son, nodding along to his conversation like the fond parents they obviously were. Had they really been such disapprovingly devout people that an eighteen-year-old Gerardo had been frightened to face up to his responsibilities? Or was he just weak in comparison to Tori who'd given birth then driven back across Europe to show him his baby?

His baby the inconvenience. He hadn't wanted to get married nor to face the next eighteen years of paying child support. He'd seen Zia not as his daughter but a life-altering negative. Mechanically, she smiled when everyone else laughed but the noise of her blood rushing in her ears was so loud it half-drowned it out.

Gerardo, whatever kind of man he was, obviously held Lucia in affection, kissing her cheeks when he bade farewell to her and his parents. Zia's eyes followed his progress as he went off to join another group – not his wife and children but a bunch of men with a cooler full of beer.

Zia turned to listen to Fiorella, who had fallen into her usual rapid rate of speech. As she tried to follow, she found herself wondering whether Fiorella and Roberto would have accepted Zia if Gerardo had owned up about her. Vicky had not only accepted her but fought for her, apparently.

When the elderly couple finally drifted away to pitch their chairs before every inch of space on the cobbles was taken, Lucia pressed Zia's hand across the table, squeezing her fingers almost painfully. 'There. It is done. You didn't choose it but perhaps it was the best way. Like a tooth that needs to come out – oof, all at once.'

Moistening her lips, Zia nodded.

'And?' Lucia prompted gently.

Zia shrugged. Dimly, she realised that the hand Lucia wasn't holding was shaking and she glanced down at where it lay on the table. Perhaps Lucia noticed too because she signalled to the waiter and ordered wine. When he'd hurried off, Zia croaked, 'You've avoided inviting your family to your home. I'm sorry. Maybe I should ask Sister Paola and Sister Priscilla whether they have any vacancies at the monastery.'

'Zia-Lucia,' Lucia crooned as if Zia was still a baby, stroking the back of her hand. 'It is not your fault. Nothing of this is your fault.'

Zia nodded but the feeling of being an unlucky black cat jinxing others washed over her again. On the stage, a man began to talk into the microphone. He introduced the mayor, who seemed young for the task, a short man with mid-length curly hair. After a short welcome he introduced the first band and the audience clapped and whistled. It was Durante's friends' band. Zia didn't catch the name, boomed out in sensational style. Six musicians arrived on stage. One sat at an electric piano, one at the drums, the rest carried their instruments – saxophone, clarinet, double bass and some other kind of horn. The vocalist ran on last, a tin whistle in his top pocket.

As the jazz combo crashed, *tarrum-tan-dah-dah-de-DAH*, into the first number, Zia sipped wine and watched the rangy, scruffy-round-the-edges Gerardo Costa, laughing uproariously with his buddies, a beer bottle like an extension of his hand.

The bottle was swiftly emptied and exchanged for a full one. Was Gerardo always this way? Or just enjoying the festival? Piero's words floated back to her. *He's not good at keeping a job or looking after money and doesn't spend much on new clothes or haircuts. He has a favourite bar.* She turned to Lucia. 'What's his job? Gerardo?'

Lucia's lower lip tightened. After a hesitation she said, with the air of one owning up, 'I do not think he has a job at the moment.'

'Does he love his wife and children?' Zia demanded.

The older woman's face cleared. 'He does,' she said firmly. She paused again, obviously gathering her thoughts. 'Gerardo is Gerardo. He's not a bad person but he lives life on the surface. He likes the easy way.'

Slowly, Zia nodded. That fitted. 'And his wife, Ilaria?'

Lucia smiled. 'Oh, Ilaria, she has a manager's job in an office and she's a good mother, too.' So, he liked strong women but what did strong women see in him? Ilaria obviously looked after the family and Tori had once gone to huge lengths to try and get him back.

All the nebulous feelings of curiosity and restlessness she'd experienced not just since she'd discovered her natural mother's birth and death certificates but, to some degree, all her life, coalesced into a deep, burning need, a fierce urge to know the story of how she came about. She leaned across the table to Lucia. 'The investigator sent me Harry's address last night. I need to see him.'

Slowly, Lucia's face sagged. 'You're leaving?'

Rocked by a wave of regret at the desolation in the voice of the woman she'd begun to hold in deep affection, the idea of leaving her and this beautiful place made her throat stiff with tears. 'I don't know!' She felt as if her feelings had been ripped from her and flung on the ground for everyone to trample on. To her horror, her facial muscles gave an involuntary spasm and a sob wrenched itself from her throat. It was such an ugly, alien sound that everyone at nearby tables swung around. Snatching up her napkin, she buried her face in its folds, biting back the convulsions.

Vaguely, she was aware of Lucia calling for the bill and explaining that her friend was feeling ill. In a daze of grief, Zia let Lucia take her by the hand like a child and lead her away from the playing band and clapping people to where they'd left the car. Ten minutes later, they were back at Bella Vista and Zia was curled in a corner of a squashy sofa in the coolness of the salon, eyes swollen, vision blurry, throat aching, sipping iced water and trying to calm down.

'Sorry,' she sniffled. 'I never go to bits like that.' She blew her nose, dismayed at the boiling tears still lurking at the backs of her eyes, ready to gush out again if she didn't force them back. Knowing she'd upset Lucia, she hiccupped a laugh. 'What a drama queen. If you want to go back to the festival—'

'No.' Lucia stroked her hand, her silver-streaked hair waving around her concerned face. 'I would not enjoy leaving you so . . .' She gestured to Zia's face, presumably blotchy and puffy from the tear storm.

Zia's breathing began to even out as she sipped water and groped for logic. 'I feel torn. I love it here but I need to get answers from my mother's – from Vicky's – old friend.'

'Write to him,' pronounced Lucia with the air of one solving a puzzle. Then she sighed. 'But I remember this Harry. He is good at keeping secrets, I think.'

'Yeah. My instinct is to see him in person.' Zia wiped away a tear with the back of her hand.

Lucia stroked her hair back. 'You could go, then return here.'

Throat constricting once more, Zia nodded. 'If that would be OK,' she said, half-shyly. 'I don't have a job to go home to at the moment. To spend a nice long time in Italy would be wonderful.'

'You still want the Italian passport?'

Zia waved that away. 'Wanting citizenship brought me here in the first place but it doesn't seem so important now. I wouldn't disrupt everybody's lives just for the right paperwork.' Her voice thinned as her throat constricted again. 'I think I started out with the idea I was entitled to it, if my father was Italian. But I've realised that he's a real person. His relationships, your relationships, they could all be changed and maybe ruined, if I start blabbing secrets. Especially when I don't know what all the secrets are.'

'But, Zia.' Lucia's hand continued its rhythmic, soothing movement, passing lightly over her head, smoothing back her hair. 'What about you? What do you want and need? You will not return to England and never tell anyone but Durante and me who you are?'

Zia sighed. 'I haven't made that decision but I suppose I'm trying the idea out. But I don't have to make up my mind about everything all at once, do I? I could leave my car here and get a cheap flight home for a few days. Get the train to Chichester. Less exhausting than driving both ways on my own.'

191

A delighted smile took over Lucia's face. 'Then when you're home here again you can take time to make up your mind,' she agreed.

Zia managed to smile back, as much over Lucia's use of the word 'home' when referring to Montelibertà as at making some kind of plan. They made coffee and by the time Durante returned from the festival, puffing after his day as a roadie, Zia had booked a flight from Perugia to Stansted on the following Friday, the 16th of July. Rome-Gatwick had been an option but Lucia insisted on driving her to the airport and Perugia was half as far as Rome.

With a rush of affection, Zia hugged Lucia. 'Thank you. I'll work out the return journey once I know how long I need to stay.'

Lucia hugged her back. 'If you leave your car here then you will definitely return.'

'Oh, I'll come back.' And, sitting out on the terrace and drinking wine with Lucia that evening, watching the stars pop, Zia found that she was looking forward to coming back to Bella Vista before she'd even left.

Chapter Fifteen

Since the scene with Nicoletta in Piazza Lucia, everything in Piero's life had turned to crap.

Zia was treating him like a mistake. He felt like his twelve-year-old self in California, yelping at the pain of messing up a bare-handed baseball catch. Coach Brady would cry bracingly, 'Smarts, eh, kid? Bet *you'll* be smarter next time.' While resenting the smug play on words he'd always vowed that next time, yes, he would play smarter. But Zia was giving him no opportunity.

At first, he'd tried not to change his habits, calling in to see Durante and Lucia for an after-work drink, only to find that within minutes of his arrival Zia generally seemed to remember something she meant to do in her own rooms. And she'd hosted a meal and ignored the obvious opportunity to return the hospitality he'd shown her . . . even without the sex.

Sex. Sweat prickled his brow whenever he thought of sex with Zia. Her long naked limbs, her flowing hair and flushed skin, the way they'd fitted together. Sex that was in the past, she'd told him, in the tone of one who wished it had never happened.

He wasn't happy with his own behaviour, from failing to prevent Nicoletta from dispatching Zia in a flurry of insults, to letting Zia leave alone, to freezing when Zia explained she'd be in Italy for several more weeks. No wonder she'd closed herself off.

He found himself calling at Bella Vista less often.

At least Lucia and Durante seemed to be off the hook with the Binotto Group for the time being.

He wished he was.

Every day at Tenuta Domenicali tension pinched his neck and stamped frowns into the brows of Emiliano and Salvatore as the family remained in deadlock.

Emiliano hadn't pinned down solemn, slick Alberto Gubbiotti on the matter of his contract but it hadn't altered his willingness to sell. Graziella was in the office less and never at Salvatore's computer alone but apart from that, not much seemed to have changed. She continued to share Salvatore's house and Piero couldn't discount her influence on his father.

Salvatore was subdued, which Piero wasn't sure how to interpret. Salvatore was never subdued! He might be quiet sometimes, but then he was always observing and enjoying. Now he just seemed dull and jaded. Was he exhausted by the strain and turmoil and by Graziella's grumbles that Piero was dragging his feet? If Piero agreed to Binotto's buying Il Rifugio would Salvatore spring back to his normal self when that pressure had been released?

On this scorching Thursday morning in mid-July when the sun burned from a sky of cloudless blue, a family meeting was scheduled for ten o'clock. Salvatore had called it. Piero arrived a few minutes early to check the espresso machine was on. He filled his coffee cup and took a seat, popping his laptop on the closest corner of the desk. A moment later, Emiliano arrived. He clapped Piero on the shoulder as he sat down. 'What's this about? Do you know?'

Piero shrugged. 'Whatever it is, I feel antsy.'

With a sigh, Emiliano slapped his laptop onto the desk too. He smelled of outdoors, of the vines and perspiration. It reminded Piero how hard his brother worked and how much a part of this place he was – whereas the best thing about Thursday, to Piero, was that tomorrow was Friday. He wouldn't be here. He'd be finishing the elderly Englishwoman's summer house. The base for it was already laid in her garden and soon she'd have her shady spot for summer. He hadn't prioritised the glazed panels for winter because if she had them fitted now she'd curl up and expire like one of the flies on the office windowsill.

The outer door rattled and Graziella stalked in, Salvatore behind her with his moustache neatly trimmed and hair cut. '*Ciao*, Papà,' Piero murmured, then tacked on a greeting for Graziella, too.

Replying genially, Salvatore positioned himself behind the desk and took the chair. Graziella poured coffee for herself and Salvatore then made as if to roll one of the office chairs to join him behind the desk. Salvatore waved her back to sit with his sons. After an exaggerated pause and look of wounded reproach, Graziella sank gracefully into the chair.

Salvatore folded his hands on the desk and lost no time in small talk. 'I have discovered that, against my instructions, Tenuta Domenicali was marketed to no one but the Binotto Group.'

Piero almost dropped his coffee cup.

Emiliano's head swivelled accusingly in the direction of Graziella and Graziella jumped. 'Salvatore—!'

'Don't,' he said flatly, without looking at her. 'It was easy to make a few calls and check whether you had ever sent the emails we composed together.' His brows drew down over his eyes, making him look fierce as his gaze moved between his sons. It settled on Emiliano, whose mouth was hanging open. 'I believe we owe it to Piero to properly market the estate and see whether other buyers come forward.'

After a hesitation, Emiliano agreed. 'That's fair.'

Piero's agile mind was already looking at the other side of the story. 'If we sell to someone other than Binotto's, Emiliano might not keep his job as Tenuta Domenicali's winemaker.'

Salvatore gave a single nod.

Emiliano grimaced. 'That's a generous thought, Piero, considering I was prepared to let you sacrifice your home.'

For several seconds the only noise came from the whirring of the fan behind Salvatore and the rumble of the tractor on the slopes of the vineyard. Then Salvatore prompted, 'Are we agreed to market it properly?' He added, deliberately, 'The three of us?'

Piero nodded. 'The right deal might be out there.'

Emiliano nodded too, but more slowly. 'I agree,' he said on a sigh, the knowledge that he might be voting himself out of a job obviously on his mind.

Salvatore sat back. 'My vote is also yes. Graziella, would you leave us, please?'

From the moment Salvatore had revealed her meddling, Graziella had sat frozen and pale. Now, giving Salvatore a jerky nod, she stumbled to her feet and from the room.

After the door closed behind her, Salvatore sighed,

slumping in his chair as if the past couple of minutes had knocked the stuffing out of him. 'This is difficult. She's acted badly and tried to make me a puppet but I should have been paying attention. I apologise and I won't let it happen again. But . . .' His hands rose and his eyes softened. 'If you don't object too much, I don't want to end the relationship. She had a fixed vision of our joint future and I don't think she saw much wrong with taking a shortcut to achieve it. She was selfish but it's not as if she was trying to pocket our money.'

Another silence. The vineyard tractor roared into the yard outside and paused, its engine idling. Piero smiled to take any sting from his next words. 'I think she'll always want to spend your money for you.'

His father half-smiled in return. 'And if I'm a stupid old man who chooses to indulge his younger girlfriend with trips to the Azores then that's my business. My sons will already have extracted their fortune from Tenuta Domenicali.'

Emiliano nodded. 'Your decision.'

Piero agreed, adding, 'But you're not a stupid old man. You care for her.'

Salvatore gave a short laugh, his moustache turning up at the ends. 'I'll speak to the agent now, while you're both present, and agree that any of the three of us can communicate with them.' *But no one else* hung in the air. Although none of them said it.

They completed the transaction on speaker and Salvatore left the office for the day, presumably to have a difficult conversation with Graziella. Neither Piero nor Emiliano saw either of them for the rest of the day but both of their cars remained outside the house.

Emiliano buried himself in the cellars and Piero only

sought him out to say goodbye for the day, finding him as subdued as Salvatore had been earlier, perhaps sampling the hollow feeling that came from facing losing something you loved. Fatigued by tension and upheaval, Piero drove home with the air conditioning blasting as if it could soothe his heavy heart.

He parked his car and made for the gap in the cypress trees, bound for Bella Vista. Did he hope to see Zia? Part of him tingled at the prospect but part simply yearned for a beer and a grumble with his friends. When he climbed up onto the terrace he found Durante alone, in the shade, a crossword book in his hands, a pair of gold-rimmed glasses on the end of his nose, one foot elevated and bound in a wet tea towel.

Piero regarded the foot. 'What's up?'

Durante tossed book and glasses aside. 'I fell down the steps.' Gingerly, he unwound the tea towel, dislodging several cubes of ice, and exhibited a puffy purpling from ankle to toes. He rewrapped it and looked at Piero hopefully. 'Lucia's lying down because she's unwell. Fancy fetching us both a cold beer?' He smacked his lips.

Piero was a willing errand boy when it concerned cold beer on a hot day. He fetched bottles of Moretti and fresh ice cubes for the wounded ankle before pulling up another lounger. 'What's wrong with Lucia?'

Durante frowned. 'A stomach pain. She's trying to sleep it off.'

Piero refused to let himself ask after Zia. The past weeks, knowing she was just the other side of the cypress trees but completely withdrawn from him, had affected him more than he would've thought possible. While he respected her right to pull back, he was conscious of a constant desire to talk to her alone. Although she seemed stubbornly inclined to blame herself for Binotto's outmanoeuvring him he wished he could discuss today's developments. She was used to the machinations behind large acquisitions and after being so blind over the access laws he was nervous of anything else he might have missed. So, despite his resolve, he asked, 'Where's Zia?'

Durante, in the midst of a long draught of beer, had to pause and wipe his lips before answering. 'Packing.' He took another gulp while Piero's heart did a slow somersault. *Packing*? Then Durante added, 'She's flying back to England for a few days to meet that man Harry who knew Vicky and Tori, then coming back.'

Piero hadn't realised he was holding his breath until air poured back into his lungs. *Then coming back*. Why had those three words meant so much? He gave an inner sigh. Same reason the last three weeks had been so crap. He wanted to see her, talk to her, be with her, make things right again. Ironic that he'd viewed tourists as safe after Nicoletta, because they went home. *This* tourist . . . he didn't want her to go at all.

Durante gestured to his bound foot. 'I was going to drive her to Perugia Airport tomorrow but I can't, with this. We'll have to hope poor Lucia is better.'

At that moment, Piero caught a glimpse of Zia taking a step onto the terrace from the little apartment she'd moved into. Then, hurriedly, she retreated indoors. At this galling evidence that she was still avoiding him, his imp of mischief jumped into the conversation. 'I'll drive her,' he offered casually. 'I need to visit the builders' merchant in Perugia.' He was pretty sure Zia hadn't confided in Lucia or Durante about their starry night of sex so they'd take his offer at face value. He hid a grin at imagining how Zia would take it.

'That would be wonderful, if you're going anyway.' Durante beamed, clinking bottles with him.

Piero clinked back. 'My pleasure.' He changed the subject, updating Durante on the remarketing of the vineyard, skating around Graziella's part in bringing that about. Durante and Lucia had known Salvatore for a long time and he didn't want them to know his father had been, in his own words, a puppet.

Durante was instantly diverted. '*Amico mio*! If Il Rifugio was safe too, I'd sleep soundly at night.'

'Yes.' Piero could barely imagine being free of that anxiety. It clung to his skin. Shadowed his patch of land. They drank another beer, then after checking that his friends wouldn't starve that evening – Zia had already offered to cook, apparently – Piero rose to leave. 'What time does Zia fly tomorrow?'

'At 11.20. We'd planned to leave at eight,' Durante replied.

'Tell her I'll pick her up then.' Piero took himself home to wind down at the end of an emotional day.

And wait for Zia.

It took a couple of hours for her to appear, striding through the trees in the luminous dusk of Apennine Umbria, some of her hair tied up on top of her head and the rest flying loose around her shoulders. By then Piero had showered, changed, eaten, and was lounging on the paved area outside the kitchen with his fourth beer of the day, a few unopened bottles of Ichnusa, the Sardinian beer he liked, beneath his canvas chair. His bare feet were up on the chair's twin, a movie playing on the phone in his lap. When he spotted Zia, he paused the movie and called out to her in case she missed him in the twilight.

She turned like a missile. As she homed in on him, he

200

removed his feet from the spare chair and gestured to it, politely inviting her to sit. '*Buona sera.*'

'*Buona sera,*' she returned shortly and all but threw herself in the chair, turning it so it faced the view rather than him.

Solemnly, he broached what he gleefully knew to be on her mind. 'I understand I'm to have the pleasure of your company in the car tomorrow.' He reached beneath his seat, pulled out a beer, tweaked off the cap and offered her the bottle.

She took it automatically. 'Durante shouldn't have agreed to you taking me. I suspect you only offered to make me uncomfortable.'

He threw back his head and laughed. 'Not only.' He sobered. 'I have to visit the builders' yard so why not? You wouldn't make Lucia drive you if she's recovering from stomach ache?'

'She's still got it, unfortunately,' she said. 'So, I'll drive myself and leave my car there.'

He made an expansive gesture. 'But if you're to be away for several days it will cost forty or fifty euros. Would you really do that to avoid an hour in the car with me?'

With a sigh, she settled back, raising the beer bottle to her lips and taking several healthy swallows. 'It's not that,' she said eventually. 'If Lucia's still ill and Durante injured when I return, I don't want to impose on you to fetch me back.'

'Impose on me,' he said quietly, his laughter gone. 'I'm sorry for the way things are between us and want to make amends.'

She sighed. 'I'm sorry, too. I could have invited you for supper on Friday. I felt bad when you turned up. Petty.'

'You're cross,' he said understandingly but his heart lifted at this small step in the right direction.

Her finely marked brows quirked. 'I was,' she amended. 'And uncomfortable that my well-meant advice rebounded and you were angry—'

He cut in gently. 'How many more times? I wasn't angry with you. I was angry with Graziella and Binotto's and for being wrong-footed.' Then taking advantage of the thaw between them he updated her on the events of the day. He was even transparent about Graziella's manipulation.

'That was . . . misleading,' she said diplomatically.

'She lied,' he corrected forthrightly. 'But Papà seems able to attribute her manoeuvrings to a yearning to be with him on a round-the-world cruise so I think he intends forgiving her, once he's set some boundaries.'

They sipped companionably, watching the mountains darken and streak with pink, a promise of yet another boiling day to come. Piero wiped his forehead with his T-shirt. 'It'll be a pleasure to spend some of tomorrow in an air-conditioned car.'

'Like, I'd actually be doing you a favour?' She laughed. She was halfway down the beer now and had kicked off her flip flops, letting her bare feet rest on the weed-strewn paving.

He replied with gravity. 'Yes. You've agreed to give me the opportunity of being with you.'

Her eyes turned towards him, gaze both wary and thoughtful. Her hair hung long and heavy and he remembered how it had felt tumbling silkily around their naked bodies. He remembered everything about her: her slumberous gaze when she was about to give into sleep; the noises she made; the way her body felt around his. She took his breath away.

'In fact,' he pressed gently, 'I'd be happy to travel with you to England. I should imagine the summer's fresher there.'

'Drizzly,' she said drily. 'You wouldn't like it.'

He could have repeated he'd like being with her but she was obviously wary of him and he was still coming to terms with his own hankering to be in her company. He opted to be truthful without coming on strong. 'I like England. Haven't been for ages. It would be interesting to be your companion on your quest.'

She snorted. 'To suggest going to England with me you've obviously drunk too much.' She polished off her beer and made to rise.

He protested, startled. 'I'm not drunk. This is only my fourth bottle – about two pints in a British pub.' He sat forward but made sure not to crowd her. 'I haven't drunk too much,' he said emphatically. His suggestion to go with her had been off the cuff but now it was growing on him. 'I could fly tomorrow and stay at least until Monday. But only if you want.'

She stared at him, her bare arms still tensed as if ready to propel her to her feet. 'Sorry,' she said eventually, relaxing back into her seat. 'For an instant I just thought of Brendon saying men will say anything when drunk.' She smiled apologetically.

He thought about the man she'd left behind in England, someone who'd been stupid enough to lose her. Piero had half-forgotten about the unknown man who'd loved Zia but now he found he didn't much care for her quoting his words. 'Are you still in contact with him? Will you see him in England?'

She wrinkled her nose. 'He's big friends with Ursula's husband so I suppose we'll always see each other.'

There was 'seeing' someone and then there was 'seeing' someone. Piero suddenly wished she'd accept his offer to go to England with her. But then she rose to leave and he rose too, reaching out to trail his fingers down her arms, wanting to delay her, to get closer to how they'd been before. 'I'm not drunk. I only want your company.'

She looked up at him thoughtfully but didn't yank herself away.

Slowly, giving her plenty of opportunity to withdraw, he slid his arms about her. She continued to study him, her eyes catching the last of the light, and he dipped his head and brushed her lips with his. A long moment. He held his breath as if something powerful and valuable hung in the balance. Then she pressed a tiny kiss to his mouth in return. He opened up to her, kissing her deep and long, and she sank against him, her softly searching lips making his spine tingle. It went on. And on.

Finally, she withdrew just an inch, breathing quickly. 'Maybe,' she began. But then something must have caught her attention. Her head turned and her gaze fixed. She turned to wood in his arms.

Without looking back at him she pulled away, scuffing into her flip flops as he stood frozen and astounded, and spinning on her heel and heading off towards Bella Vista. In the last light, she almost seemed to skim the tips of the grass in her flight.

Stung and confused, Piero cast about in the twilight, trying to see what had made her bolt like a nervous horse.

And then at the corner of the house he caught sight of a figure. Nicoletta. She was watching Zia leave, the corners of her lips curving with satisfaction. As if feeling the weight of his regard she switched her attention back to him. In a flash, her face crumpled and she began wiping her eyes on the backs of her hands, the very image of a wronged, tearful woman. 'Piero?' she called in a long-suffering voice.

'Nicoletta!' he groaned. He took in her midnight mane of hair tumbling loose, her top unbuttoned to reveal the swell of her breasts, the short skirt. Dressed to lure.

He thought of how he'd made the wrong decision in response to her tears before out of consideration for their joint past, staying to renew earlier, kindly explanations that they had no future together. But he'd made the right decision a year ago when he'd refused to bow to her ultimatum and he was going to make the right decision now. He broke into a jog. After Zia.

Adrenalin gave Zia's feet wings through the dry grass and occasional thistles. She caught Piero's groan of, 'Nicoletta!' as the cypress trees seemed to rush towards her.

She was angry. *Furious* . . . with herself, because she'd fallen into that kiss as if it were a vortex. Her disappointment at Nicoletta's appearance only compounded her ire at her own gullibility.

It was time to stop acting on her attraction to Piero.

Having not heard any rustle of footsteps behind her over the noise of her own flight through the scrub, she gasped as a warm hand settled on her arm when she'd almost reached the gap in the trees that felt like her portal to safety. He didn't halt her or spin her around but simply slid his hand down until their fingers linked and he fell in beside her. In the neater environs of Bella Vista the encroaching darkness was countered by lanterns slowly coming to life. He turned right, drawing her with him, and made for the gazebo that faced the twinkling lights in the valley below.

She could have snatched her hand back and stalked off

to her apartment. Instead, she found herself seated, facing him across the table where she and Ursula had often eaten. He grasped both her hands, expression grave and sombre. 'Don't,' he urged her. 'Don't quit at the first bump in the road. Nicoletta's in the past. I didn't invite her to Il Rifugio.'

Shock warred with indignation. She blurted, 'I'm not a quitter! Life hasn't exactly cosseted me. I've learned to deal with it.'

His eyes narrowed challengingly. 'Then why take one look at my ex and run away?'

Heat burned her cheeks. She paused to give her pulse time to settle into its usual rhythm. Did he have a point? When she'd seen Nicoletta watching them, she'd obeyed her flight instinct just as she'd whirled and fled the room when she'd discovered Brendon *in flagrante*. Had that shock and humiliation catalysed a new behaviour in her? She frowned, not enjoying that view of herself.

His thumbs stroked her fingers. 'Exes have a special ability to unsettle us, I think. When you stopped trusting your own ex, you stopped trusting all men. Your instincts make you attempt to avoid situations where a man can hurt you ensuring you automatically think the worst of me. In the same way, when Nicoletta thought she could force commitment on me she made me commitment shy.'

'Oh,' breathed Zia, wrong-footed by such raw honesty. Her brain calmed and began to work logically. 'So, Nicoletta's spoilt you for any but casual relationships?'

His forehead puckered with surprise. The area in front of the cottages near the gazebo was lit at intervals for the convenience of the guests and one side of his face was in sharp relief, making his brow and eye socket blacker. 'I'd hate to think so.' He paused before adding honestly, 'But I have been avoiding involvements.' His voice became husky. 'Until I met you, that is. I feel something for you, Zia. I don't know what it is or if it can go anywhere but I want you. I think about you all the time.'

A warm feeling uncurled in the pit of Zia's stomach. Fairly, she admitted, 'I think about you too.' A smile blazed across his face so quickly that she added, 'But I think we should take things slowly.'

The squeeze he gave her fingers before he let them go was like a retreat. 'If that's what you want.'

Unsure if she'd wanted him to agree quite that readily, she went on, 'I'm going to drive myself to the airport tomorrow. With Lucia and Durante's ailments and your two jobs, I don't want to be worried whether there will be anyone around to pick me up when I get back.'

'You want to feel in control,' he amended calmly in a *come on, admit it* voice.

She felt a flicker of surprise that he'd read her so accurately. 'OK. Maybe I do. And I think we need to remember I have to be looking for a job by September.'

He leaned in close. 'But in which country?'

She sighed. 'It's not going to be here, not any time soon. Working in Italy isn't as easy as it used to be. It's the very reason I came here, remember? In case I could get my birth father to acknowledge me and pave the way.' Her shoulders rose and fell on another, gustier sigh. 'I hadn't realised it would turn into a series of dilemmas.'

'About your Italian family?' He lifted a hand and cupped her face.

The insect life around them had broken into full song to welcome the approach of night-time and Zia felt as if the thrum was the pulse of this place, passing through her, reminding her how much she wanted to belong. Still, she forced herself to remain pragmatic. 'Biologically they're my family. In reality, I'm a blank in most of their lives. It's not a nice feeling. But maybe I'll at least fill in some of the gaps in my history, particularly the English part, if I can talk to Harry Anstey.'

'But will that help you know how to feel about the Costas?' he asked.

Again, she realised how he was reading her, demonstrating understanding on a level she hadn't experienced with other men. 'I don't know but talking to Harry is something I can do and be fairly comfortable that nobody will be hurt.' She sighed. 'Here in Montelibertà I feel as if I have to tread softly . . . and not just because it's earthquake country.'

Chapter Sixteen

Less than twenty-four hours later Zia unlocked the door of her Brighton apartment and paused. She could hear a noise exactly like someone having enthusiastic sex.

She must be hearing things. She was fuddled from the journey. Her flight had been delayed and passport control had been a frustrating test of patience. The express train out of Stansted had been OK but then she'd had to stand on both the tube across London and the train to Brighton.

The noise became louder. Banging – in all senses of the word – panting, groaning. Her heart went trippy. Had squatters moved in? Randy squatters, by the sounds of things? She glanced at the open exit behind her, checking she had a quick escape. The door of her bedroom stood ajar too, all-too obviously the source of the bumps and moans. Sweat cold on her spine, she crept a few feet nearer. The rhythmic thumping sped up, heading towards its crescendo. When Zia steeled herself to peep around the doorway, she got an eyeful of pumping hairy male buttocks and female legs and arms wrapped around the body that came along with it.

One of those female arms wore a familiar sleeve of tattoos.

'*URSULA!*' Zia cried in outrage.

The buttocks halted, mid-pump.

'Zia?' Ursula's panicky voice emerged from beneath the male body.

The man executed a hurried, clumsy dismount and, face flaming, Zia belatedly turned her back as she caught a glimpse of way more of him than she needed to see.

Seconds later, a flustered, panting Ursula joined Zia in the hallway, a sheet gathered hastily around her, pulling the door closed. 'What are you doing here?' she gasped.

Zia glared at her. 'I *live* here! What are you doing here? Oh, shit, you don't have to tell me,' she spat in disgust. 'Ursula, what the fuck? Why are you meeting someone here for sex? You promised me you didn't cheat on Stephan. I stuck up for you!'

Ursula, hair tumbled over her eyes, turned puce with embarrassment. 'It's like this—'

'And in *my bed*!' Zia hissed. 'I don't care whose arse I saw flashing up and down, you can just get him out of my flat *now* and you can go as soon as you've changed the bed. I'm sick of people cheating. Holy fuck, if I ever trust you again—' She halted as the door behind Ursula swung open.

The man, fully dressed and breathless, face every bit as fiery as Ursula's, stepped out – burly, sandy-haired and familiar.

Zia gaped. 'Stephan?'

'Sorry,' he mumbled.

Ursula cleared her throat. 'It was, like, a fantasy thingy. Y'know, like stranger sex . . . but with your husband.'

Stephan snorted with sudden laughter, burying his face in Ursula's hair.

'Ah,' said Zia, abruptly dismounting her high horse. '*Ohhhh* . . .' Then, regarding her friend severely, 'Did it have to be in my bed?'

Ursula hung her head but she was beginning to shake with suppressed laughter. 'That was a terrible abuse of your hospitality and I will change your bedclothes straight away. But, y'know the fantasy. It wouldn't have worked in our bed, now would it? He, like, picked me up in the Black Dove . . .' Behind her, Stephan gave a strangled gasp.

A reluctant smile tugging at her mouth, Zia let her backpack slide down her arms and thump to the floor. 'Well, I didn't warn you I was coming so that I could surprise you and I certainly did that. I'm going to have to bleach my eyes.'

Stephan let out a roar of laughter.

Tacitly agreeing that the best way of getting past the embarrassing episode was by pretending it'd never happened, after a rapid change of sheets Stephan and Ursula offered to treat Zia to chips on the Palace Pier. The sun peeped out between rain showers as they claimed three blue-and-white striped deckchairs in the centre of the pier, the churning sea visible through the gaps in the old boards. Close by, the dodgem cars clashed and flashed, screaming tourists clung on to the twister and the Horror Hotel ghost train while small kids wailed on the cup and saucer ride. The sugary smell of doughnuts fought with greasy fish and chips and an undernote of weed. Seagulls stretching their wings on the wind cried, 'Aar!' like the pirates they were with hooked beaks ready to snatch snacks from unwary hands. It was all comfortingly typical of the British seaside, like the teenage girls they could see inshore on the pebbly beach, obstinately wearing bikinis as if the sea breeze wasn't freezing them. Children paddling in the shallows were garbed far more sensibly in wet suits.

Snatches of conversation rose over the blustering breeze.

'Mummy, I want to go to the arcade!'

'No, not the stupid machines, let's go on the roller coaster!'

'Do you think I'm made of money? Those things cost a fortune . . .'

Zia, Ursula and Stephan settled companionably shoulder to shoulder eating salty chips with wooden forks and sheltering pints of lager in plastic glasses between their feet so they wouldn't blow over. Zia recounted her unexpected meeting with Gerardo.

Ursula listened, a chip poised halfway to her mouth, blonde forelock blown up above her head like a question mark. 'Did you not tell him who you are?'

'I froze,' Zia admitted. 'I'm getting really worried about how much I could upset his wife and kids.'

'You're his kid, too,' Ursula reminded her, though she didn't sound as convinced as her words suggested.

Zia crunched a particularly crispy chip, her favourite kind. 'I'm here to see Harry. I've begun a kind of timeline for my backstory from the letters and what Lucia's told me. I want to see if I can get him to fill in the blanks. He's living in Chichester so I can go straight through on the train.'

Ursula's blue eyes lit up with enthusiasm. 'I have a day off tomorrow. I could drive you. Stephan's working.'

Zia beamed, pleasure flooding through her at the chance for them to spend a day together. 'If you don't mind giving up your day off, that would be brilliant.'

'And how did you leave Piero?' Ursula queried, wiping

212

up the last of her ketchup with a chip. 'Have you done the deed again?'

Zia's face flamed as she caught Stephan's sudden scowl. 'No, I haven't.' She chose not to mention that they'd talked in the gazebo till nearly one this morning, which might have contributed to her fatigue today, but neither of them had tried to take the other to bed. Maybe he was right about Brendon making her wary or maybe they'd been exploring what there was between them apart from sex.

Then, this morning, she'd said goodbye to Durante, who'd been distracted by the worry that Lucia's stomach cramps were showing no sign of improving, and found Piero waiting at her car. 'Just here to wish you a safe journey,' he'd murmured, looking and smelling deliciously, freshly showered. His goodbye kiss had been thorough and she'd driven away feeling like one shivering erogenous zone, regretting not taking the opportunity to go to bed with him the night before. Though maybe she'd have missed her flight . . .

Stephan was still frowning. 'Are you seeing Bren while you're here?'

The question was a rude awakening from her daydream. 'No plans to,' she said briefly.

His expression turned faintly accusatory. 'You know he's sorry.'

'Yes, but it doesn't change anything.' She didn't try and hide her lack of appreciation of the note of censure in Stephan's voice and any companionable warmth he'd been showing cooled noticeably. After making arrangements with Ursula for the following day Zia left the couple to enjoy their newfound closeness and headed to the New Steine and the apartment she'd always loved. It was odd to pass elegant pastel-coloured town houses instead of

213

homes built from stone and terracotta; Marine Parade and gardens behind railings rather than mountains and a valley full of vines.

She'd barely turned her key when her phone rang and she saw *Brendon* on the screen. 'Didn't take long for you to get the news I was here,' she answered disagreeably as she shoved the door shut.

He hesitated. 'Um, I was going to get in touch anyway.' Then he went on more enthusiastically, 'Thing is, I got a call from Elise Stokes.'

The affection with which Zia remembered Elise made her continue more moderately. 'Really? How's she doing? She was just about the best boss we ever had.' Elise had managed their team with a mix of warmth and efficiency. Her time as their colleague was also too far in the past for her to have been at the party where Brendon got caught cheating.

Brendon pronounced significantly, 'Recruiting.'

She hesitated in the doorway of the kitchen. 'Recruiting?'

'And she was interested to hear you might be available,' Brendon added with the air of producing a rabbit from a hat.

'Is she still with that private equity firm in London?' Zia wandered over to the small kitchen window from where she could see pigeons on nearby rooftops, lined up to watch wheeling seagulls like spectators at an air show. The benches in the gardens were almost hidden by white and blue agapanthus exploding from the flower beds. A small child threw a cheap kite at the sky only for the wind to spit it back onto the grass.

'Headley Whiterow, yeah. Doing very well,' he answered. 'She asked me to give you her number. I'll send you her contact card now.'

Moments later her phone pinged as the message was received. 'Right,' she said. Part of her brain knew it was a good opportunity. In October her apartment's annual management fees and ground rent would be due. Her redundancy money was draining and she'd soon be burrowing into her savings. She gathered her thoughts. 'Sorry, you took me by surprise. Thank you.'

He sounded boyishly eager. 'So, you'll contact her?'

'Of course.' She didn't like the feeling of accounting to him for her time, even though he was helping her with a job opportunity, so added bluntly, 'Before I go back.'

The lightness faded from his voice. 'Back to Italy?'

'Yes.'

With a gruff farewell he rang off.

She heaved a sigh. Whether he'd been trying to curry favour by helping her, hoping to keep her in the UK or trying to be a nice guy, he'd obviously been disappointed by the knowledge that she wasn't back in the UK to stay. Maybe Stephan had forgotten to relay the brevity of her visit.

She smiled wryly. Brendon would have been even less pleased if she'd accepted Piero's offer to accompany her. On the flight she'd found it hard to keep her attention on her Kindle because her mind had kept floating back to Piero and the idea of the two of them visiting Chichester together. It was appealing, imagining his reassuring warmth beside her as she tried to unlock the secrets others had kept about her life. The time was growing nearer for her to turn up at Harry Anstey's door and her tummy flipped like an acrobat whenever she thought of it.

She texted Elise Stokes to distract herself. Elise called and soon Zia was agreeing to meet her at her company offices in London on Monday morning at ten o'clock. 'It's an OK commute from Brighton,' Elise pointed out enthusiastically. 'I do it myself. The offices are close to Victoria Station.'

'It sounds like an amazing opportunity,' Zia returned with automatic enthusiasm, stifling annoyance that she now couldn't return to Italy until Tuesday. They chatted for a while then Zia was finally able to search out a ready meal from her freezer and put it in the oven. While she waited for it to cook, she decided to call Lucia to ask if she was any better.

It was Durante who picked up Lucia's phone. 'She's sleeping,' he said in a worried whisper. 'This pain, it wakes her many times in the night.'

'Has she seen a doctor?' Zia asked.

'She says it is something bad she ate and this is why she shivers and feels sick,' he reported, sounding aggrieved. 'She does not like doctors.'

He didn't have much more to say apart from to call Lucia stubborn so Zia rang off, wandered out of the kitchen and picked up a pile of mail shoved aside on the hall floor, apparently ignored by Ursula and Stephan as they acted out their stranger-sex fantasy. For Ursula's sake she was glad they were enjoying a full relationship again. Making use of her actual bed was a bit yuck but she supposed the spare, which had been Ursula's for a few months, was only a single. It was still a gross abuse of her hospitality, though, she thought as she sorted through junk mail and brochures, which made it even more irritating that Stephan must have let Brendon know she was in town literally the moment her back was turned.

The only good thing about the evening proved to be Piero calling her from his upper terrace where he said he was lying looking at 'Italian stars'.

She wasn't sure if what happened next qualified as phone sex but it certainly stopped her thinking about anything else. Even the secrets that might be revealed the following day.

The morning was a different matter. Without the distraction of Piero, Zia woke at 5 a.m. and lay awake, obsessively running scenarios as to how Vicky's old friend Harry would react to her uninvited visit. She dredged up memories of how he and Vicky had interacted on his long-ago visits and wondered how Tori fitted into it. That freckly English rose frozen in Lucia's photographs must have been a flesh-and-blood person to him; he'd have known her voice and the way she'd moved and laughed and cried. As far as she knew, Harry was the only person alive who'd properly known the two Victoria Chalmers – Vicky and Tori. She prayed he hadn't lost his memory.

Ursula picked her up at 10 a.m. A sea breeze chasing puffy white clouds around a china blue sky, they drove slowly along the teeming seafront, turning right in Hove and left onto Old Shoreham Road, passing the cemetery and homes crowding every street.

'So, have you anything to tell me?' demanded Ursula as she drove, her long lock of hair tucked behind the arm of her sunglasses.

Zia tried to keep her mind off her nerves by teasing her. 'Your yellow lacy top doesn't go with your tattoos. It's like clashing patterns in a quilt.'

'Sod off,' said Ursula good-naturedly. 'I meant something in your life? To do with . . . a job, maybe?' She waggled her blonde eyebrows and changed down a gear to overtake a minibus.

Zia had been peering left to catch glimpses of the sea

but now she turned back to her friend with a frown. 'So, the Brendon–Stephan news exchange has been active.'

Ursula brushed her dryness aside. 'Exciting, though, eh? Have you spoken to your old boss?'

'Elise? Yes, we're meeting in Victoria on Monday.' Zia tried not to sound prickly. 'Ursula, is it possible to discourage Stephan from keeping tabs on me for Brendon, do you think? It was good of Bren to pass Elise's number to me but we're not together.'

Ursula shot her a surprised glance before returning her attention to the road ahead, slowing as they joined a tail of traffic. 'I wouldn't say Steph's "keeping tabs".'

'No?' Zia settled deeper into the car seat. Ursula's car was an aged Audi and it was like being driven around on a sofa. 'But I left you and Stephan yesterday and Bren called ten minutes later. And he's obviously told Stephan about the job, otherwise you wouldn't know.' Zia touched her friend's arm. 'I get that he's your husband and I talked about Gerardo in front of him yesterday myself without thinking too much about it but now I'm going to be more guarded. Brendon's taking more interest in me than is appropriate for an ex.'

'OK. I can see that's not cool.' Ursula sighed. 'I miss the days we were a foursome though.'

'It was only a few months,' Zia said quietly. 'Before that, Brendon was just one of Stephan's mates and now I wish I'd kept it that way.'

Their route was slow as they navigated the built-up areas up to Brockenhurst Hill, after which they bowled beside a patchwork of green fields. They speculated as to whether they'd find Harry Anstey and what kind of reaction might await them, until they reached the next built-up area from Fontwell to Chichester.

Zia knew Chichester to be a pretty town with a grey stone cathedral and ornate buildings, such as the beautiful octangular Chichester Cross, but the satnav missed all that out. As her heartbeat picked up, they drove off the bypass past the retail park and Lidl, then north of Oaklands Park. In ten minutes, amongst a forest of twenty-miles-an-hour signs and the between-the-wars houses of The Avenue, they found a newer community.

Ursula drew the car to a halt right next to the sign that said Herbert Road.

Zia felt as breathless as if someone were hugging her too hard. 'Whew.' She wiped sweat from her brow. 'Suddenly terrified.'

Ursula gave her arm a comforting squeeze as she glanced around. 'Yeah, they're posh places. In Brighton you could build a small block of flats on one of these plots.' The homes in Herbert Road were big new-builds of pinkish brick, solar panels glinting on steep roofs above bay windows. Each house had a double or triple garage.

'It's not a million quid's worth of house I'm scared of,' Zia commented.

Ursula reached across to envelop her in warm arms and a cloud of FCUK Friction. 'Are you more scared of finding Harry or not finding him?'

'Not sure.' Zia wiped sweaty palms on her jeans then rubbed her chest, trying to erase the squeezed sensation of panic. 'Maybe I should have written after all.'

'But now we're here we might as well find 4a,' Ursula responded pragmatically. 'Then if you don't want to ring Harry's doorbell we'll go home.'

They climbed from the car. Zia felt as if her butterflies had invaded her entire torso as she and Ursula trod smooth pavements, the newness of the development indicated by the lack of tree roots heaving up slabs. The nearest house was number 39. The numbers reduced as they progressed past smooth lawns and tidy walls, checking out the even numbers across the way.

'Did you think he'd be rich?' Ursula asked, eyeing the Mercedes and Aston Martins lined up in paved and patterned driveways.

'Don't know. I only met him a few times when I was a kid and he seemed ordinary,' Zia mumbled. They were opposite number 12 now and her heart was trying to beat its way out of her chest. 10. 8. 6. 4. The last house was number 2. They paused on the corner. No house boasting the characters 4a. 'Oh,' she said flatly.

'Let's walk back,' Ursula urged, physically turning Zia round by one arm as if it were her handle.

Numbly, Zia let herself be tugged along, gazing at the imposing homes and landscaped gardens.

'There!' they whispered in unison. From this direction they could see a white wooden sign with '4a' in black lettering and an arrow pointing between numbers 4 and 6.

They halted to gaze up a paved path with lawn on one side and a fence on the other. Zia tried to summon moisture to her mouth. She could leave. She didn't have to confront anything or anyone. She'd lived this long without knowing the secrets of her past . . . Her feet took an involuntary step back.

Then she halted. Piero had called her out on taking flight rather than facing things. If it was a new bad habit she needed to scotch it. Without giving herself another moment to freak out she squared her shoulders and started up the path, hearing Ursula's footsteps hurrying to catch up. They rounded a trellis and a flower garden burst into view, every colour jumbled together in jam-packed flower beds as if someone had given a pack of cub scouts an unlimited number of bedding plants and begun a growing competition. At an angle to the path stood a long, low wooden building.

'A cabin,' Zia murmured, pausing to admire the way French doors were set in the walls of broad horizontal boards. Beneath a gable was a green front door with a chrome knocker. She strode up and rapped smartly. Then, washed with a fresh wave of apprehension, she exchanged wide-eyed, 'Eek!' grimaces with Ursula.

A rattle from the door and she held her breath. Five seconds passed. Ten. The door opened. A man regarded them through silver-rimmed glasses.

What was left of his hair was grey and his lined face was pale. He leaned on two sticks, a droopy fleece open over a T-shirt and paunch. Then he smiled and his eyes crinkled. 'Hello, ladies.'

Memory stirred as she looked into his kind blue eyes and Zia let out her breath. 'Harry Anstey?' She hadn't realised she'd remember his eyes or the way they'd twinkled when he'd produced Dip Dabs and Fizz Wizzes for her from his pockets.

The smile broadened. 'I am! But you're going to have to remind me who you are, I'm afraid.'

She had to clear her throat. 'I'm Zia-Lucia Costa Chalmers. You used to know—'

'Zia!' The bark of surprise was so loud that it seemed to make Harry totter on his sticks.

Relief dissolved some of Zia's tension. She half-laughed. 'I remember you from when I was a kid. This is my friend, Ursula.'

He darted Ursula a wide smile but returned to staring

221

at Zia with an air of incredulity. Then he visibly shook himself. 'Come in, come *in*. This is wonderful!' Beaming like a child at a party he helped his stiff legs along with energetic taps of the sticks as the two women followed him through a square hall that opened into an open-plan living area furnished with reclining armchairs, a sofa, a dining table and a modern kitchen to the side.

'I didn't think I'd ever see you again,' Harry crowed, executing a pirouette on his sticks and one foot. 'Zia!' A slow, beatific smile broke over his face. 'How did you find me? You must think I'm bonkers, flapping about like this. What a wonder!' He put both his sticks in one hand to reach out and pat Zia's arm as if reassuring himself she was real.

For a few flustered minutes he rambled in the same smooth Devon accent that used to echo in Vicky's voice as he made them coffee, explaining his cabin was in the grounds of his daughter Mandy's house and Mandy had 'made a bob or two in property'. Finally, they were all seated in the airy living area with a view of the riotous flower beds through the French doors.

Then Harry fell silent, gazing expectantly at Zia. The moment to plunge into her bewildering past had plainly arrived.

The mug in her hand began to shake. Carefully, she placed it on the low table. 'I'm here because I'm hoping you can fill in some blanks for me.' A laugh emerged, breathy and tremulous as she looked at Harry. His kindly face alight, he sat forward in his chair as if vibrating with eagerness to hear more. She said, 'I always thought my mum was Vicky Chalmers but now I believe there was another Victoria Chalmers known as Tori. Tori was my mother, not Vicky. Vicky was my grandmother.'

Harry nodded, light glancing off his specs.

Though she felt Ursula twitch beside her Zia carefully avoided too much of a reaction. But, oh, the *relief* Harry's matter-of-fact acknowledgement brought. She could hardly believe she'd found this old family friend whose memory could illuminate her life like light flooding into a long-forgotten cave. She ventured, 'And my father was Gerardo Costa from Montelibertà in Italy.'

Again, he nodded.

Her heart thudded with excitement. He *knew*, he knew the lot! Huskily she said, 'You know Mum – Vicky – died when I was ten, don't you? You were at the funeral.'

Every line of Harry's face sagged. 'Yes, my handsome,' he said, voice sad despite the sweet Devonian endearment he used. 'Poor little you, so bewildered and white. You broke my heart. You remembered me, though I hadn't seen you for a couple of years. Vicky had kind of . . . fallen out of touch.' Hand unsteady, he pushed his glasses up his nose. 'We'd been friends for so long. We used to live together, for goodness sake! But, there, I said the wrong thing and . . .' He made a helpless gesture.

It was Zia's turn to nod along. 'Was that "wrong thing" that Lucia Costa had come looking for me?'

His expression cleared. 'You know 'bout that?'

'Yes.' Unwilling to say she now knew Lucia well for fear the conversation would go in too many directions at once, she drew in a breath and tried to order her questions. 'When did you first know my mum? Vicky, I mean?' she clarified, as he'd already confirmed knowing Tori to be her birth mother. 'I don't know much about her life between seventeen and thirty-five.'

'Those were the years Vicky and me had together,' Harry said simply, rubbing one knee as if it pained him. He'd propped his sticks against the forest green chair. He could only be in his early seventies so mobility issues had obviously come to him quite early.

Zia blinked, wrong-footed. 'Do you mean . . . as a couple?' Although Ursula had pointed out that Harry had addressed Vicky as 'babe' in one of his old letters her childhood memories suggested no more than a friendship.

'No,' he answered, though maybe on a wistful note. 'I'd known her always because she was friends with my younger sister Karen. We all lived in Exmouth in Devon.'

Zia licked unaccountably dry lips, feeling her way in the conversation. 'I know Vicky got pregnant at seventeen.'

'Weren't mine,' he answered with a waggle of his eyebrows. 'Though Tori was like my daughter, she wasn't, not biologically.'

Zia halted, her words strangled as she realised he might be thinking she'd come here to ask if he were her grandfather.

Before she could decide whether she needed to clear that up he leaned forward, voice dropping. 'If you only knew how much I've thought about you, yearning to see you again and give you the story from my side,' he declared. 'I had no idea what your grandparents would tell you.'

'Not much,' Zia managed, choked by the longing in his voice and echo of long-ago grief in his eyes. 'Please tell me everything, *anything* you know.'

Those eyes became pensive. 'Well, now. Your grandparents Alf and Joyce were disappointed when Vicky got pregnant with Tori at seventeen. Most parents would have been in the Seventies.' A grin flashed. 'I was seven years older than Vicky and divorced so they wouldn't have chosen me for the father, neither. What happened was,

224

Vicky soon had enough of bringing Tori up under the beady eyes of her parents. It was hard for single parents to get enough points for council accommodation then but by pretending we were together we qualified for a house. I needed someone to look after my kids. My ex rarely wanted to see them, let alone look after them.' He shook his head as if this was still a mystery to him. 'It worked a treat. I earned, Vicky looked after the kids – my kids Mandy and Leon as well as Tori. They were all blonde so we looked like a family and we were – except for, you know . . . bedrooms. Vicky was a wonderful, wonderful friend.' He broke off to take off his glasses and polish them on his fleece. Zia suspected it was to give himself time to control the tears that had glinted for an instant in his eyes.

When he'd once again restored his glasses to his face, he managed a shaky laugh. 'Joyce and Alf told Vicky she was acting like a hippy.'

Zia laughed too. 'I can hear them saying that.'

'Vicky was practical,' Harry went on, easing his legs stiffly. 'I can see her now in jeans and a T-shirt, always busy with some project, smiling, laughing. She used to plait her hair and it swung as she bustled about.'

A lump jumped into Zia's throat. He was describing the mum she'd loved so much.

He went on. 'When all three kids were at school, she took part-time work when it suited her but she lived cheaply. Grew veg. Made clothes. Did our decorating. Men were put off by her living arrangements but that was OK because she was happy with things as they were.' He smiled tremulously. 'So was I but you could practically hear Joyce's teeth grinding. She called our house "The Commune". We were quite pleased. Communes were cool and there we were, practising communal living like the proper hippies in Totnes.' He smiled reminiscently. 'She was a hell of a woman, our Vicky. Lovely. We lived together for eighteen happy years.' He digressed for several minutes, nostalgic for Vicky's delicious dinners and how much the three children had adored her.

Presently, Zia brought him back on track. 'Wasn't Tori's father around?'

Harry shrugged. 'He was some guy she met at a festival – a one-night stand. Vicky's parents were scandalised that he'd "walked away from his handiwork" but Vicky never made the least effort to find him—' he gave another of his short, mischievous laughs '—because she didn't know his full name. I expect they were drunk or high when it happened.'

Ursula sniggered.

Slightly wide-eyed at this candid sketch of a young, wild Vicky, Zia just said, 'Gran made similar "walked away from his handiwork" remarks to me. It was probably a catch-all phrase for the man who'd fathered Vicky's baby *and* who'd fathered Tori's, but I didn't realise it at the time. I didn't know Tori existed.'

Sorrowfully, he shook his head. 'I suspected that would be the case.' He added with a wry smile, 'Joyce was fit to be tied when Tori got pregnant in her late teens, just as Vicky had. They were great people, Joyce and Alf, but held traditional views. "Over-sensible", Vicky used to call them.'

Ursula, who'd been listening quietly, slanted Zia a look. 'You can be like that.'

'Gran and Pap brought me up from the age of ten so it's not surprising,' Zia protested. A pause for thought, then, 'I've always wondered what kind of a person I'd have become if Vicky had lived longer. Or if Tori had,' she added huskily. She turned back to Harry. 'Things might have been less confusing if mother and daughter hadn't both been named Victoria Chalmers.'

Harry laughed and gave a delighted slap to his chair arm. 'That was Vicky being a strop-box. She went into labour too early for her to have made a final decision on a name. Exhausted after the birth, she just went along with it when the midwife told her the mother's name went on the baby's wristband when parents hadn't decided on a name yet. When Joyce turned up, she read "Victoria Chalmers" and said, "I *do* hope you're going to change *that*!"'

'Let me guess,' Zia finished for him. 'Mum refused. She said if *she* wanted the baby to have the same name as her it was *her* decision. Gran had an unfortunate habit of making suggestions sound like orders. Mum would get stubborn.'

'Exactly. Defiant, that was our Vicky.' Harry's jowls lifted as he treated them to a beaming smile. 'She told me it made her feel important and excited to see "Victoria Chalmers" on the wristband, a sign her daughter was absolutely and completely hers. She decided the baby would be called Tori and she'd stay Vicky.' He grinned. 'Vicky and Joyce loved each other but when Joyce and Alf retired to Spain about the time Tori went to senior school, things became more peaceful.'

Then he sobered, slowing his delivery as if less keen to tackle the next part. 'Tori was as lovely as her mother. Not the same to look at, really, as she was finer built and even fairer, but just the same kind of warm, wonderful person. She and Vicky got on wonderfully. Vicky was lost when Tori finished A Levels and went off with friends to work their way around Europe. Then Tori fell for Gerardo and she stayed in Italy after the others moved on.'

The jaws of tension bit into Zia's spine. Quietly, she said, 'I think what you know and what I know are about to overlap.'

His eyes bored into her keenly. 'I would love to hear your side because there's so much I only guessed at. Such turbulent times we had.' He took up his coffee cup and drained it, though the contents must surely have been tepid. 'Vicky supported Tori's wish to travel but it left her adrift. She looked around for what to do next and decided on fixing up property. Her parents had sold their UK house by then and given her a part of the proceeds. She bought a rundown place.' He wiped his forehead with his sleeve. 'I was heartbroken it was in the Midlands. She said she couldn't afford Devon prices.' Painfully, he added, 'I suppose that house being far off came in handy, in the end, when she wanted to disappear.' Face slackening and eyes unfocused, he seemed to sink into his memories.

'Disappear?' Zia prompted eventually. She couldn't bear to be left hanging at such a poignant part of the story.

He blinked like a sad old owl. 'Well, first Tori came home pregnant. Vicky supported her, of course, but poor Tori was lovesick for that Italian boy.' He shook his head. 'I realise he's your father but that arse, he just didn't want to know. We loved Tori so dearly. She was like a daughter to me and a sister to my Mandy and Leon. We all prepared to welcome the baby – you – but whenever Tori wasn't around to hear us, we called Gerardo "Il Bastardo".' He blew out his lips, glancing into his cup as if surprised to find it empty. He added grimly, 'I hoped Vicky would think she should stay in Exmouth with Tori but she went ahead

228

with that bloody house purchase as if she knew what was coming.'

Pulling out a tissue, he blew his nose. Giving him a moment to compose himself, Zia fidgeted. It was like reading a foreboding thriller when you knew evil was about to pounce but couldn't look away.

'It was a horrible time.' Harry's voice was tight. 'We'd been such a happy bunch. Then we lost Tori. Vicky was lost, too, to all intents and purposes. Mandy was at university and Leon had moved in with mates. After being part of this busy household, I was left alone. Just me.'

As if he wasn't quite ready to go there, he backtracked. 'Tori had coped with the pregnancy well but had a terrible time at the birth. Her head was all over the place, afterwards. They kept her in hospital for several days. When she came home she was worse. Shouting. Agitated. She registered you with that enormous mouthful of a name. Vicky said nothing but Tori flew into a rage. "At least I gave my baby her own name!" she yelled. "Did you want me to make her Victoria Chalmers the third?" Vicky was in despair. Stunned. Tori's personality had changed overnight.'

Cautiously, Zia added to the story. 'Lucia Costa's husband Durante said when Tori turned up in Italy she was "crazy".'

His eyes fastened on her. 'Are you in touch with those Italians?' He sounded incredulous and put out.

'Only recently.' Briefly, Zia recounted how she'd discovered that Tori had existed and what had sent her to Italy. Harry listened intently, the lenses of his glasses reflecting the light. Ursula rose and, quietly finding her way around Harry's kitchen, made more coffee. Zia saw it was nearly two o'clock but it seemed the wrong time to suggest a

229

break for lunch. Everything she'd longed to know for so long was almost in her grasp.

When she'd finished her account, Harry shook his head. '"Crazy" is misleading and wrong. Tori had developed postpartum psychosis, a rare and horrific condition. Poor love was delusional. She accused us all of odd things and scribbled furious nonsense in notebooks. She was obsessive in her care of you . . . for a long time, anyway.'

'Postpartum psychosis?' Zia echoed. 'I'm not sure I've ever heard of it. That's mental illness after giving birth, is it?'

Harry had to blow his nose again. The tissue dropped shreds all over his navy-blue trousers. 'Severe mental disturbance, yes. We'd never heard of it either. She'd be up all night, ranting and crying. Vicky had to watch you were taken care of but there was no problem with that, in the beginning. She talked about wanting to escape and feeling as if she was on speed. Sounded like a bad trip,' Harry added, making Zia reflect on how colourful his 'hippy' life seemed to have been. 'Vicky tried to help but Tori threw it back at her till she decided she wanted to visit her grandparents in Spain. Then Vicky did the paperwork and suggested you had your own passport instead of being added to Tori's. That way, either of them could take you to see Joyce and Alf, in the future. I think she just envisaged that she'd need to give Tori a break, sometimes, not that Tori would leave you somewhere and Vicky would have to bring you back.'

A silence fell as Harry sank back into his memories, face woebegone. All was quiet apart from birdsong in the garden. Then he rubbed both hands across his face. 'But she never intended to go to Spain. It was Italy. Tori vanished with you, leaving a disjointed note saying Gerardo was searching for his baby and she had to take you to him. In her disturbed state I think she probably had a dream and thought it was real life. Anyway, you were both gone. Vicky was gibbering with fear.'

The room became still again. It was a lovely room; its walls, ceiling and floor of honey-coloured wood glowed in the afternoon sun. Zia broke the hush. 'She got to Montelibertà somehow and asked Lucia for help.'

'So, you know what happened there?' Harry leaned forward in his seat, eyes gleaming.

She told him what she'd been able to piece together from Lucia and Durante, bringing out of her bag the family tree Lucia had created and the photos of young Tori and Gerardo.

His breath caught as he gazed at them, touching one with a fingertip. 'Oh, Tori. You were so lovely.'

Ursula, who'd barely said a word, rose again and fetched kitchen roll, popping it into Harry's hand in place of his mangled tissue. She patted Zia's shoulder as she resumed her seat. Silently supportive.

Harry used the kitchen roll to wipe his eyes. 'Tori came home defeated and exhausted. Really, truly barely able to stand from fatigue. She didn't know how long she'd been driving or when she'd had any rest. You could look in Tori's eyes and she just wasn't in there any more.' His voice was thick with tears. 'And she came back without you. Said she'd left you with this Lucia woman. It seemed that Gerardo hadn't offered her a happy ever after, not even for a baby. She was remarkably clear about that.'

'Lucia and Durante looked after me for five days,' Zia supplied sombrely, chilled at what could have happened if Tori hadn't kept her grip sufficiently to leave her in safe hands.

It was terrifying.' Harry sniffed noisily. 'Vicky got this Lucia's address from Tori's address book but had no idea if she'd keep you safe. I did suggest getting the police but she said she could catch a flight and be there in the time it would take to queue up at the police station.' He gave Zia a sidelong look. 'We weren't conservative types. A bit anti-authority, people said.' His lip quivered as he returned to his narrative. 'So, I agreed to stay in Exmouth with Tori. Vicky got the first plane to Rome and rented a car to drive to the town – what did you say it was?'

'Montelibertà,' Zia murmured, hearing her voice as if from an echo chamber.

'Well, Vicky was frantic that with you being in Italy with your Italian father's family, somehow they could keep you. And 'parently that Lucia was not at all keen to give you up,' Harry declared, picking up one of his walking sticks and tapping it nervously on the floor. 'She spoke good English and Vicky said she was very possessive of you and asked a ton of questions, like where was Tori? Why hadn't Tori come back? Could Vicky prove Tori wanted Vicky to take charge of you? Vicky went into desperation mode. She took you, jumped in the car and drove off to the airport. There was a hullaballoo because you weren't booked on the flight but she convinced them it was a mistake. Your passport gave your next-of-kin as mother Victoria Chalmers so her story added up. Then when she got home . . .' He halted, tears starting in his eyes.

'It was the worst day of my life!' It was almost a sob. 'Tori had gone missing in the night. I had to call the police and by the time Vicky got home with you they'd already recovered . . . her body. Our lovely Tori. She was found

232

at the foot of a cliff. And it was me. My fault. I went to sleep. I had to tell Vicky.'

Zia only realised that she was crying when Ursula ripped off some more kitchen roll and stuffed it into her hands, sliding an arm around her shoulders and squeezing in wordless support.

Harry blew his nose hard then went on with a gasp. 'No one ever knew if she jumped or fell. There's documented cases of people with postpartum psychosis thinking they could fly.'

'Fly?' Zia echoed thickly. 'Seriously? What a terrible condition it must be.'

He nodded. 'Awful. There was no getting a handle on it.' He choked on another sob. 'I think Vicky blamed me for not looking after Tori properly and maybe she was right. But I thought she was safe in bed and I could finally get some sleep. I was that tired.' He blew out a long, gusty sigh. Ursula got him a glass of water and after a few sips he was able to carry on. 'Afterwards, Vicky and Tori's doctor said that if a mother with postpartum psychosis leaves the baby it's a big red flag, like the maternal bond is the final tie with reality. If I'd known . . . maybe I could have stayed awake.'

Zia's throat felt raw with pity for the desolation in his voice for the events of thirty years ago, for heart-broken Tori and overwrought Vicky taking the law into her own hands. 'It wasn't your fault,' she whispered. But a nightmare vision of the English rose's young broken body below the cliffs danced before her eyes, making bile rise in her throat. If Harry had known about that 'red flag' and made sure Tori stayed at home would Tori have recovered? Would Zia have known her mother?

Ursula gave Zia's shoulders a squeeze. 'Maybe we should give this a rest,' she suggested, anxiety lacing her voice. 'Come back another day? Honey, you're ripping yourself apart.'

'There's not much else to tell, really.' Harry gave his nose another blow. 'You were about five weeks old when Tori died.'

Numbly, Zia nodded. 'The death certificate says the 22nd of November 1991.'

'It was a nightmare when that Lucia turned up a week later. Bloody spitfire. Vicky had you somewhere, dealing with the arrangements. I'd taken time off work to be with Mandy and Leon – they were only just adults. Cried for Tori all day long, the pair of them. Then Lucia marches up, insisting to see Tori. I had to tell her she'd passed away. White as a sheet she turned and I wondered if she thought I was lying to get rid of her. Once Vicky heard Lucia had called round, that was it. After the funeral, no more ado, she packed up and left.' He removed his glasses to blot his eyes. 'She only ever came back to Exmouth a couple of months later to scatter Tori's ashes in Sandy Bay where we'd taken the kids when they were young. She was petrified, said that Lucia was capable of making trouble. You were a British citizen all right and tight but that Lucia was fierce.'

Zia managed a watery smile. 'Lucia's nobody's fool but she's actually lovely.'

The look Harry gave her was sceptical. 'Well, that's as may be but Vicky packed her grief with her other possessions and ran off to this fixer-up house in Northamptonshire.' He gave a great sniff and his voice dropped. 'I only saw her a few times after that.' The old hurt deepened the lines on his face.

Ursula chipped in. 'But why pretend she was Zia's mum? That's what's always puzzled me. To look after her daughter's daughter would have been what most people would have expected.'

The smile Harry gave was nearly a grimace. 'Because it was easiest, dear,' he said simply. 'Vicky never met a formality but she wanted to avoid it. She refused to look into whether she'd done anything unlawful taking Zia home from Italy. She had the same name as the birth mother so it was easy to fudge things with the health visitor and the school.'

Zia laughed ruefully. 'She wasn't brilliant with rules.' Her mind drifted back to her lovely, strapping, no-nonsense mum. 'Poor Mum, to have lost her daughter like that. Now her occasional sadness and the times I caught her crying make sense. She was mourning inside.'

'More than occasional, dear,' Harry said sombrely. 'She used to wait till you were asleep to cry. She told me that. She called it her "daily fix" or her "midnight medicine". If she had that release, she could get through the days.'

A hot tear slipped down Zia's cheek. 'I never even suspected,' she said, her voice hoarse.

He cleared his throat. 'Very protective of you, she was. Ultra-protective. Obsessive, some might say. She created a world for you and she lived that story.' He managed a watery laugh. 'Joyce said to Vicky, "You can't go on pretending forever," and Vicky said, "Why not?" The downside was that she carried on being scared of Lucia catching her up and maybe spilling the beans to the authorities. I think that was why you two moved around so much.' He sank back wearily in his chair. 'Then I made a stupid mistake. Lucia Costa turned up in Exmouth again and I told Vicky. She stopped writing and when I finally drove to the house you'd been living in, you'd moved on.' He sounded terribly, ineffably sad. 'She should have known I'd never, ever have told Lucia where you were. I would have done anything for Vicky.'

After a moment of silence, Harry's eyes pink with emotion and distant with memories, Zia spoke again. 'Would that have been in 1991?'

Bleakly, he nodded. 'About then. Two years on, Joyce and Alf contacted me to say she was dead.' He paused to swallow. 'At least they *did* tell me, so I could go to the funeral. Later, they brought her ashes and we let the tide carry her out to join Tori. Never saw any of you again till today.'

Zia fought through her memories of that horrible time. 'I was left with a neighbour one day and didn't know why. Gran and Pap got back very late. I wonder if it was then.'

Harry's face was pouchy and tired. 'Your grandparents were old-fashioned and probably thought it would upset you to be there. They came back from Spain for good to look after you, didn't they?'

She nodded. 'I wonder why they didn't tell me I wasn't Vicky's child, once she was dead?'

'Well, exactly.' His Devonian accent thickened for a moment, making the word a rolling 'egzarkly'. He narrowed his eyes at Zia as if assessing her ability to hear what he had to say next. 'But mental illness . . . some folk see it as a stigma, don't they? Alf was particularly shaken by the word "psychosis".' Harry paused, his eyebrows twitching as if in time with his thoughts. 'I reminded Joyce of her earlier words about not being able to pretend forever. She jumped on her high horse and snapped that you'd

236

had *quite* enough upset, thank you very much. You were ten, distraught and frightened so they were going to carry on as Vicky had arranged things. Can't say I blamed her, really.' He added reflectively, 'I think they suddenly understood Vicky's fears about you being taken away because the rules hadn't been followed. Whether the pretence did more harm than the truth, I don't know, but it was all for your protection, dear.'

He pushed his glasses up his nose, eyes swimming with tears once more. 'Joyce said they'd write with their new address but damn if they ever did. There was something Joyce and Vicky had in common – they felt I knew too much. They shut me out.'

By the time Ursula pointed the car back towards Brighton it was rush hour and Zia felt as limp as last month's lettuce.

They'd eventually enjoyed a tea shop lunch with Harry then spent the rest of the afternoon in his sunny cabin, filling in Zia's timeline. Harry had given her four old, tatty photograph albums. 'These are Vicky's own,' he'd said, turning the old, board-like pages with glue going brown beneath the film. 'On one of my last visits to you both she asked me to keep them for her. Said they were too painful to look through and you were getting old enough to find them and ask tricky questions. Said she'd kept a few other things of Tori's.'

Zia nodded. 'Like school reports? We didn't understand why there were so many at first. Then we realised they belonged to two different Victoria Chalmers.'

Harry managed a smile as he closed the last album and gave it a last pat before handing it over. 'Were Tori's good and Vicky's full of exasperated comments?'

Zia had laughed, though her eyes stung with tears. 'Actually, yes.' Throat tight, she leafed through Vicky's albums, poring over images of Tori in her carrycot, her high chair, at school, laughing during a family day on the beach or beaming from within a group of friends.

The icing on the emotional cake had come when Harry's daughter Mandy arrived home from work, a coiffed woman in her fifties driving a Lexus. The moment Harry explained who Zia was Mandy had dragged her into a hug. 'I loved Tori and Vicky so much. Tori was like my sister and Vicky was just the most wonderful, warm human being. My brother Leon will hate that he wasn't here for this. Are you really Tori's darling little baby?'

Her words had wrenched a sob from Zia that dragged at her heart.

Now, exhausted by emotion, she gave a great yawn and Ursula sent her a quick look. They were in a queue of cars waiting to get onto the A27 so she didn't need to concentrate on the road. 'Take a nap. You look like crap.'

'Thanks,' Zia said drily.

Ursula put the car in gear as the vehicle in front inched forward before its brake lights came on again. 'I never appreciated quite how hard all the moving around was on you as a kid till I heard you telling Harry.'

'Don't know about "hard".' Zia felt disloyal to Vicky if she'd made it sound that way. 'I just couldn't make lasting friends.'

'But that horrible girl who invited you to her party and when you turned up you found the family was away on holiday!' Ursula's was the first car in the queue now and she craned forward, waiting for a gap in teeming traffic.

'Her mum had made her invite me when she hadn't

wanted to,' Zia pointed out reasonably, trying not to remember how humiliated and left out she'd felt. 'Writing the wrong date on the invitation probably seemed the obvious solution. She needn't have worried. I was leaving soon anyway.'

'That makes it even more crappy of her.' Ursula spun the steering wheel and whipped out into a space between the cars.

Zia's stomach felt as if it had been left back at the junction. 'It wasn't that bad.' She really didn't want to go through the whole poor-Zia-finds-it-hard-to-make-friends thing all over again so she murmured, 'I suppose there must be medical records and a coroner's report for Tori.'

'I suppose so.' Ursula sounded struck by this idea. 'Are you going to track them down?'

Zia considered, swaying with the movement of the car. 'I don't know. Would paperwork give me any more insight into Tori than the memories of Harry, Lucia and Durante? Add anything to the photos treasured by people who loved her?' She had to swallow hard to get the next words out. 'It's shitty enough to realise my birth led to Tori's death without seeing the recorded evidence.'

'Oh, Zia.' Ursula crooned softly. She groped for Zia's hand and gave it a squeeze before returning to the steering wheel.

'When I'm back in the UK in September I'll go to Devon and throw rose petals in the water of Sandy Bay for my two mums.' Zia closed her eyes, trying to uncurl her hands and soften her spine into the car seat. Tears leaked from beneath her closed lids and her head, full of whirring thoughts, ached.

Today had exaggerated all her feelings. Overwhelming

sympathy for Tori as well as sorrow and loss. Gratitude to Lucia and Durante for keeping her safe when her psychotic young mother abandoned her. Grief that Vicky had interpreted Lucia's search for Zia as a threat. Immeasurable thankfulness for Vicky, Joyce and Alf who'd all given up their own plans to care for young Zia.

At some point this afternoon she'd made the decision never to identify herself to Gerardo. It had come from an instinct to protect herself from disappointment rather than from structured reasoning but the decision was a relief. Couldn't trust him. Could do without him.

Her head lolled and the engine noise warbled in her ears as she began to drift. She slept the rest of the way home, only waking to the sound of Ursula's phone as she double parked outside Zia's building. She scrambled for her bag and jacket, interrupting the conversation Ursula was having with Stephan only to bestow a kiss on her cheek and whisper her thanks. After yawning her way up to her apartment, she made her first job to call Lucia, thinking she might be waiting anxiously to learn how things had gone.

Once again, it was Durante who answered. 'Lucia is sleeping. She is quite sick, I think. Maybe I get the doctor tomorrow, no matter what she say.'

He sounded so unhappy that Zia felt a wriggle of unease. She'd expected Lucia to have been fighting back by now. 'She began this on Thursday so that's three days. I think maybe you're right and it's time to get help.' After checking everything else was OK Zia rang off. Durante didn't seem to like speaking English on the phone and she felt too drained to make the effort to speak Italian. She'd recount her meeting with Harry and tell them about her Gerardo

240

decision when she got home and Lucia, hopefully, was better.

No, not home. Italy. Funny how much it felt like home even though she was in her own apartment in Brighton.

She threw herself on her bed and called Piero to share what she'd learned and his warm, welcoming, sexy, American-Italian accent instantly made her feel closer to Italy.

Chapter Seventeen

A few months ago, Zia would have spent a Sunday in Brighton with Brendon, Ursula and Stephan wandering the passage-like streets of The Lanes, sauntering up to North Laine for breakfast at Komedia, listening to buskers in Churchill Square or crunching along the pebbly beach.

In contrast, Zia saw this particular Sunday as just a day to pass until she could get the job interview over on Monday.

She phoned Durante and was disappointed to hear Lucia seemed to be getting worse. 'I worry lots,' he announced succinctly. Luckily, Durante's twisted ankle was getting better or Zia might have cancelled the interview and gone straight back. Instead, she contented herself with going online to book her flight for Tuesday . . . then discovered there was no flight to Perugia till Wednesday. Flying into Rome would have worked beautifully if she hadn't left her car at Perugia airport.

She dusted and vacuumed her apartment then cleaned her windows, leaning out high above the New Steine and breathing in briny air that rang with the gulls' peevish cries. The waves were deep blue and she was watching their white tips blowing towards shore when her phone rang. She drew her head back indoors on a buzz of excitement, hoping for Piero. It was only Brendon. 'Bleurgh,' she said aloud. She had to remind herself that, now Ursula was back with Stephan, it would be awkward if she and Brendon couldn't at least be polite to one another. Then she answered the call.

'So, how'd it go?' he asked expectantly.

She wrinkled a puzzled brow. 'The interview isn't until tomorrow.'

He laughed. 'I meant meeting your mum's old buddy yesterday. Was he able to tell you all you wanted to know?'

Slowly, she said, 'I don't remember discussing yesterday with you.'

A hesitation, before he breezed, 'On Friday you said that's what you were here for.'

'No, I didn't. But I did tell Stephan,' she added pointedly.

His tone became wounded. 'Look, no need to be snitty. I'm being friendly. I know it was important to you and hope it went well.'

Zia snapped the window closed, shutting out the whistling breeze. 'I wasn't snitty.' She wasn't friendly, either, and she didn't tell him whether her visit had gone well.

Brendon changed tack. 'Are you excited about tomorrow? It sounds like a great job to me. I told Elise—'

Zia stopped listening, a chill slithering into her stomach. Brendon's chummy chattiness felt manipulative, as if acting as though they were close would automatically make it so. She cut in. 'Brendon, we're not in each other's lives now. I'm surprised you expect me to share things with you.'

243

He seemed taken aback. 'But I got you that job!' he protested.

'You can't have, because I don't have the job,' she pointed out. 'I have an interview. Elise just asked you to pass her number on.'

'I didn't have to do it.' He sounded like a peeved child who expected a gold star on his chart because he'd made a parent a meal. 'You'd be able to continue to live in Brighton. You love it here.'

It was only the obvious unhappiness underlying his bluster that allowed Zia to maintain even a cursory level of courtesy. 'Thank you for doing so. Yes, Brighton's a great place. I'd better go, Brendon.' She said goodbye.

An hour later, Ursula called. By then Zia was striding along Madeira Drive between the touristy part of Brighton and the marina, passing the faded grandeur of the nineteenth century Madeira lift that once gave halfpenny rides up to Marina Parade, enjoying the dilapidation of Madeira Terrace Arches and ignoring beer-fuelled shouts from a group of men.

'Hey, Ursula.' She jammed a finger in the ear not pressed to her phone as she strode alongside the tracks of the Volks Electric Railway as the train prepared to chuff off in the direction of Black Rock Station.

'Just checking how you are after your emotional day.' Ursula sounded relaxed and happy.

Zia almost said, 'Bored!' but it might have sounded as if she wanted Ursula to invite her round and Zia wasn't sure if either she or Stephan would like that. She'd had Ursula to herself during Ursula's marital break and now she must butt out of Ursula's time with her husband. 'Fine,' she said cheerfully. 'I've caught up on chores and now I'm walking towards the marina. Poor Durante's despondent because Lucia's tummy pains aren't going away. I wanted to tell them I've decided to leave Gerardo in the dark about my identity but it wasn't the right moment.'

'You've made that decision?' Ursula sounded surprised.

Zia dodged a family of cyclists making full use of Madeira Drive being closed to motor vehicles and almost stepped into a clattering skateboarder instead. 'I fell asleep mulling it over in the car and then couldn't tell you when I jumped out because Stephan had called. I think the negatives of telling Gerardo outweigh any possible positives.'

Ursula said doubtfully, 'I suppose nothing Harry said put Gerardo in a good light.'

'No. Any romantic notions I had about finding a daddy have faded. I felt nothing when we met and he was obviously no more than an accidental sperm donor who didn't want to face the consequences. I've met Fiorella and Roberto and even allowing for thirty years of mellowing I can't see them as such ogres that he should have abandoned Tori and me. Lucia and Durante stepped up and that's where I'm placing my loyalty. I'm making life easy for them.' Zia moved away from the railway tracks as the distinctive combination of humming, gliding, clanking and tooting grew louder and the Volks train tootled by.

'I see your point. Her nephew doesn't really deserve the soft spot she has for him.' Ursula changed the subject. 'Are you excited about tomorrow's interview?'

Zia laughed. 'Don't you start. Brendon called earlier, trying to make me thrilled about it and take credit for setting it up at the same time.'

Ursula sounded horrified. 'No, really? Don't go thinking I'm in cahoots with him.' Then she giggled. 'Am I allowed to want you to get the job and stay here in the UK, though?'

'Suppose so.' Zia grinned. 'Bloody Brendon also wanted to know about our trip to Chichester. I wish I hadn't talked about it in front of Stephan.'

'Crap,' said Ursula guiltily.

Zia hastened to reassure her. 'I'm not trying to create difficulties with your husband. If we both just watch what we say in front of him the problem will go away.'

But Ursula's tone turned to dismay. 'It's tricky, honey. Y'know, couples have conversations. If he asks me something and I don't answer it seems like I've got something to hide.'

'He asks you about my life?' Zia clarified, dismayed in her turn.

'Kind of,' Ursula muttered, sounding cornered. 'You're his friend too, aren't you? He's concerned for you.'

'Is he? Right. Um, I understand.' Zia didn't really. Neither did she believe Stephan was her friend. He was Brendon's friend and seemed to have no compunction in feeding Brendon's proprietorial illusions. What she did understand was that there was a danger in asking Ursula to take sides: Ursula couldn't take hers. Shaken by this unpalatable truth she strode faster, dodging dogs off leads and adults pushing buggies, half-wishing she hadn't confided her decision about Gerardo.

'Will you let me know how you get on tomorrow?' demanded Ursula with the air of someone wanting to move the conversation on.

Zia knew she took a beat too long to answer. 'Of course.'

Another beat before Ursula said stiffly, 'Not so I can pass the information along.'

'I didn't think that,' Zia protested guiltily, knowing that for an instant she had thought that. An uncomfortable, alien thought, it was one she wished she hadn't admitted to her brain. Ursula was her rock, her constant, her best friend.

Except Ursula had been destroyed by losing Stephan and lit up with joy at getting him back. Zia wouldn't, for anything, return the shadows of anxiety to Ursula's eyes. Yet Stephan was in the habit of asking direct questions . . . and Ursula had said not answering them was tricky.

Monday morning. Crowded train from Brighton to London Victoria. Yuck.

Trying to read over the clatter of the train and people talking too loudly, Zia, trussed in her blue-grey suit, could only think of summer dresses and sun-drenched days, especially when she received a text from Piero.

Thinking about you. x

It was the kind of message that didn't demand an answer but after watching English fields and hedges flash by, she replied. *Lucia still seems quite poorly. x* Caution prevented her from saying, *I'm thinking of you too and want to be in Montelibertà instead of imprisoned on a frigging commuter train with a mob of coffee-breath commuters.*

She is, he confirmed. *Want to speak later? x*

She paused for thought, rocking with the train as they rumbled over points, watching the landscape change to apartments and office blocks, billboards advertising private medical care and vodka. She hadn't deliberately withheld the news about the interview during phone conversations since she'd been here. It was more that she'd wanted to talk about Italy, starry nights and happy things. She replied: *I'm on my way to a job interview in London. Should be home this evening. x*

A pause in communications. She wondered whether he needed time to absorb the information or if he was just busy. Finally, as the train slowed for Victoria in a grey, tunnel-like closing in of buildings and glass, she received: *Have you decided to return to the UK permanently? x*

She answered honestly: *Don't have a choice from mid-September. The rules say I can't stay in Italy past then and I'll need income. Living in Italy would require a longer-term strategy. x* She grabbed her bag as the platform glided up alongside the window and the train jerked to a halt, making passengers already on their feet stagger. When the doors opened, she joined the flow of people alighting. Victoria Station's roof of curved metalwork and transparent sections seemed lower than usual and the announcements about trains and security boomed too loudly. She halted, hunting out her phone again despite the tuts and tsks of hurrying commuters forced to skirt her. She reopened the conversation with Piero and texted: *Thinking about you, too. x,* then she rejoined the noisy flood, jostling elbow-to-elbow through the chrome barriers then picking up speed as she plunged from the station into an even noisier London, hustling along the crowded streets to Lower Belgrave Street.

She found Headley Whiterow in a gracious Edwardian building of tawny brick with bow windows behind black railings. At the top of the steps Zia was buzzed into a white and grey reception area. A young guy with brown curly hair showed her to Elise's office.

'I'm so excited about this!' Elise cried, long blonde hair and short skirt making her look like a little girl who'd got into her mum's clothes and make-up. From that effusive greeting to her introductions around the bright, comfortable offices, everything about the Headley Whiterow setup seemed perfect. Even the directors Tim and Aneka, who welcomed her in a conference room of squishy leather

248

chairs and a walnut table, seemed as if they'd be good to work with.

'Elise speaks highly of you,' said Tim, taking off his jacket, perhaps to demonstrate that they were already comfortable with her.

'We trust her to handpick exactly the right person for the role in our highly effective team,' added Aneka, who wore enormous black-framed glasses as if she were an emoji of someone trying to look clever.

They began on the long, discursive interview process. At 12.30 they crossed the road to a convenient restaurant where they ate salad and drank spritzers. Elise's hair remained a glossy sheet despite the best efforts of the summer breeze that teased tendrils from Zia's plait. Elise offered earnestly, 'The Brighton–Victoria commute's pretty doable and so's Brighton–Blackfriars but you could work from home two days most weeks. The role's varied and with travel, although—' she pulled an apologetic face '—only in Europe. No North America. But it's exactly the field you've been so successful in before and it's Italian that's your second language.'

Zia tried to get carried along by their enthusiasm and the sound of familiar terminology. After lunch they crossed back to the office to watch a systems presentation and talk about client portfolio, experience, and future visions. The job was, effectively, what she'd been doing in Brighton but in London, a smaller company, more responsibility and a salary that would not only compensate for commuting costs but allow her to make payments on a new car too. The role was made for Zia.

'So,' Elise said. 'There's more we could talk about but I already know your commitment and capabilities. What I'd like to do is put together a formal offer and email it to you.' She must have already got the nod from Tim and Aneka because they all assumed identical anticipatory smiles. 'What do you think?'

A few months ago, Zia would have asked when she could start. But what came out of her mouth today was: 'When would you need to know?'

The fixing of Elise's smile spoke of her surprise. 'Soon, to be honest. I need someone I trust to coach clients through the deal process.' She hesitated. 'Do you have a holiday booked or something?'

'Not really. But my car's in Italy and so's a lot of my stuff.' She assembled her words carefully, rawly aware that she ought to be grabbing the opportunity. 'I'm staying with a great-aunt who's ill at the moment and I'm expected to be there for most of the summer.'

Elise dropped the smile. 'Ah.' She closed her laptop and pointed a remote at the AV screen to close it down. 'So, when would be the soonest you could join us?'

Zia made a judgement from financial need and the lawful limit to her current stay in Italy. 'Third or fourth week in September.'

Elise's expression lightened and she exchanged a look with Tim, who nodded. Elise's smile returned. 'Not ideal, but we can work with that.'

They rounded out with enticing prospects for advancement and finished at five o'clock. Zia felt jaded. She'd heard of people finding it hard to return to the workplace after an absence but hadn't given it much credence till subjected to a day-long interview. She trudged, rather than walked, back to Victoria.

The commute home was a pain. After not getting a seat until Haywards Heath, alighting at Brighton station she barely had the energy to battle along the crowded narrow pavements of Queens Road. Glad to turn off, she passed the Royal Pavilion Gardens with tourists crowding the lawns and then clopped across Old Steine with a herd of other pedestrians. Her phone sounded when she was trudging along St James's Street. The screen showed that it was 19.20 and the caller was Brendon. 'Yeah?' she said, less enthusiastically than ever. If she didn't think Ursula would suffer the backlash, she'd just block him.

'So? How'd it go?' he chimed cheerfully.

'OK.'

'Only OK? Elise seemed enthusiastic.' Brendon sounded as if he thought Zia might be holding out on him.

She stopped so suddenly a Goth girl bumped her shoulder and gave her a sour look down her pierced nose. 'You've spoken to Elise about my interview?'

'Obviously, I gave you a great report—'

'*What?*' She half-shouted. 'What the hell do you mean, "a great report"? She was my boss and you and I were the same level. Don't be so bloody presumptuous.'

'Oh, you know what I mean,' he said, in a joshing tone, as if Zia was being purposely prickly and he was the man to jolly her out of it.

'No, I don't.' Zia realised pedestrians were tutting as they danced side-to-side to get by her but fury was fizzing up her spinal cord and shutting down the part of her brain labelled 'manners'.

Brendon persisted. 'You're going to take the job. Right?'

'None of your business!' she exploded. Three women in front of her looked round.

His tone slid into resigned pleading. 'Oh, Zia, stop being precious! If you insist on me spelling it out, here it is: I want you back. I did a bit of cheerleading to Elise because if you have a good job in the UK then—'

'It's nothing to you whether I'm in London, Italy or Timbuktu,' Zia interrupted, stepping out again, faster and faster as if her frustrations were rocket fuel. '*Nothing*. Your drunken sexploit ended my feelings, which were going the wrong way anyway. We're done.' Now pedestrians were dodging her, pressing themselves against walls as her fury propelled her through them like a wrecking ball.

'Look,' answered Brendon with a kind of forced calm. 'Stephan had Ursula back—'

She halted suddenly, ignoring a hot pain in her calf as someone bounced into her with a wheeled bag. 'IT'S NOT THE SAME FUCKING THING!' she bellowed.

'But I wanted you to move *in* and instead you're moving *on*,' he cried, as usual shifting tack when he didn't want to answer. 'Don't you care I'm upset?'

'Less and less every time we speak, if I'm honest, so there's no point trying to guilt-trip me,' she snapped bluntly. 'I don't know if I'd ever have committed to you if you hadn't cheated but you *did* cheat so it's tough shit if you're unhappy. Now back off.'

A silence. Then Brendon's voice turned into a furious hiss. 'A mistake from me means it's OK to hurt me? I don't *think* so, Zia. Banging that woman had no bearing on how I felt about you and you know it.'

Zia winced. 'But it most certainly had a bearing on how I feel about you. However crudely you put it, you had sex with another woman when we were meant to be exclusive. The end.'

Silence. Awareness of the hustle and bustle of St James's Street gradually returned. She realised she was almost at the turning for the New Steine when she'd meant to stop at the supermarket. Then Brendon came again, this time in a low, dangerous drawl, 'You'll be sorry.'

Zia was left clutching a silent phone, ashamed she'd lost her shit but relieved the row had brought things to a head.

She half expected his last dramatic words to have been a threat to put in a bad word for her with Elise but the job offer arrived later in the evening along with a warm email. *I'd LOVE to have you, hence the promptness of this offer. Can't keep the job open for long, though . . . and I sense your heart's not yet in this country.*

As Zia had already arranged to say bye to Ursula on her lunch break tomorrow and was booked on a train to Stansted afterwards for an overnight stay ahead of an early flight, she had to admit Elise had called it right.

Chapter Eighteen

Piero hated the atmosphere at Tenuta Domenicali whenever Graziella was around but refused to be discouraged from getting his afternoon espresso.

Graziella gave a great sigh when he entered the big office and Salvatore beetled his moustache, his expression imploring Piero, as if to say, 'Try not to have a problem with my girlfriend. You know how she is.'

Piero had a list of problems with Graziella but he had a bigger problem with upsetting his father so he paused to chat, displaying a sleek black device around his wrist. 'I bought an Apple watch.'

Salvatore smiled shrewdly. 'You have a sudden interest in counting steps? Or have you fallen out of love with your Dolce and Gabbana watch because it was a gift from Nicoletta?'

Piero grinned. 'I sent the Dolce and Gabbana back to her.' Nicoletta had acknowledged its return by text and he hoped that she'd also acknowledged the symbolism of the action. He was not on the market.

'And she returned all the jewellery you bought her?'

Salvatore's eyes twinkled, obviously having a good idea of the answer.

Piero rolled his eyes, enjoying the gentle banter rather than perpetual talk about the vineyard sale. 'I didn't expect it.'

Salvatore chuckled. 'So, you weren't disappointed.'

Graziella gave a sniff, tap-tap-tapping on the computer. She didn't join the conversation but Piero couldn't imagine her sending back so much as an earring that a man had bought her. She was too damned acquisitive.

He headed back to his own office reflecting idly that being with a man fifteen years older didn't fit with Graziella's designer gear and highly glam image.

His steps paused.

Was she hoping his father would die soon? Salvatore might have left her money in his will. Or if they married and Salvatore passed before Tenuta Domenicali was sold she'd inherit a quarter of the vineyard. He shivered at the nightmare thought that if she got Emiliano onside, they'd outvote Piero.

Back at his desk he glanced at his new watch and turned his mind to happier things. Zia's plane should have landed. He pictured her driving her red car along the dusty state road and wondered when she'd arrive at Bella Vista. In the next couple of hours he could get away.

His gut tightened with pleasurable anticipation as he sped up completing a batch of computer files and rang the systems guy at a distributor's to ask whether they were likely to be implemented today. Receiving an unequivocal '*No, non posso*' he raced through his inbox. By 4 p.m., he was scooting through the now-empty outer office and out through the door.

The wheels of his mind turned as he drove away from

the vineyard. How would things be with Zia? The six days of her absence had passed slowly. Whenever he closed his eyes, he saw Zia's taut, naked body and her full, sexy mouth on him.

That one amazing night of making love to her seemed to have switched on something he'd thought Nicoletta had switched off – openness to something more than 'casual'. The memory of their calls while she'd been in England . . . the car's air conditioning was barely able to cope with the heat level of his thoughts.

Then, swinging left to circumvent the centre of town, he frowned. How had she ended up attending a job interview? That text had caught him unawares. But what else had he expected? That somehow Italian law would make an exception for her and she'd stay indefinitely? She'd need a job to go home to.

The thought made his chest constrict as he drove up Via Virgilio and out of town until he reached where the rock towered on either side. He wished for more time, more flexibility and opportunity for something to grow naturally between them. They were both . . . what was that American expression he remembered from his childhood? Gun-shy. With Nicoletta and Brendon in their fairly recent pasts, neither was necessarily ready for plunging straight into commitment.

In a few short weeks they'd be living in different countries. He couldn't imagine himself selling up – even if that would be particularly easy right now – and moving to the UK. To live there for a year had been great but it was cold in winter and winters seemed to last about nine months.

Turning into his own drive he mentally shook himself. One hot night and he was letting his mind wander into moving-in territory? He was a grown man, not a lovesick teenager. He parked in the shade and slid out of the car. Like a grown man, he would shower and change then stroll through the trees to Bella Vista. He might get a coffee or a beer. Or a chance to talk to Zia.

Then, alerted by the slow crunch of tyres behind him on the gravel of the shared segment of drive he glanced round to see a big white vehicle nosing out of Bella Vista. It took him a couple of seconds to grasp the significance of the red cross but then the lights flashed and the siren began the distinctive *deedle-dee durr, deedle-dee durr* of an ambulance siren and it shouldered its way into the traffic with Durante's small grey car following so closely it could have been on tow.

Fear sizzled up his spine. Who was in the ambulance?

Then he saw Zia, frozen in the now-empty drive. Grown-man status forgotten, he turned and ran towards her.

She turned her gaze on him as he pounded up, her eyes huge and horrified. 'It's Lucia! Her stomach pains have gone crazy. I got back to find the ambulance already here. They're going straight to the hospital at Perugia.'

'Ospedale Santa Maria della Misericordia,' he supplied automatically, catching his breath.

She nodded. 'Durante's chasing the ambulance. He asked me to stay and look after things because guests are due to arrive to stay in Villino Il Pino this afternoon.' A phone was in one trembling, white-knuckled hand. 'He left me Lucia's phone so I could look after them. She looked . . . awful.' Her breath shuddered. 'Her skin was so sweaty and she was writhing. If not for her age I might have thought she was about to give birth.'

Stifling that unlikely image Piero slid an arm about her. 'She's getting emergency help. Did the medics give any clues about what's wrong?'

She turned into him, her cheek moving against his shoulder as she shrugged. 'No, but they weren't hanging about so I don't think they liked what they saw.'

'Shit,' he murmured impotently, a horrible, hollow fear taking over his insides at the thought of Lucia being seriously ill. He'd never known her suffer anything worse than a cold. Sliding his other arm about Zia he held her, her hair tumbling silkily over his hands, her breast pressing against his pounding heart, seeking comfort as much as offering it.

Despite his chilly anxiety he became aware of heat. Not just from the sun pounding down on them but from Zia. Her trousers had probably been suitable for the aircraft but were asking for trouble in the Umbrian sun in the third week of July. Temperatures soared into the thirties every day. He dropped a kiss on her hair. 'Let's get you in the shade.' Their hands somehow linked naturally as they turned and headed back towards the house. He grabbed bottles of cold water and, seeing Zia's pallor and dazed expression, guided her towards a terrace chair to drink.

'It was horrible,' she murmured between sips.

He sat down and rested his hand comfortingly on her thigh. 'I'm sure.'

'I knew she was still poorly but I didn't expect to come back to this. My flight was delayed and there was a hold-up on the road. Another two minutes and I would have missed them.'

He let her talk, understanding the human need to express what had just happened, search for answers and check for errors.

Finally, she began to blink her way out of her shock. She gestured towards the valley turning hazy in the late afternoon. 'I've missed this.'

'Good.' He felt immeasurably reassured by her simple statement but at that moment the awaited guests arrived in a dusty blue SUV, a man and woman with an adult daughter who tried valiantly to communicate in laboured Italian until Zia said, 'We speak English, if that's easier.'

The young woman fanned her face with relief. 'Awesome! We're booked into Villino Il Pino.'

While Zia got them settled in the cottage Piero jogged home, showered, changed, then returned with a chicken pasta dish he'd prepared before leaving for work this morning in the hopes he might have the opportunity to share it with Zia. He'd slipped it into the oven and was wrapping garlic bread in foil by the time Zia returned.

She dropped a backpack by the kitchen door as she joined him. 'That's the guests sorted.' She looked less shaken now, as if the small task had settled her down. She washed her hands then checked the oven. 'Good job someone's organised.' After giving him a hug, she took out plates and cutlery, evidently taking it for granted that they'd dine together, then emptied the dishwasher and refilled it while Piero wiped down surfaces. Presumably Fiorella hadn't been in for a couple of days and Durante, preoccupied with Lucia, had let chores slip.

Zia paused to sigh. 'I wonder when Durante will let us know what's happening.'

He checked the time. 'It's an hour at least to the hospital, even with sirens. They also have to admit her and get some idea of what the problem is.' He took a bottle of wine from the rack and put it in the fridge, adding wine glasses to the table setting.

Zia sliced fresh tomatoes to toss in oil and basil to go with the bread and pasta and presently they ate at the terrace table, burning a citrus candle to discourage the evening insect attack.

'Depending on how you look at it,' she said thoughtfully. 'I either haven't known Lucia very long or I've known her all my life. Anyway, I'm scared for her.' She lay a hand over her abdomen as if to indicate where her fear lay.

He took her other hand, her fingers hot and slender in his. 'By finding her, you made her very happy. She told me about you years ago but didn't think she'd ever see you again. It was always a sadness.'

Her eyes swam, tears spiking her lashes, but she smiled as if comforted. 'Vicky's friend Harry said they were all scared of her. They thought she'd create trouble by involving the Italian authorities.'

'But you're British,' he pointed out. Her skin had lost the overheated feeling of this afternoon and he circled his thumb on the silky back of her hand.

'But Mum took me from Italy,' she returned. 'Apparently, she was very bold.' Then, as if she needed to fling open her mental filing cabinet and empty it, she gave more detail of the story Harry had poured into her ears. Darkness gathered. Fireflies flickered gold and the stars silver. Zia's voice was the only sound apart from the rhythmic whirr of the cicadas. Piero found himself under the spell of her voice as she brought the chapters of her story together. She breathed life into a young Vicky as a defiant single mother in a less tolerant society, Vicky and Harry bringing up their kids in one household and later sharing the misery of Gerardo failing to love Tori as she yearned for. Her voice dropped as she talked of the psychosis that had sent Tori careering off to Italy, only to leave her baby with Lucia. Vicky snatching back Zia then arriving home to news of Tori's death. Lucia clamouring for information.

Vicky fleeing, living the lie she was Zia's mother. Gran and Pap eventually perpetuating Vicky's lie because telling the truth seemed too fraught with difficulties.

'You know Lucia now. I'm sure Vicky didn't need to be so scared,' he murmured when she finally showed signs of winding down.

Zia nodded. 'Perhaps grief for Tori and guilt she'd snatched me from Lucia magnified the situation and brought Vicky to desperation stakes.' Quietly, she added, 'I wish she hadn't had to live with those feelings. She was a special woman. Loving and capable. Kinda quirky.'

Softly, he laughed, enjoying sharing this time with her beneath the stars. 'She sounds special.' He lifted her hand and pressed a kiss to her fingers. 'You're special, too, Zia. You've literally had people fighting over you from the day you were born.'

He watched as her gaze fell to his mouth. For long seconds the world stopped still.

And then her phone rang in the darkness and she snatched back her hand to grab it. 'Durante?' Her voice was high with anxiety. 'How is she? Piero's here. I'll put you on speaker and you can use Italian, it'll be easier for you. He can translate any bits I miss afterwards.'

She made the necessary on-screen adjustments and set the phone down, gazing at it with fierce attention.

Piero said, 'Durante?'

Durante's voice hovered between strain and panic. 'She is gravely ill,' he cried. 'Piero, my Lucia! She rolls and gasps and holds her belly.' The words flooded out as he described the controlled urgency of the hospital staff, what they'd said, Durante's feeling of helplessness as he drank in their grave expressions while they gave pain relief and arranged a scan.

261

Piero tried to reassure his friend, though the gravity of the news gave him chills. 'Lucia's a fighter. We were just talking about how she doesn't give up easily. And the miracles of modern medicine . . .' But they all knew he was issuing platitudes.

Briefly, Durante informed them he was staying with a cousin near Perugia so he could get to the hospital if needed and then issued a breathless goodbye.

Piero reclaimed Zia's hand, knowing from her face that she'd understood. 'So, the news isn't good.'

Her eyes were wet. 'No. Could it be appendicitis?'

He stroked her fingers, wanting to soothe her anxiety. 'I don't know. Maybe tomorrow we'll learn more.'

'Durante mentioned surgery?' she whispered, fresh tears tipping slowly from her lashes.

His heart felt as if a cold hand was closing on it at the terror in her eyes but her understanding that much of Durante's half-hysterical Italian made it pointless to shield her. 'Possibly.'

She gripped his fingers. 'I'll text Durante and tell him I'll help any way I can. I'll look after the rentals or take a bag of his things to his cousin's house or . . . absolutely anything.'

'I'll do it.' He texted Durante in Italian. Then he rose, pulling her to her feet and into his arms, wishing he could do more to make her feel better. 'What about you? Will you be all right? It's getting late.' He hesitated, not sure whether asking if she'd be OK alone would sound opportunistic.

But Zia beat him to it. She held him very hard and whispered, 'Will you sleep with me? I don't want to be alone tonight.'

Chapter Nineteen

Zia heard her words on the air almost as if someone else had spoken them and her breath caught in horror. 'I don't mean—' She gulped. 'I sound like a cold-hearted bitch, as if I'm propositioning you when Lucia and Durante are in such a bad place.'

His arms fit naturally into the curve of her waist and she was reassured by the lightness of his touch. 'I understand. Let's just be together.'

They cleared the table and closed up the main house then she took him to the little apartment she'd enjoyed smartening up, stepping within the white walls as if into a sanctuary. Her body felt like lead, exhausted by a 7.30 a.m. flight and a shit-storm return to Italy.

'It looks fantastic in here.' Piero glanced around approvingly at Zia's temporary quarters. She took a quick shower and when she stumbled out, he was waiting to enfold her in a towel. In her bedroom he pulled back the sheet and tucked her beneath it, shucked off his own clothes and wrapped his body around her.

He spoke with his mouth against her hair. 'Durante

interrupted our conversation. Are you glad you found Harry?'

She turned her face against his skin, taking comfort from his presence. 'Yes.' But her heart performed a skippity-skip and she knew she'd drawn out the word doubtfully.

He drew away and resettled himself so he could look into her face. 'Sure?' He sounded puzzled. 'I thought you were relieved to know more about your history. Glad to speak to people who knew Vicky and Tori and could make them feel real to you.'

'Yeah.' She began to stroke his chest where his body hair was at its silkiest. 'That's true and it was fantastic. I know my birth mother, Tori, will forever be a teenager and I missed out big-time but it was bliss to speak to someone who knew and loved them both.' She sighed. 'I feel everything you'd expect – joyful, reassured, relieved that the mystery is finally, *finally* cleared up. Wistful and regretful that Tori suffered, that my birth prompted that suffering and, of course, immense sorrow at what I lost as soon as I had it. More regret that Mum – Vicky, I mean – and Gran and Pap couldn't have told me about Tori and given me a share of their memories. Sorry there's no video that would have let me hear her voice and see how she moved. But . . .' She let her eyes drop to the pulse beating at his throat.

His frown curled one eyebrow. 'But?'

'There's an anxiety.' Her throat had tightened as if trying to squeeze back the words. 'I've read up on postpartum psychosis on the internet now.' She paused, heart hammering so hard it made her feel shaky. 'Although only one or two women in a thousand get it, there's a familial link. If I ever have kids, will I be one of those women?'

'Oh, Zia!' He pulled her closer, harder against him,

264

stroking her hair down her back. After a few seconds, he said, 'It's obviously a rare condition. I'd never even heard of it before. Had you?'

She shook her head.

He went on, gently, persuasively. Comfortingly. 'And the world has advanced in thirty years.'

She sniffed. 'Not enough that mental illness always gets sympathy.' But her heart steadied a little at his compassion and good sense. She would have hated him to dismiss her worry as not real or, conversely, been horrified to the point of leaping from the bed and running. Instead, he just held her and stroked her.

Gradually, feeling secure with his body wrapped around hers, fatigue took over. Drowsily, she reflected that she'd never realised non-sexual nakedness could feel so comforting and a goodnight kiss on the shoulder so sweet.

Sleep swept up to claim her.

Morning came at six when they were both jerked awake by Piero's phone bursting into life. Zia's heart pounded as she listened to his end of the conversation and realised the caller was Durante. Squinting against the early sunlight burning through the curtain fabric she searched Piero's handsome face for clues as to whether the emergency had deepened. A calm, '*Sí, sí,*' did a lot to assuage her fears, however. Piero nodded. His eyes flicked to her as he said, '*Poi dico a Zia di chiamarti.*'

She remained silent until the call ended then burst out, 'Is everything OK? Why did you tell him you'd ask me to call him?'

He dropped the phone on the bedside table and kissed her neck. 'Lucia passed a stable night but there's no improvement. Durante wants me to gather his clothes and sponge bag and take them to his cousin's house in Torgiano,

265

just outside Perugia.' His phone beeped. 'That's probably him texting the cousin's address. I can combine taking the bag with visiting a distributor in that direction. He wants to FaceTime you when you're in the office so he can talk about the guest side of things. Both Villino La Quercia and Villino Il Tasso have changes of guests today so Fiorella will be coming to help with cleaning and linen changes.' A sudden grin transformed his face. 'He didn't want to disturb you this early but knew I'd be getting up for work. I thought you might prefer me not to mention we were in bed together.'

She flushed. 'Ah. Thanks. That would definitely have felt like over-sharing. I'll get dressed and try him from the office.'

She made to roll from bed but Piero hooked his arm around her waist. 'You OK?' He nuzzled her neck.

'I'll cope.' The nuzzling felt like exactly the right level of contact: intimate without being sexual. Despite her anxiety over Lucia, her arms twined themselves around him and she pressed close.

His breath was hot on her skin. 'That feels fantastic but you're completely taking my mind off what we have to do.'

Her hands slithered down to cup his buttocks. The feel of his skin took her breath and she shifted to bring herself fully against him, discovering from his hardness exactly where his mind had gone. She murmured, 'But maybe we have a few minutes . . .?'

He dropped his mouth to her breasts, making her gasp and arch against him, body pulsing. 'A few minutes is enough?' he breathed.

She groaned. 'Sometimes, it's exactly right.'

He gave her what she wanted – hot, hard and furious

266

but *exactly* right. Then she stood beneath the cool shower once again, trembling with aftershocks as she tried to reassemble her brain. Piero, with a last lingering kiss and a promise to catch her later, went to pack a holdall for Durante. The scary events of yesterday had swilled away their previous wariness over how much they could relax with each other. Last night, Piero's arms had felt like the most secure place in the world and this morning desire had hit her so hard she'd acted on it without thought.

Now it was time to force strength into her limbs by spooning up cereal and drinking coffee. Then she slipped into shorts and a T-shirt and plaited her hair and hurried along the terrace, exchanging the bright morning sun for cool dimness as she stepped into the hallway to the office. She switched on the computer then FaceTimed Durante on her phone. He flashed up on her screen at a peculiar angle, looking rumpled and exhausted, the bags beneath his eyes seeming to drag down his entire face.

'Now I go to the hospital,' he said, walking as he talked if the swinging of a car park and buildings in the background was anything to go by. 'Dear Zia, I ask you to look after everything. I am so sorry.' He had to raise his voice over those of passersby.

'I'm happy to help. Just tell me what I have to do,' she said comfortingly. A busy ten minutes followed as Durante furnished her with the computer password and, with a mixture of explanation and her showing him the screen via the camera, she learned where to find the bookings and guest contact details.

At the door to the hospital now, he became visibly anxious to be off. 'Fiorella arrives at ten and she knows what needs doing for new guests.'

Zia felt a tingle of alarm. 'And I've helped before but

267

does she know about Lucia's illness? Or do I have to break the news?'

Durante nodded, his hovering finger enormous as he prepared to end the call. '*Sí*, she know. I go now. *Ciao*.' His image disappeared even as Zia tried to tell him to give Lucia her love. Blinking back tears, she supposed that if Lucia was still in pain she might not care for solicitous messages anyway.

The day began to pick up speed. Zia saw the Villino Il Pino guests to ask them not to bother Durante for anything they might need but to call Zia on Lucia's phone. The departing guests from Villino Il Tasso and Villino La Quercia threw their things into their car with the resignation of those at the end of a holiday and Fiorella arrived, her gap-toothed smile absent for once and the seams of her face deepening as she clucked about Lucia. Zia had to concentrate hard to follow her Italian as she said that it was frightening how a hitherto healthy person could be attacked by mystery pain. 'Where do these things come from?' Fiorella demanded. 'Why Lucia?'

Zia agreed, her eyes prickling as she thought of poor Lucia lying in a hospital bed . . . but also at the distress in Fiorella's expression. The tiniest tendril of connection began to unfurl but, ruthlessly, she snipped it off. Much safer not to let those feelings develop.

When the guests from Villino La Quercia left with a toot of their car horn, Fiorella gathered fresh bed linens and towels and Zia began to strip the beds then Zia continued cleaning the cottage while Fiorella worked on the main house.

They broke for a lunch of bruschetta – mainly because the only bread was stale – then they readied Villino Il Tasso for guests, too. It was hot work but the cottage smelled pleasingly of fresh linen and kitchen spray when they'd finished.

Fiorella wiped sweat away with her overall. 'What about your apartment?'

'My responsibility,' Zia assured her. 'The guests at Villino Il Pino are only staying three days so there will be another cottage to service on Saturday.'

Fiorella looked doubtful. 'There is a wedding in my family that day.'

An irresistible thirst for information surged through Zia. 'How wonderful! Your close family?'

The older woman's gappy smile flashed. 'The daughter of Roberto's niece. They're to marry at the small church near our home. I haven't bought a new dress as I have several. There are many weddings in my family.'

Zia smiled, wondering how many of those at the wedding would share Zia's DNA. A lot, by the sound of it. 'I'll look after the changeover at Villino Il Pino on Saturday. Can you come again on Thursday, a week from today?'

Fiorella agreed as she gathered her things but added, sagely, 'The garden will grow.'

It took Zia a moment to understand that this was more than a philosophical non sequitur. She glanced out at the flower gardens surrounding the house and realised Fiorella was right. Already weeds were daring to take root in the gravel and dead heads spotted the rose bushes, probably because Durante had had other things on his mind in the past week. She groaned. 'I'd better remind myself how to look after plants.' In her childhood, Zia had helped Vicky thin carrots or trim climbers but Joyce and Alf had employed a gardener so Zia's horticultural education had ended there.

Fiorella left and Zia awaited the new guests. The couple for Villino Il Tasso arrived promptly, but the others, a French family, were late. Zia had barely used her school-girl French since her GCSEs so laboured along with Google Translate to show them around Villino La Quercia and respond to the enthusiastic questions about the region. She was, at least, able to tell them a little about the vine-yard they overlooked, which seemed to satisfy their interest.

Finally, she escaped to the supermarket, buying lots of salad because it would be simple to prepare and flexible around interruptions. She was beginning to get the idea that being the sole person responsible for Bella Vista could be a tie.

All day she itched for updates on Lucia but refused to pester Durante, imagining the effect if all of Lucia's big family – which included Zia, if you were precise – kept bugging him for information.

Piero turned up earlier than she'd expected, freshly showered and bearing a picnic. Zia suddenly realised how exhausted she was and flopped onto a terrace lounger in the shade. 'You're awesome.'

He squeezed onto the lounger with her, which he accomplished by pulling her into his lap and curling about her. 'That's very true.' Though he joked, his smile was dim.

'What?' She pulled back to look up into his face, taking his sunglasses off his nose so she could read his dark eyes.

He sighed. 'Durante telephoned. Lucia's scan showed a peptic ulcer, hence her pain. Then the situation worsened abruptly this afternoon and she was rushed into surgery. He's waiting for news but obviously scared stiff.'

Fear rippled through Zia too. 'Is she in danger?' She fought to keep her voice even.

A tiny hesitation told her she wasn't going to receive much comfort. He said, 'We don't really know anything, yet.' But he held her closer. Cuddling up was uncomfortably warm, though it was early evening, but Zia didn't want to detach herself from his reassuring heartbeat.

As a distraction from wondering how poor Lucia was faring, she asked him how things were going at Tenuta Domenicali.

'Graziella's a pain,' he complained, tracing the shape of Zia's hand with a fingertip. 'She's like a creaking gate, going on and on about how "we" should take the Binotto deal. Papà and I almost had an argument about her today. I suggested he just retire and take Graziella out of my hair. I apologised straight away but we ended up cross with each other, which made Graziella smirk.'

Zia's conscience stirred. 'If there was another avenue to explore about the vineyard, would you want to hear about it?'

He closed his eyes and groaned. 'I'm sick of the whole thing, to be honest. We must have explored everything by now. My family seems to think of nothing else and talk of nothing else.'

He sounded so irritated that Zia took that as a 'no'. It wasn't her business, after all.

It was a while until they felt like eating the picnic. After, to escape the multitude of moths flittering around the terrace lights, they retired into Zia's apartment, safe from creepy crawlies behind fly screens. Piero made love to her with such tenderness that she had no idea why she'd ever thought letting him get close to her might be a mistake. That night they slept fitfully, each waking often to check their phones for news of Lucia.

When there were no messages by morning, Piero went

off to spend Friday in his workshop and Zia began on Bella Vista's garden, trying to pick shady areas in which to weed and chugging cold water to combat the summer heat . . . and checking for messages.

Just after ten o'clock the awaited text came from Durante. *I ring Piero now.* She returned *OK* then threw down her trowel and dashed to Il Rifugio through the heat haze, not heeding the bleached grass that scratched her bare ankles.

She found Piero sitting in the dappled shade outside his workshop, phone to his ear, his gaze welcoming her as she approached but his expression grave. He moved up so she could join him on the bench and listen to his end of the conversation but as Durante was doing most of the talking it wasn't enlightening. Finally, he ended the call, frowning. 'Damn. The ulcer caused a perforation before they could get to it, which caused peritonitis. She came through the surgery safely but it's a critical condition. She'll have a rough time for a week or two while they get on top of the infection.'

Zia felt as if the world gave an extra spin and she had to inhale hard, getting a hint of the scent of fresh wood on his skin. 'Poor, poor Lucia. That sounds horrific.' She gulped and added in a small voice, 'Poor Durante, too, of course. I'm being selfish, but I've only just found her and now . . . well, sometimes you don't realise how much you care about someone until you're scared they might slip away.'

'I know.' He sat back, drawing her against him, and kissed her hair. 'It's not the same thing . . . but when you were in the UK,' he made a gesture with his free hand, 'you felt a long, long way away.'

His admission tingled through her. 'It was about eleven hundred miles.'

'Not geographically. Emotionally. You were back in your old life.' He brought his other arm around her, his voice low and husky against the sound of birds singing in a nearby shrub. 'When you were in England I moped like a teenager. My stomach hurt. It's not a situation I'm used to.'

Zia's heart fluttered. 'That's quite an admission.'

His smile twisted wryly. 'And you have nothing similar to admit?'

She tried to be scrupulously honest. 'A lot was happening to me. I discovered the gaps in my own backstory. I had a row with my ex. I went for a job interview.' She smiled at the apprehension in his eyes. 'But I kept thinking of here as "home". I wanted to be here. And I thought about you a lot.' She smiled. 'I'm not sure how connected those last two statements are.'

He gave her plait a tiny tug. 'But *maybe* connected?' His eyes were teasing now.

'Maybe,' she conceded. His dark hair blew in the hot breeze and she brushed it back from his eyes, recognising as she did so that it was a proprietorial, girlfriendy gesture.

He didn't seem to mind but just kissed the end of her nose. 'How about dinner this evening? I'll take you to one of my favourite places in Montelibertà and you can tell me about the row with your ex.'

'It's not a restaurant where Nicoletta's likely to spring up and scream at me, is it?' She waggled her eyebrows.

He laughed. 'In the unlikely event that our paths cross, I think she understands the situation now.'

'Then I'd love to. Though there's not much to tell about Brendon. I just had to explain again – and at high volume this time – exactly how over we are.'

'I hadn't realised you would be seeing him.' Piero lowered his mouth towards hers.

Zia closed her eyes. Waiting. When the kiss didn't come she opened her eyes again. 'We only spoke on the phone,' she explained. Then she brought his head closer and gave herself the sublime pleasure of kissing someone who knew exactly how to make it good. As his soft, warm lips moved over hers she realised she was beginning to trust Piero and his feelings for her. He was a good man, a true friend to Lucia and Durante, a good son even though his dad's girlfriend was making his life a misery.

And, as his hand slipped beneath her T-shirt, hot, gentle, questing, trickling like silk over her skin, he lit her up like the Italian sun.

Chapter Twenty

That Friday evening began a week of what Zia came to think of as the new normal. The restaurant where Piero took her was in a cellar, filled with gorgeous smells and antique glass. The manager, who knew Piero well, drank a glass of wine with them, asking Zia about England and Piero about the vineyard.

On Saturday, Zia serviced Villino Il Pino on her own ready for the next guests, thinking about the family wedding Fiorella had mentioned. Would Gerardo be there? If the bride was Roberto's niece's daughter then she thought that made her Gerardo's cousin once removed. It wasn't a close relationship but probably enough in a small community. And he'd struck her as the type to be attracted to free booze. A wedding in Italy wasn't something she'd experienced but, in Sorrento, she'd once watched a young bride and her attendants walk through the square to church and everyone had clapped the procession of beautiful young womanhood. She wondered if that would be happening down in Montelibertà today.

Then the picture faded from her mind because the new

British couple arrived to occupy Villino Il Pino and asked a hundred questions about things Zia would have thought quite straightforward.

On Sunday, Piero took her with him to Emiliano's home on the other side of Montelibertà. The house had a pool and the terrace was edged with tubs of white geraniums. Passionflowers climbed over a pergola and bees hovered lazily over the waxy blooms with filaments as purple as emperors' robes. Emiliano's wife, Jemma, was sunny and easy-going and the children, Cristian and Camilla, swarmed over Zio Piero like puppies. In minutes, Piero had stripped off to swimming shorts and was throwing the shrieking kids into the pool and dive-bombing in after them.

Zia laughed as he let Cristian and Camilla duck him and clamber on his shoulders, wet hair black and plastered to his head. Emiliano joined in at an equally boisterous volume and Jemma settled down with Zia to spectate while the delicious scent of barbecued meat and vegetables wafted from the nearby grill. 'Men are always boys at heart,' Jemma said indulgently. She shot Zia a speculative look. 'Do you have children?'

Zia, understanding that it was natural for Piero's sister-in-law to be curious about Piero's date, said easily, 'No. I haven't felt the urge and I don't even have a job to support myself at the moment.'

Jemma began to ask her about that and then broke off as a thickset man with a beige hat and a big moustache let himself into the garden. A woman in her fifties with a mass of curls and a sour expression clutched his hand possessively. 'Salvatore!' Jemma exclaimed, leaping up to kiss the elderly man's cheeks.

Salvatore beamed at her and then at the children, who clambered from the pool to greet their grandfather, 'Nonno,

Nonno!' and edify him with demonstrations of how they could bomb his sons, who remained in the water and shouted greetings.

Zia was introduced to Salvatore and the fabled Graziella, watching with frank curiosity as the unsmiling woman accepted a glass of wine and then sat herself apart from everybody else.

Salvatore, on the other hand, accepted an ice-cold beer then regarded Zia from under thick grey brows. 'Piero mentioned you. You're staying with Lucia and Durante? You're from England? You look Italian.' Like his sons, his Italian accent was mixed with American. *Yur frum Inglan?*

Zia thought it best that as few people as possible knew her reason for being in Montelibertà so answered, 'Gran always said my father was Italian,' then went on to tell him how beautiful she'd found Tenuta Domenicali.

He shot Piero a quizzical look, making Zia think her visit was news to him, but he just observed, 'You know Zia means "aunt" in Italian, right? But I guess Brits are like Americans and will call their kids any damn thing they like the sound of.'

'Exactly,' Zia agreed, liking his rolling, if rusty baritone and the occasional smiles that lifted his moustache at the corners, as if his mouth was doing a curtsey.

After they'd chatted for several minutes, Piero joined them, his swim shorts plastered to him and water glistening on his body. 'Hey, Papà, you moving in on my date?'

'You wouldn't stand a chance if I did,' Salvatore retorted, brushing droplets of water from his arm as they dripped from Piero's hair.

Though it was the jokiest of remarks, Zia noticed Graziella's mouth tightening. Seriously? She thought Zia might be making a play for a man about forty years her senior?

Salvatore and Graziella didn't stay for the meal. In fact, Zia formed the opinion that the done-up, made-up Graziella would have avoided sitting down even long enough for a single glass of wine if she could have. Jemma had been welcoming but Graziella soon bore Salvatore off as, apparently, they were expected at the house of friends. Her friends.

It was the only slightly sour note in an otherwise glorious day.

After the weekend, Piero was chained to his desk at Tenuta Domenicali and Zia spent time on the garden, fretting about Lucia even though the news indicated she was holding on, punctured by drains and drips. Her temperature was still high and, of course, she had pain from the surgery. Her favourite condition was asleep but, unfortunately, her discomfort tended to triumph over her exhaustion. Visitors other than Durante were not yet recommended.

The British couple in Villino Il Pino were constantly seeking Zia out to grumble about something. 'Just thought you'd like to know that the shower mat has a rip,' the man pronounced weightily.

'And there are bird droppings on the loungers,' the woman added, wrinkling a freckled nose.

Zia didn't mind sloshing water over the loungers to vanquish evidence of avian incontinence and buying a jolly blue shower mat so the man didn't have to look at the one-inch tear in the old one but when Wednesday brought a cloudy sky and the woman sighed, 'You can't even see the tops of the mountains,' Zia was stumped. What did they expect? That she'd get a long broom and sweep the clouds away? She didn't mind the housekeeping work that came with the cottages but how did Lucia and Durante put up with nit-picking guests?

Then she noticed that Elise had sent a chasing email to ask whether Zia had had time to consider her job offer. Hurriedly, she returned an apology, explaining how ill her great-aunt had been on Zia's return from the UK eight days ago. She paused to ponder. It was an excellent job offer, but Brendon had made it sound as if Elise felt comfortable discussing Zia with him, so she finished with, *It's such an uncertain time that I feel it would be unfair to expect you to hold the position open. I hope you find exactly the right person for such a great role.* Her days were busy enough without entering into the palaver of contracts.

The nights . . . the nights Zia spent with Piero.

His bed. Her bed. Wherever they ended up the air crackled when they touched, whether it was slow and tender or like colliding thunderclouds, they were on each other until, finally sated, they curled up and slept.

On Thursday Fiorella came to help with the servicing of Villino La Quercia and Villino Il Tasso. 'Also, my son is here to do the garden,' Fiorella announced. 'Durante agreed it.'

Zia, who'd been standing on the terrace waving goodbye as the blue car of the enthusiastic French family drove slowly up the drive, swung around. And there stood Gerardo Costa, staring back at her, looking less down-at-heel than when Zia had seen him the first time. His hair was washed and drawn smoothly into its short, grey-streaked ponytail. He'd shaved recently and his T-shirt and shorts were clean. He smiled. '*Buongiorno.*'

'*Buongiorno,*' she replied. It was a shock seeing him

when almost two weeks ago, after listening to the damning things Harry had had to say, she'd made the decision not to interact with him. And now . . . was there a meaningful glint in his eyes as if he were recognising some connection between them? She tried to shake off the fanciful notion but her smile felt stiff as her inner voice told him: *Yeah, here I am, buddy. You wanted me gone but I made it without you and I'm doing fine.*

She addressed herself to Fiorella, leaving it to Durante whether Gerardo was there as an affectionate nephew or paid labourer. 'OK, we'll leave your son to the weeding. Let's begin Villino Il Tasso.' She fished the key to Tasso from her pocket and grabbed the caddy of cleaning equipment but her heart took up an unpleasant rhythm as if it didn't know what it was meant to be feeling. She'd developed a shy liking for Fiorella, the woman she was coming around to mentally labelling 'grandmother', but Gerardo? She couldn't attach to him at all.

Energetically making up beds while Fiorella squirted bleach in the kitchen, her mind wouldn't leave him alone. Maybe he *had* caught on to who she might be. Her skin and hair were right for a British-Italian and even a man who hadn't wanted anything to do with his baby would probably remember she'd been named Zia, a bizarre choice of name to an Italian – as so many people had told her. So what? It made no difference now. She'd been disappointed when she met him at the Montelibertà Festival, Harry hadn't had a good thing to say about him and even Lucia and Durante were aware of his weaknesses. A shower and a change of clothes didn't make up for all that.

When lunchtime came around, she put out meat, cheese and *pane di Terni*, a round, rustic loaf. A blue bowl of green leaves and sliced red tomatoes provided colour to the repast and water and orange juice sparkled in their jugs. She couldn't say she felt the degree of pleasure she would have felt if her companions had been Lucia and Durante – or Piero – but the meal passed off OK. She was getting better at understanding Fiorella and Gerardo seemed genuinely concerned about Lucia.

'She is my favourite aunt,' he said. 'She and Durante lived in town when I was a boy and I would visit them often. They worked, of course, but at the weekend Lucia would bake cakes for me and sometimes they took me to Lake Trasimeno.'

'But not your brothers and sisters?' Zia couldn't help asking.

'Sometimes.' He nodded. His T-shirt was grubby following the gardening. 'We are a big family but special relationships sometimes grow.'

Special enough that he could turn to them for somewhere to secretly meet his Brit girlfriend, Zia thought. 'Oh? I grew up with few relatives.' Her reply piqued Fiorella's curiosity and she asked for more. Zia hesitated. Which version should she give? The version she'd known most of her life? Or the one with the additional mother she'd just discovered?

Driven by curiosity to see Gerardo's reaction, she embarked on the second, though her palms sweated uncomfortably. 'My mother was young when I was born and died when I was five weeks old. The man who got her pregnant didn't want me. My grandmother brought me up and I used to think she was my mother. She died when I was ten and then her parents looked after me.'

Fiorella's wrinkles arranged themselves in an expression of concern. 'No brothers or sisters?'

Zia smiled. 'Not on my mother's side, anyway.' She

risked a glance at Gerardo. He was watching her with an unreadable expression, not noticeably worried by this conversation or appearing anxious he might be outed after all this time. She decided to push. 'Fiorella how do you feel about the British visitors to Montelibertà?'

The elderly woman looked mystified. 'Fine. Tourists are everywhere. They like the sun and bring money to the area. They create jobs.' She gave her high-pitched laugh. 'I haven't learned English, though. I never liked it.'

Politely, Zia laughed, too. Then she turned to Gerardo. 'And you? Have you had much contact with the British visitors?'

This time, something flickered in his eyes. But he shrugged. 'Like my mother says, Montelibertà relies on the tourists. My generation all learned some English.'

Zia let it drop but she didn't miss him easing his palms down the fabric of his shorts as he turned the subject to Lucia's health. Zia cleared the table while they chattered about Durante sending Roberto bulletins, as he did to Piero, and Roberto disseminating the information within the family. She wondered whether the tell-tale signs she'd caught were the work of her imagination or whether her birth father, sitting right in front of her, was only pretending not to know who she was.

Maybe, like her, he'd decided to remain anonymous.

It was late afternoon when Zia's phone sounded its FaceTime alert. She'd just showered and was lying naked on the bed and letting the air cool her still-damp body. When she saw it was Ursula calling, she pulled on her T-shirt then answered. 'I meant to call you. Ooh, love the hair!'

Ursula grinned as she flicked her fingertips through the hair that had been cropped of its long lock at the front and was boasting red-gold highlights amongst blonde spikes. 'It is ultra-cool, isn't it? But three quick texts in eight days, Zia, that's pants. How's Lucia?'

'Eight days! Then that's how long she's been in hospital. I've been caught up with stuff.' Zia brought her up to date with poor Lucia's painful lack of progress and Durante's raging anxiety. 'It's great to see you looking so happy and relaxed.'

Ursula beamed. 'Yeah, things are going pretty well with Steph. He's at work right now. By the way, Brendon's being the Incredible Sulk. He said you were a bitch to him.'

It wasn't lost on Zia that Ursula was calling when Stephan was out but she had no objection. Stephan had picked a side and it wasn't hers. 'Let Brendon sulk,' she declared. 'He's been overstepping the mark so I told him to butt out. Shame he had to explode and sour things more than necessary. You'd think he'd realise that as he was the one caught with his pants down he doesn't have a leg to stand on.'

Ursula snorted a giggle. 'He was standing on both his legs from what I remember.' Then she sobered and a shadow entered her eyes. 'To be honest, I'm worried about him causing issues between Steph and me. He lashed out again with his bloody silly complaint about me being forgiven and him not. Steph told Brendon the cases weren't the same but he still got grumpy with me.'

Zia was alarmed at this new direction. She could imagine the kind of pit of despair Ursula might be hurled into if things once again went wrong with her marriage. 'Don't let Brendon poison things between you two.'

'You don't need to worry about that,' put in an unseen voice, before Stephan loomed into shot over Ursula's shoulder. Judging from his shirt and jacket he was fresh in from his job in procurement at Brighton & Hove City Council.

Ursula swung round. 'Steph! Where did you spring from?'

Steph grinned and ruffled her new haircut. 'Just came in from work. You were obviously yapping too loudly to hear me. Hi, Zia!' he said to the screen.

'Hi, Stephan.' She smiled but it was creepy that he'd appeared out of thin air like that. People heard both sides of a conversation of a video call. Oh, well. She hadn't said anything that wasn't true, even if she might have been a touch more tactful if she'd known Stephan was earwigging.

She and Ursula talked about other things for a few minutes, then Ursula said she had to go. Although Zia didn't regret returning to Italy, she couldn't help feeling wistful as her best friend's smile flashed off the screen. Ursula had been the best thing in her life for twelve years but evidently circumstances had changed when Zia dumped Ursula's husband's best buddy.

She suspected Stephan wouldn't want Ursula to see so much of Zia when she returned to Brighton.

It was a horrible thought.

Time rippled along like a gentle stream. Zia did what had to be done at Bella Vista but the holiday cottages had been designed as a retirement business so, now she was in the rhythm, she had free time to play with.

Piero already filled her evenings and nights. On Fridays and weekends, she sometimes sat in the corner of his workshop, watching while he made a play house – in kit form, it looked to her, but he explained that the parts would be assembled on site. His drawing and measurements were on a board on his wall. Larch filled the workshop with its sweet scent and a haze of fine golden sawdust. When the machines weren't roaring he had Formula 1 coverage playing on his laptop.

'You follow Ferrari?' she asked, one Sunday when his eyes kept being drawn from his nail gun to the race.

His eyes laughed. 'I'm Italian so I'm *tifoso* – a fan. I didn't let my time in the US or UK change that.'

At last Lucia began to respond to treatment, although Durante said on the phone that she was still fighting the remains of the infection. To help him out and improve her grasp of the local accent, Zia had told him to speak Italian and she'd stop him if she didn't understand. He went on, 'She wants to read but she can't hold a book comfortably because of her surgery.'

Struck by an idea, Zia sat up. 'What about her Kindle? She can hold that in one hand. Give me your cousin's address and I'll bring it over tomorrow. It'll give me something useful to do.' Bella Vista was beginning to feel solitary without Lucia, Durante or Ursula and Piero would be driving south to meet a buyer who supplied the busy restaurants of Rome and expected to be late back. It would be nice to do something more practical than sending daily texts to Durante for Lucia to read from her hospital bed.

'*Perfetto*,' exclaimed Durante and Zia put it on her calendar along with the cousin's address. It would be the 4th of August, two whole weeks since Lucia had been taken away in the ambulance. She hurried off to take the Kindle from Lucia's bedside drawer and put it on charge.

The next day saw her driving through Montelibertà and taking the winding road down the mountain until she reached the dual carriageway where she could whizz past the sunflower fields to Torgiano, close to Perugia. She was thrilled to arrive at the cousin's white-rendered house and find Durante awaiting her.

'*Ciao, ciao*!' He managed a beaming smile as he kissed her cheeks though he looked drawn, had visibly lost weight and needed a haircut. 'The doctors think she may be home in another week and now it would be good to receive brief visits from others. You want to come?'

'You bet!' Zia cried, so much relief flooding through her that she embraced him all over again. She followed his grey Fiat to the hospital where he showed her the way to Lucia's ward, shared with three other women.

When she finally saw Lucia, propped up in exactly the hospital bed Zia had imagined, pallid and exhausted, normally curly hair flat and new lines graven on her face, Zia's throat filled with tears. 'I've missed you,' she croaked.

Lucia held out hands that looked like waxed parchment. 'Zia-Lucia,' she murmured. 'What a mess I am. Look at this horrible tube in my nose. I have needles in my arms and staples in my stomach.'

Zia laughed, dizzying relief at Lucia sounding exactly the same as she always had, turning her hot all over. 'Thank goodness you're getting better,' she choked. 'You scared me to death!' Then she forced a bright smile and switched to Italian, saying she wanted the practice but actually because she thought it might be less tiring for Lucia. 'Bella Vista's just waiting for your return. The guests are all behaving. Fiorella and I are looking after the cottages.' It was better not to mention Gerardo's gardening in case it made Lucia worry how Zia was coping or whether the shit was about to hit the fan. After ten minutes she kissed Lucia's soft cheeks and left the couple to hold hands, the Kindle safely stowed in Lucia's locker.

She drove back singing along to Ava Max, her heart the lightest it had been since the ambulance bore Lucia away. Back at Bella Vista she found Gerardo spraying weeds on the drive and Fiorella heading for the cottages with her arms full of clean towels. 'I've seen Lucia,' she shouted through her open car window and they both hurried over, Fiorella in a striped overall today and Gerardo's shirt flying open. Zia found herself beaming at their eager expressions. 'She doesn't look well, hooked up to tubes and things, but she's kept her sense of humour and Durante says she might come home next week!'

Gerardo whooped. '*Grazie a Dio! Grazie a Dio!*' and after he and Fiorella had hugged he returned to the weeds with a definite spring in his step.

Watching him go, Zia was hit by doubts. Had she been too judgy? For all his faults he loved his aunt and had worked hard in the gardens. Durante might be transferring money into Gerardo's bank account, as he did for Fiorella, but that was fair. Help would be needed for a while. Lucia's recovery would be gradual and Durante would need to look after her, as well as recovering from the weeks spent haunting the hospital and losing sleep.

Taking a seat on the terrace where bees bumbled around twilight-blue stephanotis, Zia opened her phone calendar and counted ninety days from when she'd arrived in Italy. It took her to the 14th of September. Accounting for the recent four full days spent on UK soil meant the eighteenth would see the end to her permitted stay in Italy, just over six weeks away. Then she had to stay out of Italy for at least another ninety days. *Permesso di Soggiorno* took three to six months to come through and it was hard to decide whether to apply without a clear idea of what the step afterwards would be.

She stared out over the valley where a handful of workers scurried between the vines like ants, working their way downhill. It was the end of their working day judging by the mountains shimmering blue-green beneath the watercolour sky of late afternoon.

In a few weeks she'd be leaving.

The reality sank through her like wet cement, dragging with it her joy at Lucia's progress on the road to recovery.

Piero. She'd have to leave him too. Just as she'd long ago fallen hard for Italy, now she'd fallen for Piero.

There was no other explanation for the way her heart bungee-jumped whenever they met. He'd made no more remarks about not wanting to be entangled. They spent time together whenever possible. Sex was off the scale as they learned more about what drove each other crazy.

If only she had some certainty about how best to plan . . . her stomach performed a sudden pirouette. An idea had sprung, fully formed, into her mind; an idea she hadn't considered before but which now seemed blindingly obvious. She revolved it in her mind, assailed by a thousand doubts that it could really be that easy.

Perhaps she'd discuss it with Piero and see if he saw any flaws she'd missed.

Up the hill, Il Rifugio almost in sight, Piero willed the car in front to stop dawdling. 'Come on, I've had a shitty day.' The traffic in Rome had been the usual nightmare, the buyer had been difficult to enthuse and Salvatore had phoned asking him to call in at the vineyard on his way home. When he got there, he'd found that, out of the blue, his father had decided to set a limit on how long they'd keep the vineyard on the open market before returning to Binotto's offer. The following heated conversation had ended with Salvatore upset and Piero needing to mend a fence.

At least Zia had volunteered to have a meal waiting for him. He liked knowing she was in his house, the window open to the buzz and whirr of insects and the breeze rustling the dry grass. It made his stomach skip about.

It was nearly 9.30 p.m. when he finally let himself through the front door and jogged down the steps to the kitchen, dumping his laptop bag en route. He found her perched on a stool, reading, her hair spilling down her back, cool and sexy in a short dress of denim blue. She glanced up and smiled and he swept her up into a kiss from which they both emerged breathless. 'That's better,' he murmured and brushed another kiss on her temple. 'Long day and Graziella set Papà on me. Even with the air con I feel like I've been in an oven instead of a car. Wait for me while I jump in the shower?' He deposited her back on the stool and pulled his shirt over his head without unbuttoning it, her laughter following him as he ran up the stairs.

Once in the cool stream of water he thought he should have invited Zia to join him, giving 'jump in the shower' a whole new meaning, but a growling stomach persuaded him to hurry back to where she was setting out a cold meal on his classically simple white plates.

Her liquid eyes smiled at him as he cannoned back into the room. 'What happened with Graziella?'

He grabbed water from the fridge. 'Papà asked me how long I'd feel comfortable leaving the vineyard on the market and she jumped in, whining that I was dragging my feet and—' he rubbed his nose sheepishly '—I told her to buy some fucking patience along with her next Gucci handbag. Papà wasn't happy.'

Zia sat down and helped herself to moist balls of mozzarella and focaccia sprinkled with herbs. Slowly, she said, 'I know I said I wouldn't offer any more unasked-for but well-meant advice about the vineyard but—'

He groaned and dropped a kiss on her shoulder, which was naked but for the strap of her dress. 'Do you mind if we forget the vineyard tonight? I just want to enjoy your company and hear how your trip went today. Durante hasn't called me.'

Zia's wide smile flashed. 'I saw Lucia! She looks wrung out but she's very much herself.' He ate rice salad and a cheesy pastry while she recounted every detail about Lucia's condition, her ward and what she'd said, her eyes mirroring each emotion as she flipped through joy, worry and compassion.

When she reached the end, he took her hand. 'I wish I could have gone with you. I miss Lucia and Durante – even if their absence has allowed us to spend so much time together.'

'Same.' Her smile flickered but her mind seemed to have drifted from the subject. Carefully, she laid down her fork, holding his gaze. 'By the way, I've had a crazy idea about Gerardo.'

'Oh?' He took a bite of focaccia as he waited for more.

She propped her chin on her palm. 'Today I worked out how much longer I could stay here and it's September the eighteenth.'

He swallowed, stomach diving in dismay. This last couple of weeks he'd almost been able to forget that Zia couldn't remain in Italy indefinitely. 'As soon as that?'

Slowly, she nodded. 'You know I decided not to come out about who I am in case it rubbished things for Lucia and his wife and kids?'

'A selfless stance I'm not sure everyone in your position would take,' he commented drily.

'It's kind of unfortunate that I have a conscience about them,' she agreed philosophically, if sadly. 'You know the options. I could simply return to living in the UK. Or I could, as I quite want to, apply for the temporary permission to stay so that after two years I can apply to be permanent.'

Anticipation raised the hairs on his arms. 'And . . .?'

She laid down her fork. 'To properly consider the second option brings me back to my starting point – people with an Italian parent or grandparent have a much better chance of success.' She took a long, slow breath, a new light creeping into her eyes. 'But today I realised I was assuming a worst-case scenario . . . that if I approached Gerardo then it was inevitable others would be involved and hurt. But what if I could persuade Gerardo to acknowledge paternity to the necessary authorities *and them alone*? His family need never know.'

He stopped eating as the simplicity of the plan hit him. 'I hadn't thought of this either.'

A smile tugged at the corners of her mouth. 'If I've been a secret till now, why not continue the same way? It would circumvent the Costa family trouble I've worried about.' The smile dimmed. 'It would be cynical to use him like that but if I'm correct that he's worked out who I am, does that matter? Is there a downside? Is the idea crazy? As Ursula says, he hasn't done anything else for me.'

He found himself grabbing the nearest of her hands. 'It's not crazy if it means you'd stay here.'

The smile widened shyly. 'Well . . . I came here with the intention of discovering whether that was possible—'

He took the other hand too. 'Zia, it could really work.'

She gazed at their clasped hands, frowning uncertainly. 'Having the actual conversation would be tricky. I'd need to think about the best approach.'

Jumping up, he rounded the table, pulling her to her feet and into his arms, warm and soft against him. 'Do it, Zia!'

She nestled into him, her voice trembling. 'Thanks for being so enthusiastic. But I have to be honest . . . it's scary to think about asking him.'

'Do it,' he repeated more softly. 'I'll help if you need it. I'll do whatever it takes.'

Chapter Twenty-One

It was the first Saturday in August and the landscape shimmered in a heat haze, the grass so dry it looked like spun gold. It was too hot to sleep easily and last night Piero had grumbled when Zia had rolled away from him to seek a cool spot on the sheets, his small air conditioning unit defeated by the stifling air.

The day promised to be hectic as new guests were due for all three cottages; the young couple departing Villino La Quercia had requested late checkout and incoming guests for Villino Il Pino an early one. Zia and Fiorella were working with the front and back doors of Villino Il Pino open but Fiorella's grey hair was dark with sweat. Zia had given her the bathroom to clean because splashing water about was cooler than changing sheets but the older woman was moving slowly. '*Fa troppo caldo,*' she complained. *The heat is too much.*

Zia paused in the bathroom doorway. 'Would you like to go home? Villino Il Pino's almost done.' She'd step on it despite the oven-like temperatures and get Tasso and then Quercia done alone rather than threaten Fiorella's health. Or . . . Gerardo was harvesting the last of the apricots from a tree on the other side of the house before the wasps spoiled them all. Might he turn his hand to cleaning bathrooms to give his elderly mother a rest? Zia had passed only a few words with him today. She was working up the courage to approach him but, though her imagination had conjured up various scenarios, she hadn't come up with the right way of saying, 'I'm your daughter. I think you might have guessed. Will you admit paternity to make my paperwork a little easier? We don't need to tell anyone.'

Fiorella straightened up with a groan but didn't meet Zia's eye. '*Sto bene.*' *I'm fine.*

Alarm rippled through Zia. She knew Fiorella relied on her cleaning money to augment whatever pension she had but it was tricky to convey 'I'll make sure you still get paid' in a way sufficiently diplomatic to render it acceptable. Instead, when they'd washed the surfaces and swept the floors of Villino Il Pino, she wiped her forehead emphatically. 'Phew. I need a cold drink. Let's take ten minutes in the shade.'

Relief flashed in Fiorella's eyes and she followed Zia to the terrace, plumping down into a chair in a way that told Zia she'd made the right call. She fetched cold water and took the next seat. Automatically, the two of them turned to survey the view. The vineyard was quiet and still, the mountains hazy. Nothing seemed to stir in the oppressive heat apart from slowly buzzing bees drawn to white geraniums and blue plumbago.

Then a man's voice tore the air in a volley of irascible Italian.

Zia swung round in time to see Gerardo almost falling through the door to her apartment growling, '*Merda*!' and swatting at a wasp that whizzed threateningly around his ears. Astonished, she leaped up. 'Gerardo?'

He halted mid-stride, obviously as surprised to see her as she was him. A hank of his hair had fallen from its ponytail. He smiled awkwardly. 'Ah, Zia. Um . . . my hands are covered in apricot juice and it attracts the wasps. I went in to wash.'

'In my apartment?' she breathed in blank astonishment. Anger propelled her feet towards him, then she got close enough to smell alcohol, sour and strong. She halted. 'Have you been into Durante's stash of liquor?'

Gerardo assumed an injured air. 'This is the home of my aunt and uncle. I'm always welcome to refreshment here.'

Zia had to accept the truth of this but persisted, 'But nobody made you welcome in my apartment.'

Then Gerardo completely changed tack. He treated her to a conspiratorial smile and assumed a syrupy croon. '*Lo sapevo. Volevo solo essere sicuro.*' She gaped at him, unwilling to trust she'd heard him correctly, so he repeated it in English. 'I knew. I just want to be certain so I look at the letters.'

All the moisture dried from her throat. 'You looked—?' she croaked.

He took an eager step. 'I understand. You search for *passaporto Italiano*. I will sign the forms so you get.'

She blinked at him. 'You'll help me get an Italian passport?' she clarified.

'*Sí.* I know you want. I help you.' He made an extravagant, arms-wide gesture as he returned to Italian. 'You have a thousand euros? I know you have the money.'

'A thousand euros?' It was as if her lungs had filled with sand. It wasn't that she didn't comprehend the words but she was robbed of speech that he'd said not a single thing on a human, personal or emotional level. He was talking *business*. He was speaking to *his daughter* but all he saw was a euro sign. Nausea rolled and sweat popped on her forehead. She stared at him with revulsion, this grubby man, this reluctant sperm donor, *this little shit*. She recalled her pleased surprise when he'd rocked up to help at Bella Vista. Had it all been an act? An opportunity to look good in Zia's eyes before he made his move? 'How—' she licked her lips. 'How do you know who I am? And about the letters?' There were only three people in Italy who knew her story and two of them were currently in Perugia.

'Your man,' he said simply. 'Your man told me. I have a wife and children and he said—'

Zia's blood turned to ice and the pain that lanced through her was worse than anything she'd ever known. 'You bastard,' she interrupted bitterly. 'You're not a father. You're a disgrace. You never wanted me. You didn't help Tori when she was ill and desperate. And now you want me to pay you to acknowledge your paternity?' In English she added, 'Piss off.'

His face sagged into lines of ludicrous dismay. 'But Zia . . .' He halted.

Trembling with rage and sick with disappointment, she locked the apartment, uncaring that Gerardo was still staring stupidly. Then she halted.

Fiorella was no longer in her chair at the other end of the terrace. She was gazing from Zia to Gerardo with wide, thunderstruck eyes. Zia was ashamed to realise she'd forgotten the older woman was nearby. Unable to remember what was said in Italian and what in English and gauge how much Fiorella might have understood, she stalked across the terrace leaving Gerardo and Fiorella standing as if turned to stone. Ignoring the scratch of scrub on her bare ankles she crossed the drive and stormed through the gap in the cypress trees towards Il Rifugio.

Your man told me.

I'll help if you need it. I'll do whatever it takes.

Fury boiled inside her. If she'd known that he'd meant *Piero* would decide if she needed help and, behind her back, inform Gerardo who she was and even about Vicky's poignant collection of letters, she would have made it clear how unacceptable that would be. How dare he? How *dare* he? In feeling entitled to assume control he'd forced her to confront exactly how shitty her father was.

Half-blinded by tears, she followed the noise of Piero's woodworking machines. Inside the door to his workshop, she halted. He was shirtless, a sheen of sweat on his skin despite the open doors.

He must have caught sight of her because he completed passing a piece of timber through the machine and turned it off, its roar diminishing to a moan. 'I'm glad to see you. Papà and Emiliano—' He broke off. Then frowned. 'What's the matter?' He reached her in five strides. 'Not Lucia?'

She shook her head. 'How could you?' Her voice was so broken it hurt her throat. 'How could you tell Gerardo I had money and I wanted him to get me an Italian passport? Now he's put the two things together and asked for a fee.'

'*What?*' His eyebrows clanged down to meet the bridge of his nose.

'It was up to me,' she cried, clenching her fists in helpless fury. 'It was my decision when, or even if, I talked to him. How do you think I felt when my own father asked me for money to sign a form or two? Didn't you care, so long as you got what you wanted?'

Piero's dark eyes looked almost black but his skin paled. He took a step back. 'How do you know I talked to Gerardo?'

'He *told* me!' she snapped. 'Shame you didn't anticipate him demanding a fistful of euros or you could have bought his silence in advance. I would never have needed to know that greed's the only emotion I arouse in my father.' Her lip trembled. 'And that you would go behind my back.'

Silence. Piero took a step away, flipping his T-shirt from a hook on the wall and pulling it on as if he needed the layer of cotton between them.

His refusal to defend himself added oxygen to her fire. 'I know you want me to make my home here but this is my business, not yours.'

The gaze he turned on her was like a stranger's. 'I don't even know if I'll have a home here myself,' he put in without emotion. 'The others have just been up to ask me to accept the Binotto deal if there has been no interest in the vineyard in three months. Three months!'

Zia did hear his words. She did see his dejection. But the last few months of discovering everyone she loved had lied to her all her life had coalesced into a rage that stripped her of rational thought. She bundled away his anxiety as if consigning a troublesome dog into another room. 'Holy crap, haven't you seen the obvious *yet*?' She heard the contemptuous words as if someone else had said them.

His eyes narrowed, his voice suddenly as tight as hers. 'The obvious?'

'Leaseback!' she burst out. 'I've mentioned it in front of you till I'm blue in the face and you never got it. Approach an asset finance company for a leaseback deal on Tenuta Domenicali, for goodness' sake! You all get your dosh, Salvatore can retire, Emiliano can run the business and you can leave the company. Sorted. Il Rifugio doesn't even come into the equation.'

Fury wiped every other expression from his face. 'I must be slow,' he said with icy sarcasm. 'Not only did I not figure it out but I assumed you'd know I'd want to hear how to save my home and family relationships.'

His biting anger was so uncharacteristic that it brought Zia back to herself.

She licked her lips, trembling in the aftermath of her unaccustomed loss of control and, suddenly stricken, replaying in her head the way she'd been yelling at him. Shame trickled down her neck and she made her wavering voice calmer. 'When I butted in before, it went badly. I told myself not to interfere again. But twice I've asked if you'd want someone to tell you if there was another avenue to explore and you said "no".'

'OK, I was sick of the subject,' he ground out. 'But from a couple of fucking oblique hints, I'm supposed to figure out my lover's withholding vital information that could save my home?'

Zia flinched. Regret washed over her. 'You're right. I should have persisted. I could give you a contact—'

'Brendon?' he spat incredulously.

'I was thinking of Elise,' she replied evenly. 'But, on second thoughts, in case I ever end up working for her, I think you should identify the right company yourself.'

'Yeah, because I'm definitely on my own,' he snapped. Then his phone rang and he snatched it up from his workbench. After a steadying breath he began talking to someone about a garden arbour. When, instead of drawing the conversation to a speedy conclusion, he turned his back and asked after the caller's wife and family, Zia, heart like lead, took it as her invitation to leave.

Hollow and trampled, she dragged herself back to Bella Vista. She found Fiorella and Gerardo gone, meaning she had just over an hour to service two cottages. The Villino Il Pino guests had already arrived but she didn't have time to introduce herself and go through what they needed to know. She armed herself with linens and cleaning things and subsumed her misery in a whirlwind of work.

The guests arrived full of questions and she had to fake a smile as she responded with information about the supermarket and went off to research whether there was a synagogue in Montelibertà.

Intending to ask, but calmly this time, for an explanation as to why Piero had blabbed to Gerardo, she returned to Il Rifugio after a few hours . . . only to find the Alfa Romeo absent and house and workshop shut up. She sent him a text asking to talk. By the time she fell into bed that evening she felt as if someone had filled her veins with ice.

No answer from Piero.

It was odd to be alone in bed. Tonight, for the first time she'd locked the apartment door, probably a reaction to Gerardo calmly walking in and looking through her things. Sleepless, the hot darkness seemed to press on her and the only sound was the hum of cicadas outside. For the first time it annoyed rather than soothed her, getting inside her head, a constant creaking she couldn't switch off.

She checked her phone, the screen creating a brief oasis of light. Nothing from Piero. She settled back onto her pillows, her thoughts pulsing as incessantly as the cicadas.

Shame was a cold companion. She'd taken her hurt out on Piero without even acknowledging how much he must want her to stay to have gone behind her back. She should have listened to his explanation. Been calm and clear about why his high-handed piece of meddling had been worthy of Brendon at his worst. Sickening disappointment had been inevitable but furious accusations had not.

She rolled onto a cool place on the sheet as her mind slid to the confrontation with Gerardo.

I have a wife and children . . . 'Yes, I am aware,' she should have answered. 'The irony of you saying that to me, your eldest child, doesn't seem to have entered your avaricious little mind.' She'd have had to stop to look up the Italian for 'avaricious', though, so would probably have had to settle for 'greedy'.

Restlessly, she tossed and turned. She must be considerate of Lucia and make sure no antagonism prevented her from picking up the reins of her family life once she was well. Six weeks from today Zia had to leave Italy anyway.

She wasn't even sure if that was such a bad thing now.

Chapter Twenty-Two

Emotional roller coasters had no safety restraints and Piero had been thrown around on one since Zia had stormed into his workshop that morning, paralysing him with her accusations then casually tossing him a get-out-of-jail card called 'leaseback'.

Or maybe that should be a 'stay-in-your-home' card.

Too wounded to decide what to do about her wrath he grabbed his laptop and drove to Emiliano's lovely house. 'We need to talk,' he said, entering without waiting for an invitation when Emiliano answered his knock.

'Yeah, come in,' Emiliano said ironically, closing the heavy wooden door in Piero's wake. But when he heard the highlights of Zia's disclosure – Piero didn't feel like pressing on his bruises by confiding the accusation part – he beamed. 'This has huge potential! Why hasn't our agent suggested it?'

'Because there would be nothing in it for him?' Piero hazarded.

Jemma, grasping the importance of Piero's errand, took Camilla and Cristian to play with their cousins and the

302

brothers settled into researching leaseback – or sale-and-leaseback, as they soon discovered was the full title. 'I want to know everything there is to know before we talk to Papà,' Piero said grimly.

Emiliano had fetched cold beers and the American cookies he baked to relax. He fired up his laptop and placed it opposite Piero's on the table. 'Graziella can't know about leaseback either or she would have suggested it by now.'

Piero nodded. 'How about you research asset finance companies and I'll look for downsides and test cases?' He began an internet search and the brothers worked in companionable silence.

When Jemma returned home with the children Piero and Emiliano broke off long enough to eat pizza and join the conversation. Cristian and Camilla had gone up to bed and Jemma was relaxing in front of the TV before Piero sat back from his laptop, screen-fatigue stinging his eyes. 'I believe leaseback's a prospect for Tenuta Domenicali,' he pronounced.

Emiliano nodded. 'All the downsides I've read about are from the other side of the fence to us. People who invested in a property and then the tenant left, went bust or there was some messy legal wrangle. I think it comes down to the quality of any prospective deal.'

Anticipation prickled like a ball of thistles in Piero's stomach. 'So we talk to Papà? He'll be in the office on Monday morning.'

Emiliano beamed. 'Freaking right. This could be the answer to our prayers. I wonder why Zia didn't say something earlier? It could have saved a lot of aggravation.'

Piero nodded, closing his laptop with a snap. 'Good question.'

Though he drove home exhausted he didn't sleep well. He'd grown used to Zia's lush nakedness against him and the movements she made in her sleep. He left his shutters open so he could see the stars but could find none of his usual pleasure in them.

How could Zia think he was capable of pulling the sneaky stroke she described? How could she? Why would she? How dare she? He got that her ex had tried to be controlling – he never understood the 'women are property' thing himself – but that was her ex. Piero had done nothing to deserve that. The heavy, disillusioned thuds of his heart seemed to fill the room.

On Sunday morning, stale and out of sorts, he buried himself in his workshop. The fresh, resinous scent of wood filled his nostrils as he turned a finial for the play house roof on the lathe. At lunchtime he ate with little appetite, gazing out at the glorious view of the vineyard that had caused all the problems. Not feeling as excited as he should about preserving that view for himself, he spent the afternoon preparing a presentation on the sale-and-leaseback of Tenuta Domenicali. Furious as he was at Zia questioning his integrity she had – eventually – pointed out a potential solution.

In fact, his opening words when he began his presentation on Monday morning were, 'This may be the solution we've been looking for.'

Emiliano was almost bouncing in his seat. 'I think so, too.'

Salvatore looked interested. Graziella looked indifferent.

An hour later, Piero felt optimistic. Salvatore had become more and more engaged, firing questions without voicing a single negative. Emiliano was already talking about recruiting to fill Piero's and Salvatore's shoes if sale-and-leaseback could be achieved.

Piero laid down the pen he'd used for pointing at his screen. 'It seems a gateway to us all getting what we want.' He didn't add *including Graziella getting her life of luxury via Papà* but he thought it.

It was a surprise to realise she was wearing a stony expression. 'I still vote for the Binotto deal,' she said simply.

Piero glared at her perfectly made-up face. 'It's good to know how you'd cast your vote if you had one.'

Something flashed in her eyes, making Piero pause before he replied. Had that been . . . fear?

'Papà?' he said, still eyeing Graziella with the uncomfortable feeling he was missing something crucial.

Salvatore was also staring Graziella's way, a half-frown on his face. 'Of course, we must explore this option.'

Graziella's knuckles turned white.

Now Emiliano's gaze was on her, too. 'I think we should approach asset finance companies directly. We don't seem to be having much luck with agents.'

Graziella cast her gaze down. Piero looked from her to his father.

Salvatore wore a perplexed frown but said, 'Great work, Piero.' He rose, a signal that the meeting was over and, after a pause, Graziella followed suit.

Piero watched Salvatore take her hand as they left the office, smiling but with an enquiring lift of his brow. Then they passed from Piero's view.

How odd. But Piero shrugged the apparent anomaly off and got on with his day's work.

It was well into the afternoon when Salvatore re-appeared. He had Emiliano with him. The latter was wearing the black frown he usually reserved for interruptions when he was blending wine. The morning's good humour had vanished from Salvatore's face, too. He shut

305

the door and seated himself stiffly. Emiliano propped a shoulder against the wall.

'Alberto Gubbiotti has just called me,' Salvatore said heavily.

Piero's heart plummeted at the sound of the name of the man he'd come to think of as his nemesis. 'Oh?'

Salvatore rubbed his hand over his mouth, rasping his moustache. 'He offered me more money for my share if I committed to his deal now. Right now.'

Silence.

Piero's pulse kicked up. He prayed his father hadn't decided this was one of the opportunities in his life that needed grabbing. 'Like a . . . a sweetener because you're the major shareholder and he thinks you can force his deal through?'

Salvatore inclined his head, the grooves around his mouth making his expression grim. 'There are uglier words but "sweetener" will do.' His eyes flicked between his sons.

Piero swallowed. 'What did you tell him?' Despite the air conditioning, sweat prickled between his shoulder blades.

'That I needed time to think.' Salvatore sucked air in then puffed it out as if he'd suddenly developed asthma. 'He urged me to act. Said the offer wouldn't remain on the table for long.'

Piero murmured, 'Hardball.'

Emiliano muttered unhappily, 'This feels off.'

Outside, the tractor clattered across the yard.

Only one explanation suggested itself to Piero. It would open a can of worms but he was prepared to act as tin opener if it might save his home. 'It's exactly as if Gubbiotti knows we're exploring another solution and is acting to head it off.'

A great, exaggerated *oh, I get it . . .!* look shot Emiliano's eyebrows up to his hairline.

Slowly, Salvatore nodded. 'I think so too.' A tiny bead of moisture formed at the corner of his eye. 'Someone has passed information to Gubbiotti. Gubbiotti, and possibly the "someone", sees me as the one most easily influenced.' A flush of rage suffused his face. 'Me!' he barked, making Piero and Emiliano jump. Then quietly, brokenly, 'They think I'm a stupid old man to be manipulated.' The moisture formed into a tear and followed a wrinkle down his cheek.

'I'll get you a drink.' Piero dropped a comforting hand on his father's shoulder as he passed, feeling the bones and sinews that might be aged but were still strong. He hurried to the water cooler, thoughts flying, hopes rising – so long as Salvatore's anger proved not to herald a false dawn.

On his return, Salvatore sipped the water, frowning unseeingly at Piero's desk until the beaker was half-empty. Then he raised a hand and Piero thought he meant to dash it against the wall . . .

But he paused.

His gaze became fixed, almost as if seeing something Piero and Emiliano couldn't. Then slowly, slowly, he let his arm drop. And groaned.

'Papà?' Piero had retaken his seat but now he half-started up again.

Salvatore covered his face with his sinewy, age-spotted hands. 'I can't hide it any more. There's a reason we can't go ahead with Piero's leaseback idea.'

'What?' Piero couldn't stifle the cry of dismay, though he could see there was something badly amiss with his father.

307

Salvatore shook his head violently as if throwing off something vile. 'I have been keeping something from you. Bad news about my health.'

'*Merda*,' Emiliano breathed. He slipped slowly into a chair and stared at his father, eyes enormous.

Salvatore continued in the same weighty, sorrowful manner. 'I'm losing the use of my left arm. The doctors tell me I have a condition that affects the brain. My body will gradually break down, my muscles spasm. There will be problems with recognition and with speech.' He groaned. 'It's an unpleasant condition. But at least I have Graziella to care for me. She'll nurse me. And—' he drew in a deep breath '—I'll have several years before I die.'

Piero gasped a shocked, 'Papà!' He felt as if someone had reached in a giant hand and given his world a spin.

Salvatore reached out and grasped his sons' arms. 'I've been trying to pretend it isn't happening but it's time to face facts. We should take Tenuta Domenicali off the market. If I die as a deal is going through it will cause you horrible complications. Wait until . . . I'm not here.' His face worked and he swallowed hard. 'When you inherit my part of the property, you'll own half each and can choose the right deal then.'

Piero thought he was going to throw up. The warm hand clasping his forearm was the one that had looked after him all his life, guided him on his first bike, taught him to fish. It felt as strong and vital as it always had. Surely his father couldn't have received this sentence of death? Yet, here he was, right in front of them, sounding hoarse and unlike himself as he broke the news.

Then the office door flew open and Graziella stood on the threshold, her complexion waxy, eyes bulging in horror.

Maybe she does love him, Piero had time to think as he absorbed the shock stamped on her every feature.

But her next words dispelled that pleasant myth. 'What? You're leaving everything to them but I'm to *nurse* you?' she cried. 'Be your *carer*? While they inherit *everything*?'

Salvatore looked surprised. 'Graziella . . . I'm sorry. I didn't know you were nearby. I had meant to break this to you much more softly, *cara*.' He heaved another of those long, sorrowful sighs. 'At least we can afford medical people to help you. I know it's not easy to care for a terminal patient—'

A harsh laugh tore itself from Graziella's lips. 'I'm not nursing anyone. Especially if there's no—' She halted.

Silence.

'Nothing in it for you?' Salvatore suggested quietly. Then he rose, straight and tall, with little sign of the regretful old man of seconds before. 'Emiliano. Piero,' he said. 'I apologise for frightening you. I'm not ill, except maybe a little heartsick. And now I need to speak to Graziella.'

'What?' Graziella's curls flew as she gazed wildly between the three men.

'What?' echoed Piero and Emiliano. 'You're not sick?'

Salvatore was already bearing her inexorably out of the door. 'Only of being lied to. Come, Graziella.'

As the sounds of their departure echoed down the corridor Piero and Emiliano were left staring at each other in shock.

Piero swallowed. 'The old bastard. He must have heard her out there or caught sight of her. He nearly gave me a fucking heart attack. I hate it when he goes his own way and leaves the rest of us to follow if we can.'

Emiliano, looking equally dumbfounded, fetched a

309

bottle of Orvieto Classico and two glasses from his office and poured them each a measure. 'Holy shit.' For once he swigged his cherished wine like a teenager drinking supermarket plonk. 'He did say it was a trap for her, didn't he? He's not really ill?' His eyes appealed to Piero.

Piero emptied his glass, wiping sweat from his forehead. 'He said he wasn't. He's a hammy actor but, hell. He had me going.'

Emiliano topped up their glasses. 'The old fox.'

After a couple of glasses of wine, they switched to coffee, waiting until, what seemed like hours later, Salvatore reappeared, face grey and fatigued. They jumped up and he slid his arms around them both exactly as if they were still little boys. 'I'm sorry, that was a crappy thing to do to you. I'm sorry to put you through it,' he said hoarsely. 'But I caught a glimpse of her hovering out there through the crack in the door and seized the opportunity to let her show her true colours.' He cleared his throat. 'She's packing.'

Relief melting his muscles, Piero still demanded reassurance. 'And you're not ill?'

Salvatore gave them a last squeeze before releasing them and lowering himself into a chair. 'No. I made up every word.' He let his head fall back and closed his eyes. 'I had to shock the truth out of her. She was going to get a big finder's fee from Binotto's.' Salvatore's voice was thick with disgust. 'Greedy bitch. When she realised my "illness" would mean I wouldn't sell the vineyard and she wouldn't inherit a share either . . .' He hesitated, seeming not quite able to meet their eyes. 'It was her ex-husband who had all the money when they got together, yet she managed to walk from the divorce court with half the proceeds of three hotels. I should have remembered that.'

Emiliano made an inarticulate noise of rage.

Piero snapped, 'Shouldn't you be calling the police? She deserves to be punished.'

Salvatore pulled an apologetic face. 'I'm not sure that taking an old man for a ride is a crime. It was a clumsy attempt, now I look at it.' He gave a bitter laugh, the noise perilously close to a sob in the still air of the office. 'I thought she made me happy. But it was expedient for her to make me believe a younger, glamorous woman loved me. I'm sorry.' He put his hand over Piero's. 'I was a bad father. I let her persuade me that you losing your home was an acceptable sacrifice.'

'No,' Piero protested and leaped up to slide his arms around his hurting father. 'You're a good father. We all let ourselves be blinded by a woman, sooner or later.' He seemed pretty good at it himself. First Nicoletta and then Zia.

Salvatore patted his shoulders. 'Thank you.' Gently, he freed himself. 'I'd better go and make sure she's not stealing the family silver.'

Piero and Emiliano were left gazing at each other again, silenced by their father's pain.

But Piero was conscious of relief, too. Graziella and her manipulations were leaving. Il Rifugio was feeling safer by the moment.

Chapter Twenty-Three

Lucia returned home on Wednesday just as all Bella Vista shimmered a welcome in the afternoon heat haze.

At the first sight of Durante's car Zia raced across the terrace to hold the door open while Durante helped his wife from the vehicle. Throat clogging to see Lucia still looking pallid and drawn, stooping protectively over her abdomen as if worried something would fall out, all Zia could offer was a beaming smile and welling eyes.

'*Ciao*, Zia-Lucia,' Lucia whispered. Her smile was pained but at least it was there. 'I felt every bump in the road. And there are many.'

'You do look as if you need to rest,' Zia said sympathetically. She and Durante took an arm each to help her up the terrace steps and then indoors to a sofa. When she laid herself down with exaggeratedly ginger movements and closed her eyes, Zia kissed her forehead and melted away.

Zia was hovering on the terrace when Durante reappeared and pulled her into a hug. He said, 'She will improve but it will take time, the doctor said. She is back to sleep.'

'You're shattered too,' she choked. 'Are you hungry?'

'I could eat,' he answered vaguely.

She gave him a squeeze. 'You've lost weight. Why don't I make you some quick pasta? We'll eat together then you can flake out.'

He hesitated. 'Do you mind if I eat beside her? I feel as if I must watch. There are no doctors now.'

Zia could understand anxiety after such a grave illness. 'Of course.' She rustled up pasta with pine nuts and tomatoes and had to wake Durante, already settled on a chair and footstool in the salon.

'*Mi dispiace*,' he apologised, scrubbing his face in an obvious effort to wake himself before taking the fork and plate.

Zia left the couple alone, thinking wistfully of previous meals on the terrace with Lucia and Durante and Piero dropping by . . . something he'd conspicuously omitted to do for the four days since their confrontation. Visions of his clean-cut face, blank with astonishment, presumably that Gerardo had spilled the beans, then grim with fury, spoiled her lunch. Afterwards, to turn her mind to things other than her tantrum she went into the office and reminded herself of the next guest changeover.

Tomorrow, Thursday, Villino Il Pino's current guests would leave. The new lot wouldn't arrive until Friday, giving Zia plenty of time to service Pino. She made a supermarket shopping list then drifted outside again seeing, through the salon window, that both Lucia and Durante appeared to be sleeping. Lonely and suffering from a feeling of anticlimax she went into her apartment, switched on the air conditioning unit she'd bought for the bedroom and tried to get Ursula on her lunch break. She made it an ordinary phone call as the parlour premises had a 'no video calls' rule in case a door opened and the caller got a flash of naked body parts being inked.

'Hey, you!' Ursula sounded both happy to hear from her and keen to know all about Lucia's homecoming.

Zia felt soothed just to hear her best friend's voice. 'Poor Lucia looks ragged after her surgery and Durante's hovering over her. They've both gone to sleep, bless them. I'll go to the supermarket in a minute while they nap.'

Ursula made a sympathetic noise then asked casually, 'No Piero to welcome Lucia back?'

'Busy, I expect,' Zia said vaguely. Inwardly, she sighed as she realised she'd instinctively avoided confiding in Ursula about the shittiness of Gerardo after Piero's high-handed interference and Zia steaming over to fling it in his face. Bloody Stephan bleating to bloody Brendon had affected what she could say to her bestie. Instead, she directed the rest of the conversation to Ursula's life in Brighton.

On Thursday Zia awoke early, a ball of apprehension that Fiorella was due to come to work, the first time they'd see each other since the scene with Gerardo. Was the secret Gerardo had kept so long finally out? Had Fiorella, who Zia was becoming fond of, fished enough from the shouting match conducted in a muddle of English and Italian? If so, what happened now?

Was she emotionally resilient enough to deal with it if Fiorella and Roberto were cold or dismissive? On top of worrying over Lucia and losing Piero, she wasn't sure.

As her apartment's door was standing open, she heard Fiorella arrive shortly before 10 a.m. and the jangling of

Zia's nerves was only heightened when she heard Roberto's voice too, asking Durante if Lucia was up to visitors. Durante replied that Lucia was sore and easily tired. Roberto agreed to keep the visit short. Their voices faded and Zia heard a door shut.

Silence, but for the whisper of the breeze and the buzz of insects.

She let out a breath she hadn't realised she'd been holding.

As the Brits who'd stayed in Villino Il Pino had already begun their trek north she decided to shoot off to begin on the cleaning while Fiorella was indoors with Lucia. Squaring her shoulders, she smoothed her hands down her shorts to dry her palms and stepped out onto the terrace.

Fiorella was sitting outside, her gaze trained on Zia's door.

Zia halted, heart banging like the bass in a metal band. Slowly, Fiorella rose, smoothing her palms down her flowered dress in an echo of Zia's own gesture a moment before. 'Gerardo told me,' she said simply.

Zia nodded. If Fiorella was about to say she wanted to sweep their relationship under the carpet she'd probably break down and cry. Zia wasn't what Pap would have termed 'a leaky female', weeping and wailing her way through life, but tears were already blocking her throat. She knew her grandmother now, had worked alongside her in Lucia's absence. She'd tuned into Fiorella's rapid Italian muffled by her missing tooth and devoured news of her unknown family, smiling over the remarriage of an aunt and the exam results of a younger cousin. She swallowed. 'I only discovered who my father was five months ago.'

'Ay, ay, ay,' said Fiorella. A tear brimmed from her eye. 'You are my granddaughter.' She made a small, uncertain movement of her arms.

Zia took a step, then another. Her grandmother's arms reached out and she closed her eyes as they closed gently about her.

'Zia-Lucia,' Fiorella whispered. 'With a good heart you helped Durante and Lucia. Roberto and I liked you for it. We never dreamed who you were.'

The hot tears trickled down Zia's cheeks as, for the first time in years, she knew what it was to be hugged by a grandparent. She just couldn't let go. Fiorella sniffled, patting Zia's back. Ten, maybe twenty seconds passed before another, larger body loomed beside them. Zia wiped her eyes and turned to find Roberto hovering. He drew her gently from Fiorella's arms and kissed both her cheeks.

'We wanted to come straight away when Gerardo told us,' he murmured. 'But we decided to wait, as we knew my sister and Durante would soon be home. Our English . . .' He gave a rusty laugh. 'We wanted someone nearby to translate if needed.'

Zia wiped her cheeks with the backs of her hands, laughing too. 'I might have managed. My Italian has improved while I've been here.'

Fiorella gave her high-pitched laugh between the tears. 'I told you. She nearly always understands me now.'

Durante emerged from the house where he must have been awaiting the right moment, beaming, kissing Zia's cheeks. 'Let's talk together. Between us, we have the whole story.'

The conversation lasted for the rest of the morning and right through lunch, though Durante carried his upstairs to eat with Lucia in their bedroom. Working along the timeline as best she could, Zia put together everything she'd learned of her history.

As they listened, Fiorella and Roberto shook their heads or winced and exchanged pained looks. 'Perhaps we were too strict,' Fiorella sighed. 'Too unbending. Gerardo was inclined to want the liberty of adulthood without the responsibilities. We were frightened of him getting in, in . . . a *situation*.'

'A situation like making his girlfriend pregnant?' Zia asked drily.

Fiorella looked troubled. 'It was not so common then. Not always accepted.'

Roberto cleared his throat. 'And if he'd fallen in love with his English girlfriend and left to live in England we didn't know how we would have been able to see him. We had little money. He had little money.'

Zia smiled, though she couldn't smother a sigh. 'You didn't have to worry about Gerardo falling in love with Tori, apparently.' She went on to tell them what she knew of Tori's death and later Vicky's. Fiorella's eyes brimmed more than once. 'You don't hate us?' she asked Zia hoarsely.

Emphatically, Zia shook her head. 'Of course not. But you can see why I didn't tell you who I was. I had no idea how your family would greet me or if I'd cause trouble between Gerardo and his wife and kids.'

Roberto and Fiorella sighed in unison. Roberto lifted his hands. 'It's possible. You understand,' he added, 'that it's up to Gerardo if he confesses to them?'

Zia grimaced. 'I don't think we need worry about that either. He won't.'

They talked for a little longer and then, after Zia had shyly exchanged kisses with her grandparents, Roberto took Fiorella home. Fiorella hadn't helped out today but she looked exhausted and Zia didn't mention work. There was only one cottage to service and she was well able to whizz through it by herself.

She set to stripping Villino Il Pino's beds feeling as though she was in a dream, the knowledge that Fiorella and Roberta were *glad* to discover another granddaughter gradually sinking in as if her heart were a sponge expanding to soak up the joy.

Once the cottage was clean and redolent with the scent of fresh linens, she wiped her eyes one last time then carted the laundry bag of last week's sheets up to the house, moving slowly in the August heat. As she rounded the olive grove, she saw Durante on the dusty drive, talking to a taller man.

Piero, his mouth set, brows knit in a frown.

Both men glanced up at the sound of her footsteps on the gravel. Durante lifted a hand and beamed and she could do little but wave back. Piero lifted a hand also. Perfunctory. No smile. Sunglasses hiding his eyes.

Pulse hurrying, Zia headed for the laundry room behind the kitchen feeling ashamed all over again that she'd hit Piero with that unacceptable burst of temper on Saturday. Hands clammy, she took her time stuffing the white cotton sheets into the washing machine, telling herself it was best he knew she wouldn't be manipulated. *Damn* him for trying, just as Brendon used to; it was an unacceptable fault.

Once outside again she found Lucia and Durante in the shade of the terrace on loungers, Lucia looking several degrees brighter than the day before. Zia had played down her dust-up with Gerardo to the couple, not wanting them to worry, and hadn't mentioned the money aspect at all.

318

They probably knew Gerardo would do that but she didn't want them to know Piero would. Stupid to protect him when he'd let her down so badly.

Wiping the thoughts from her mind so they wouldn't show on her face Zia dropped a kiss on Lucia's head. 'I'm glad to see you out of bed.'

The older woman grimaced and managed a breath of a laugh, though it made her put a protective hand to her abdomen. 'I came out to see Piero and have stayed for some fresh air.'

'Has Piero gone?' Zia asked casually. She'd lingered in the laundry in that very hope.

Lucia nodded. 'He's busy. He says Graziella has left Tenuta Domenicali.'

Zia glanced at her in surprise. 'Oh? Permanently?'

Durante nodded. 'She's been working hand-in-glove with Binotto's so Salvatore has bid her goodbye. And they think they've found a solution without that deal. He didn't go into detail but he hopes to keep Il Rifugio.'

Zia said, 'That's fantastic. Big shock about Graziella, though.' She wondered if the 'solution' was the one she'd hurled at Piero in rage and scorn. Despite everything, she was glad to know things were looking better for him. When she was back in Brighton's seaside grandeur and English autumn had taken the place of sultry Italian summer, she would take comfort from knowing he was secure in his beloved home above the valley. Il Rifugio – the escape.

Friday, Saturday and Sunday passed quietly. Lucia's phone remained in Zia's pocket so she could continue to be the one to deal with guests. Lucia, even under the anxious and watchful eye of her husband, had a wobble when her temperature shot up. Durante called the doctor and he

319

and Zia waited, chilled by new dread. Fresh antibiotics soon returned Lucia to the slow road of recovery but Durante was almost as exhausted as her and asked the family to resist visiting. The exception was Fiorella, who came to help with Saturday's guest change.

Secretly, Zia acknowledged relief. She didn't want her last few weeks at Bella Vista to be a boiling pot of angst as she came up against relatives who may or may not know who she was . . . and may or may not want to.

Life at Bella Vista was quiet. Sister Paola and Sister Priscilla brought a basket of peaches from the monastery but left them with Zia when she explained Lucia's need for rest. 'She is in our prayers,' Sister Priscilla said with a smile, then they rumbled off in their little car.

Piero called again on Saturday and had a word with Durante. Zia caught sight of his rear view disappearing in the direction of Il Rifugio. A bundle of emotions fell on her – grief, disappointment, regret . . . But she didn't call after him.

On Monday afternoon she was enjoying the coolness of the office when she heard a car crunch to a standstill on Bella Vista's drive. As she heard Durante attend the front door she ignored it, continuing with her check of future bookings, which were solid until well after October half-term. She nibbled her lip. She'd better suggest Durante get someone else lined up to help Fiorella service the cottages after Zia's mid-September leaving date. He and Lucia weren't going to be up to it for a while. As she could still hear his voice outside she noted it on her list of things to discuss with him.

Several minutes later, Durante appeared at the office door. Zia began to smile a greeting but felt it slip as she caught his troubled expression. 'Is everything OK?'

Durante's gaze was circumspect. 'Gerardo is asking to speak to you.'

Zia's stomach gave a great lurch. Gerardo must be the caller Durante had been speaking to. 'Oh. Do you know why?'

'To apologise, he says.' Durante gave an awkward shrug, as if feeling caught in the middle.

'Oh.' She fidgeted. Somehow, she hadn't anticipated this. Gerardo had been so blatant in his attempt to extract money that she'd assumed him not to be troubled by a conscience. Mentally, she'd written him off, certain he'd got the message not to approach her. For Durante's sake she'd hoped he'd continue in the garden for a while but Bella Vista's grounds were large enough that she could avoid him. Now Durante was hovering, eyes large and worried, as if wary that she might explode. She sighed. She'd done enough exploding. 'It'll be easier for everyone if we clear the air, I suppose.'

'Shall I get him?' At Zia's nod, Durante turned and vanished and Zia rose, feeling she needed to give the impression of meeting Gerardo head-on.

Then there he was, framed by the doorway, sober and spruced up. He looked her in the eye and cleared his throat. 'I am sorry,' he said in English.

'What for?' She had no intention of making things easy.

'Everything,' he answered, then switched to Italian. 'I'm sorry I wasn't good to your mother. Sorry I asked you for the money. It was wrong to consider it.' He drew in a long breath. 'I'll sign the forms to agree you are my daughter.' He hesitated, then added soberly, '*Non so perché a volte mi comporto male.' I don't know why I sometimes behave badly.*

Zia shrugged. 'Alcohol?'

He dropped his gaze. 'Maybe.'

Just for a moment she thought wistfully how great it would have been to have a dad who was a wonderful, positive presence, as some lucky people had. The nearest for her had been Alf, a kind and loving man but divided from Zia by generations. It was as well to face facts, though. The man who'd provided fifty per cent of her DNA was weak and self-orientated. Her instinct was not to rely on him in any way. She said, 'Let's go back to pretending you don't know who I am.'

Gerardo, looking surprised and maybe relieved, mumbled, 'OK.' In moments, Zia heard the front door snick closed behind him.

Durante popped his head into the office and raised enquiring eyebrows. She gave him a smile as she sank back into her chair. 'We're not going to have anything to do with one another. I don't know how to feel.'

His old smile flickered, replacing the careworn frown he'd worn since Lucia had fallen ill. 'Your feelings will settle, no? You want ice coffee?'

She smiled at his gesture to make her feel better. 'Absolutely! Let's make it with hazelnut milk for a treat.'

The three of them – her, Lucia and Durante – settled in the shade outside to enjoy the cooling drink. Zia talked over Gerardo's unexpected appearance with the kindly couple she was finally letting herself think of as her great-aunt and uncle.

Lucia, plainly wishing Zia could see Gerardo a little more as they did, offered tentatively, 'He has a tendency to take the easy way out of situations and is capable of selfishness . . . but also of kindness to those he loves. He doesn't always think how getting what he wants will affect others. If he told you he's sorry then he is. He's realised he was wrong.'

In the privacy of her mind Zia added, *or someone has persuaded him to apologise to make me feel better.* It could have been Fiorella or Roberto.

Or Piero had been at work again, maybe trying to make amends. For several days a need had been growing in Zia to end the horrible cold silence between them. This could be a good excuse. The damage was done between them but if she extended an olive branch – she had a whimsical vision of snapping one from the olive grove as she passed – it would make his proximity more bearable. After dinner that evening, without questioning herself too closely on why she'd showered and put on her red-flowered dress, she picked her way slowly through the trees towards Il Rifugio.

Fireflies flickered like defective fairy lights. The rose-mary-scented evening was windless after another blazing August day. Nearing the house she caught the familiar undulating wail of woodworking machinery. Though her heart faltered she continued across the paving towards the workshop beyond the house, moss springy beneath her flip-flops. Little was visible down the valley but lights from Tenuta Domenicali and a darker dusk where the mountains awaited dawn to once again reveal their majesty.

The workshop doors were rolled back and she stepped hesitantly into the light, pulse racing. Piero, wearing his protective gear of red ear protectors and a white dust mask was guiding timber through the planer, a fountain of sawdust being caught in mid-air by the extractor. *Neeeeee-oowwww.* His torso flexed as he leaned into his task. *Neeeeee-oowwww.* He turned to add the machined piece to a stack and froze as he caught sight of her. For several seconds he stared. Then he pressed a switch and the machine rumbled into silence. He pulled off the mask and hung the ear protectors around his neck. 'Anything wrong?'

A couple of steps further into the room and then she halted again. 'Lucia's OK, if that's what you're asking.' She watched his shoulders relax a notch. 'I came to tell you something.'

He waited. The mask had left tracks in the stubble either side of his mouth.

She licked suddenly dry lips. 'Gerardo has repeated his offer to acknowledge paternity to the authorities but this time with no fee attached.'

He made no reply.

'So,' she went on doggedly, aware he was making this hard work. 'I thought you ought to know he's done it. Thank you if you put him up to it but I won't be taking him up on his offer. I don't want to owe him a favour. Sooner or later, he might try to call it in.'

Still Piero said nothing.

She stepped close enough to catch the smell of his skin. 'I'm sorry I was so unreasonably angry. I've come to hate men trying to control me and I viewed your attempt to help in that light. I overreacted.' She ground to a halt.

After a few seconds he gave a nod. 'OK. Excuse me. I have a schedule. I wish you happiness, Zia,' he added. Then he restored mask and ear protectors to their proper places and switched the machine back on.

Stung, she wheeled about and strode back to Bella Vista, using her phone as a torch as darkness threw down its cloak. Her cheeks burned. Why the hell was Piero behaving as if he had the moral high ground? It had been like talking to the wood he'd been working. Was he one of those people who reacted to being in the wrong by shutting down their emotions? Yet she remembered all the times she'd read his feelings in his eyes, in bed together, laughing over a meal.

It felt as if he were bitter. Resentful. Accused of something he hadn't done.

She halted as if the thought was a giant hand blocking her progress but Gerardo had plainly said *your man . . .*

But when had Gerardo proved himself so reliable?

Knees trembling, she hurried to her apartment on the end of the house and searched the contacts on Lucia's phone, which was still in her custody. She shared the *Gerardo Costa* contact to her own phone, picked it up and, not giving herself time to chicken out, pressed *call*.

He answered cautiously. '*Pronto.*' There were a lot of voices in the background. It sounded like a bar.

'This is Zia. Can I talk to you again?' About to suggest tomorrow, she hesitated. If he'd had a couple of beers, he'd be less guarded. 'Are you in town? I'll pop down.'

'OK.' He sounded sluggish and surprised. He told her the name of the bar, Antiche Mura, which translated to 'Old Walls'.

Antiche Mura wasn't in the centre of town, she found when she googled it, but was more of a neighbourhood place. She picked up her car keys and followed her sat nav to the given address in Corso Mescolini and pulled up outside a tavern of aged, uneven stone. She locked the car, and, holding onto her keys and phone, thrust her hands in her pockets. Judging by the scene of dilapidated houses and beaten-up cars the neighbourhood wasn't a great one.

At one of the tables scattered on the broad pavement

she saw Gerardo lounging amidst a group of men, beer bottle in one hand and cigarette in the other. He caught sight of her as she crossed the ill-lit dusty street and waved the bottle, which looked empty. 'You can buy a drink inside,' he called genially.

She wondered if he was hoping she'd buy him one while she was at it. 'I've brought no money,' she said truthfully, halting on the pavement several yards short of him. 'I just want to talk to you.'

All his table-mates were men of a similar age and appearance to Gerardo. They turned to gaze at her but he made no introductions, just pulled himself to his feet and joined her, leaving the bottle on the table but bringing the cigarette.

Zia maintained a small smile and spoke in Italian, deliberately making herself non-threatening so she could feel her way towards the information she wanted. 'I'm guessing Piero gave you money so that you'd make that offer to help me with the authorities today. As I'm not going to take you up on it, I'm afraid you'll need to give it back to him.'

He narrowed his eyes over a contemplative drag on the cigarette. 'Nobody gave me money.' He blew the smoke out again then flashed a boyish smile, giving Zia a hint at what Tori might have once seen in him. 'My parents talked to me.'

'Your parents suggested you help me without asking for money?' she clarified. A chill trickled down her spine.

'Yes.' Looking hurt that she had to be quite that blunt, he cast a longing look back to his table full of buddies and a fresh round of drinks that had appeared in his absence.

She went on quickly in an attempt to keep his attention

for a few more seconds. 'But it was Piero who suggested you ask me for money originally. Yes?'

Gerardo turned back to her. 'Piero who?' One of his eyebrows jumped higher than the other in his puzzlement and her stomach lurched as she recognised that quizzical lift from her own repertoire of expressions.

The chill trickle became a cold sweat. 'You said my man had suggested you ask me to pay you to acknowledge me.'

His face cleared. 'Yes, your English boyfriend. Brendon. On the phone he said he wanted to grant your wish for an Italian passport. He also said he wanted to compensate me because one day I might be his father-in-law and if you had Italian citizenship it would make it possible for him to live in Italy too. He was going to send a thousand euros by PostePay but then he said PostePay wouldn't work because he was in the UK so couldn't have a Poste Italiane account. He said you would give the money to me if I ask you.'

Zia stared at him in shock, unwilling to believe her ears. '*Brendon* got in touch with you? How did he get your number? And he told you to ask me for a thousand euros? Why would he do such a crazy thing?' Jeez, Brendon and Gerardo didn't have a moral compass between them.

'It was meant to make you happy,' Gerardo replied sullenly.

'I doubt it,' she answered grimly. Any further questions she might have conjured up were interrupted by a young man in his early twenties sauntering up the street, dark hair curling above dark eyes. He gave her a fleeting, awkward smile then took Gerardo's arm. '*È ora di cena*, Papà.' *It's time for dinner,* Papà.

'Riccardo.' Gerardo tried to shrug him off but the young man nudged Gerardo around and began to propel him up the street repeating, '*È ora di cena*, Papà.'

Gerardo's cronies around his table laughed and slapped the table, sing-songing after them, '*È ora di cena*, Papà!'

Zia, rooted to the spot, watched them go, Riccardo keeping a firm grip on Gerardo. They turned a corner and out of sight, Gerardo still sulkily protesting and Riccardo resignedly coaxing him along.

She'd just watched her half-brother fetch their father home from the pub.

Her knees wanted to buckle. She'd just seen her *brother*. Her brother! Twenty-two maybe, he was a little taller and thicker-set than Gerardo. He looked as if he could be a good guy, handling his tricky father with good humour and holding his head up in an embarrassing situation.

On unsteady legs she turned and headed back for her car. Once inside, she sat for a long time staring at the yellow streetlights and the peeling paint on nearby buildings. Heart racing, she tried to process the sighting of her younger brother. Riccardo.

Then the enormity of what Gerardo had told her about Brendon filtered in.

She forced herself to face the truth. She, and she alone, had caused the chasm between herself and Piero. She'd accused without checking a single fact. Not one. No wonder he'd stared at her so blankly. So silently. It had been a refusal to lower himself to answer such a challenge to his integrity.

She was an idiot. She must apologise, and not the tempering half-apology she'd offered him tonight but an unreserved, wholehearted acceptance of fault.

But there was something she needed to do even before that. She took out her phone and dialled.

Brendon answered, 'Hey,' in a smug, *I've been waiting for this call* tone.

'What the fuck?' she said flatly.

'Well, good evening to you, too,' he purred mockingly.

'How did you get hold of my birth father? How do you know who he is? And why would you encourage him to ask me for money?' She thought she knew at least some of the answers but needed to hear it from his own lips.

Brendon laughed, obviously pleased with himself. 'It's been interesting, following your little adventure second-hand. Especially the private investigator stuff. Who would have thought it's so easy and effective? A few quid and I had your father's address. I wrote, including my contact details and the offer of a reward, and he was on the phone like a punter with a winning lottery ticket.'

Disappointment shrank Zia's skin. 'You mean you've been fishing for information about me via Stephan, who gets it from Ursula? Like . . . stalking.'

His laugh was astonished this time. 'That's not stalking.'

'Maybe it's just harassment,' she corrected herself. 'Using underhand methods to obtain information about someone which you then use to cause them distress. In this case, to spoil any chance of me having a good relationship with my father by getting him to reveal himself as a weasel. I think it counts as deception to "discover" that PostePay doesn't work from outside Italy and then tell him to ask *me* for the "reward" you'd promised. I could check with the police about that,' she added thoughtfully. She knew how to press his buttons. Just as he'd been unable to accept her ending things because it made him look bad, he'd recoil from her illuminating this latest shitty thing he'd done.

'It's not deception or harassment either,' he snapped, but she didn't miss the tremor of uncertainty in his voice. 'I told you you'd be sorry you were a bitch to me so when Ursula said you'd decided not to tell your old man who you were . . .' There was a lack of conviction in his voice as it tailed off.

'You told him for me, hoping it would hurt me. You pathetic little shit.'

Defiantly, he burst out, 'You shouldn't have told Steph I was poison. I was upset.'

Her mind flew back to that WhatsApp video call with Ursula. Stephan must indeed have been listening in as she'd suspected – and then run straight to Brendon. 'I think what I actually said was not to let you poison their relationship. But going to such lengths to find my father to hurt me *is* poisonous, Bren. Isn't it?' she pressed. Then, not giving him a chance to disagree, 'What a narrow escape I've had. I'm disappointed in myself for letting you fool me into thinking you were a nice guy. Everything you've done since I caught you cheating has shown me who you really are. At least I know what real love is now and that I never felt it for you.' Her mouth gathered speed, expressing her thoughts uncensored. 'Why don't you pursue the woman from the party? You and she had sparks . . . the way I do with Piero. You and I never had that,' she said shakily.

He was silent as she ended the call.

She sat in her car alone, staring into the night, hearing the increasingly raucous noise from the tipsy patrons of Antiche Mura. It was nearly eleven. Zia knew her unavoidable conversation with Ursula was going to be tricky so she wouldn't rush into it tonight.

And that went double for Piero. In her head, she heard the echo of what she'd just said to Brendon and broke out in a sweat.

I know what real love is now.

Chapter Twenty-Four

It was the next morning before Zia gathered herself to contact Ursula. Her heart took up an uncertain rhythm. 'I'm not sure how this conversation is going to go,' she said before Ursula could utter more than a greeting.

Ursula giggled uncertainly. 'That sounds as if you expect something bad to come of it.' Then, uneasiness creeping into her voice, 'Do you?'

Zia leaned on the terrace railing. Below, clumps of crocosmia had dropped their petals like flickers of flame. She tried to be honest. 'It's one of those occasions where speaking up could cause problems but keeping quiet could cause problems too.'

'Hang on.' The sound of a door being closed. 'Go on,' Ursula said. She sounded downright worried now.

Though she'd rehearsed this call half the night Zia felt as if she were about to jump across a crevasse with no certainty of firm footing on the other side. 'Brendon put Gerardo up to asking for money to acknowledge me,' she said bluntly. Briefly, she summed up the chain of events that had led to her confronting first Gerardo and then Brendon last night, omitting the part about seeing Riccardo. She hadn't properly absorbed her jumpy feelings over that herself. Like an online transaction, her 'share' button wasn't available because processing wasn't yet complete.

Ursula squeaked in horror. 'Shite! Before you asked me not to, I talked to Stephan about Gerardo and you using a private investigator to track down your mother's friend.'

'I know,' Zia sighed, glad that, unprompted, Ursula had made the connection between Brendon's actions and how he must have come by the underlying knowledge necessary. 'And then Stephan overheard us FaceTiming.' The midday sun had burned every cloud from the sky and honey buzzards spread their wings to circle slowly in the deep blue, likely spying out bees' nests to raid.

'I'm sorry,' Ursula said miserably. 'Stephan asked me what else we'd been talking about and got funny when I was evasive, so I told him. He promised he wouldn't tell Brendon. He *promised*.'

'I can see how it happened.' Zia did understand, even if she didn't like it. 'He felt slighted by you keeping my secrets from him. Unfortunately, his loyalties lie with Brendon.'

'That's no excuse,' Ursula broke in hotly. 'He *promised* not to tell. I'm his wife. A promise to me should trump his bro code.' She sounded close to tears.

'Oh, Ursula,' Zia breathed in distress. 'I don't want to cause trouble.'

'Don't you be sorry. You're right to tell me about my husband's breach of trust and its consequences. I need to know,' Ursula retorted bitterly.

Zia groaned. 'I don't want to split your loyalties and

I understand that you're married to Stephan, not me. But you're right . . . how could I have let you think your confidences to your husband are respected if they're not?

Ursula's emotionally impulsive nature sometimes made her cave rather than cope so it was an immense relief when she replied quietly, 'You're not the problem here, Zia. I'll just have a quiet word with Stephan and then it won't happen again.'

Cheered by this calm pronouncement, Zia felt her shoulders loosen. 'We're all guilty of saying stuff we shouldn't, sometimes. I hope this won't sour things.' She meant between Ursula and Zia but equally it could mean Ursula and Stephan. She transferred her gaze from the honey buzzards to the track through the cypress trees towards Piero's property. She was all too achingly aware that she'd already soured things between Piero and Zia. She didn't share that particular heartbreak with her friend though . . . because if Brendon got to hear about it he'd be ecstatic.

And if Brendon *did* get to hear about it it would mean that Ursula had overshared with Stephan again and Stephan had gone running off to bleat to Brendon. Zia wasn't going to open herself up to that kind of pain.

Piero knew he'd acted like a dick when Zia visited him the evening before. He'd been seeking solace in his workshop and was too heartsore to accept her apology well. The knowledge of how he'd all but blanked her had marred what should have been a good day at Tenuta Domenicali today.

Once home after work, he headed straight over to Bella Vista, intent on trying to clear the air. Though he was seeking Zia, his heart lightened when he stepped out from between the trees to see Lucia taking a turn up the drive on Durante's arm.

'Piero! It must be time for afternoon coffee.' She smiled and looked less haggard than when she'd first returned home but still wore her recent illness like a mask.

Gently, he took her shoulders and kissed her cheeks. 'Fantastic to see you up and about.'

Durante pretend-wiped sweat from his forehead and grinned. 'At last!'

They ambled together to a shady spot on the terrace. Piero updated them on progress with the finance company; they told him that two of Lucia's sisters had visited today and Lucia hadn't been too fatigued. When he'd drained his cup he asked casually, 'Is Zia in her apartment?'

Lucia looked interested. 'Try her door and find out.'

Feeling conspicuous beneath his friends' gazes he strolled down the terrace and knocked. When he received no reply, he had no choice but to turn around and trail all the way back to where Lucia and Durante still sat. 'I'll catch her another time. *Ciao.*' He'd better text her and ask to meet. He must apologise. At least she could blame uncontrollable anger for her hurtful words whereas he could only blame pique for failing to meet her halfway as she tried to clear the air.

Dispirited, he headed home through the cypress trees where bees buzzed and cicadas pulsed, unbuttoning his shirt as he went. In this weather he could change three times a day and still feel sweaty.

Then he saw her, sitting on his back doorstep, watching his approach.

Fingers on the final button, he froze like a stripper on his first night.

Shorts hugged her hips and her top rode up to give a

glimpse of smooth stomach as she rose from her perch. 'I've come to apologise,' she said when he was still ten feet away. She removed her sunglasses so he could see her eyes.

He left his on. Last night it had been as if she could see into his soul when their gazes locked and it had made him realise how vulnerable he was to her. 'You apologised last night and I . . . wasn't particularly polite.'

Her smile flickered. 'But you knew something I didn't – that when I raged at you originally you'd done nothing wrong. That kind of thing tends to piss a person off.'

'Pissed off' didn't begin to describe the pain he'd felt or the nights he'd failed to sleep. Every time he thought of Zia his stomach had dropped as if reaching for a rung on a ladder and missing it. He used his shirt sleeve to wipe sweat from his face. 'Let's go inside. I'll put on the air con in the kitchen and you can tell me what's on your mind.' She followed him in and he took down tall glasses, filled them with ice, poured water over and handed one to her. She'd settled on one of the barstools and he took another, on the other side of the breakfast bar so he could see her but not be tempted to touch. Then he waited.

She sipped before speaking, as if her throat needed the lubrication. 'It was Brendon who got in touch with Gerardo. He called himself my English boyfriend but Gerardo paraphrased and referred to him as my man. I thought you'd been trying to interfere, to manage my life, just as Brendon used to try to. I've had plenty of time to think since then, to realise I should have asked whether you were involved, not just believed the worst of you.' She shrugged one smooth, brown shoulder. 'Now I'm thinking straight, I doubt Gerardo even knew we'd been seeing each other.' Puzzlement crept into her eyes. 'Why didn't you just tell me it wasn't you?'

He didn't want to reveal how his throat had completely closed in horror that she'd think him capable of such a thing. Mortification that she'd accuse without question had caused a gut reaction not to defend himself – and that had proved as damaging as her rage. 'Why would Brendon do anything so shitty?'

She let her folded arms slide forward wearily. 'I told you we had a big quarrel. He made some "You'll be sorry" threat and I laughed at him. That set him off.' Straightening, she sighed. 'Finding out from Ursula's husband how easily a private investigator located Harry, Brendon used one to contact Gerardo. He made Gerardo think he was concocting a brilliant surprise for me, lining up Gerardo to agree to confirm paternity as a kind of gift. He even pretended he saw Gerardo as his future father-in-law and wanted to send him money using PostePay . . . but it didn't work so he should ask me for it. A thousand euros.' Her smile was so raw with pain that Piero had to fight not to drag her into his arms. She made a noise that was half-sob, half-laugh. 'It was genius-level cunning. Brendon knows all about my avid curiosity about my father. He wanted Gerardo to present himself to me as a greedy git specifically to disappoint me.'

Such calculated cruelty hit Piero in the heart. 'So, Brendon didn't even do this because he thought it would make you leave Italy and run back to him?'

With a sniff, she shook her head. 'No. Just plain, old-fashioned spite.'

'Wow.' Piero absorbed her words. 'What a shit.'

'Yeah.' She propped up her head as if there was too much inside it for her neck to support. 'Gerardo's gracious offer to officially acknowledge me free of charge came because his mum told him to, not because he's had an attack of generosity.' She paused to take a gulp of water. 'He hasn't mentioned Tori to me or even asked who looked after me when she died. There's no caring in him. Zero.'

Then she straightened and curved her mouth into a smile that wasn't reflected in her eyes. 'Anyway, I still have until the middle of September and it's only the 17th of August today.'

He tried to imagine her in rainy England. He'd visited Brighton but it had been a stag weekend so his memories were hazy. A pier, a pebbly beach and a plentiful number of clubs had been involved. 'So, you're abandoning your hopes of living here?' The thought made him feel as if he was losing his grip on something precious.

'Maybe the moment's passed,' she answered and he thought he saw her lip tremble. 'I don't like my father much. Last night I had the dubious pleasure of watching my half-brother collect him from a bar . . . a half-brother who looked right through me. Fiorella, Roberto, Lucia and Durante have reached out to me but they know I could be the proverbial cat amongst the family pigeons.' She gave another of those bleak smiles. 'An unlucky black cat who brings bad things. Most of my connections here are in my imagination and it's time I accepted that. I can go home and have a good life.'

Although her words were brave her eyes spoke of hurt and disillusionment so deep, he spoke without considering his words. 'You could stay if you married an Italian.' Then he checked, shocked to hear what he'd said, groping for what he'd actually meant.

Her skin paled and she hesitated for several seconds before giving a short laugh. 'Actually, that's a fallacy.

338

Marriage gives me no automatic right. It might make my case stronger if I apply for residency and then citizenship, that's all.' She smiled sadly. 'But "by descent" makes just as strong a case, if not stronger, and I'm pretty sure Fiorella and Roberto will acknowledge me as their grandchild in place of Gerardo acknowledging paternity, if I ask them. Maybe I will ask them one day but live in another part of Italy. I doubt it can be Montelibertà.'

'I see,' was all he could manage in response. His emotions were in such a hopeless tangle that he couldn't think, judge, know what he wanted. He was reeling from hearing that remark about marriage dropping from his lips. Where had *that* come from?

Wordlessly, he watched her slide her feet to the floor, scrabbling instinctively for a way to keep her with him for a few more moments. 'While we're exchanging apologies, I'm sorry for going off on one about you not opening my eyes to leaseback sooner. You weren't responsible for pulling me out of a business sewer. I'm a big boy and I should have done my homework instead of waiting for a miracle and perhaps being prickly when I followed one of your suggestions and it didn't go well. I'm sorry.'

She hesitated as interest entered her long-lashed eyes. 'So, leaseback might work?'

'We've had a real promising meeting today. The deal-makers have gone off to crunch the figures. I can't tell you what a relief it is to be sharing a goal with Papà and Emiliano.' He watched the gold flecks in her eyes, picked out by the early evening light that slanted through the window. 'Graziella's left. Turns out she was trying to pick up a finder's fee from Binotto's.'

Her hair gleamed under the light too, tendrils dancing

beside her cheek bones. 'Durante told me. I was shocked. Are you relieved?'

He tried to smile. 'Like getting rid of a hornet in my underwear. Except that Papà's hurt. He'd been alone for a long time and had feelings for Graziella. She was a user but she also made him happy.'

'It's a shame for him.' Her voice dropped, softened. 'How about you? You must be relieved to know you can keep your home.'

He smiled faintly. 'I daren't count that chicken until we know we've got a suitable deal.'

She took a step towards the door. 'I think it will be OK. You'll get what you want – leave Tenuta Domenicali and create beautiful garden structures, here in Il Rifugio, forever.'

He sucked in air as if someone had elbowed him in the stomach. This beautiful, intelligent woman cared he had stability even though she didn't know what her own next step would be. He wasn't sure he'd cope as well in her situation. Slowly, testing the words, he said, 'It's what I've longed for.'

'Then I hope you get it.' She smiled. 'I'm glad we cleared the air. I expect we'll meet at Bella Vista when you call to see Lucia and Durante because I want to stay till my very last day. Then I'll drive home to my own life.' For a moment, the smile reached her eyes. 'I wish you happiness, Piero.'

He watched the open door long after she'd stepped out through it, wondering if she'd felt this lack of satisfaction when, last night, he'd been the one to say 'I wish you happiness' to her.

'I wish you happiness' was easy to say. Being happy was harder. The road to happiness was strewn with obstacles and traps, doubts and difficulties, choices, conflicts and sacrifices and he felt as if he'd just hit standing water in a summer storm – he could aquaplane right off into the scenery.

He needed time to think.

Chapter Twenty-Five

Zia resolved to wring whatever enjoyment she could from her last few weeks in Italy.

Lucia was pottering about nicely now. Durante had begun keeping the Bella Vista grounds again. Zia still serviced the cottages with Fiorella but that didn't absorb all her time. She hiked around the country park, finding steep outcrops that gave a view of the town as well as the mountains, providing a different perspective to the one she was used to. Sometimes she drove into the centre of Montelibertà to eat at a trattoria and once she FaceTimed Harry from there and showed him the piazza. Another time she took the train to Rome and strolled the streets, dodging scooters.

Her constant companion was disappointment, heavy as a rock in her stomach. Her father was a disappointment. Getting to know her family had stalled. Apologising to Piero had gained her little but an apology in return.

Every couple of days she saw him, helping Durante with a heavy job or grabbing coffee and a chat. He invited all of them for a meal at Il Rifugio, an invitation Zia side-stepped. It would stir too many memories of them making love on the upper terrace, beneath the stars . . . or in his bed, his kitchen, or on his stairs. The gentle, unhurried seduction of his kisses. She'd replayed his comment that she could marry an Italian so many times it drove her crazy. Especially because, for one *yes-I-will, we'll-find-a-way-to-make-it-work* moment she'd thought he was proposing. Her heart had leaped so hard it had nearly burst out of her chest.

Almost as fast, she'd caught his what-did-I-just-*say* expression. This man who'd been unable to marry a woman he'd had a two-year relationship with proposing to someone he'd known since June? The man who'd turned his entire energy to staying where he was proposing to a woman about to leave?

Erm, no.

Although she tried to avoid Gerardo, now she almost understood his relationship with alcohol because every day she had to fight the temptation of suggesting to Piero that they resume their affair, if only for the time she had left.

But she'd already given Piero up once. She could only imagine giving him up again would be harder.

August ended. September brought no noticeable let-up in the heat and Lucia said, 'We need storms.' She was still taking a good nap after lunch each day but otherwise was up and about. Her wound had healed but was sore and her appetite was variable. She was well enough to begin advertising next year's ceramics courses and Zia had shared them on her social media feeds and got Ursula to do the same. Lucia even felt well enough to join Zia and Fiorella for a few minutes as they readied cottages for new guests, wiping the occasional surface but mainly just joining in the chat.

Tenuta Domenicali looked to have secured an acceptable leaseback deal. In a few months Piero would be free and Zia would have the comfort of knowing he, like Lucia and Durante, would be secure on the rocky plateau above the valley.

Life in Italy would go on without her. Brighton's pastel buildings and pebbly beach would welcome her again, lovely in September with enough tourists to keep it lively but not mobbed. The succeeding British south-coast winter would be rainy enough to wash away heartache. She'd sign up with a recruitment agency and update her profile on LinkedIn.

On the 11th of September, Zia serviced the cottages for the last time.

By late afternoon Lucia and Durante were indoors, Fiorella had gone home and Zia was lounging on the terrace. Her Kindle was in her hands but she was gazing down into the vineyard and wondering how large the grapes had grown when she caught a movement in her peripheral vision. A woman of around fifty, dressed in stylishly cropped trousers, her glossy hair upswept into a clasp at the top of her head, was climbing the terrace steps, peeping into the kitchen and then the main terrace doors.

As Zia didn't recognise the woman, she called, '*Buongiorno.*'

The woman looked round, shading her eyes. '*Buongiorno.*' An infinitesimal pause then she added, '*Sono* Ilaria. *Sono la moglie di* Gerardo.' *I'm* Ilaria. *I'm the wife of* Gerardo.

Zia gazed at her in shock. As the wife of Lucia's nephew, Ilaria might easily be paying a family visit. Or . . . she might be there to challenge Zia. 'Oh,' she said.

Ilaria stepped nearer, her smile polite. 'Zia-Lucia?'

'Yes, I'm Zia.' Zia offered Ilaria a seat, giving her wits a chance to gather themselves. 'I didn't know if I'd ever meet you.'

Ilaria clasped her hands, making her rings flash in the sun. 'I doubt Gerardo intended it.' She gazed at the view for several seconds. Then she turned to Zia with a rueful twist to her lips. 'When a husband receives letters he does not share and his telephone record shows calls to England, a wife wonders.'

'Oh!' Zia breathed. 'You thought . . .'

Ilaria shrugged. 'Maybe.'

Zia almost laughed at the idea that she'd be mistaken for Gerardo's 'other woman'. 'I never wrote to him,' she said instead. 'It was someone trying to make mischief for me. I've tried not to interfere with your family but, at the same time, I wanted to know the truth about myself.'

Ilaria nodded, her long earrings keeping time. 'He told me. I knew he had an English girlfriend once. Gerardo and I, we have known each other since school, you understand? The girlfriend left and later we married. Gerardo, he has not a strong personality. I am tough enough for two and we love each other.' Softly, she added, 'You cannot help who you love.'

Zia thought of Piero and said, 'No.' Presumably this was the woman who'd sent Riccardo to fetch Gerardo from the tavern. He probably liked being looked after like a child, Zia thought.

A silence grew. At last, Ilaria said, 'I am not angry to know you exist but I am not happy.'

With her words, a pinprick of light at the end of the tunnel – one Zia hadn't even realised she was holding out hope for – was extinguished. She let bitterness creep into her voice. 'You can't help who you love; I can't help who

I am. It must be an enormous thing to discover your husband has a child from before your marriage. I can see why you wouldn't want to have to explain me to your own children or bear the gossip.' Along with her bag of letters from the past she'd carried dreams with her to Italy. But now she said goodbye to them with one steady, resigned sentence. 'Don't worry. I'm going home in a week.'

The lines on Ilaria's face relaxed. She said simply, 'Thank you.'

Then Piero raced up the terrace steps. He hesitated when he saw Ilaria. '*Buongiorno.*'

The older woman nodded. '*Buongiorno.* I will leave now,' she added in Zia's direction and was soon striding purposefully past Piero. In a minute they heard her car tyres crunching down the drive.

He frowned as Zia let her breathing even in the wake of her unexpected visitor. 'That's Gerardo's wife, isn't it? Are you OK?'

For a second she let herself wonder how it would have felt if, instead of thanking her for leaving, Ilaria had asked Zia if she'd like to meet her siblings. Impatiently, she shook herself free of such fruitless fantasy. 'I'm fine,' she said brightly.

Then Lucia and Durante appeared and demanded Piero stay for dinner, falling into their familiar easy ways with each other. Zia escaped into the kitchen and took fish from the fridge ready to grill and serve with sautéed potatoes.

Ilaria wasn't happy to know she existed. Ilaria seemed a sensible woman – except for the marrying Gerardo thing – and Zia could completely see her point of view. She couldn't help a stray tear.

Piero came into the kitchen just as she was wiping it away. 'Zia,' he began, his deep voice rich with sympathy.

But Durante barrelled in behind him. '*Birra o vino?*'

Zia plastered on a smile because if she had to talk about the meeting with Ilaria just now she'd howl. '*Vino, grazie,*' she said in as cheery a voice as she could dredge up. A huge glass of wine would be great right now.

She drank several with dinner, in fact, listening to the chatter around her without often contributing. Aware of Piero and not looking at him. Her phone rang twice but the screen advised her it was from an unknown number and didn't connect. She dismissed them as probable nuisance calls. Eventually she excused herself for an early night. 'I've always been a lightweight with alcohol and I've pushed my limit.'

It was later, after she'd gone to bed and was trying to lose herself in a book that another of the phone calls came and this time it connected. It was a man and as Zia had been expecting the recorded voice of some attempted scam it took her by surprise when he addressed her by name. 'Who is this?' she asked, drowsy and tipsy and not instantly able to place the voice.

'I'm Ursula's boss. We've met at the parlour,' a rumbling voice reminded her. Then he explained sombrely that the 'quiet word' Ursula had tried to have with Stephan about passing information to Brendon had become a screaming, catastrophic row.

She breathed, 'Oh, no!' And as she listened with horror to what Ursula had done next panic and regret threatened to choke her.

She shouldn't be in Italy.

Ursula needed Zia.

Piero had gone home on Saturday evening filled with plans to get Zia alone on Sunday. For the past couple of weeks, she'd acted as if, emotionally, she'd already left. He needed to break through that invisible, yet formidable, barrier. They needed to talk. When he awoke on Sunday morning to a text from Zia his heart gave a hopeful hop.

But then he read the message.

Piero, I have to leave early but I'll never forget this summer. Wonderful things happened and also some that were horribly real. I hadn't planned to go without saying bye but maybe it's for the best. What we shared was like a skydive. We flew, we floated, almost as high as your 'Italian stars'. It was exhilarating, exciting, glorious, addicting, joyful . . . but then the ground rushed up and we didn't know how to land. It's best for everyone that I've decided not to try and live in Montelibertà, isn't it? I'm so, so happy that it looks as though you'll keep Il Rifugio. I might visit Lucia, Durante and my grandparents next year and, if I do, let's meet as old friends. xx

As if his muscles had turned to cooked spaghetti he fumbled through dressing and stumbled out of the house, birds singing their welcome to the mellow morning light as he hurried across the uneven ground between the cypress trees. There was no red car parked behind the gazebo.

He found Lucia alone on the terrace, her eyes heavy.

'Zia's gone already?' he demanded incredulously, as if it were Lucia's fault.

She nodded. 'Very early. Ursula's boss telephoned Zia last night to say Ursula's in hospital. Her husband locked her out of their house.' Her eyes widened. 'She took pills.'

'Oh, no,' he murmured, trying to imagine willowy, sassy Ursula doing anything so desperate.

Lucia's eyes filled. 'Zia-Lucia, she said, "I only have a few days left here anyway," and—' Lucia had to pause to blow her nose '—and "in my real life, Ursula is all I have".' A sob convulsed Lucia's throat. She covered her face, shoulders shaking. 'We let her keep to the shadows so she didn't upset the family.'

His legs failing him, he half-fell into a chair, realising with sickening clarity that he'd helped make Zia feel that way too. 'I let her think my home's the most important thing to me,' he murmured.

They'd all played their part in letting her believe that Ursula was all she had.

Never had anything ever felt so final. And she hadn't even said a proper goodbye.

Chapter Twenty-Six

Zia had been home for a month. Her spare room was once again 'Ursula's room', which was the least she could do. Stephan had locked Ursula out of her own home for blowing up at him about blabbing details of Zia's life to Brendon. Stephan had responded with a bitter 'marriage over!' plunging Ursula into the black despair that had led her to the paracetamol bottle.

After Ursula had left hospital with no lasting damage to major organs but a psychiatric appointment to keep, she'd spent a week gathering her strength before Zia accompanied her to a solicitor's office. Any day now Stephan would discover that in the twenty-first century changing the locks to keep your wife out didn't entitle you to keep her half of the house. Already two of Ursula's most alternative, tattooed colleagues had accompanied her to fetch her personal possessions from the erstwhile marital home, positioning themselves between her and Stephan and wearing poisonous glares that Ursula said, in a flash of her old self, 'quite took the fucker aback'.

In helping make life bearable for her friend Zia had kept her mind from her own life's unbearableness – especially Piero never responding to her goodbye text.

Not a word.

She'd checked compulsively, not sure whether to expect a *Hey, that's a shitty way to say goodbye!* or *OK. I understand. At least we can still be friends.* Or, what she secretly hoped for: *I'm not letting us end like this. We must be able to make this work. Apply for temporary residency. Three months will soon pass . . .* Yeah, right. 'Can't live without you' messages were a bit Hollywood. Zia hadn't sent him one, even though it was what was written in her heart, because here she was, living without him. Her sadness was like lead-lined guts but she was breathing and eating so she was living without him.

She'd got as far as a second interview for a job she quite fancied with an investment company and was sure the raw feelings of loss would go eventually, if she kept busy enough.

Lucia had called to say the first ceramics course would be in June next summer and she'd put a reserve on Villino Il Pino for Zia and Ursula and was hoping they'd come. The idea filled Zia with mixed longing and dread.

She and Ursula had been to Chichester to pick up Harry and they'd all driven down to Sandy Bay in Devon to throw rose petals into the sea for Vicky and Tori. All three of them had cried – Zia and Harry for Vicky and Tori and Ursula because everything set her off. The process of finding her single identity after being part of a joint one for so long was emotional. Afterwards they'd gone into Exmouth and met Karen, Harry's sister and Vicky's old friend. She'd been able to track down three more of Tori's school friends, including one who'd been with her in Italy.

Harry's kids, Mandy and Leon, had completed the party gathered to remember Tori and, together, they'd helped Zia with her sense of who Tori had been.

One friend, Steffi, had even managed to find an old video on YouTube of her eighteenth birthday party. 'I borrowed my parents video camera for my birthday, just before we took off for Europe,' she explained. 'My parents tried to show us a dance from their day called "the bump" and Tori laughed till she cried.' She'd passed the link to Zia who'd pored over the fuzzy old footage, watching her rosy, freckle-faced mother cough and hiccup, tears of mirth destroying her mascara. She'd watched it over and over, laughing and crying along with Tori Chalmers. She'd rarely been more grateful for anything than that YouTube link.

It was with a happy and sad yet more settled heart she returned to her flat in New Steine.

It was a Sunday morning halfway into grey October when Ursula answered the apartment doorbell and Zia heard her say, 'Wow! Surprise.' Her tone was so wary that Zia presumed that it must be bloody Stephan until Ursula raised her voice. 'Zia? Visitor.'

Zia emerged from the lounge to see Piero standing in the doorway, huddled in his coat, his hair on end from Brighton's horizontal winds. His dark eyes flew to her and blazed.

All she could do was stare back. 'Piero?' In England?

Ursula looked from one to the other and reached for her coat with a mischievous, 'Just remembered somewhere I have to be,' but Zia barely registered her tactful exit.

'What are you doing here?' she asked him stupidly.

A tiny smile flickered at the corner of his mouth. 'You left without taking your wine. I've brought you three bottles each of Orvieto Classico and Sangiovese.' He pulled a capacious backpack from his shoulders. It clinked as it reached the floor.

'You came to England to bring me wine from Tenuta Domenicali?'

'No.' He jammed his hands in his pockets. 'I'm here to sort out my life.'

Cautiously, she turned this idea over, feeling as if she was on one of the fairground rides on the pier and if she made a wrong move she'd go flying off. 'And what does that entail?'

He raised thoughtful eyebrows. 'First, I ask if I can come in.'

She flushed as she realised she'd kept him standing on the grey laminate of the hall that served her apartment and the one next door. 'Sorry.' She laughed unsteadily and showed him into the airy lounge overlooking New Steine gardens, which were empty but for a man and a black poodle.

Piero removed his coat. 'The leaseback deal's going through. Papà's talking about visiting cousins in America. Emiliano's recruiting to fill my role. It's taken me a few weeks to get to a point where I felt I could come here. It's OK to put my workshop in mothballs because I still get a quarter of the profits from the wine-making. It's just the premises we're selling.' He sat down on her sofa.

She licked dry lips, drinking in the sight of him along with the news from Montelibertà. 'I know roughly how leaseback works.'

He gave a sudden, genuine smile, rubbing his jaw which looked to be freshly shaved. 'Of course. Sorry.' He waited a beat then added, 'So, I've taken an apartment here in Brighton.'

Shock flashed through her. 'Where?' she asked blankly. 'St James's Street. Parking's a bitch.'

'Round the corner?' She almost got up and peeped out of the window to see if St James's Street still ran across the top of New Steine.

'Yep. If you were happy to leave me behind I'm going to feel really silly.' He jumped to his feet and began to pace, the sentences racing out of him as though if he didn't speak fast he'd forget what he meant to say. 'Lucia kept me in touch so I knew you and Ursula were both OK. But your goodbye text . . . Well, you sounded as if you weren't happy with the way things ended. As I'm certainly not, I looked into things and found out I can stay here for six months.' He paused. 'There's a chance of residency after that.' Another pause. 'Though I might have to get a job.' When she continued to gape at him, so shocked that she couldn't process all he said, he took a tentative step closer. 'If you think there's some chance we can be together we can figure it all out. If you can't live in Montelibertà it can be here or in another part of Italy. If we can be together.'

'But you didn't even reply to my text,' she objected.

He gave a rapid, exasperated shake of his head. 'I daren't. I was scared I'd say the wrong thing. I wanted to look you in the eye and talk. I'd been trying to get you alone back home but it was like trying to creep up on a wild bird with a net. You kept flitting away. Then I got that text and my heart just about broke. I realised I had to be a lot more fucking determined.'

Inside Zia, a tiny shoot of hope began to grow. 'Renting an apartment here is definitely that.' She took a step towards him, her heart beating so fast it felt as if it were lifting her off the carpet. She saw him relax, begin to smile, and the shoot of hope grew like a beanstalk as she closed the last few inches between them.

Sliding his arms about her he pressed his lips to her cheeks, her eyelids, her mouth, pressed himself against her so she could feel the gallop of his heart. 'Marry me, Zia. I'll live wherever you're happiest.'

She drew back to look into his face, finding it hard to take in his words. 'You don't want to get married.'

His smile flashed. 'I didn't want to get married to Nicoletta. I want to be married to you.'

'You've fought tooth and nail to keep Il Rifugio.'

'I love it there,' he admitted stroking her hair aside so he could nuzzle her neck. 'I love you more. You're more important than a house, even one with a world-class view. You're a world-class view all on your own.' His mouth moved to the place beneath her ear that set her skin on fire.

'But,' she stuttered, tipping back her head and closing her eyes, 'living in England will freeze your arse off.' But inside her the beanstalk of hope was going crazy, blossoming with relief and joy.

He sighed as if she were just creating obstacles. 'I'll wear thermal boxers.'

Then her phone began to ring and she snatched it from her pocket to silence it . . . until she saw the name on the screen. Slowly she showed it to Piero. *Gerardo Costa*.

He lifted his hands. 'Nothing to do with me.'

'I realise that.' To emphasise her trust in him she looped her spare arm around his waist so he couldn't leave while she answered, holding the handset so he could hear. '*Pronto*.' She felt her shoulders hunch as if to ward off something unpleasant.

'*Gliel'ho dovuto dire*,' said Gerardo without preamble.

Zia hesitated. 'You had to tell them? Who? What?'

'Ay, ay, ay,' grumbled Gerardo, uninformatively. 'Riccardo, he complained I was always in a mood these days. Caterina and Laura, they joined in. So, I told them about you.'

Zia's breath caught. '*You told them about me?*' It was so unexpected that she responded with the first thing that came into her head. 'Had you been drinking?'

He laughed. 'You must have taken lessons in scolding from my wife! No.' Then he amended, 'Or not much. All my life I thought I felt nothing for you but when you left? My stomach felt sick.'

'Wow,' she said, at a loss. Totally, utterly, unable to decide what to feel.

He cleared his throat. 'When you come back, they want to meet you.'

It was so unexpected that Zia let out a gasp and Piero's arms tightened around her like walls that wouldn't let in anything bad. 'Seriously?' she choked. Then, on a misgiving, 'But do they hate me?'

Gerardo's voice turned almost husky. 'No, Zia-Lucia. They want to know who you are.' As if feeling the need to persuade her he added, 'They're nice people. More like Ilaria than like me.'

She laughed, but then asked cautiously, 'And what about Ilaria? What does she think?' She hadn't forgotten his wife thanking her for keeping away from her family.

'If the children are OK then Ilaria is OK.' He didn't sound quite so positive on that score but Zia decided she could work with that.

She looked up at Piero and felt suddenly shy. 'I think I might be returning to Italy, after a while.' A slow smile spread over Piero's face and he cocked his eyebrows as if to say, 'Really?' She kissed the hollow of his neck. 'Tell Riccardo, Caterina and Laura that I look forward to meeting them. Very much.'

'Good,' he said, sounding gruff this time. Then, 'I'll see you soon.'

Zia was left with a silent phone and a crackle of astonishment. 'Who would have thought *Gerardo* would be the one to remove the big obstacle?'

Piero's eyes were alight and though he smiled he said, 'There are just two problems left.'

Her shoulders sagged. 'What?' When things seemed too good to be true, they usually were.

In a voice weighty with sorrow he pronounced, 'You haven't told me you love me. And you haven't said whether you'll marry me.'

Laughter burst from her, the kind of bubbling, joyful explosion that she'd thought she'd forgotten how to make. Then she sobered because actually this was deadly serious stuff. She cupped his face. 'Of course, I love you. And I'll marry you any day, any place.'

Then their mouths found each other, gasping at the touch of tongues, the kiss going on and on, pulling them closer and closer together, deepening, exploding. And just to make really certain nothing had been lost in translation Zia said against his mouth, '*Ti amo, caro.*'

And he returned, '*Ti amo anch'io.*'

I love you, darling.

I love you too.

Epilogue

Zia and Piero drove to Montelibertà after keeping Ursula company for her first few months post-Stephan, and then waving her off for a spring holiday in Ireland. In a few weeks she'd be coming back to live in Zia's apartment while the sale of the marital home went through. Stephan had made himself unpleasant when she'd filed for divorce but with Zia's support and that of her counsellor she'd refused to let 'such a douche' drive her out of Brighton.

Zia drove her car ahead of Piero's and the first thing she saw when the two vehicles turned into the driveway of Il Rifugio were the waving arms and beaming smiles of Lucia and Durante. With a whoop, she stopped her vehicle and leaped out to fling herself into their arms. 'I'm back!'

The next few minutes were spent wiping happy tears, grinning their heads off and kissing cheeks. Finally, Lucia gave her a last hug. 'I must go home and prepare dinner. You will be there?' She bent a stern eye on Zia.

Zia clasped one hand over her heart. 'I will. But it's scary.'

'No, no.' Durante waved her worries away. 'It is family.'

'It can be the same thing,' put in Piero, drily, preparing to unlock the door of Il Rifugio with an eagerness which told Zia that no matter how much he'd put her first, a large chunk of his heart belonged to this house up above the valley.

They took a couple of hours to unpack the car and settle in. Piero took a nap after their long journey but though Zia lay down and cuddled into his warm, familiar body her butterflies refused to let her sleep. Instead, she watched spring sun peeping in the windows and wondered whether the vines in the valley had begun to sprout their leaves.

When the sun went down it was time to shower, to put up her hair and pull on a dress. Piero hugged her close. 'Don't look so worried. It's just a dinner party.'

They both knew it wasn't 'just' a dinner party and Zia was glad of his hand as they made their way through the dear, familiar cypress trees, the grass spring-green instead of the golden straw of summer. Several cars were parked further up the drive but they took their usual route up the steps and over the terrace.

In silence they walked up the hall and into the dining room, where the table had been set for a buffet and all the chairs brought in from the salon. Zia clutched Piero's hand tighter. '*Mamma mia*,' she breathed, the Italian exclamation for any situation.

First, she focused on Gerardo. Uncertainly, he came forward with Ilaria holding his hand but he was smiling. Equally uncertainly, he kissed her cheeks and Zia found herself closing her eyes. She wasn't sure of her emotions but the gesture made the blood roar in her ears. Ilaria only nodded and smiled at Zia before she stepped back to let Fiorella and Roberto bestow on her much more exuberant and noisy hugs and kisses. 'Zia-Lucia, you are back!'

Then Gerardo cleared his throat. 'And here are Caterina, Laura and Riccardo to meet you. *Le tue sorelle e tuo fratello.' Your sisters and your brother.*

Zia swallowed and turned to three people who'd been hovering in the background, all younger than her, all offering tentative smiles. Almost in a trance she gazed at them, recognising Riccardo, who'd had his hair cropped into spikes, and two young women, one with long hair and one with short.

They gazed back.

The oldest female, about Zia's build, stepped forward. 'I'm Caterina. This is Laura, and this is Riccardo.'

'I'm Zia,' she managed huskily, feeling her cheeks lift in the biggest smile she thought she'd ever smiled. 'Zia-Lucia Costa Chalmers.' A shaky laugh emerged. 'It must seem an odd name to you but I think my mother was trying to keep all my options open.'

They laughed too, moving closer, eyes lively with curiosity. For several seconds nobody knew what to say or how to react to one another.

Then, instinctively, Zia opened her arms. Caterina was the first to step in and kiss her cheeks, then Laura, then Riccardo. Zia cleared the tears from her throat and pulled back to introduce Piero. 'I'm not sure if you know my fiancé.' Then as they laughed and talked together activity burst around her, breaths exhaled, bottles opened and glasses clinked. Gerardo hugged each of his kids in turn – including her.

Piero poured champagne and lifted his glass in a toast. '*Alla famiglia! Salute!*' and suddenly she was in tears.

When Riccardo muttered, 'Girls!' disgustedly, her tears turned into laughter.

'They're happy tears. *Alla famiglia*!' she cried, wiping her face with a napkin. Even Riccardo looked dewy-eyed at that and everyone talked at once, testing her Italian and showing her their more-than-passable English.

Then, surreally, Laura gave Zia her phone. 'Please . . . your number?' she asked shyly, as if she half-expected to be refused.

They swapped contact details then Riccardo and Caterina held their phones out too and she exchanged numbers with them all, sniffing all over again. 'This is the strangest moment of my life. But one of the happiest.'

Then Piero whispered something in her ear and she added, 'Oh, yes. Will you all come to our wedding in the summer?'

'Of course, of course,' cried Caterina and Laura. 'A wedding!'

Riccardo pulled a face. 'Do I have to wear a tie?'

Piero clapped him on the shoulder. 'A man after my own heart. I do, so you do.'

Zia laughed and threw her arms around Piero because she was just so joyful that she wanted to share every atom of it with him. 'We want it to be at Santa Lucia church . . . of course.'

'Of course!' cried Lucia, who looked back to her old, healthy self.

By the end of the evening so many toasts had been drunk that even Gerardo had had enough. At least – under the watchful eyes of wife, grandparents, aunt, uncle and children – he said he had.

It was late when Zia and Piero got home to Il Rifugio. Zia didn't know if she was giddier with champagne or with joy. 'Laura, Caterina and Riccardo all seemed to have a lot of affection for Gerardo, just as Lucia and Durante do,' she chattered as, hand-in-hand, they climbed the stairs up to Piero's bedroom – her bedroom too now.

Piero kissed her hair. 'I thought the same. Maybe he's not all bad.'

'I doubt he's all good though.' Zia sighed. 'I hope one day I'll stop being wary of him.'

They reached the bedroom, the bed still rumpled from their siesta earlier. Zia turned to Piero and undid his top button so she could kiss the skin at the base of his neck. 'Maybe we'll form a bond or maybe he'll disappoint me all over again. Who knows? At least searching . . .' Another button, another kiss. ' . . . for him . . .' Another button, another kiss. ' . . . led me . . .' Another button, the longest, slowest kiss of all. ' . . . to you.'

Piero pointed to the next button. 'Don't stop, *cara*. I like where we're going.'

Loved

Under the Italian Sun?

Then why not try one of Sue's
other sizzling summer reads
or cosy Christmas stories?

The perfect way to escape
the everyday.

Sparks are flying on the island of Malta . . .

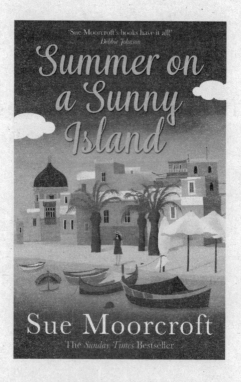

An uplifting summer read that will raise your spirits and warm your heart.

Come and spend summer by the sea!

Make this a summer to remember
with blue skies, beachside walks
and the man of your dreams...

*In a sleepy village in Italy,
Sophia is about to discover a
host of family secrets . . .*

Lose yourself in this uplifting
summer romance from the
Sunday Times bestseller.

What could be better than
a summer spent basking
in the French sunshine?

Grab your sun hat, a cool glass of wine,
and escape to France with this
gloriously escapist summer read!

Hannah and Nico are meant
to be together. But fate is
keeping them apart . . .

A heartwarming story of love, friendship
and Christmas magic from
the *Sunday Times* bestseller.

This Christmas, the villagers
of Middledip are off on a
very Swiss adventure . . .

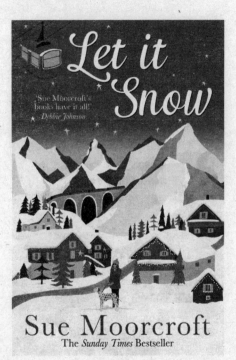

Escape to a winter wonderland
in this heartwarming romance from
the *Sunday Times* bestseller.

One Christmas can change everything . . .

Curl up with this feel-good festive romance, perfect for fans of Carole Matthews and Trisha Ashley.

It's time to deck the halls . . .

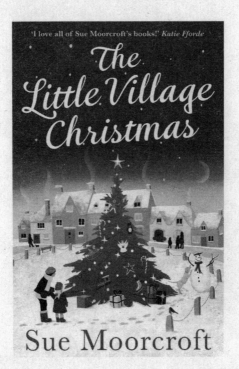

'I love all of Sue Moorcroft's books!' *Katie Fforde*

The Little Village Christmas

Sue Moorcroft

Return to the little village of Middledip with this *Sunday Times* bestselling Christmas read.

*For Ava Blissham,
it's going to be a
Christmas to remember . . .*

Countdown to Christmas as you step into
the wonderful world of Sue Moorcroft.